W9-CFK-370

"FULTON COUNTY SHERIFF'S DEPARTMENT ... I GOT A WARRANT TO SEARCH THE PREMISES."

"Come on in," I said. "You might as well start in the kitchen." The young guy came in. Three older cops trooped in behind him. The last cop stood in front of me, watching, his hand near his gun. That was when I noticed the crowbar lying next to my feet, halfway under the couch. It had a rag wrapped around the end, and it was black with blood. Roger's blood. I didn't have to think hard to figure that my prints were all over the handle.

In the kitchen one of the cops said, "Aw, look at that."

Another voice said: "Raw deal, huh?"

It took the cops about half a minute to get the cuffs on me and explain my constitutional rights ...

Avon Books are available at special quantity discounts for bulk purchases for sales promotions, premiums, fund raising or educational use. Special books, or book excerpts, can also be created to fit specific needs.

For details write or telephone the office of the Director of Special Markets, Avon Books, Dept. FP, 1350 Avenue of the Americas, New York, New York 10019, 1-800-238-0658.

POWER

OF

ATTORNEY

WALTER SORRELLS

AVON BOOKS ◆ NEW YORK

If you purchased this book without a cover, you should be aware that this book is stolen property. It was reported as "unsold and destroyed" to the publisher, and neither the author nor the publisher has received any payment for this "stripped book."

To Patty, of course

POWER OF ATTORNEY is an original publication of Avon Books. This work has never before appeared in book form. This work is a novel. Any similarity to actual persons or events is purely coincidental.

AVON BOOKS
A division of
The Hearst Corporation
1350 Avenue of the Americas
New York, New York 10019

Copyright © 1994 by Walter Sorrells
Published by arrangement with the author
Library of Congress Catalog Card Number: 93-91666
ISBN: 0-380-77167-5

All rights reserved, which includes the right to reproduce this book or portions thereof in any form whatsoever except as provided by the U.S. Copyright Law. For information address International Creative Management, 40 West 57th Street, New York, New York 10019.

First Avon Books Printing: February 1994

AVON TRADEMARK REG. U.S. PAT. OFF. AND IN OTHER COUNTRIES, MARCA REGISTRADA, HECHO EN U.S.A.

Printed in the U.S.A.

RA 10 9 8 7 6 5 4 3 2 1

PREFACE

The camera crews call it a perp walk.

The reason they love a good perp walk is because all they have to do is line up outside the courthouse, point and shoot, while the marshals hustle the guy, the perpetrator, out to that unmarked Crown Victoria they always have waiting down at the curb. If the cameramen are lucky, they get a shot of some jerk with cuffs on, a raincoat pulled up over his head, looking guilty as hell.

This is what the defense's bar snarls and moans about when they say their clients are getting *tried in the court of public opinion.* My lawyer complained about it just like everybody else. Fact is, though, when I did my perp walk down at the Richard B. Russell Federal Building in Atlanta, I *was* guilty. Fair's fair.

I have a videotape, 11 Alive News, the day they sentenced me. My wife sent it to me in prison after the divorce papers came through. I guess that was spitefulness, but I'm not sure. Maybe she thought I'd want it as some kind of memento.

My perp walk included all the classical elements: I came out the glass door with a windbreaker over my head, cuffs on, two great big federal marshals steering me by the elbows, all these people sticking microphones in my face, the whole nine yards. The reporter did a voice-over, saying that Bobby Vine—a principal deal maker in the boutique investment bank of Hawley Vine & Co.—had been convicted in federal court today on four counts of securities law violations after a month-long trial.

Bobby Vine, formerly an attorney, would be sentenced by Judge Reggie C. Leaphart on Monday in courtroom 1603.

That was how the reporters always described me—formerly an attorney—like being a lawyer was something to be ashamed of. Or maybe it was the *formerly* part they liked, the fact that I'd been disbarred. They never used the word *disbarred* though. I don't know why. I would have if I'd been doing their job.

The videotape showed a pastel sketch of my lawyer, one hand in his pocket, the other waving around in the air. The artist had made his face look blue for some reason. It had only taken the jury about an hour and a quarter to reach a verdict, all four counts.

After that, a shot of another guy traipsing after me while I did the perp walk with the marshals. The guy had on a thousand dollars worth of pinstripes and a big smile. The reporter said this was Bobby Vine's partner, Roger Hawley. She also said it was rumored he would have to close down Hawley Vine & Co. in the wake of this trial—like, gosh, wasn't that hard luck for him?

But old Roger bounced back. As always. I don't have a videotape of it, but three months later he opened what he called a merchant bank. It was named Excor, Inc., and he set it up in an unusually nice suite of offices, big expensive place downtown. Nobody was quite sure where he got all the money.

The last picture, they showed me getting stuffed into the gray Crown Vic, a federal marshal putting one hand on my head as I sat down in the backseat. The reporter wound up the story taking a couple lazy shots at Greed and Fast Money, wondering if this trial signaled a change in the air, a big comeback for Down-Home Values, the Eternal Verities, etc.

Thinking back on it, starting life over after two and a half years at the federal camp down in Alabama, I look at myself on the tape and think: Who the hell was that guy?

1

Roger's Last Deal

CHAPTER 1

"Ay, Vine. You want to know my philosophy of sales?" It was Ray talking to me.

Ten-thirty, Monday morning. We were in Ray's office at Ray's Rent-2-Own—his main store over there on the Buford Highway strip, northeast of Atlanta. The walls of Ray's office were cinder block, painted gloss white. One wall had a two-way mirror in it so Ray could look out onto the showroom floor, make sure nobody was dragging off a sofa without paying for it.

The only decoration was a life-sized cardboard poster of Ray leaned up next to the filing cabinet. Maybe *decoration* is the wrong word. *Eyesore*—that would pin it down a little better.

The poster showed Ray standing there in his polyester fat-guy suit, wearing a smile that would put you in mind of one of those African dogs—a hyena, say, or a jackal. He had a kinky permanent that made his face look even wider than it was already. His arms were crossed and he had a bunch of big shiny rings on his fingers. I noticed they had air brushed the tattoo off the back of his hand.

MAKE A DEAL WITH RAY! That was the slogan on the poster. It was a terrible slogan. Ray's business, basically, is renting furniture. Meaning he buys two-hundred-dollar sofas and rents them to deadbeats for seventeen months, $9.99 a week. Payable each Friday, right after the paycheck comes in. If there's anything left of the couch after seventeen months, the customer gets to keep it. You do the math; it's pretty profitable.

Ray had hired me after I got out of prison. He had been in the federal prison camp at Maxwell Air Force Base once, too—tax evasion, fraud, conspiracy to commit, that kind of thing. But now he was an honest guy, full of charitable impulse. His big thing, after he had gotten out, was hiring ex-cons to work in his stores. He called it mainstreaming. Mainstreaming was his *Contribution to Society.* That's how Ray sees the world, I think: capital letters, italics.

Don't get me wrong. I like Ray. Ray is a good man.

"No, Ray," I said. "I don't know what your philosophy of sales is."

Ray was pontificating, leaning back in his Naugahyde Execuchair (on special, $6.89 a week, today only), and looking up at the ceiling. There was nothing to see on the ceiling. "You sell anything yet today, Bobby?" he said. Ray didn't like getting to the point. He liked teasing the point, poking it, prodding it, tiptoeing around it until something kind of congealed.

"Couple of nibbles," I said. "Did a demo, one of those Korean stereo systems. Had a guy said he'd be back on that used La-Z-Boy."

"You didn't close, huh?"

"Come on Ray," I said. "Ten o'clock in the morning, nobody closes a sale."

Ray pointed his finger at the ceiling, talking straight up in the air like I was floating somewhere over his desk. "See, Counselor, that's where you're wrong. You got to *assess* the need. That's step one. Then you got to *meet* the need. That's step two. Then you got to *ask* for the sale. That's step three. You want to know the problem? Everybody forgets step three."

"That's your philosophy of sales?"

Ray looked at me all of a sudden, like I'd surprised him. "Who said anything about philosophy? We talking basic, old-fashioned, normal, everyday, roll-up-your-sleeves, get-down-to-basics *selling.* Sales 101, you know what I'm saying? They don't teach Sales 101 in law school, I guess."

"Not where I went," I said.

"Well!" Ray said. "What the hell *did* they teach you?"

I shrugged. The truth was I had not learned much in law school. Not much that had ended up being of any value to me. I learned a lot of *how* . . . but not much *why.* This didn't matter to Ray, though. Law school, damn, that was the big time to him.

Ray, you see, had a yearning for Higher Things, whatever the hell that meant, and The Law was up there on the mysterious and inaccessible plane of Higher Things along with Art, Good Taste, Fashion, and Golf. These were things from which Ray had been shut off—by birth, training, inclination, fate. He knew that these things existed, but he thought that somehow they were unreachable and inaccessible to *him*. Not in this life, I guess, was what he thought.

He'd reach out for them, then pull up short at the last minute. For instance, he had bought a set of clubs once—genuine Pings—metal woods, triple wedges, boron shafts, you name it. Cost him a young fortune. But he'd never had the courage to go out and use them. It was just too much for him. Someday, he kept telling me, someday he was going to have the time to get out there and Shoot Some Golf. But it just never happened.

In the meantime Ray had charity-case convicts like me that he could teach about Selling and Negotiation and stuff like that. Real World Skills, he said. Mainstreaming.

"Here's the psychology," Ray said. "You got a guy. You with me, Bobby? You got a guy. He's an idiot, a jerk. Lazy, don't pay his bills, can't keep a job. But he wants him a stove. Hell, Bobby, he *needs* him a stove. Man, he's eating out of cans, eating out of bags, right? He got no credit, got no friends, he damn sure got no money. But he just *got* to have him a stove! You with me?" Ray had purple bags under his eyes, looking at me like a bloodhound with an Afro. He was pleading to be understood.

"I'm with you, Ray."

He was happy. He was teaching me Skills, letting me in on how to make it in the Real World. "So he's got—what?"

"A *need,* Ray. He's got a *need.*" After a while with Ray you catch on.

"That's right, Counselor. He's got him a *need!* Now he comes in here and we got—what? *A solution!*" Ray was getting worked up, leaning forward in his chair, and rubbing on his homemade prison tattoo like he was finally going to make it go away after all these years. "We got him a solution!"

"Right, so he puts down a month's rent and walks out with the stove."

"Wrong. Wrong, Counselor! You got to overcome his psychology. He got a natural suspicion of you. You got to overcome it. Whap! You got to tip him over the edge! That's the psychology. Come on, Bobby, you got a buyer-psychology situation here."

"Okay," I said. I was looking at the poster of Ray, wondering what dumb, vain fit ever made him think that a picture of himself was going to make anybody want to rent a refrigerator here. MAKE A DEAL WITH RAY! Ray was a bright guy, an extraordinary guy in his way. But not an honest-looking guy. Not even with the homemade prison tattoo airbrushed off his hand.

"You got to *close* him, Counselor. You got to *close* him! And you can't close nobody if you don't ask for the sale. Get it?" He counted the words off on his small tubular fingers: "Ask ... for ... the ... sale."

"Ray," I said. "I'm thirty-seven years old. I was a successful businessman once upon a time, a semisuccessful lawyer, so I'm not a total stranger to the concepts here."

But Ray wasn't listening anymore. "You can go with your assumptive close," he said, "say, *'Where would you like your stove delivered, sir?'* Okay? That's a good clean one. Or *'Can we step over to the register, complete the paperwork?'* Or this one's hard to pull off, you got to have a feel for the guy— You listening, Bobby?"

"Absolutely, Ray." I wasn't really—but it didn't matter too much. Nothing seemed to make much difference to me these days anyway. I'd just been kind of marking time since I got out of Maxwell.

"Or, hey, here's one. Little more aggressive, like if you got a fence sitter. You say, *'Sir, do you got thirty-nine dollars and ninety-six cents in your pocket?'* They say, yeah, you say: *'Great. Let's step on over to the register, quit fooling around, get you taken care of.'*" I was nodding, not really thinking about selling stoves.

"But you know what I really like, Counselor? I like the direct approach. Come right out and say it! *'Sir, do you want to carry home that stove?'* Come right out and say it! It's the greatest thing in the world! *'Ma'am, would you like to take home the love seat and the matching end tables? Folks, y'all want to carry home the dryer?'* That's all it is to it. You don't never use the word *buy* 'cause they ain't buying. They don't got no time for that word. They just want to get home, let all their friends come over and set on that brand new modular couch." Ray kept on like that for a while, and I kept nodding.

Then it came over me—that sick, choking, shut-in feeling I used to get down at Maxwell. The Big Fear. I felt like I couldn't breathe and my vision started to get dark around the edges like I was going to faint. My internal organs were filling with tumors, expanding, ready to pop like wet balloons. It wasn't Ray's fault, really. It was just something that happened to me every once in a while.

I'd been out of Maxwell six months now, but I hadn't been able to shake these spells of—I guess you'd call it despair. I just thought of it as the Big Fear. It was like being dead suddenly, looking out at the world through dead eyes, feeling that your life had just ebbed away, and there was nothing left. The Big Fear was the most bleak, terrible thing I'd ever felt and it happened to me once, twice a day.

The psychologist at Maxwell had said it was just a panic attack. White-collar crime, he said, it's a sure road to panic attacks. Something to do with the fracturing of your value system. Or the disintegration of your motivational schemata. I forget. It was something along those lines. The prison psychologist was kind of like Ray: He had a lot of words, but after a few minutes, sometimes you stopped listening to them.

"Hey, Ray," I said. "I got to get a breath of fresh air."

"What?"

"Fresh air," I said, and I walked out of the office. Ray was yelling something at me as I went away, but I couldn't make it out. Just the tone—pissed off, because I wasn't showing enough enthusiasm about sharpening my Real World Skills.

I wandered through the warehouse, feeling weak and beat down, then out onto the loading dock—a flat concrete riser with some shredded tires bolted on the edge that stuck out into the empty parking lot. It was about ninety-eight degrees out there, the air dull, heavy, lifeless. I watched the heat shimmer up off the blacktop.

There was nobody on the loading dock, no cars in the parking lot. It was completely still out there, completely empty. I looked around, waiting for something to come to me, some kind of answer. But there was just nothing there. The heat, the dust, the scarred green dumpster, the old boxes and potato chip bags blown up against the building. That was it. No answers. No explanations. No solutions.

See, until recently I had lived my life according to the principle that the less you thought about things, the happier you'd be. I don't mean that I didn't believe in the use or exercise of the mind—I'm not saying that at all; what I'm saying is I figured if you hewed diligently to the rules and regulations, stayed inside the lines, did all the stuff your teachers and trainers and breeders had scrimshawed onto your brain then, hell, you'd be fine. You wouldn't have to suffer any pain or hurt or uncertainty or hard times. Man, you'd be set.

Turns out, this was a bunch of shit.

Maybe it works for some people, but it didn't work for me. See, lawyers get trained to see both sides of every issue, to see all kinds of fine distinctions about good and evil, so that the varying degrees of personal morality and the ethics of professional conduct start merging into one another. Problem is, they aren't the same thing. Legal ethics are a tricky web of rules, of all these wherefores and conditionals and dependent clauses: If A is true, then Z follows; but if A is true and B is *also* true, then all of a sudden Z doesn't follow anymore. Truth, under the law, is damned malleable stuff. And if you start to internalize that way of thinking, I mean really *believe* it in your bones the way I did, it starts to cut you loose from your moorings.

Because law is not morality. Law is not about truth and justice and all that crap you read about in junior high school civics class. It's not about saving the innocent man from the gas chamber, about Perry Mason jumping up in court and pointing his finger at the guy who *really* committed the crime. Law, the way I was trained anyway, is about manipulating rules and procedures in order to bag the big game for you and your clients.

What that means—if you're the kind of lazy-minded shit I

used to be—is that the law comes down to this: *What's right is what you can get away with!*

And this mind-set starts sloshing over into everything in your life. Friendship becomes barter; love becomes a transaction; marriage becomes a contract: you know, *in the event that the party of the first part does fail to perform certain services herein enumerated such that the party of the second part. . . .* Well, you see what I'm saying. What happens is that your view of reality gets all twisted up, and life, which is so goddamn uncertain and fragile and complex in the first place, is cheated; the heart gets surrounded and choked off by this carapace of rules and subtleties and too-fine distinctions; love and tenderness and care and all the integuments of human connection and conduct, they wither and become corrupt.

And I let this happen to myself. *Fool! Fool!*

So I sank down on the concrete, dangled my legs off the side of the loading dock, feeling the sun and trying not to think or feel anymore. It hurt too much thinking about it, thinking about the things that had slipped away from me—my lovely wife, the fine children that I hadn't seen in two and a half years.

I swung my feet back and forth, trying to block it all out, but still seeing the vague images in my mind: the trial, the divorce, the disbarment proceedings. Thinking about my old partner, Roger Hawley, about what I'd like to do to that asshole. Every now and then I had the urge to confront him, to drive over to his office at Peachtree Center and see what he had to say for himself, ask him why he sold me out the way he did.

But I never went. What was the point? If there was one thing I had finally learned, it was that you never got a satisfactory answer out of Roger Hawley. That was just the way he was built. He was sliding away from you all the time, without you even knowing it. You kept thinking he was right there in your face, right there giving you the absolute lowdown. And then all of a sudden he was gone, out of reach, nothing left to hold onto.

The sky was a white glaze of light. Nothing moved.

There was something about the heat and the sun at the

loading dock that started bringing me back. The fear, the disgust, the sense of being dead slowly washed away, and I could feel my heart stomping around on top of my stomach. Maybe the Big Fear was just too much effort in that baking sun. And then pretty soon I was okay, just another ex-lawyer, ex-banker, ex-scumbag, coming up for air.

After a while a car pulled into the parking lot, a long champagne-colored Lincoln Town Car, about ten years old. The coupe with the opera windows, an exquisitely ugly model. There was glare shining off of it, shining so bright that it seemed almost like it was driving around in a cloud of light. It glided by the loading dock slowly, turned around, and stopped about thirty feet from where I was sitting—close enough for me to see the chrome mud flaps and the curb feelers, close enough to see the windows, tinted almost black. The car sat there for a couple minutes, gleaming, with the engine running. I could see the air tremble over the hood, could feel someone in the car looking at me. I couldn't see them, though; the windows were too dark.

I waited. There was nothing better to do.

The driver's-side door opened and a big black guy got out. I put my hand up, trying to block out the glare off the car so I could see him better. He had a Fu Manchu mustache and his hair was jeri-curled, dripping in wet ringlets out of one of those green and yellow guru caps.

"I know you," he said. It wasn't a question. He had a weird voice, like the whine of bees, and his eyes were hidden behind little round sunglasses. A scary guy.

"I don't remember you," I said. I was thinking maybe he'd been at Maxwell. Or maybe I rented him a couch, matching end tables. He wasn't the kind of guy you'd forget, though. I didn't get it.

"Bobby Vine," he said. He was standing next to the car, his hands crossed over his chest.

"That's right," I said. He just stood there looking at me. "Is there something I can do for you?"

"Come here, my man, check this out." He put his key into the trunk of the Town Car. It was so bright I could hardly see him.

"You got to fill out a return voucher," I said.

He looked up at me, made a sleepy, hard-guy face. "Do what!"

"If you got a return, you need to go up front to the register, fill out a voucher, and then the guys in the warehouse sign the yellow copy, pick it up for you."

He looked confused for a minute. "Nah, man," he said. "I just want you to *look* at it." He pointed at the trunk.

I shrugged and walked out to the car. Curious, I guess. He opened the trunk all the way, and we looked in.

"What?" I said. There was nothing to see particularly—just the spare, a jack, a crowbar, some greasy pink rags like they use at filling stations to wipe the oil off a dipstick.

He picked up the crowbar, hefted it in his hand, wrapped one of the rags around it two or three times. Then another one. When he was finished tying the second rag around the crowbar he said, "How's that look?"

"Fine," I said.

"Good," he said. "Good."

Then he hit me with it, once, in the head.

It didn't hurt. There was just the shock and then a feeling like my blood was shooting through my veins at twice the normal speed. I felt calm.

The last thing I remember thinking before I blacked out was, Did Ray ever tell me what his philosophy of sales was or not?

CHAPTER 2

I woke up slowly, rising into a pulsing womb of pain, a pain that came before consciousness, before thought, before personality—a total, all-encompassing pain. After a while I got past the pain enough to pay attention to what was around me. I wasn't sure at first where I was. All I could see was the smudged, close ceiling. Was it prison? The blood started going, buzzing through my head. I tried to sit up, but couldn't. Nothing seemed to move right.

Not prison. It wasn't prison, but I still couldn't remember where I was. For a minute I wasn't even clear on *who* I was. Just confusion and pain. My head pulsed with every heartbeat, the veins twisting, writhing, expanding, full of poison juices.

Again I tried to sit up. But it wasn't just my head. My right arm didn't quite respond the way it should, and my ribs felt smashed. It was like somebody had beat me up with a baseball bat.

Or maybe a crowbar.

I felt sick to my stomach, then the blackness rushed in.

When I woke up the second time, there was dried puke on the sheets and a horrible, dead smell filling the room. It was my own room, that's where I was. A gnawing emptiness expanded in my gut. The sun was shining through the window.

There was something strange about the sun, something I couldn't place at first. Then I realized: The sun only came into my room in the morning. When I woke up the first time, there was no sun. It must have been yesterday afternoon. So I'd been here for almost a day. Fifteen, twenty hours, minimum.

I sat up, taking it slow. My stomach clenched, tried to back up on me; my ribs complained; the veins in my head went crazy, twitching and writhing. A concussion, maybe? Half my brain leaked out into the pillow by now? I sat still until the pounding in my head eased a notch.

I felt my ribs with my good arm. Nothing seemed to be broken. Same with the shoulder. Just a big gash coming down toward my elbow. I unbuttoned my shirt, slowly, with my left hand. There was a purple bruise, six inches long, running diagonally across the left side of my chest.

I was thinking, How do you tell if your ribs are broken? The blood from the gash on my arm had fused with the shirt. After some slow-motion wriggling and peeling I got the shirt off. My right arm looked ugly, blood caked down the side. There'd been just one whack there, too, glancing off the shoulder and tearing the skin down to the elbow. Nothing too serious, but it hurt like hell.

I got up, slowly, and went into the bathroom to clean myself.

Taking off my pants, I noticed my wallet and keys were still in the pockets. I opened the wallet, looked inside. Driver's license, Social Security, no credit cards (I don't have those any more) and fifty-seven dollars cash. So it wasn't robbery. Mr. Crowbar didn't want my money. It was weird.

I stood in front of the mirror, feeling kind of empty and bewildered and hollowed out. Bad news. Greenish-white skin. Little rivulets of dried blood stuck to my face. Hair glued up in all directions. *What's going on, man? What's going on?* I had this bad feeling—the Big Fear coming on again—accompanied by the sense that some shameful thing out of my past was creeping up on me ... but I couldn't figure out what it could be.

I got in the shower, figured I'd get some thinking done: who-what-why kind of things—keep it on a nice analytical plane, push the emotions away. While I worked all the crusted fluids off my skin and out of my hair, let the water warm my body, I went over the details. The problem was there weren't many details. I go out behind a furniture store. An old land barge drives up. A guy gets out. He recognizes me, pretends he wants to show me something, hits me over the head. I wake up a day later in my own bed, my own room. Nothing stolen, nothing disturbed. Period. End of story.

There was something missing. Each time I went through the story I thought about what I should have done. Gone back inside. Or blocked the crowbar. Savage chop to the throat. Knee to the groin. Well. It played okay in the shower, anyway. *Don't get mad. Don't do it. You get mad, the Big Fear starts coming back. Easy, man, easy: analytical, remember? Cool, calm, collected.*

A missing piece. That was the important thing. The guy didn't want to kill me. He wanted me to end up here, otherwise he would have left me out behind Ray's store. Why? What about the face? The voice? I kept thinking, going back and back, but I couldn't place him. Mr. Crowbar, he just wasn't a guy you would forget.

What about before I went to Maxwell? That was a whole different life. Back then I was pretty successful—a happy, pillar-of-the-community jerk. Pretty wife. Nice kids. Good school district. Smoked chicken in the backyard. Golf on Saturday. Decorative law degree hanging on the wall. It was all so nice I could hardly even think about it without feeling sick and rotten about myself.

Stay cool, Bobby. Stay detached.

The one little chink, the one minor flaw in the facade of my life back then (if it was a facade), was that I was rigging stocks on the side. Very profitable, very illegal. I didn't like thinking about that much, either. Still it wasn't the kind of sport where people came after each other with crowbars.

The only name I could come up with, the only guy I really had bad blood with, was Roger Hawley. But if anything, it was me who ought to be splitting *his* head open. Just another one of those things not to think too much about. After he handed me over to the U.S. attorney, I don't imagine he ever gave me a second thought. "Don't worry, Bobby. Just deny everything. This kind of thing, worst that can happen, you get a suspended sentence. As soon as it's over we'll take care of you." Roger always said *we* when he talked about himself. He was that kind of guy.

It wasn't until well into the trial that I started to get suspicious, to wonder why the SEC and Justice hadn't gone after Roger, too. By the time I figured it out, I was a goner.

But that still didn't answer any of my questions about Mr. Crowbar. Much as I'd like to blame Roger Hawley for all the shit that had happened to me in the past few years, this obviously didn't have anything to do with him. I didn't have anything he wanted anymore. No money, no influential buddies, no cute wife, no adorable kids, no deals in the making. *Breath in. Breath out. Nice and calm, that's good, nice and easy.* I was traveling light now, a man with no baggage.

I toweled off, put on a pair of jeans, and went to get some breakfast. I was feeling better now that I was clean, and the thought of having some food was putting me in a better mood. Screw Mr. Crowbar. Who cared what the missing piece was? I was alive. I was hungry. I was a free man. Things were looking up.

I walked into the living room. No problem there, nothing disturbed. Everything was in its place: One brown vinyl Bark-a-lounger, one coffee table made of shellacked two-by-fours, one Samsung TV (rented—at cost—from Ray), a couple shelves of decent books about sales and the history of war and various other simple, pleasant things. It wasn't exactly *mine*. I hadn't entirely staked it out just yet. But it was a start. And so I was thinking, Okay, okay, this isn't so bad is it? Nice little house, nice little job, a few nice diversions. Life isn't so bad. Got the whole thing under control.

Time to get something to eat. Bacon, four eggs over easy, couple of English muffins, big mug of coffee, maybe a slice of grapefruit . . . and the world, once again, would be set right. Then I'd call the cops, report this thing, get this whole business behind me.

I went into the kitchen, jiggled the light switch. The bulb seemed to be burned out. It took a few seconds for my eyes to adjust. Then I saw. What I saw made me realize that I did not have life under control. The world had no intention of being set right.

And I'm not talking about the dreary bachelor's tableau—the dirty dishes in the sink, the half-eaten tortilla, the empty bottle of Texas Pete hot sauce that I still hadn't gotten around to throwing away—not any of that, but the other thing: the thing that made the Big Fear come welling up again. For a minute I couldn't move, couldn't even think, couldn't let what I saw pass across the threshold of my brain.

Slumped on the linoleum, was a man, dead, with his head beat in.

Somebody had hit him in the face a bunch of times, hit him enough to throw his whole head out of shape. There was a lot of blood—in his lap, on his shirt, on the linoleum, smeared across the door of the refrigerator. The blood had gone black as old creosote. Just enough of the face was left to make the dead man recognizable.

It was Roger Hawley.

I went back into the living room, sat down, and turned on

the television. I was paralyzed, my mind so clogged up by the whole thing, that I didn't know what else to do. Time sort of stretched out for a while, and it seemed like if I just sat there in front of the TV and didn't move or even think about anything, then maybe nothing would have actually happened and everything would stay the same forever.

Phil Donahue was interviewing three married lesbians, asking them about their children. After "Donahue," I watched "Geraldo." He was doing lesbians that day, too. I didn't really pay attention to what they were saying, all the questions.

I was thinking about Roger Hawley, the stuff we had done together. I couldn't really associate that thing in there, that dead *thing* in the kitchen, with Roger. He had always been in motion, always going, always talking. He never stopped. I couldn't think of him as dead. Even now, even though I can't think good things about him anymore, I can still say he was one of the most alive people I ever knew. He had that spark.

The sad thing about Roger is that I don't think he ever realized this. Sometimes it seemed like Roger didn't exist except in other people's minds. He was like a blank slate, letting you scrawl your dreams and aspirations all over him. What I mean is, he could ferret stuff out of you—what you wanted to do with your life, what you wanted to be, what you believed in—and then turn that knowledge to his own purposes, make you into his tool by convincing you that he was the best route to your dreams. And so you'd do anything for him.

I know *I* did anyway.

But the point is that Roger got lost inside of that psychological acuity, that uncanny understanding of other people that he had. It was like he couldn't see himself at all, except in the mirror of everyone else's desires. He didn't have much of anything left over for himself. Nothing but ambition and energy and this restless, crazed, insatiable need to be whatever the person across the table wanted him to be. Smart, funny, wise, rich— it didn't matter. He was game for it. Yeah, old Roger was game as hell!

And that's some vain shit, man, because nobody can pull that off. It ends up turning into one parlor trick after another, nothing real about it, my whole life degenerating into a cheat and a sham and a lie.

Did I say *my?* I meant Roger, of course. It's *Roger's life* I was talking about.

After "Geraldo," the noon news came on, then a soap opera with a dead guy lying around in the first scene. I started laughing, I don't know why. It was funny how different this soap opera guy looked from a real dead person. I kept laughing, couldn't stop, like something in my head had popped.

I was still laughing when somebody started banging on the door.

"It's open," I said softly—and I could feel the Big Fear rising inside me in a sudden rush, everything finally bursting the dams and pouring into my head with sure and terrible clarity. They knocked again. "It's open!"

The door squeaked, let in about eight inches of light. A face cut into the sunshine, a young cop, eager, with a blond forelock. "Fulton County Sheriff's Department," he said. "I got a warrant here says I can search these premises."

"Come on in," I said. "You might as well start in the kitchen." The young guy came in—three older cops, serious-looking, trooping in behind him. The last cop stood in front of me, watching, his hand near his gun, while the other three went into the kitchen. The cop's eyes never left my face.

That was when I noticed the crowbar lying next to my feet, halfway under the couch. It had a rag wrapped around the end, the kind of rag you use to clean a dipstick, and it was black with Roger's blood. I didn't have to think hard to figure that my prints were all over the handle.

In the kitchen one of the cops said, "Aw, gracious, look at that." Quiet, like a deacon talking in the back of the church.

Another voice, a funny guy, said, "Raw deal, huh?"

It took the cops about half a minute to get the cuffs on me, explain some things about my constitutional rights.

Outside, the cop with the forelock was making throw-up noises under the dogwood tree.

2

Jeannie's Deal

CHAPTER 1

I was in the Fulton County Jail, a big, pink star-shaped building, seven stories, with Plexiglas windows. My cellmate was a black kid named Bug who had just gotten back from the ninth floor at Grady Hospital. He had tried to hold up a liquor store with a penknife. The guy at the register had laughed at Bug, shot him twice in the chest, once in the neck.

"Yo, you get arraign yet?" Bug said.

"Murder One," I said.

"Damn!" Bug shook his head. "You got a lawyer?"

"Public defender, guy named Jackie Shane."

"Little chubby-face black dude? Man, he a fool. He got the worst record in the whole PD office." Bug was smiling at me, acting nice. Figuring he'd take advantage of me.

"Yeah, well," I said. "I was framed."

"Uhhh," Bug said. Every third guy in jail says he was framed. And the other two say they're innocent, victims of some kind of conspiracy or perverse bad luck.

"I didn't hit the bastard thirteen times in the head with a crowbar," I said. "I'd never do a thing like that."

"Uhhh," Bug said.

"Or smash his head all over the refrigerator? I look like the kind of guy who'd do a thing like that?" I was squinting my eyes, trying to seem a couple bricks shy of a load. Unpredictable and dangerous.

"Nah, man," Bug said. He shrank into himself, trying not to take up any of my space.

I gave him my best Maxwell smile.

CHAPTER 2

The interrogation, duly videotaped and transcribed, was conducted by a Fulton County Sheriff's Department homicide investigator named Claude G. Handlin. My public defender just sat there, not saying much. What follows is toward the end, straight off the transcript, after we'd talked for a few hours.

HANDLIN: Let me ask you again, Mr. Vine, you want to tell me why you killed Roger Hawley?

VINE: How many times I have to tell you? I mean, really.

HANDLIN: Okay. Okay. Let's back up a little. Let's back up, calm down. Tell me a little about you and the decedent.

VINE: The decedent? Me and Roger go way back.

HANDLIN: How way back is way back?

VINE: College. Both of us were at Clemson, pledged Sigma Nu. Accounting majors, ROTC. The usual stuff. We were junior deal makers even in college; we ran a couple of little businesses, taking pictures at proms, selling gimmicky booster crap to rich alumni before the football games, that kind of thing. He was my best friend.

HANDLIN: Okay.

VINE: I'll tell you the thing about Roger, about why he was a great deal maker: He could con you into thinking that the dumbest thing in the world was actually a great big adventure. Printing up a T-shirt to sell outside the stadium at the USC game, he'd make it out to be a holy crusade. What he did later on, the investment banking, it was more of the same: A staple manufacturer buys a string manufacturer, my friend, it's the second coming of Christ. It's that important, you know? He gets you that fired up. The deal, it's like the deal turns into a kind of sacrament, some ritual of salvation.

HANDLIN: You're losing me here, son.

VINE: Okay. Okay. Roger wasn't a steady guy, but he had a lot of ideas. And he was so smooth, always knew what to say, girls hanging around all the time. Whereas I was quieter, steadier, more analytical. I tended to kind of watch people, wait to see what they were going to do. But we got along okay. That was our secret, working together. He had ideas, energy, the gift of gab; I got things done.

HANDLIN: See? Stick to simple English, I understand.

VINE: After graduation we kind of went our separate ways. I got married, went to law school at Vanderbilt, moved to Atlanta. I was working for a big firm downtown, mostly corporate stuff. Lot of my clients were financial-service outfits. Banks, you know, small brokers. Roger ended up in Philadelphia doing investment banking, kind of a medium-sized regional firm. He came into investment banking just before it turned into a hot business—before the LBO scene really heated up.

HANDLIN: LBO?

VINE: What planet you been on for the last decade? You know, leveraged buy out?

HANDLIN: Oh, sure. I heard of that.

VINE: So anyway I got married. College sweetheart, the usual. Carla was a good-looking woman, a Tri Delt and all, but I guess I never figured her out. That a wedding band?

HANDLIN: Yes.

VINE: How long you been married, Deputy?

HANDLIN: I don't believe that's germane here, frankly.

VINE: Alright, I don't give a shit, sir. My point, the point I was going to make is it's amazing how long you can go on living with somebody, and you still don't know who they really are. Me and Carla—well, looking back I'm mystified. It's like I saw everything on the surface—you know, how she smiled at certain times when it seemed like there was no reason to smile or the look of concentration on her face when she played solitaire at night after the kids went to bed—but I couldn't see any deeper, couldn't understand who she was or what she was all about. It was that way with Roger, too. In retrospect I realize I never knew the guy. Not really.

But to finish the story, one day Roger shows up out of the blue. On my doorstep. I mean literally. No call, no nothing. I just open the door and there's Roger standing on the front porch with a big Hartmann suitcase. Saturday afternoon, he's wearing a handmade suit, Italian necktie, nice shine on his shoes. We sit down, have a couple drinks, turns out he's kind of at loose ends. They made him resign up in Philadelphia. He gave me some reason why it had happened—office politics, maybe. Later I found out the truth was that he'd been cooking the books on some deal. I never really got the whole story, though.

He was going on about how Atlanta was the growth capital of America, all the fortunes you could make here. He wanted to start a little investment bank. He called it a merchant bank, you know, because it had that European kind of feel to it. You know what an investment bank is, Deputy?

HANDLIN: A bank, I know what a bank is. You loan money.

VINE: Not exactly. An investment bank arranges for people to raise money by issuing stocks, bonds, debentures. It's a whole different thing from commercial banking. See, the Glass-Steagall Act. . . . Forget it, it's not important. Anyway, what happened, Roger caught me at a weak moment.

HANDLIN: Weak in what sense?

VINE: You ever worked in a whole building full of lawyers? They're the most insufferable bunch of assholes. All this pious crap coming out of their mouths. All these delicate distinctions. All this talk. But they never *do* anything. It's ridiculous. As long as you've got a logically defensible position, as long as you've got your ass covered, it doesn't matter whether you've accomplished anything. Or on the off chance you actually accomplish something, you've got a fifty-fifty shot of doing something that's evil and wrong and totally fucked up. But you've got to go a long way to find a lawyer who'll admit this to you. Lawyers, they're always bowing down in front of the system, the law, like it's some kind of magic shrine. They say, "Hey, sorry but that's just the way the law works. Start disregarding the law, start fudging the system, and next thing you know the Gestapo's going to be dragging your family off in the middle of the night." This is a real handy argument when you're milking the magic titty for a hundred and half a year. I was sick of the whole thing. Or maybe it was just that I was getting the impression that they weren't going to make me a partner.

Anyway we hooked up together, me and Roger, went in debt up to our eyeballs, and started Hawley Vine & Company. Our mainstay was underwriting stock issues for small companies. Real bush league as investment banking goes. But man was it fun! We were deal makers now—wheeling and dealing, making things happen—instead of scurrying around cleaning up somebody else's mess. It was the most fun I've had in my life. The adrenaline, the pressure, the crazy hours, the feeling of power when everything comes together.

I'm getting off the point. Anyway, we were lucky. We did okay. Roger's Mr. Outside; I'm Mr. Inside. We expanded, brought in a couple more people, some analysts, some secretaries, moved to a new building. Roger started to get obsessed with the whole thing. More, more, more. Expand, expand. He had always been that way, I guess, but what had been kind of charming in college started to seem a bit obsessive. He just couldn't be satisfied. And we kept going further in debt.

See when you expand this way, you run into trouble. The money's there ultimately, but you're always operating three, four months behind the next check. Cash flow becomes . . . problematic. Eventually Roger dreamed up a way to get us out of our fix by manipulating stock prices. You know how stocks work, Deputy?

HANDLIN: Buy low, sell high.

VINE: Yeah, well. No magic to it. The price of a stock is nothing more than what somebody is willing to pay for it. If I buy a stock in some company for ten bucks, there's a buyer and a seller. We agree on a price, that's what it's worth. If I find a guy the next day who's willing to pay fifteen, then it's worth fifteen, okay?

HANDLIN: Take your word for it.

VINE: My point is, there's a thousand little companies out there, market value of maybe a million, two million dollars, where there might be only a few hundred people who own shares. It's easy for a small group of people to manipulate the price. You sell your stock to me, then I'll sell it back to you, then you sell it back to me. You see where I'm going?

HANDLIN: What's this got to do with you and Roger Hawley?

VINE: Watch. Just watch. You're going to like this. I buy from my buddy at six dollars, I sell it back at six and a half. At the end of the day, some little guy at the *Wall Street Journal* writes down six and half, and there it is in the paper the next morning. Stock's worth six and a half dollars. It must be true, hell, it says so in the *Wall Street Journal.*

Day after that, my buddy sells those same shares back to me for seven. Next day in the *Journal* it says seven. Now it's worth seven. Next day I sell back for eight. You see what's happening?

HANDLIN: The price is going up.

VINE: Wrong. It looks like the price is going up, but it's not. It's bogus. People get fooled. They read the *Wall Street Journal,* they say, "Hey, look this stock's going up; let's get on the train." They start buying. More people want to buy than want to sell. You get a stampede and the price skyrockets. Now me and my buddy, let's say, for the sake of argument, we bought in with a hundred thousand bucks. Well the price is going up, let's say it's at eighteen now. That means our stock is worth three times what it was at the beginning. Three hundred thousand. As long as we can find a buyer. So we divide it up and sell it. If we're lucky we sell while everybody, all these speculators, are still trying to buy. Boom. We net a hundred, two hundred grand for a couple weeks' work.

HANDLIN: Smart. How come more people don't do that?

VINE: It's illegal. Why you think I went to jail?

HANDLIN: Fill me in here, why it's illegal. That type thing isn't my strong suit in terms of law enforcement.

VINE: Because I basically conned people into thinking something was happening that wasn't. The whole principle, the thing that makes the market work, is that people trust it. Everybody out there is supposed to be making square deals. If people are making deals that aren't really deals, that aren't what the lawyers call arm's-length transactions, then the whole thing falls apart. We took advantage of the mechanisms here, making it look like something was happening that wasn't. We ripped all these guys off.

HANDLIN: So you and the decedent came up with this idea?

VINE: No. Roger came up with this idea. The basic idea's been around for as long as people have traded stock, but Roger put a little spin on it, some tricks that kept the SEC from knowing what was going on, suspending trading, all that shit.

See, Roger didn't tell me what he was up to the first time he did it. I found out, though, and told him to stop, gave him the legal-beagle speech about how it wasn't ethical, legal exposure, blah, blah, blah. He said no way, he had put all of our spare capital into the deal and if he unrolled our position in the middle of the deal, we'd take a loss. We had some obligations due at the bank, a balloon note on a lease, some other things. If Roger came up short, we couldn't pay. And then the bank would push us into Chapter 11, maybe even go after our assets. My house, my car, you name it. If he had pulled out, it could have put my family on the street.

So I said, okay, finish the deal ... but just this one time and never again. Two weeks later, he comes into my office and puts a check on my desk. Special dividend, he says to me. Seventy-five grand.

HANDLIN: This point, what happens to Mr. Legal Ethics?

VINE: Lawyers can argue anything. That's the way we're trained. Back then? For seventy-five grand, hell, I'd argue anything. White's black, black's white. There are economists out there who claim that insider trading is good, that it actually transmits information to the market more quickly than conventional financial reporting and in doing so increases the efficiency of the market. I boned up on that line of reasoning, convinced myself that what I was doing was no big deal. See? Logic in the service of convenience. That's what legal training does for you.

HANDLIN: They sent you to jail for that?

VINE: No. They never caught me on that particular one. I don't have to tell you I'm not going to go into it any further, you being an officer of the law. But basically we did it a bunch of times, then we got caught.

HANDLIN: So it's all his fault you got sent to jail?

VINE: No. It's my fault. I could have said no to him, just put my foot down. But I never did. I never said no.

HANDLIN: How come he didn't go to jail, him being the chief honcho of this operation?

VINE: I don't know the exact answer to that. What happened, I went to him after the indictments came down, said I was going to plead guilty, tell them everything. I assumed, you know, that they were going to indict him, too. Roger says no way, don't plead guilty. You've got to fight them. He had some money salted away offshore, down in the Caymans or Panama. He said he'd pay for my lawyer, take care of me, all that kind of thing. Just sit tight, old buddy boy, it'll all be okay. I say okay fine, Roger. Whatever you say.

But the other shoe never drops. No indictment against him, no subpoenas, no depositions, no nothing. I mean absolutely zippo. It's like this crashing silence. Meantime, the SEC and the U.S. attorney are building up a real detailed case against me. I thought we'd covered our tracks real well. But they're coming up with bank records, confirmation slips, you name it. Chapter and verse. Funny thing was, they only got the stuff for a few of the deals. The really juicy deals, they had a few suspicions, some odds and ends, but zero documentation. Nothing they could use in court.

Anyway, Roger comes to the trial every day, sits right behind me. The whole time he's patting me on the back, smiling like a son of a gun, telling me everything's going to be fine. What a fucking prince of a guy.

What happens, they've got me up on the stand, on redirect—the prosecutor's asking me something, a question about some document, people's exhibit eight zillion by this time, and she screws up, asks me about the wrong document. Looking at the wrong page of her notes, maybe. No big thing, but she gets kind of flustered, just for a second, like she's lost her bearings. And at that moment she looks around, looks for something to grab onto. Something to steady her.

That's when it happens. She and Roger, I see their eyes meet, making some kind of connection. Just for a second. Just a fraction of second, maybe. Right there, man, I see what's been going on all this time. He was feeding her. I wanted the earth to open up, swallow me alive. It was him, it was Roger, giving them all the goods they needed to put me away.

HANDLIN: I guess you got a strong resentment here.

VINE: Hold on, Deputy. Hold on. Not strong enough to kill him.

HANDLIN: And I guess looking down on his dead body lying there in your kitchen, it must have felt pretty good.

VINE: I don't know what I felt. It was like I was paralyzed. Maybe I didn't feel anything.

HANDLIN: Nothing. This fellow gives you the shaft, ruins your life, he's lying on the floor bleeding to death, and you don't feel nothing, no emotional type reaction.

VINE: How many times do I have to say it?

HANDLIN: Mr. Iceman. Cool as a cucumber. Dead man don't mean diddley-shit to you.

VINE: You don't know what it was like. You don't know a goddamn thing about me.

HANDLIN: All right, Mr. Vine, let's take it from the top. How come you killed Roger Hawley?

MR. SHANE: Deputy, we've been going here, what, about

three and a half hours? How about you give me a moment of time with my client?

CHAPTER 3

Ray was sitting on the other side of a dingy counter in the room where you meet with your lawyer. He had come to see how I was doing, I guess. "It's funny, Ray," I said. "The last thought, the last thing that crossed my mind when that guy hit me in the head was what you were talking about in your office. Your philosophy of sales? You remember that?"

"Yeah," Ray said. "I don't recall you was listening."

"Maybe I wasn't. Did you ever tell me what it was? Did you say what your philosophy was or not?"

Ray was looking around the room. "You know this ain't such a bad place," he said. "Back when I was in, everything, you know—it felt like somebody'd pissed on it. You wanted to wash your hands all the time."

"I guess," I said. To me everything still had that feeling.

"You ever read that book," Ray said, *"The Art of the Deal?* By that guy, what's his name?"

"No," I said. "Never got around to it."

"Nah, I didn't neither," Ray said. "I don't read books as a rule. I seen a thing about it on TV. Kind of liked that name, *The Art of the Deal.* It's got a ring to it."

"Uh-huh."

"Started to think about it, though, after a while I decided this guy's full of shit. He had a good name for it—art!—but he was still full of shit." Ray was rubbing the back of his hand again, the place where he had the tattoo. It said RAY with quotation marks around it. "The thing is . . . ." He trailed off, working on his hand. "The thing is, it makes it sound like a deal is—I don't know—like it's some damn sculpture, some hot rod you spent all your weekends on till you got it all chromed up, four-barrel carb, sixteen layers of clear coat on it. Like there's just you and the deal. You, here; the deal, there." Ray pointed. Here, there.

"But it's not that way, Counselor. There's you. And then there's some other guy. The deal, okay, that's something between the two of you." He looked at me. "See what I'm saying?"

I nodded, thinking about it.

"Sales. Deals. It ain't no work of art. It's just you and him. Either you can go in there, fuck him over, may the best fucker win, right? Or you can find some common ground. I used to take that road. Fuck 'em. Fuck 'em. Fuck 'em all to hell." Ray was waving his arms around. "That was my whole philosophy. Bend over, boy, I'm driving you home." Ray was staring up at the tiny window on the door, six feet up, all of a sudden looking like an angry kid. A kid with an old man's face.

"But after a certain point in time—not in prison, it was later than that—after a certain point in time, I realized, hey, that's a philosophy for assholes, for people who ain't gonna sleep too good at night." We sat there for a while.

"So what happened, Ray? Some big thing happen to you, thunderbolt out of the sky?"

"Nothing particular," Ray said. "I just got me a new philosophy."

"That's it?"

"That's it."

I didn't say anything. I had never had a philosophy, I guess, a worked-out system of what matters and what doesn't. I had just played good boy—or good lawyer, maybe—and followed the rules. And then after a while even the rules had lost their power to keep me in line, and I had nothing left to guide me. Break one rule, you make up a new one. I was trying to figure out what the difference between us was, how he'd managed to keep a consistent take on life and somehow I hadn't. Or if I had, it had been consistently the wrong one.

The guard stuck his head in and pointed at his watch. "Two-minute warning," he said.

"It came on you all of sudden?" I said.

"No," Ray said. "Hell, no. It just happened. One day I woke up and realized I was different somehow."

"Well. What *is* your philosophy, Ray?"

Ray put on his look like he was going to lecture, looking out into the middle distance like some tweedy law school professor in a bad movie. "Common ground. Just got to find a little common ground." Then the professor look went away and he shrugged. "You know the word *commerce?* I seen a thing on TV one time—rarely watch the education channel—but anyways this fellow says that back in old history days that word, *commerce,* meant something more like *friendship.* Like doing a guy a favor. Hanging out and doing favors. That's what being in business ought to be. I do you a favor, you do me a favor. Integrity, trust, honor. That's what it's all about."

"Like the Mafia," I said. Then I felt like a jerk.

Ray didn't think I was funny. He just looked around the room like he needed to wash his hands after all.

He stood up suddenly, took his hat off the counter. It was a bright yellow baseball cap, mesh, that said *Indian Creek C.C.* on the crown, with a picture of a guy really whacking a golf ball stitched above the words. Ray stared at the hat for a while. "I can't bail you out, Bobby," he said.

"Look, Ray," I said. "It's okay. Three hundred and fifty grand, that's a lot of money."

"I got the money, it's not that. It's just . . . I can't do it."

"You got philosophy about bail, too, Ray?"

"Yeah," he said. "I got a philosophy about a lot of things."

Ray walked over to the door. "How about your lawyer?" he said. "He any good?"

"He's an idiot," I said.

Ray flinched, like a father watching his kid get beat up on the playground, but knowing in the long run it did the kid no good to intervene. "You're a lawyer. You must have some friends. . . ." he said. "Lawyers. People who could help you out."

"The folks I knew didn't practice this kind of law," I said, gesturing around the room. "Besides I'm a disbarred lawyer now. I'm untouchable. As far as my old friends are concerned, my ashes are scattered to the wind. I'm dead to those people."

Ray said, "I wish. . . ." Then, whatever he was going to say, he decided not to. I couldn't tell what he was thinking.

He stood next to the door, rubbing his tattoo.

CHAPTER 4

"Vine. Somebody here to see you." The guard unlocked the door. I wasn't expecting anybody.

I guess I must have looked puzzled. Bug said, "Yo, maybe it's your lady."

"I don't have a lady," I said.

"Don't got no lady?" Bug looked at me funny. "Gotdamn!"

We went down to the talk room, the same place I'd met with Ray. There was a guy about my age sitting across the counter from me. He wore a fruity-looking houndstooth check suit, custom made, and his tan was a little too deep. A Phi Beta Kappa key hung from a chain that dribbled down from the buttonhole of his vest. I hadn't seen a guy that young wearing a vest in years. He wasn't fat, but there was something soft and overfed about him. His eyelids drooped, like he was bored or put out with you. Behind the act I could see he was a little nervous. Who could blame him? The last time we'd met, it had not been a real congenial affair.

"Jordan Foote, Esquire," I said. "What a pleasant surprise."

He raised one eyebrow, looked at me for a second, then looked away. It seemed to cause him mild physical pain to look at me for any length of time.

"Mr. Vine, I had no choice in the matter," he said. "In a case such as yours, the guidelines were crystal clear. Breach of fiduciary duty, flagrant violation of law. It was very dis-

tressing and exceedingly clear." His accent was Southern prep
school, a little airy sounding—like he'd eaten too many
breath mints.

"Was your speech the one about the inviolate sanctity of
the law?" I said, thinking back to my disbarment hearing. He
had been second from the left in a row of gloomy-looking
lawyers. Gloomy until they decided to go ahead with the disbarment anyway; then they'd gone ahead and cranked up the
flame of righteous indignation. "Or was yours the one with
the quote—"

"Judex damnatur cum nocens absolvitur."

"That's the one. I was wondering for months what that
meant." I smiled at him. "See, I don't speak French."

Foote gave me a look, not sure whether I was kidding or
not. "Condemned is the judge when the guilty is acquitted."

"I couldn't agree more," I said. I turned off the dumb grin.
"Now what do you want, Jordan?"

Jordan Foote sighed heavily and took a legal pad out of his
document bag. He took a long time. "In the matter which we
are about to discuss, I am representing Ms. Jeannette
Richardson. I presume you know Ms. Richardson." Foote had
a stiff way of talking, like he was reading out of a book.

I shrugged, not committing to anything.

Of course I knew who she was. She was big, big money.
Atlanta Ballet Board of Directors, social registry, old indus-
trial family money. My law firm had had some dealings with
her family business—a commodity chemical company called
RichCo—when I was with them back in the late seventies.
She was the chairman of the company now. Jordan Foote
smiled faintly at me, like an aunt who has never bred with
her own species.

"Ms. Richardson," he breathed, "is a private investor. A
woman of substantial means. *Substantial* means." Foote
stopped and wrote something in small neat letters on his vir-
gin legal pad, letting this revelation sink in. You could see his
teeth through a tiny crack in his lips, like he was trying to
smile.

"Okay," I said.

"She is prepared to arrange for payment of your bail in return for your assistance in a certain confidential matter." The same little teeth, gleaming through his lips.

I crossed my arms and watched as Foote wrote more small letters on the legal pad. He had a gold fountain pen—not a Mont Blanc, skinnier, but something along those lines. He kept writing. The legal pad had the name of his firm printed at the top. I outlasted him, and finally he looked up at me, a tight frown on his face.

"If I may offer a word of free counsel, this is not the kind of opportunity that comes around every day."

I looked at him. "Free advice," I said. "Must be my lucky day. What's an hour of your time worth? Two hundred, two twenty-five an hour? That must have been six or eight bucks worth of advice."

He started writing again. More neat letters. I pulled the pad out from under his long, thin hands and set it down out of reach on the Formica table. "You want to write an appellate brief, go home and do it. You want to talk to me, get started."

"I am not here to play games, Mr. Vine, but rather to convey the wishes of my client."

"Convey. By all means, convey."

"Very well. This is her proposal." Foote studied his fingernails. They were buffed and shiny. He took good care of them, you could tell. Roger used to do that, too, get his nails manicured. I never saw the point of it. "If you agree to meet with Ms. Richardson, we will arrange bail. She will explain in greater detail what she expects from you in return for her generous assistance. If you do not wish to aid her in this matter—and she assures me she can see no reason why you should not—then we shall arrange to recover our bond and you will be allowed to return to this lovely resort." He drew a delicate circle in the air with his pen.

"That's it?"

"With one small exception. You must agree in advance that Ms. Richardson's name will not be connected with yours in any way, shape, or form. And that includes particularly the matter of payment of bail."

"No hanging around with riffraff for Miz Richardson?"

"It's a very generous offer, Mr. Vine." He smiled again, the same faint row of teeth. "I don't imagine that you have many alternatives." Foote hoisted his fountain pen like he was go-ing to write something terrifically important and then set it back down again. He had forgotten I took his stage prop away.

It was a weird situation. I'd been eating myself up for two days now trying to figure who would want to trump up this case against me. And now someone I didn't know was going to bail me out. Why? What was her angle?

"When do I start?" I said.

A couple of minutes later, he was writing a check for three hundred and fifty thousand dollars to the treasurer of Fulton County. It was a hell of a lot of money. I took the liberty of looking over his shoulder. The name of the company printed on the check was Turnkey Investment Ltd. It had the sound of one of those dummy corporations that millionaires use to avoid paying taxes.

We drove up through Buckhead and out to West Paces Ferry Road in Jordon Foote's Vanden Plas. West Paces Ferry is big-house country: hundred-year-old trees, porte cocheres, servants' quarters, four-car garages, old stables converted into artists' studios. A lot of these places, you couldn't touch them for less than a few million.

We drove past the governor's mansion, then turned up a long, long driveway made of crushed stone. There was a point, halfway up the driveway, where all you could see was trees, old mossy hardwoods. You'd never have guessed there were two million people living within a few miles of that spot. The sun glinted through the foliage, catching a fern here, a sapling there. The air was black-green, shot through with flashes of white, flares of pale green. We could have been in the mountains, for all you could tell, miles from any-one.

I had grown up in the foothills of South Carolina in a little town where you could just wander out the back door and walk for miles through the pines. It kind of took me back, thinking about what life was like when I was a kid. I was a little grind, always doing my homework. But not ambitious really. Just getting by, doing what I thought I was supposed to do—never giving much thought to anything in particular.

I had never had a clear idea about what I was going to be when I grew up. Maybe some vague images: pretty house, pretty wife, pretty kids, cooking out in the summertime. Somewhere along the way I'd gotten it in my head to be a lawyer. It sounded great: You'd get to stand up in a courtroom, point at the guilty party, make a nice thundering speech. Of course the way it ended up I never even saw the inside of a courtroom. Most lawyers don't.

What a trap, what a goddamn crock it had turned out to be. Not just law, not just investment banking. I mean something had gone wrong with my whole life. And yet I couldn't say exactly why it had turned out that way, what it was that had gotten so fouled up. It's like some kind of connection between me and the world had snapped—and now that it was gone, I couldn't remember what it was, didn't even know where to look for it.

Sometimes I'd try and figure it all out, try and look back on my family, my life, things I had done. And there'd be glimmers here and there, brief sharp memories: the feel of my son's hair or the starchy, cottony smell of my ex-wife or this strange sucking sound my daughter used to make while she was sleeping. But they never seemed to add up to anything. And always, if I thought about it for more than a little while, the Big Fear would start in again, and I'd be drowning again, death seeping in on me from all sides.

Even with the air-conditioning turned on in the Jag, I could smell the rotten loamy odor of forest. We drove on slowly, the gravel crunching like smashed Cheerios under us. Out of the corner of my eye, I saw some kind of wildflower, bright purple, lit up in the dark belly of the woods. I turned to see it, but it had disappeared. What had happened to me? What was it that I had lost? Everything good seemed to vanish when I got close to it.

The house loomed in front of us. It was an old stone house, a mansion really, that looked like it had been built maybe a hundred years ago. Somebody had tarted it up and expanded it later, though—maybe in the twenties or thirties. There was a widow's walk and a goofy cupola on the old part and then a newer section, stuffier looking, glommed onto the side.

We drove up to the front door, and I got out. Jordan Foote

drove away without saying a word or even looking at me. I climbed the steps, and the door opened before I knocked.

"Miss Richardson is expecting you," said the maid—or whatever she was. She was soft-spoken, racially indistinct, well dressed but casual. Her skin was the color of semisweet chocolate.

I followed her through the house. The rooms were full of excessively trendy decor: lots of big round shapes and ugly maroons and blacks and bluish-grays. It was like walking through the middle of a bruise. We went through three or four rooms and came to the back of the house. The chocolate woman opened a sliding glass door to a patio and pointed to a couple of white chairs sitting under a beach umbrella.

"Please sit down. Miss Richardson will join you shortly." I walked over to the chairs and sat down. "May I offer you a refreshment?" The chocolate woman sounded like she had learned how to talk in the restaurant at the Ritz-Carlton.

A pitcher of something that smelled like martinis sat in front of me. "Thanks, no," I said, and the chocolate woman left.

I sat there feeling tense and out of place. The patio was about half a block long, made of huge black flagstones, which gleamed like they'd been vacuumed about five minutes earlier. Off to the side of the patio was an old swimming pool, tile, shaped like a kidney, built to the same giant scale as everything else on the property. Next to that was a stone cabana with two windows set close together, so it had a kind of cross-eyed look.

Stretching out in front of me was a whole lot of lawn, grown close and tight as a putting green. A tennis court, grass, squatted in the dead center of the lawn, surrounded by a high chain-link fence with little green ribbons threaded through the links. At the far side of the lawn, maybe a hundred yards away, were more trees. You got the feeling the place had been designed by engineers who just fit all the pieces together in a utilitarian way and didn't care how it looked, whether it gave some kind of unified impression.

Out beside the cabana there were two people wrapped up in black cloth outfits. They looked like guys in a ninja movie, only they had oval basket things on their heads, helmet contraptions that looked like fencing masks. The two ninjas were whacking each other with sticks. Even in the late afternoon, it was probably ninety degrees. I couldn't imagine a hotter, stupider thing to do than stand out in direct sunlight in a ninja outfit, getting hit with a stick.

They seemed to be going through a series of exercises, starting in a kind of stylized lunging position with the sticks pointing up in the air. Each time there was a freeze frame for a second and then they'd jump: whack, whack, whack, whack, whack! Then back to the starting position. The taller ninja looked like he was the student. Or at least he wasn't as good as the smaller guy. He was getting the shit knocked out of him, catching it in the head a few times.

At first it was kind of interesting, seeing the different moves, different positions. Then it got boring. What it boiled down to, it was just a couple of people swatting each other with sticks. You can only watch that for so long.

There was a stack of magazines on the table next to the pitcher of martinis. *Euromoney, The Economist, Institutional Investor*—all the macho finance magazines. Plus *Forbes, Fortune, Inc.*, and *Business Week*. At the bottom was a thick magazine made out of heavy brownish paper called *Transactions of the American Philological Society.*

I leafed through *Institutional Investor* for a while, reading about hedge strategies with forward currency contracts, Eurobonds, that kind of thing. Not especially interesting stuff, so I picked up *Transactions of the American Philological Society*, looked inside. The first article I turned to was called, "Franz Jungencranz: Towards a Hermeneutical Topology of the Spirit." It didn't mean anything to me.

After a while the ninja twins broke off their exercises and one of them, the taller of the two, walked over to the table where I sat. He took the basket contraption off his head and wasn't a *him* at all. It was Jeannie Richardson.

The most striking thing about her was her hair, which was jet black, a white streak running through it about two inches above her right ear. At first glance you would have thought she was just the other side of forty, but I happened to know she was a good bit older. More like fifty, fifty-five. You could tell she'd had some surgical assistance with her face—the eyes had that skinny Chinese look to them. And if you looked carefully, you could see the age in her hands: They were thinned out, the tendons snaking visibly up into her arm, the flesh loose and starting to blotch a little. But for all that, she was still a damn good-looking woman.

"Bobby Vine," she said. Her smile was perfect, the perfect Southern lady with the perfect Southern finishing school smile. And yet there was something masklike about her face, as though her pleasant smile were floating on top of something more interesting and complicated. Her finishing school, I think, had been Wharton, not Sweet Briar—maybe that accounted for it.

"You know, Bobby," she said, "I've been keeping an eye on you for some years."

"Is that right?" I said. I felt jittery, impatient. Whatever was coming, I wanted to get it over with.

"Oh, yes. Since your days at Hawley Vine. You had quite a reputation, you know."

"For what?" I said.

"Competence. Resourcefulness." She raised her eyebrows slightly. "Discretion."

"Among other things," I said drily.

"We all have our lapses, Bobby. God knows, I have." She laughed, high and monotone, like an electric organ.

The chocolate woman came out and started unlacing Jeannie's ninja suit. The suit had a lot of laces, lots of arm guards and stuff. "Do you know kendo, Bobby? Japanese fencing? Marvelous sport." She pointed at the other ninja standing near the pool. "That's my *sensei,* my kendo master, Mr. Sugiyama. A very spirited little man. In Japan he taught kendo to the young girls. It's considered part of their breeding over there, you see—so they can control their husbands." She laughed again, this odd, humorless laugh.

Yes, there was definitely something a little too studied about her: Maybe she was just too quick or even too thoughtful to really pull off that old, circuitous, Southern-lady snake dance. You know what I mean, the way women down here can sometimes squeeze you to death with charm? I could see something moving around behind that mask. Intelligence? Toughness? Loneliness? But I couldn't make out what it was.

The chocolate woman finally finished all the unlacing, unstrapping, and unbuckling, poured two martinis out of the pitcher, and took the ninja suit away.

"I guess I need to thank you," I said as Jeannie Richardson sat down.

"Let me look at you," she said. And she did, staring right into my eyes. From most people this would have seemed rude, but from her it seemed genuinely curious—if a little unnerving.

"Anything in particular you're looking for?" I said after a while.

"Integrity," she said.

"Okay," I said. "This is one I've been working on myself lately. Have I got it or not?"

Jeannie Richardson looked away into the distance somewhere above the pool. "Oh, darling, I wouldn't have a clue," she said, shrugging. "I've tried for years, you know, divining people's character. It never works." She gave me the finishing school smile again. I didn't smile back.

Sugiyama had peeled off his ninja suit and wandered over, not exactly to where we sat—but close enough. He was standing at the edge of the patio with his hands behind his back, looking placidly upward, thirty degrees above plane. Mr. Sugiyama, I supposed, doubled as a bodyguard.

"So," I said. "Ex-con. Busted lawyer. Barred from the securities business. Under indictment for murder. What use could you possibly have for me?"

She laughed, flashed me the Sweet Briar smile. "A reasonable question, Bobby." Then she looked away for a minute, the smile fading, like she was collecting her thoughts. I fooled around with *Transactions of the American Philological Society.* "You've studied philosophy?" Jeannie said.

"Can't say I have. I was an accounting major." I smiled mirthlessly. "You know—credits, debits."

Jeannie Richardson lifted her eyebrows a tiny fraction of an inch. "Too bad," she said.

"Yeah," I said. "Well, that's the way it goes."

"Bobby. . . ." Her nails clicked a couple times against the wrought iron table. "You seem a little . . . defensive."

"Who's defensive?" I nodded my head toward Sugiyama, the tough-looking kendo guy. "At least I didn't bring a bodyguard."

"You know *exactly* what I mean." She frowned at me, puzzled. "You're smarter than you act, Bobby. Why is that? Usually it's the girls who act dumb."

"I don't know," I said. "I'm not strong on self-analysis these days." I was feeling itchy, antsy. My left leg jiggled under the table. I knew I should be grinning and unctuous, but somehow I just wasn't in the mood to play the game.

A look of irritation surfaced briefly under her smiling Southern mask, then disappeared again. "All right, darling, let's cut to the chase. I assume you know more or less who I am, more or less what I do."

"I'm aware of the public record."

"Meaning?"

"Specifics?" I said. "Here's exactly what I know. Wharton, MBA, early seventies or thereabouts. You graduate, and Chairman Daddy brings you into the company, but he won't let you do finance; nice girls don't do finance, right? Couple years later, you're chief financial officer anyway. Nobody claims favoritism because you're the best man for the job. Let's see, 1979, your father dies, and you strong-arm the directors into making you president."

She was surprised. Actually that wasn't part of the public record at all. My old law firm had done work for a company RichCo acquired back in the seventies and I'd absorbed some inside gossip—not that I was going to give that away to Jeannie. Better to feign omniscience.

"Nineteen eighty-two. Majestyk Paper and Pulp Company. Over the counter. Trading at five and five-eighths. You go in, buy a thirty-four, thirty-five percent stake. The board gets nervous, offers you greenmail, eight and a half. You say no. Two weeks later you sell out to a Hong Kong investor group, price undisclosed. Rumor is you got over twelve, which adds up to about six million, free and clear. How'm I doing?"

Jeannie smiled—not the finishing school smile, but just a here-and-gone baring of teeth, an acknowledgement of facts.

I told her about all the other deals I was aware of. Royal Towers Partners, where she had played hide the weenie with an option on the property, made a couple million; Three Jay Master Limited, where she had made eight or ten million selling off their lease portfolio to a major oil company. There were a couple others. I quoted chapter and verse.

"Bravo," Jeannie said, clapping her hands languidly.

"Which brings us back, as we say, to the bottom line," I said. "What do you want from me?"

Jeannie trailed her little finger around the rim of her martini glass. "I have a proposition for you. I think we have some mutual interests. If we can make them dovetail—and I'm sure we can—then you and I can make a deal which will be of great benefit to both of us."

"I don't see it," I said. "Three hundred and fifty grand. That's a lot of money on spec. I might take off for Honduras tomorrow."

She did the electric organ laugh again. "You're a sketch, Bobby. Anybody can see you didn't kill Roger. You're not the type. I'm quite sure you promise a handsome return on equity."

"Equity?" I said. "You don't own me Jeannie. Not yet."

Jeannie waved her hand slowly, like she was shooing away a fly. "Just a figure of speech," she said pleasantly.

"Okay," I said. "So tell me a story."

"Ah, yes. Like, once upon a time?" She laughed. "Here's a story then, darling. Nine months ago one of my bankers came to me with an investment. It was a prospectus for a limited partnership called Health Systems 1990-II. Solid fundamentals, nice tax angle." She took a sip of the martini, rolled it around on her tongue, and went on. "The prospectus looked good. It was a medical equipment leasing deal, and it looked like a marvelous place to park a few dollars."

"Okay."

"I'm sure you're familiar with the structure of these deals, but I'll go over it briefly. Equipment leasing partnerships work this way: The manager of the deal sets up a limited partnership. He then offers units of the deal to the public. Each limited partnership unit costs, say, a hundred thousand. The general partner goes out and borrows money from the bank in an amount equal to the total contributions of the limited partners."

"Then the limited partners can charge the depreciation on the underlying assets off on their personal taxes," I said.

"Generally, yes. The Health Systems assets were CTs and MRIs, these scanner things, which they were going to lease to a hospital chain. There's one little catch, one little downside risk."

"Letters of credit," I said.

"Right. All the limited partners have to sign a letter of credit payable to the bank for the amount borrowed against your units by the partnership. If cash flow dries up and you can't make your bank payments, they call the letter of credit, and you have to make good on the loan.

"Anyway, I'll get back to that in a minute. Now, in a reputable venture of this type, the asset is always preleased. You have a customer, a supplier, and all the partnership has to do is raise the money. In this case a big hospital chain ordered a whole slew of scanners because of a change in Medicaid rules."

"Sounds like an airtight deal," I said. "Where's the problem?"

"It was a big order. The company that makes the CT scanners couldn't deliver them all in one throw, so Health Systems, the partnership, had a lot of cash sitting in the bank until the equipment was manufactured."

"I still don't see the problem," I said. "So you're late a quarter or two on your dividend distribution. Big deal."

She squinted at me for a second. "The problem, Bobby, is that the general partner of Health Systems was a crook. He cleaned out the bank account."

"Interesting," I said. "But what does this all have to do with me?"

An amused glint appeared in her eyes, like she thought she'd caught me with my hand in the cookie jar. When I didn't react, she cocked her head and said, "You really don't know?"

I shook my head.

She touched the white streak in her hair, smiled faintly. "The general partner, the crook? It was Roger Hawley."

The clouds were starting to part. And I wasn't sure I liked what I saw. "Uh-*huh,*" I said.

"Get it, darling?" she said.

"Yeah," I said. "But I still don't see where I fit in. So you lost some money—what, a couple hundred grand? Why bail me out for that?"

"Try eight million."

"Ouch."

"Ouch is right, darling. But that's not the worst of it. The worst is that the bank is going to call the letters of credit if we can't locate the money. I'll have to come up with eight million, cash. And right now I have a bit of a liquidity problem. I'm heavily invested in an ongoing deal. I've pledged these assets to support substantial borrowing. As soon as the bank finds out what happened, they pull the financing on my deal. If I pull out now, I get killed. It's that simple."

"So make the bank come after you," I said. "Let them sue. Throw some injunctions at them. Plead hardship. Make them play a little litigation tag."

"That's a page out of my book," she said. "Except for one thing. Jordan Foote's due diligence was slipshod. It escaped his attention that the bank that extended the credit line to Health Systems also happens to manage a large trust fund for me. A very large trust. You see the bulk of my inheritance is held in trust. Substantial income, but no control."

"Don't you have other resources?"

"All invested in the deal," Jeannie Richardson said. "If I don't pay, they freeze the trust. That means that the money to pay for my house, my cars, my boat, everything I own. . . ." She made a gesture with her hands: the Queen of Spades, chucking it all into the air.

"And you think maybe I ripped Roger off, smashed his head in and then called the police? And now I'm going to break down and confess to you and write you a check for eight million bucks so I can spare you the loss of your marvelous home and your spectacular European automobiles and your trustworthy family retainers and your jolly kendo teacher?"

Jeannie looked at me without blinking. "Do I seem stupid to you, darling?"

Sometimes it all builds up, the helpless, ugly feeling that the whole world is leaning on me—like I've lost all choice, all volition, all free will. And when that happens I guess I overreact a little.

I was embarrassed, letting myself get worked up like that. I didn't want to show it, though, so I just shrugged and looked away, let her think whatever she wanted.

"Okay, then let me finish," she said. "What you can do is help me look for the money. You have a history with Roger. I think that you can find out what he did with the money."

"Takes a thief?" I said quietly.

"Please, don't take it that way. I have a ... feeling about you." She was looking at me again with her intense, ambiguous gaze; she could have been getting ready to seduce me or pick my pocket, and I wouldn't have had a clue which.

"You've called in the cops? The Georgia Bureau? The FBI?"

"Of course. The FBI has already located a transferral of the stolen funds to a bank in Panama. They are pursuing repatriation through the usual channels."

I shook my head. "I still don't see it. What can I do that the Feds can't do?"

"I abhor conventional solutions. They lead to conventional results. Suppose the money's not in Panama now? What if he converted it to gold or gems, and the paper trail ends in Panama City?" A small twitch of the shoulders. "You, Bobby, are an unconventional solution. You can do things the FBI can't."

"Such as?"

"I expect we'll find that out if the need arises."

I thought about it for a while. Well, what the hell? There was something about the story that didn't feel right. There was something essential about Jeannie Richardson that eluded me. But when it came down to it, I didn't have any choice. None at all.

Jeannie Richardson leaned over and took my hand. She was close enough that I could smell her sweat, her perfume. Her raw, animal appeal caught me by surprise. "Please, Bobby. I'm not going to give you some bullshit about you being my only hope. But don't turn down a chance to clear your name and, sure, to help me out while you're at it. Don't turn it down out of orneriness. That would be monumentally stupid."

"I know. I know."

"Then it's a deal?" She opened her eyes a little too wide, like a flirtatious schoolgirl. It didn't suit her.

"Yeah, it's a deal." There were some other things I needed to know. "But tell me this: How did you find out Roger was skimming? I need someplace to start."

"I heard from Truman Shore, Roger's partner at Excor. He was, you know . . . a bean counter." She dismissed him with a small gesture of her hand. "Comptroller, something like that."

"You want to tell me what happened?"

"I was at home. I got a call, my private number, last Saturday evening. It was Truman, in a panic, an absolute tizzy. He said he had found some kind of problem with the Health Systems account. He was so confused, I couldn't get a straight story out of him, so I told him to put Roger on. But he wouldn't go to get him; he said Roger had done something with the account. Indiscretion was what he said. No, wait. I take that back. *Impropriety* is the word he used." She raised her eyebrows slightly and poked out about half an inch of pink tongue. "Well, *impropriety* . . . darling, that's not a strong word in my book."

She stopped talking, like she was thinking back on it.

"Well," Jeannie said suddenly. "You can talk to Jordan tomorrow. He'll give you the blow-by-blow. I'll instruct him to extend his full cooperation. Oh, and I'll have him give you a retainer, too. Ten thousand should be sufficient to get you started." She didn't listen for me to say yes or no, didn't even bother to smile. We had made our deal, and I guess she figured that was that.

"I'll have Louise call a cab for you." Adding, just in case I didn't get the hint: "Around front."

I stood. Then, as I started to walk away, I thought of something. "Can I ask you a question, Jeannie . . . while we're out here on the veranda, you know, being chummy and everything?" I grinned, like: no hard feelings.

Jeannie looked at me flatly. I seemed suddenly to be taxing her patience. "All right."

"You studied philosophy?"

She got a curious look on her face, trying to parse out where I was heading. "Long, long ago, yes. Why?"

"So what I'm wondering is, do you have a philosophy in your own life?"

She frowned. "I'm sorry?"

"A philosophy. You know, do you have some kind of angle, some kind of rules about how you live your life?" I paused, thinking about what Ray had said the other day. "I'm kind of taking a poll."

"I see," she said, smiling briefly, furtively. Then she looked out at her lawn, her trees, her pool, her cross-eyed stone cabana, her kendo trainer, her tennis courts—I don't know, taking everything in. The wind had started to pick up and the oaks were thrashing at the sky over on the other side of the lawn. There was a storm moving north, working its way up from the gulf. You could feel it coming.

Jeannie Richardson watched it all, maybe seeing some things I couldn't. She was surveying her kingdom, measuring it out. And I don't think she was satisfied.

"Yes, Bobby," she said finally, the white streak a gleaming dissonance in her jet-black hair. "I suppose I do have a philosophy."

She gave me her best Sweet Briar smile and tossed the rest of her martini onto the black flagstones. The drink splashed across the hot rock, evaporated. The vodka reek hit us in a close, choking cloud.

I waited for her to tell me, to explain her world view, but she didn't say another word. So after a moment I turned away, left her smiling inscrutably into the oncoming storm.

3

Ed's Deal

CHAPTER 1

The perky redhead at the reception desk on the twenty-sixth floor was studying her nails. They were radish or coral or Malibu sunset, some color like that. Her phone console looked like mission control for the space shuttle. When I came off the elevator, she looked up and smiled at me with a nice set of teeth, the orthodontia of a movie star. I told her my name, said I was there to see Jordan Foote.

She punched some buttons, effused into her mission control headset, pushed another button. "Mister Foote's in a meeting!" she told me. "Sarah Bryce will be with you shortly!"

"I was supposed to see Jordan," I said. "We made an appointment."

The perky redhead placed all ten of her Malibu sunset fingernails carefully on the countertop so they pointed at my groin, and leaned forward, confiding in me. "Sarah's the head paralegal here! She knows everything!"

I thought about it. "Okay," I said. "If you say she knows everything, that's good enough for me." I sat down on a puce leather couch over in the visitors' jungle across the room. There were a bunch of us, serious-looking guys with shiny briefcases, waiting around on couches that had been driven back into a couple thousand dollars' worth of rented ficus plants and midget palmettos.

I looked at the magazines, started to get impatient. A woman with a little brass trolley came around to tend the rent-a-jungle. She watered, pinched, turned the plants twenty or thirty degrees. Sometimes she fluffed the leaves, both hands, like a hairdresser.

Just when I was about ready to go over and badger the receptionist again, a tall, young woman came out, looked around and walked over to me.

"Mr. Vine?" She stuck out her hand. "I'm Sarah Bryce."

"Bobby," I said. We shook. Her grip was firm—not limp and crumply the way a lot of Southern women's are—and her hands, like the rest of her body, were long, taut, and angular. Her hair was the color of varnished mahogany, held off her neck in a dime-store barrette. No makeup as far as I could tell. Translucent skin, high cheek bones, thin mouth, all the muscles visible in her jaw. She wore a simple dark green dress. A nice-looking girl—sexy, in a kind of horsey way.

"Sorry for the wait," she said. "Jordan's in a meeting right now, something that just came up this morning." She looked nervously around the room—like she didn't want to meet my eye. I had gotten used to this since I got out of prison. People don't want to look at you because if they *really* see you, it humanizes all that evil stuff that you represent. Evil is easy to handle in the abstract. But when you face it in the walking, talking flesh, all those quaint nursery school moral prescriptions vanish and you start to get this uneasy thought: How come this guy seems so much like me?

I followed Sarah back into the offices. She had a nice loose-limbed walk, more shape than I'd noticed in the lobby.

We passed by a wall of smoked glass with a conference room behind it, three men inside with their jackets off sitting at a huge cherry conference table. One of the men was Jordan Foote; another I didn't recognize. The third was a guy I'd seen somewhere before, middle-aged, with a paunch and a beard. Not a friendly looking guy. I couldn't place him though.

Sarah showed me into a tiny office, overflowing with paper. Cardboard bankers' boxes were stacked five and six high along one wall, numbers written on the sides in black marker. Sarah picked up a heavy stack of manila folders off a chair next to the desk, dropped them on the floor. A little radio on her desk was playing country and western music, a song about a guy who was holding back his tears. There was a dart board hanging on the wall across the room, pictures of people cut from magazines taped all over it.

I noticed her gaze kept sneaking over my left shoulder toward the door—as though she were measuring out the distance she'd have to run if I decided to try clubbing her to death with a fourteen-pound volume of *Shepherds' Citations*.

"Have a seat," she said. But she didn't sit down herself. She paced up and down the room a couple of times.

Her eyes flicked over my shoulder again as she took a handful of darts out from among a bunch of ballpoint pens in a coffee mug on her desk. She turned and took careful aim at the target on the far wall. I recognized most of pictures, the cutout people on her dart board; they were lawyers. The bull's-eye was situated right beneath Clarence Thomas's crotch.

"Give me a second," Sarah said. "I'm thinking."

She stared meditatively at the dart board for a while, then threw the first dart. Thunk. The red feathers quivered over a famous litigator's forehead. She stared some more. Thunk. The second dart lobotomized Alan Dershowitz.

"Some kind of statement about lawyers?" I said.

Still looking intently at the dart board: "In my cosmology they fit somewhere between roaches and rattlesnakes."

"Would that put them slightly above pond scum?" I asked. When she didn't answer—much less laugh—I said, "You'll be glad to know I'm not a member of the bar."

She snuck a brief sideways glance at me, raised her eyebrows disdainfully. "Disbarment doesn't especially help your cause."

How'd she know about that?

She turned back to the dart board, took aim with a yellow-feathered dart. It was a good profile: small, high breasts; lean belly; slim, shapely legs; all the parts gracefully connected. A tendril of hair was sneaking down her long neck.

Thunk. Some guy I didn't recognize got skewered in the middle of his insincere smile.

"Who's that one?" I said.

"My ex-husband."

"A lawyer?"

"What else."

"Jordan doesn't mind you doing this? It seems a little. . . ."

"Sacrilegious? Of *course* Jordan minds." She laughed, threw another dart, which missed and lodged in the wall.

"Damn! The partners keep sending nasty memos, but I'm too valuable to fire."

"Lucky you."

"For what they pay me? No, lucky them." She zinged another dart, looking pleased with herself when it took a local ambulance chaser through one lung. There was something damn attractive about her: the sly smile, the aura of competence, the fact she didn't seem to care much what her bosses thought about her.

"Here's what I'm thinking," she said softly. She was still facing the dart board, the last dart poised for the throw. "You're disbarred, roped out of the law business; you're history in investment banking, consent orders signed with the SEC; you're just out of prison; you've been arrested for killing your partner—and then, boom, Jeannie Richardson's sending you over here like a junior accountant to dig up a bunch of stuff about some obscure investment that blew up in her face."

"You're suggesting. . . ."

"Yeah, something's wrong with this picture."

"I don't think it's so complicated," I lied.

"Then explain this to me so I can understand."

"See, I'm a recovering attorney," I said. "Attorneys Anonymous, you know. It's been very upsetting, the Bar Association taking away my secret decoder ring and everything. So Jeannie's helping me in my recovery, kind of letting me play lawyer. It's one of these twelve-step things. I think this is step nine I'm working on. Or eight, I forget."

Sarah looked at that space right above my left shoulder for a second, shrugged dismissively. Glib didn't seem to cut it.

"Okay," she said with a slow derisive drawl. "The hell with it. Forget it. Jeannie says I'm supposed to talk to some guy, give him some stuff, fine—I talk to the guy, I give him the stuff. Billable time is billable time, right?"

"Hold on! Look—"

"What?" she shot back. "I ask you a serious question and you start jerking me around. *Oh, yeah, she's just some girl, just some chump paralegal, I'll just yank her chain a little, what's the harm?*"

"Hey, that's not fair," I said.

"Oh?" She looked out the window.

I was about to say that as hard as she'd slammed me for my disbarment and so on, surely a few comeback quips were not out of order—but then I figured why get into it?

So I just said: "Truce?"

She kept looking at the dart board, at all the lawyers, their faces full of dart holes.

"Well?" I said.

"If. . . ." She tossed her last dart, and it caught Clarence Thomas square in the balls. ". . . you promise to be a good boy."

"Well," I said, "given my choices. . . ."

She hesitated, then—in spite of herself it looked like— grinned. It was a sudden, fine smile that transformed her from that neither-here-nor-there category that mothers call *interesting*—meaning almost great-looking but not quite—to being drop-dead beautiful. It was a neat trick. I felt an unexpected giddiness rush through me.

Her smile faded quickly, and she prodded a banker's box with her toe. The box said HEALTH SYSTEMS 1992-II in black marker.

"Health Systems Nineteen Ninety-Two Dash Two. It's all in there. Drafts of the prospectus, annual report, accountant's forecast, copies of the letters of credit, list of investors, partnership agreement, all the support documentation."

"You want to give me the ten-cent version of what happened?"

She nodded, her gaze sliding skittishly over me. Smile or no smile, she still wouldn't meet my eye. "Okay. Roger's bank, Excor, has done a bunch of these limited partnerships. They've also done some initial public offerings, munis, stuff like that, but partnerships were their mainstay."

I heaved the box onto my lap and looked inside. All the usual stuff: meaning about fifteen pounds of paper in various stapled, bound, rubber-banded, and paper-clipped configurations.

As I leafed through the papers she kept talking. "Basic structure of the deal: sheltered income, tax deferred. Ninety units at a hundred K per. Jeannie bought eighty units. Standard buy and lease deal. Underlying assets were eight or nine

CT scanners and one MRI. They used to call them NMRs—
Nuclear Magnetic Resonance scanners—but the nuclear thing
scared people so they changed the name. MRI stands for
Magnetic Resonance Imaging. Magnetic: you know, much
less threatening." She smirked a little, laugh lines springing
up around her eyes. "It's all in there."

"Actually," I said, "Jeannie pretty much filled me in on the
deal itself. I'll go through the documents later for the details.
What I want to know about is the people."

She probed my face briefly, then looked away. "People?"

"The players. What they did. What they're like. Tell me
about Excor. Tell me what they were like to work with."

"Ah. I see. Gossip." She smirked again, a good wiseass
smirk. "Like, greed? Fear? Maybe throw in some avarice?"
Her black eyes were shining, but I noticed she still wouldn't
look at me directly. "What's *avarice* mean anyway?"

"We could probably start with job descriptions," I said,
"work up to avarice a little later. Tell me about Roger first."

At the sound of his name, a dark expression crossed her
face—the reminder, I guess, that I was supposed to have
killed the guy. "Roger's the head honcho at Excor. Was, I
mean." She rubbed her hands anxiously on her thighs. "Chief
salesman, chief deal maker. They'd put together the partnership and then he'd wholesale the partnership units to broker-
age houses that had big retail operations. Then the
broker/dealers sold the individual units to their clients. Den-
tists, retirees, whoever. From what I understand, Roger was
the Rolodex king, the one who made the deals as well as the
one who sold the units to broker/dealers."

"And your personal impression of him?"

"He's a quick study. Charming. Smooth." She paused.
"Also totally full of shit."

I laughed pretty hard. Too bad I hadn't figured that out
seven or eight years ago. "And his partners?"

"Harv Zell's the partnership guy, the mechanic. He did real
estate syndications somewhere for a while—Florida maybe?
He knew all the ins and outs of limited partnership law.
Hawley, I got the impression, wasn't too technical, so Zell
took care of the details, the structure, the legal spade work,

the tax angles, all of that stuff. He's a tough cookie. Then you have Truman Shore. I only met him once. Bald guy, looked like Mr. Potato Head. He was the comptroller, chief bookkeeper type. My impression, he's sort of a wimpy, Nervous Nellie type."

"Anybody else?"

"There's some big money behind them, a silent partner. But I'm not sure who it is. My advice would be talk to Zell."

"Does Jordan's firm represent them?"

Sarah looked surprised. "Oh, no. Nobody told you about that? We're just Jeannie's crew. Excor uses Faulkner Keenan. They deal with Tate."

Tate. No last name needed. Tate Keenan was kind of the Darth Vader of the Atlanta legal scene. He had joined Faulkner Keenan & Williams back when it had been Faulkner & Williams. Faulker & Williams had once been the ultimate Southern white shoe firm—a bunch of worn-out old prep school boozers from Duke and Harvard and Vanderbilt; it was pleasant, well-bred, a good place for guy with a low handicap and a strong pouring arm. But it was dying. Too many old generalists, too many sons-in-law, too little nerve. Tate Keenan came in straight out of Georgia State or some third-rate place like that—he was probably the first lawyer they'd hired from outside the usual circle of Ivy League underachievers—and within three years he was a partner. Unheard of, making partner that fast.

He was a rainmaker, a guy who pulls in a lot of new business. He wasn't polished, wasn't friendly, wasn't a backslapper or the kind of guy who liked hanging around at the symphony. In short, he wasn't like most of the leaders of the Atlanta legal community. What he was, though, was tough. Tough, ruthless, smart as hell. And he never quit, never gave an inch. Tate scared the shit out of people. For this, his clients loved him.

"Tate Keenan," I said. "What do you think of him?"

Sarah rested her chin on her hand. A tiny muscle twitched in one cheek. "He's a bastard," she said finally. Her face was exquisitely blank, hiding something.

"You worked for him?"

"Nope." Like she was slamming a door.

"I see. Right. Well, do you know anything about his dealings with Roger and Excor?"

She looked around the room nervously. "No more than anybody else."

"What's that supposed to mean?"

She hesitated. You could see something back there working its way out, like a flashlight bobbing around at the other end of a dark culvert. "Look," she said finally. "I have a friend down at Faulkner Keenan. She might know something."

She didn't add anything else, so I said: "But you wouldn't want to put her job at risk by telling me things she's not supposed to let out."

She squinted at her dart board. "Something like that."

I sighed theatrically.

"Hold on," she said sharply. "I appreciate where you're coming from, but we're talking about a friend of mine. She's decent, she's honest, she's a single mother. But you, what do I know about you? I'm supposed to jeopardize a close friend's livelihood just so some . . . you know, some washed-up big shot scumbag can save himself some trouble in court?"

I couldn't blame her for feeling that way. But damn, it takes the wind out of your sails to hear it. A cold suffocating darkness ran through me—that feeling of counting for precisely nothing in somebody else's mind. Less than nothing, even: I was just a thing to be feared and gotten rid of—like a mean dog or an unpoisoned rat. I couldn't stand any more of this.

"Screw it," I said. I slammed the banker's box on the floor and stood up to leave.

"Wait!" She grabbed my wrist, squeezed it urgently. "I didn't mean . . . I shouldn't have said. . . ."

I just stood there for a second, feeling the pressure of her hand, staring at the floor, trying to keep the Big Fear at bay.

"It's not that," I said finally. "I can handle the dart board, the snide remarks about disbarred lawyers and scumbags, I can handle all of that because it doesn't cut to the heart of things." All this time, she'd been avoiding looking at me, but now when I glanced up from the floor, her black eyes were fixed on me, hard and frank. "So listen carefully when I say this: I didn't kill Roger Hawley. I *did not* do it."

She looked at me, not saying anything one way or the other.

I kept gazing into her dark, intelligent eyes, feeling a strange connection and a sudden urge to confess something. She seemed more present than anybody I'd been with in a long time. "I made some big mistakes in my life, got tangled up in some things I'm ashamed of. Roger and I did some really stupid things together. But that's in the past."

"Okay," she said, still looking at me.

Once she'd decided to take the plunge, to actually look at me and acknowledge me, it was like she couldn't let go. Her hand was still clenched on my arm. It was the closest physical contact I'd had with a woman for almost three years.

And then it was pouring through the viscera: the surging of the sap, the sucking of the taproot, whatever you want to call it. Maybe I'm getting carried away, but what I'm saying is that sometimes you see a person in a flash, like they're surrounded by light, and when that happens you feel an inexpressible power shifting around inside yourself. That was how I felt: Something was moving in me that I couldn't name.

Why her? Why then? I don't know. Maybe it was because she didn't take pains to hide who she was or what she was thinking; she just made her pitch and if you didn't like it, too bad. I wasn't used to honesty, wasn't prepared for it—and so she caught me with my guard down.

"I was trying to put Roger behind me," I said. "But I guess he just wouldn't go away. Something happened here, something I don't understand. Somebody killed Roger Hawley, made it look like I did it. I don't know who it was. I don't know why they did it. Right now, Sarah, I don't know a damn thing."

She let go of my arm, frowned skeptically. "You're saying you're being framed?"

I nodded.

The frown deepened. "And the Ten Bee Five stuff? The failure to file Thirteen Dees? The insider trading? You were framed on that, too, I suppose?"

"No. I . . . that was. . . ." I shook my head, trying to get the words out. "I was guilty of all that." Besides the cops, I had never admitted this to anyone before. Not even Ray who'd been straight and generous with me from the first day I met him.

"And the disbarment, breach of fiduciary duty, all that?"

"Guilty as charged. But murder, no way. Not murder."

Sarah kept looking at me with her frank black eyes, not saying anything. For the first time it seemed like maybe there was some sympathy there. Or if not sympathy, at least an openness to what I was saying. Right now that was enough: All kinds of strong, barely identifiable emotions were rushing around inside me. Keith Whitley's voice came out of Sarah's little radio, singing about how he was no stranger to the rain.

"I'm scared, Sarah. This is not just some deal that fell apart and now we're going to play litigation tag for a few years. This is the real thing. Something just fell in right on top of Bobby Vine's shitty little life and I don't even know why or how it happened." Still looking into her eyes. "Sarah? I'm asking for your help, okay? You don't have to like me. I'm not asking for that. I just want to find the truth here. If the truth is that I did it, then nothing you say, nothing you do, nothing we haul out of this damn box is going to make any difference. But if the truth is that I didn't kill Roger Hawley, then you might make the difference. You might, just *might* save my life." Still looking at me, no expression. "Sarah. The truth, that's all I'm after."

She finally looked away from me, hugging herself with her thin arms and looking thoughtfully at her dart board. After a minute she said, "Okay. Okay, I'll set it up. I'll talk to my friend."

"Thanks," I said. "That means a lot to me."

"But it's her call. If she doesn't want to talk, I'm not going to press her on it."

"I couldn't ask for anything more."

The phone rang and Sarah answered, made a face, set it back in the cradle. "The fearless leader beckons," she said.

"Jordan's ready to see me?"

"Yeah. Straight down the hall, then left." She stood, shook my hand soberly.

As I headed into the hallway, she said, "Bobby?"

I turned, saw her head poking around the door frame.

She was smiling shyly at me, the gorgeous smile. "I apologize for being such a jerk. But I was expecting somebody, I don't know . . . different."

"Thanks," I said, feeling a flush of embarrassment. There was something in her eyes when she said it, something that made me feel exposed and naked.

Then she looked flustered, like she'd rather not have said all of that out loud, and her head disappeared back into the office.

As I walked down the hall I heard her darts thunking into the dart board again. Beneath that, fading, Merle Haggard sang about turning twenty-one in prison doing a life sentence, no parole.

CHAPTER 2

I headed for the door at the end of the hall. There was a secretary's nook behind it and then Jordan's office through a second door. Jordan's secretary was trenched in—her desk a sort of defensive fortification in front of the boss's door.

"Just one moment, sir," she said. She was about fifty, with a hateful look in her eyes, and hair forged in an Annette Funicello flip. "Mr. Foote has just received an important call."

I didn't stop my charge for the door, so she leapt up, ready to defend the citadel even at the risk, no doubt, of bodily harm.

"He won't mind," I said and shot the gap into Jordan's office before she had a chance to clothesline me or roll her chair into my shins.

"Sir! Sir! Mr. Foote, I tried to stop—"

I closed the door to shut her up and sat down on a green leather settee across the room from Foote.

Foote was hunched over his speakerphone, trying to make out the hollow voice coming over the line. The voice was complaining about something, about a hearing that didn't go well: "—what I'm saying, you go *in camera* with some god-awful loose cannon like that, you never know what's going to happen. I tell him, Your Honor, we've got precedents out the ying-yang—"

Foote interrupted. "Len, I'm sorry, Len. Excuse me, Len, I've got company. I'll get back to you in—" He looked at his watch. "I'll get back to you in five minutes." He shot me a prissy glare. "This shouldn't take long."

"No can do," said the hollow voice. "Got to get back to this deposition. Why don't I catch up with you at Tate's to-night? You're supposed to be there, aren't you?"

"We'll chat then," said Foote. He punched the hang-up button, missed, punched again.

Jordan Foote's glance flicked toward me, flicked away, avoiding eye contact. I have a different theory with lawyers, what it is about me that makes them nervous. Evil they can handle. What bugs them is that I got disbarred. Looking at me probably brings on all sorts of spooky thoughts of profes-sional mortality, images of descending guillotines.

"Five minutes? You must be on top of this Health Systems thing, I guess, if it's only going to take five minutes to tell me everything you know." I gave him my biggest dumb-dumb smile and looked around the room. "Eight million. Some fuck-up, huh?"

"You're a rude little man," Foote said.

I didn't answer, just kept looking around the room. No blond wood, no smoked glass, no Danish furniture. None of the pink-and-green granite crap they had in most of the other offices of the firm. Nothing flashy. The desk was old maple with the original varnish, crackly looking. The bookshelves were lined with old, leather-bound books, the kind your dec-orator buys by the yard. Not law books. Plato, Shakespeare, Dickens in twenty-three volumes—the kind of stuff I always read the Cliff Notes for in college. The Persian rug was a little threadbare, just the right amount. Other than the telephone, the lamps, there wasn't anything in there that would let you know we were in the twentieth century. He even had hunting prints, originals, hanging on the walls next to the Yale Law diploma and the Georgia Bar certificate.

It was all bogus. It was too much. He was trying to look like old money, trying so hard to look like his great-granddad had been running the hounds in jolly olde someplace or other, that it had to be a fake. My guess was that Foote's father, Jeannie's dad's crony, had been a cracker straight off the farm.

Jordan Foote waited, not looking at me. I smiled sweetly.

"What a place, huh?" I said, still eyeballing the room. "How much did that desk set you back? Eight, ten grand? I'm impressed—Jesus, this place, look at it! This stuff must have cost your clients a fortune. I mean the probity, the scrupulousness, the sure moral compass and good counsel this crap must represent. . . ." I trailed off, thinking *Why can't you keep your fat mouth shut, Vine?*

Foote put his palms together in front of his face, like he was praying. He finally looked at me, arranging his face so as to indicate some sort of deep spiritual anguish. "I fail to see, given your history," he said finally, "that you are in any position to comment on my professional or ethical standing. Jeannie instructed me to assist you in your . . . investigation, which I shall do, notwithstanding your petulant attitude. But don't push me. I broke you once, and I'll do it again if I have to."

Talk about your petulant attitudes. I shrugged. "Whatever. Look, we've both gotten our licks in, so how about we start trying to get back the money Roger stole instead of pissing on each other? Something's busted; let's fix it."

Jordan Foote continued to look at me over his prayerful fingers, elbows perched on his antique desk. He didn't say anything, just made a breathy sighing noise through his fingers.

"One," I said. "What is the nature of your business relationship to Jeannie Richardson? Two, precisely what services did you perform in the Health Systems case? Three . . ." I broke off. "Three, I'll get to later."

"Mm," said Foote. "Yes. My father was general counsel to Ms. Richardson's father's company, RichCo, and we—meaning the firm—have continued in that capacity. Additionally, I am a member of the board of directors of RichCo. We have also acted as counsel to Ms. Richardson in all her major business activities outside of the company."

"Outside of RichCo."

"Correct. Finally, after her father passed away in 1979, we acted as co-executors of his will. With Ms. Richardson. As per the terms of her father's will, we are administrators of a trust containing most of what remains of Mr. Richardson's assets."

"Hold on. Jeannie mentioned this trust. What's the deal?"

Foote winced prayerfully. "The *deal?* The *deal,* Mr. Vine? I'm afraid I don't have the slightest inkling what you're talking about."

"Oh, I think you do. Let me take another stab at the question. What's the deal with her trust?"

More prayerful wincing. "I presume you mean what are the terms, the disposition, beneficiaries, etc.? In sum, the . . . *deal* is that she inherited from her father only a comparatively small number of assets. Her home for instance. Prior to his passing, her father as you may know, sold most of his interest in RichCo to the public. He was extremely liquid at his death, and those assets are, for the most part, held in trust. Ms. Richardson receives income from the trust."

"Does she control the trustee?"

"No. Barring dissolution of the trust, my firm—Foote Shelby & Foote—oversees administration of the trust." He looked over his hands at me for a moment.

"Terms for dissolution of the trust?"

"Other than a few minor technicalities? Birth of a child."

"Which won't happen. She's too old."

"That seems the likelihood."

"You said, 'minor technicalities.' Such as?"

"My death."

"So you control her money for the foreseeable future."

"Nominally, yes. We have little control over it in the sense you seem to imply, however. The terms of the trust are quite rigid. Investment in U.S. Treasury securities only."

"It generates substantial billings, no doubt, for the firm."

"Our billings to the trust are none of your business. Rest assured they are reasonable. And minimal. Despite the size of the trust, it does not demand a great deal of administrative effort."

"Size," I said. "Speaking of which, how big is the trust?"

"Again, not germane and none of your business."

"Fine. I can dig up a prospectus from the offering back in '79 and extrapolate if I have to. But the bottom line is that she's got enough cash to live the life of the idle rich. But other than that, she has to pay her own way. On top of which, inflation has probably taken a substantial bite out of the value of the assets."

"That would be a fair conclusion."

"Old Daddy didn't trust her very much did he?" I said.

Foote didn't move, just stared over his fingers at me. "With regard to women, he was a traditionalist," he said finally.

"Okay. Question two." I said. "Health Systems."

"We reviewed the prospectus and performed certain due diligence functions. End of story."

It was my turn to look at him without saying anything. I waited.

"End of story," he said.

"I think Roger might have disputed you on that one."

Foote turned a light pinkish color—like grapefruit cocktail in a tan glass, maybe.

"Okay, then," I said. "Tell me what you know about the Health Systems partnership."

He went on for a few minutes, talking through his fingers, telling me things I already knew about the Health Systems deal.

"I heard there was a silent partner at Excor," I said. "Deep pockets."

"I heard that, too," he said. He looked for a second like he was going to say something, but then he pressed his lips back into his fingers.

"You got a hunch who it is?"

"Perhaps."

"What do you mean, perhaps? Either you do or you don't."

But Foote wouldn't say anything else.

"Come on, this isn't a court of law here," I said. "I'm just trying to dig up something that might help your client get back her runaway eight million." There was a strange expression on his face. Fear, maybe. It was hard to read.

"I'm sorry, but I don't know anything," he said.

"Look—"

"I told you. I don't know anything." His voice was dull and his eyes were flat, dead, unreadable.

"Okay, Foote. Let's get the sequence of events. When did you first hear that Hawley was cooking the books?"

"Last Saturday."

"From?"

"Truman Shore, their comptroller."

"What time?"

"Early evening. It must have been about seven o'clock."

"And what did you tell him?"

"I told him to calm down, that I would inform Jeannie and send out a team to take a look the next day."

"Did you call her?"

Foote hesitated. "Actually . . . no."

"Eight million on the line and you didn't bother to tell your client? Roger could have taken off for Brazil that night."

"I thought it could keep. Besides, Truman was sufficiently upset that I thought it prudent to visit Excor with him the next morning to review the material. He was very confused. After I had ascertained the situation, naturally I intended to give Jeannie a full report."

"But he called her anyway."

"Yes. She suggested that we contact Harvey Zell—Roger's other partner. It was decided that Truman and Harvey would confront Roger and we could observe. We met with Roger at his home on Sunday morning. He denied everything of course, made quite a show out of it. How dreadfully outraged he was and so forth. Quite an embarrassing and disgusting performance. The next day he was dead. Naturally we insisted on reviewing the books with Truman Shore that afternoon."

"And what did he find in the Excor books?"

Foote smiled bitterly. "Nothing. That is to say, there was

nothing left to speak of. All cash had been transferred to Roger's own account. All securities had been liquidated and transferred. It was all gone. The FBI has since found that all funds were immediately transferred to several Panamanian bank accounts. We are currently attempting to arrange repatriation of the funds through the bureau." Foote sat up straight, took his hands out of the prayer position and laid them flat on the desk. "Which is why, quite frankly, I don't understand why Jeannie has ... unleashed you. I can only see that sending a felon to go blundering through the waters at this point will make the situation worse than it already is."

"That answers question three," I said.

"Question three?"

"I was going to ask your opinion—why you thought Jeannie had sprung me out of jail."

Foote got up and made a big sweep with his hand, showing me the door.

"I wouldn't have the foggiest idea," he said.

On the way out, I picked up a check for ten thousand dollars from the office manager and collected my box of documents.

As I was schlepping the box down the hall past the glassed-in conference room, I noticed that the two men Jordan had been meeting with were still sitting there at the huge table. The fat guy with the beard, the one I recognized, was pissed off about something. He was banging on the conference table with the flat of his hand. It was like an old movie: I could see his lips move, see him hit the table, but I couldn't hear a thing.

Where had I seen that guy before?

CHAPTER 3

Ray was in his office at the Buford Highway store, right off the I-285 loop.

"Ay, Counselor! What in hell you doing here?"

Notwithstanding my nondisclosure agreement with Jeannie Richardson, I told Ray everything. Ray wasn't the kind of guy who'd spread something like that around. I guess I'm not a real legalistically minded person. I always had a hard time with that confidentiality stuff; it just didn't sit well with me. Withholding information from somebody always seemed pretty much the moral equivalent of telling them a bald-faced lie.

I know I'm naive and all that, but I always figured you put two honest men in a room together, give them both all the facts—share and share alike—hell, they'd work something out. Or maybe strangle each other. Either way, you got a solution. The American legal system, of course, frowns on this approach. So, all in all, maybe it's just as well I wasn't practicing the law trade anymore.

"When you coming back to work?" Ray said. "We got this promo we're doing—five dollars gets you anything in the store for the first week. Beautiful? I'm telling you, is that beautiful or what? They're flocking in, man, like fucking sheep. Just bring five dollars, friends, walk out with anything in the store! I grossed a hundred and a half new bidness this week."

"I don't know," I said. "I was hoping I could kind of get a leave of absence to straighten this thing out."

"Leave a what?"

"Absence."

"Absence!" Ray ran his hand through his hair, this kind of Brillo arrangement he paid a lot of money to get reconstructed every four or five weeks. "Leave a absence! Sound like you asting me to let you go."

"Well, then can you let me go for a month or two, hire me back after that?" I said.

Ray squinched up his eyes, stuck out his lower lip. "Hell, then I just got to fill out a bunch of goddamn paperwork. Bunch of tax forms, equal opportunity, all that shit. I guess it'd be easier to just let you slide a while."

"Thanks, Ray," I said.

"Don't thank me," he said. "Don't by God thank me. Thank Uncle Sam, all them fucking forms I got to fill out. Otherwise I'd just say don't let the door hit you in the ass on the way out." He started walking out into the showroom. "Come look at here," he said. "You got to see this. I had a artist come in, do a cartoon type a thing, you're gonna love it."

"Cartoon of who?"

"Me, Counselor. We gonna do a logo, make us a big-ass sign outside." We went up to a booth with a sign that said IN-FORMATION over it in two-foot-high letters. Information, in this case, was not where you got information at all. It was where they made you fill out credit applications, put down what church you went to, five friends' names, their addresses and phone numbers, your parents' names, your job, how long you've been there, all of that. "Ay, Darlene, you looking more beautiful every day," Ray said to the girl at the counter.

"You, too, Ray," Darlene said. She was the store manager, kind of cute in that bucktooth redneck way.

"Where you put that sign? The artist one?"

Darlene dragged out a big piece of poster board, propped it up on the counter. It was a cartoon of a guy wearing a suit, a guy with orange Bozo hair and a goofy smile. It didn't re-semble Ray even vaguely. Next to the clown in the suit, it said RAY'S RENT-2-OWN. Underneath it said HAVE WE GOT A DEAL FOR YOU?

"It should be an exclamation mark," I said. "It should be: *Have we got a deal for you!!!* More like that."

"Explanation mark? That's what that artist fellow said, too. Maybe we change it. What you think? You like it?"

"Great," I said.

"That's what I think, too, Counselor. It's gonna be great as hell. We gonna make a sign twenty foot high, just the sign part, then we gonna put it way the hell up on poles—maybe a hunnert, hunnert-ten foot off the ground—so's you can see it from I-285, both directions. Man it's gonna be pulling them fools off the interstate, they gonna be wrecking their cars trying to get off."

"You could be right," I said.

"Ay, Counselor. Seriously now. You want to stay at my place? I don't guess you like staying over there where you at now. Dead guy in there and all."

"Actually I had to stay at a hotel last night," I said. "Police won't let me stay in the house yet."

"Damn. Well pack your shit up, I'll see you about seven-thirty. Here's the key."

"Thanks," I said. I hesitated for a second. "You're a good man, Ray. You know that?"

Ray looked at me funny for a second, then held the poster out in front of him, arm's length. *"Man,* that's beautiful. Gonna be pulling them fools right off the highway!"

CHAPTER 4

I decided I'd better call Ed Mance, the cop only I know. I hadn't talked to him in seven or eight years, but he still owed me for something I'd done a long time ago.

It took me a while to get through to Ed Mance's desk. He was a detective with the Atlanta police—in Crisis Intervention, whatever that was. The phone had to ring a few times before he picked up. I said hello, asked him how Tracy was doing. There was silence for a while. Then Ed said she was doing super, cute as a button, had to beat the horny little bastards off her with a stick nowadays.

"That's good," I said. There was another silence on the

line. I didn't say anything about the favor he owed me, but he knew what was coming.

It had happened maybe ten years ago, back when I was a second-year associate at the firm downtown. Carla and I were living out in Decatur and Frank, my youngest, hadn't been born. Ed and his second wife, Lucille Ball (that's the entirety of her first name, I kid you not), had some friends over next door, getting drunk and listening to Hank Jr. on their console stereo. Their little girl, Tracy, was by herself, fooling around next to this dinky little above-ground pool they had.

I was out back just by chance, standing around in the dark, thinking about things. I remember noticing how Ed's back-porch light was shining through the side of the pool, being struck by the way it looked. The sides of the pool were fiber-glass, translucent, extending maybe five feet off the ground. With the light shining through them, you could see wave patterns through the side. I heard a splash, saw a dark shape moving around against the light patterns. At first I didn't re-alize what had happened. I thought it was one of the kids playing around. All I could see was this dark shape against all these streaks of light.

I stood there for a second, leaning against the fence, just looking at the patterns, not thinking about much of anything. Then I realized this dark shape had stopped moving. It was just lying there on the bottom.

I ran through the gate, climbed up on the little catwalk around the pool and there she was, Ed Mance's little girl, Tracy, lying on the bottom, her hair gently floating around her head. The light from the porch caught her face and I could see a tiny bubble trembling in her mouth like a drop of mercury. I don't remember how I got her out, who did the mouth-to-mouth, any of that—I just remember walking into the house, all these cops and their wives looking up at me. I had Tracy in my arms, water running off her all over the carpet, her little blue bathing suit sagging off her shoulders. They all looked up at me with these drunk, suspicious cop stares. Even the wives, suspicious.

"What did she do?" Ed Mance had said.

Later that night—after he put his ax through the side of the pool a couple times and all the water drained off into the creek—he told me that, man, I had saved his baby girl's life. He said it a bunch of times, took me by the arm, holding on a little too tight with the alcohol and the adrenaline still going in his veins. He told me *anything you need, man, anything— it's yours. Yours for the asking.*

Back then, I hadn't needed much of anything.

"Son," Ed Mance said. "You in a heap of shit right now."

"Tell me something I don't know," I said.

Ed hesitated. "Look, Bobby," he said finally. "I'm City of Atlanta, not Fulton County. This one ain't my jurisdiction."

"I know," I said. Long silence.

"This ain't such a good time," Ed said. "You ate lunch yet?"

"No," I said.

"How 'bout the Varsity?" he said. "Twenty, twenty-five minutes. My treat."

I told him that would be fine, but I'd buy.

I drove down to the Varsity in my creaky Dodge Aries. The Varsity is an Atlanta landmark, mostly I think because the town is weak on landmark material. It's an old-fashioned drive-in that has a big sign outside telling you how many tons of hot dogs, hamburgers, Coke, whatever, that they sell every day. The funny thing about the Varsity is that no matter how bad all that stuff is, all that grease and glop oozing out on your hands, somehow it always tastes pretty good. I can only credit this to the involvement of some sort of gustatory voodoo.

Ed Mance was waiting for me inside. He's a short guy, maybe five-six or seven, with black hair cut in a flattop, Marine style, and ugly black-framed glasses. He'd had the same haircut, same glasses, since he left the Corps in 1968. Ed smiled all the time, not like he was happy, but like his mouth was just stuck that way. He was wearing a shiny blue windbreaker that said BRAVES across the front, a brown necktie underneath.

"You try the onion rings?" Ed said in a loud voice. "Them niggers can flat *cook* some onion rings back there." There were only about two dozen black people within hearing distance.

We got in line. The guy behind the counter said, "Whaddaya have! Whaddaya have! Whaddaya have!"

We got our leaky, greasy chiliburgers and our leaky, greasy onion rings and sat down.

"Been a while, son," Ed said.

"I've been out of circulation."

"Not *that* long."

"Yeah," I said. "I guess I just lost touch. After we moved." This was true. We had left the neighborhood a couple years after the thing with his daughter, moved to a big Williamsburg style house with an American eagle over the door. Forty-six hundred square feet. I drove an Oldsmobile. As best I can recall it was heaven on earth. These days I do my best not to think about it.

Ed didn't look at me, he just set in on that hamburger, not saying a word. When he was done, he wiped his hands off, finger by finger, leaving a pile of ten ruined napkins in the middle of the table, big orange chili smears down the center of each one.

"Bobby, let me tell you something," he said. He was smiling at me, that big empty smile. "I'm a law enforcement officer, been doing it a long time. All I see every day is dipshits, most of them a bunch of no-account nigger crackheads. They are *lined up,* Bobby, I mean *lined up* waiting to get their sorry asses throwed in jail. You put them in jail, they get out, they get back in line again. And all the time these people are lying to me. Everybody's innocent, every goddamn one of them. They didn't do it, it was somebody else, it was mistaken identity, it wasn't my gun, it wasn't my house, I don't know him, I don't know, I don't think so, I don't give a shit, I never been there in my life, I never been in jail before, never been to juvenile, never ripped off nothing in my life, it was only a half a gram, somebody planted it on me, I never seen the shit before, it was her, it was him, it wasn't me." Ed's pale blue eyes were boring into me. "You understand? *It wasn't me!* It wasn't never *me* that done it! I am an innocent man!" He had his hand over his heart.

"Okay," I said.

"I been hearing that shit day in, day out," Ed Mance said. His smile just wouldn't go away. "Day in. Day out. I get to where it don't matter. Just another lying nigger crackhead. I put it away in a little box, Bobby, lock it up, forget I had my intelligence insulted again. Again, Bobby! How many times I got to be insulted?"

"I don't know," I said.

"You see what I'm getting at? I don't mind sending a white man to prison. God knows I sent plenty of them. But what I hate, what really burns my ass, is hearing a white man lie to me. All these years, I never heard a white man say to me, yeah, Detective Mance, I'm guilty as hell, guilty as charged. You understand, Bobby? Niggers, I can take it. But every time I hear that shit out of some white man, it shakes my faith."

"Okay," I said. Hoping maybe he'd give the word *nigger* a rest for a while.

"We go back a long way!" he said. He was leaning forward, whispering, the smile stuck on his face.

"I know that," I said.

"So, I know you gonna ask me a favor. I know you gonna do it. You saved my baby girl's life, most precious thing in the world to me, so what I owe, I'm gonna give it to you." Ed Mance sat there, looking at me through his 1968 black-frame Marine Corps glasses, and for the first time since he started talking, that rubber smile slipped away. "Just one thing Bobby, awright? Just don't lie to me. Don't tell me you a innocent man. Don't tell me that, Bobby."

"Ed—" I said.

Ed Mance held his hands up in front of his face, palms out, thumbs touching. "Don't do it, Bobby. Sheriff's deputies show up at your house, responding to an anonymous 911 call. They got you in the room with the dead man, got your prints on the weapon, he's been dead sixteen hours, whatever it was, and you setting in front the fucking TV watching 'The Young and the Restless.' Don't tell me you didn't do it!"

" 'The Young and the Restless?' " I said.

"Straight from the horse's mouth," he said. " 'The Young and the Restless,' my wife's favorite. I been asking around."

"I wasn't really paying attention," I said.

"I guess not, son. I guess not." Ed Mance took off his Marine Corps glasses and polished them on his brown tie. "Just tell me what you want, Bobby. Tell me what it is you want. Anything in reason I'll do it for you. I ain't asking why. You say jump, I say how high." He looked at me, letting it sink in. "But when it's done, I don't know you no more."

"Okay," I said. "It's a deal, Ed."

"Just so you real crystal clear on it."

I nodded. "I understand. Here's what I need. Can you find out about a contract killer, a black guy, who beats people to death? Say, with a crowbar? Is there some way you can find that kind of thing?"

Ed looked at me a minute, smiling again, his cop eyes pale blue behind his Marine Corps glasses. "You really reaching on this one, aren't you?"

"Ed," I said. "I'm asking you a goddamn question. You don't want me to say I'm innocent, I won't say the word. But lay the fuck off. Okay? I'm asking you a question. Can you find this guy?"

Ed Mance thought about it. "Nigger contract killer? I'm just telling you, you stretching on this one. The white race, it seems like, got a lock on that business. Niggers are more the do-it-yourself types. Homies hitting homies. Gun for hire, I don't know."

"Can you find him? That's all I'm asking. I can give you a physical description. I can pick him out of a lineup. I can tell you what kind of car he drives if that'll do any good."

"You give all this information to Deputy Handlin over at the Sheriff's Department? You sure you wouldn't rather throw some darts at the face book? How come you need me?"

"Ed. . . ."

I must have had a pasty look on my face: Ed cocked his head and blinked. "You really got somebody particular in mind."

"I got somebody very particular in mind. One guy with a crowbar, funny voice, funny mustache, six-three, built like a tight end, drives an old Lincoln with dark glass, opera windows. I got a very, very particular guy in mind."

"I guess you do," he said. "I guess you do." Ed Mance kept looking at me with his cop eyes, thinking it over. "You sure he ain't Potta Rican? Maybe a Indian or something? Got some mean-ass Indians come outta Florida sometimes, out the swamps."

"Black. Light-skinned but black," I said. "Definitely."

"What makes you so sure he's a professional?"

"This guy did everything right, Ed. I mean everything."

"Uh-huh. I guess he did." Ed started eating his onion rings. He went through the same routine as with the hamburger, wiping each finger with a napkin after he was done. The grease off the onion rings looked like motor oil after a couple hundred miles in your engine. "I heard your story from Handlin," he said finally. "Hypothetically, the way you told it, could you see inside the car?"

I thought back to the big car, the light glinting off of it. "No," I said. "The windshields were tinted. All the windows were dark."

"Why is that?" he said.

"Why is *what?*"

"Tinted windshields. Why is it niggers always got tinted windows?"

"I didn't know they did."

"Absolutely," Ed said. "Every nigger in the world, get a extra fifty dollars in his pocket, he goes out get his windows tinted. They got sheets of this stuff, plastic, you just cut it out and it sticks to the inside of the window. Static electricity." Ed sat there a minute smiling at me. I was tired of hearing this, all this racist shit. It put me in a bad mood.

"So you couldn't see inside the car?" Ed said. "No shapes, no nothing?"

"Not that I could tell. There was a lot of glare. What's your point?"

"Point is, there might have been somebody else in the car. Maybe your nigger with the crowbar is just hired help. On his sheet, it might just be assault, you know, that type of thing. What about if there's somebody else in the car? Is he white? Is he young? Old? Tall, short, you don't know."

"If—" I said.

"*If* there was somebody else in the Lincoln," Ed said. "But I lay you big money there was."

"Okay."

"I can check the computer, see if we got a contract killer,

somebody fits your description. Heavyweight rap sheet, all that. But this boy with the crowbar, he could be a amateur. He could be working for somebody. See what I'm saying?"

"Okay," I said.

"Let's look here, take two scenarios. Scenario One. Nigger drives up knocks you out, takes you home, goes out, gets this Holly character."

"Hawley."

"That's what I said. Goes out gets Holly, brings him to your place, kills Holly," Ed Mance paused. "You see what I'm saying? One nigger, all alone—it don't make sense. Too complicated. Let me give you Scenario Two. Nigger drives up, gets out, knocks you on the head, all that. But there's somebody else in the car. A white man! You know why I say that?"

"No, why?"

"Motive, Bobby. Motive. You learn about motive in law school?"

"I think mostly I slept in Criminal. It was eight-thirty in the morning."

"Motive. Setup like this, it's got to be some kind of white man behind it. How many niggers out there want to kill this boy Holly? The answer is zero, cause Holly probably don't even *know* any niggers. So you got to find the white man that wants Holly dead. That's the other man in the Town Car. That's man who hired the nigger with the crowbar."

"Plausible," I said.

"I don't know about plausible, but it could damn sure happen. White man hires the nigger, says he needs to do a little bit of heavy-duty collections, that type of thing. Nigger don't even know murder's on the menu. He busts you in the head, keeps you asleep for a while. The white guy gives him a story—you know, they gonna make you and Holly sign something, just some kind of bullshit excuse. Night comes, they drive out to your place, take you and Holly out the trunk of the Town Car, ready to drive off, white man says hold the phone, boy, I got to take a leak. He goes back in the house, takes out a rubber glove, picks up the crowbar and beats Holly to death. Takes the crowbar back, you unconscious, gets your prints all over it, drops it on the floor. He comes out the front door zipping up his fly, the nigger don't even know nobody's dead."

"Interesting," I said.

"Motive," Ed Mance said. "You want to sell this one, you got to find out why that white man wanted Holly dead. Think about, one, why would somebody want to do Holly? Think about, two, somebody works with bodyguards, collection agents, repo men, investigators, skip tracers, them kind of people. You think about motive, about who might of done it. I'll do what I can, see can we find a nigger fits your description. I might could sneak you in, look at the city face book, too. But if I'm right about this second scenario, you ain't gonna find much. Your nigger's probably some retired third-string linebacker for the Falcons, got a couple parking tickets and that's it."

"I appreciate it."

"I hope you do," Ed said. He got up, put on his Braves windbreaker.

"Say hello to Tracy for me," I said.

Ed looked at me for a long time, smiling that rubber smile. He had the same unreadable look in his pale blue eyes that he'd had when I'd carried his drowned daughter into the living room ten years before.

"I just might do that," he said.

4

Clement's Deal

CHAPTER 1

I went back to Ray's house, got my box of documents out of the trunk of the Aries, and shagged them inside.

Ray has a huge house, maybe five thousand square feet. For a furniture guy, he doesn't have much head for what to do with houses himself, so he hired a whole squadron of overbred boys from Midtown—architects, decorators, landscapers, you name it. He gave them free rein. And, man, they used it.

The place looks good from the road. It's a kind of Tinkertoy construction, with beams and guy wires exposed. There's no symmetry, just a bunch of sharp, unrelated angles sticking up out of the hillside like pieces of some alien spaceship pitched out of the sky: long, thin windows; roofs slanted here, flat there; unidentifiable vertical pieces (chimneys? flagpoles?) sticking up at odd heights; strange cantilevers.

The closer you get, though, the more the whole conception falls apart. Like, for instance, unless you've been briefed about the terrain, you can't find the front door. It's hidden behind a big horizontal slab of concrete that looks like a leftover piece of some blown-up fortification. I could go on, but I won't. You get the picture.

Inside is where the *artistes* really got out of control. Black leather couches, neon thingamajigs in the corners, green malachite tables, lobster-eye halogen lights on long poles that sway back and forth when you touch them. It wasn't Ray. Ray is Naugahyde.

I walked into the dining room, set my banker's box on the long black marble table. It had seats for twenty, black Eurochairs with two-inch-wide backs that poked up over the table like periscopes. The dining room had a twenty-foot cathedral ceiling, little slit windows like arrow ports in a medieval castle, a sculpture off to the side made of red neon and black chicken wire. Nothing against Ray, because he had almost nothing to do with it, but I wondered who—as they say—was kidding whom.

The lunch with Ed Mance had made me depressed. Depressed and actually a little sick to my stomach. Chili cheeseburgers you should avoid when you're thinking about clanging doors, electric chairs, death row. I could feel my organs expanding, the membranes peeling back, the cancers starting to grow and fester inside of me. My heart started to go crazy.

No. Not now. Make this thing go away. But I couldn't. It was Ed that had set it off, with his dead smile and his sure eye for my guilt. I felt like this was the end of it somehow. This was *it*. Here was a guy, Ed Mance, who'd seen me haul his little girl out of a pool, seen me stave off death in another human being, and yet I couldn't even convince him that this was all a big mistake. He still had it in his head that I had smashed Roger Hawley's face with a piece of steel and then sat down to watch TV after it was over.

Thinking about it, obsessing on it, I couldn't get myself calmed down. My heart wouldn't stop going. My organs were rotting, ready to explode. I was turning inside out, dying.

I saw Roger's face, his head mashed out of shape so you could hardly recognize it. His mouth was open, hanging off-kilter like a busted gate, the flesh ripped back on the right side of his face so you could see his black-stained teeth. I just couldn't get my mind around the event. What a sad-ass, fragile thing life is. A few bags of tissue ripped open, a little fluid spilled, and the whole thing goes dim and sputters out. On the floor, that torn and broken form—it wasn't Roger, it wasn't *anything,* just a horrible nothing, a cipher, a zero. Whatever it was that was human about Roger Hawley had suddenly ceased to exist.

And I couldn't figure out what it all meant. It's just one of those barriers, I guess, that the human mind can't get over, can't cross. Which, however true, is no consolation.

I got up and walked around, went in the kitchen, drank a

beer in three pulls. It wouldn't stay down. I threw it up in the sink. God*damn,* I was so afraid.

I went into the living room, stood in the very center of the room. For a long time I didn't move at all.

I was turning inside out, dying.

And then, after a while, I was okay again.

I opened the banker's box, took out all the stuff, started going through it. Looking for something. But what? What was I trying to find? I wasn't even sure. What if the money Roger stole was just sitting down there in Panama? A couple weeks, a couple days—the FBI would get it back. Then where would I be? Back to square one.

I spread everything out along the big black table, divided it up into about fifteen piles, went through everything. It took all afternoon. I was just about done when I heard the front door open and close. Ray came into the room. He watched me work for about five minutes, then he went away again.

The deal-making juices had started to flow again, giving me an odd, nostalgic feeling. I had thought this stuff was gone from my life forever.

After a while he came back. "What you got there?" he said. He was looking down at me from the end of the table. Ray had a beer in his hand and was wearing a V-neck undershirt, a gold bracelet, a pair of yellow golf pants, plastic house slippers.

I started reading: *"Prospectus for Health Systems 1992-II (one); Financial Forecast for Health Systems—by Big Six Accounting Firm (one); Draft financials (27 pages); Due Diligence Memorandum, Bradley Douglas, Esq., of Foote, Shelby & Foote. (one)"* There was a lot more stuff on the list.

"This what lawyers do?" Ray said. "Make lists?"

"Among other things," I said.

Ray shook his head sadly. "You want a beer?"

"Thanks," I said. "I had one already."

"Well, if you don't want a beer," Ray said, "then you want to tell me what all that shit means?"

I went ahead and explained the whole deal to him, how it all fit together. This company, Valumed, made the CT scanners, and Hitachi made the NMR. A company called American Hospital Corp. was leasing the equipment. I explained the difference between a forecast and a pro forma, a lot of technical stuff. Ray caught on quick; the guy has creative financing in his blood.

"Due diligence? Explain that one to me," Ray said.

"You hire a lawyer to go out, a hundred and fifty an hour, sort of look into a deal. Scope it out. Make sure there isn't some kind of legal time bomb, no contingent liabilities, books are in order, everything's plumb and level. It's a standard part of any major financial deal. We got one here that was done for Excor by Faulkner Keenan and we got another one done for Jeannie by Jordan Foote's firm."

"Both of them doing the exact same thing?" Ray said. "Honest to Christ—a hundred and fifty an hour?"

"Basically."

He blinked. "How about this boy Zell?"

"He was one of Roger's partners at Excor. Some kind of syndication expert."

"And this prospectus thing. Tell me about that."

I picked up a forty-page document, stapled in the top left corner with a heavy-duty staple. "This is what you give to people when you're trying to sell them on the deal. Want me to read it to you? Here: at the beginning we got the name of the partnership, all that stuff. Next few pages we got all these qualifications the lawyers make you put in, stuff like, here I'll read you this: *An investment in this limited partnership is speculative and involves a high degree of risk of loss. The limited partnership units are not transferrable and no market for the limited partnership units exists or is expected to develop.* Blah blah blah. Down here we got: *The offeree, by accepting delivery of this confidential private offering memorandum, agrees to keep it confidential and return it and all other related documents received by the offeree and any copies thereof if: (i) the offeree does not. . . .* Okay? Like that kind of thing. Five pages of that. Then we got a *This page intentionally left blank.* I used to love saying that into my dictaphone—this page intentionally left blank—knowing I made enough money saying it to pay for a movie. Skipping through, here's the good stuff.

"Bold print, big letters. *Health Systems 1992-II, Ltd. (the*

'Limited Partnership') will be organized as a Georgia Limited Partnership pursuant to the form of the Limited Partnership Agreement (attached hereto as Exhibit E) upon a minimum of 80 limited partnership units (the 'Units') at $100,000 per unit ($8,000,000) and a maximum of 95 Units ($9,500,000) being subscribed for prior to November 9, 1992. The Limited Partnership plans to lease certain medical equipment to a major publicly held corporation engaged in the operation of hospital and other health care facilities. Skipping down . . . *The general partner has tentatively reached agreement with both suppliers of the equipment and with the lessee of that equipment. The general partner plans to deliver the first of nine pieces of equipment beginning in March of 1993. Additionally—"*

"Okay, okay," Ray said. "I get the picture. That's what you used to do for a living, come up with stuff like that?"

I nodded.

"Hundred and fifty an hour?"

"Give or take."

Ray shook his head. "So, give me the bottom line, Counselor. How's this gonna help you get off the murder rap?"

I looked down at all the paper and the hopeless feeling welled up again. "It could be there's something in here that'll tell me what Roger was doing, who he was working with, what he did with the money. I mean somebody must have killed him to get the money. Right?"

"You think their name's gonna be in there somewhere?" Ray waved his beer bottle over a three-inch-thick pile of paper. "Page two hunnert thirty-nine, 'Joe Blow took the money'?"

"I don't know, Ray. All I'm sure of is that somebody killed Roger because of money. It's a business thing, a business relationship. It's just got to be. Once I find that relationship, I can start to figure out why they killed him, how they framed me, the whole thing."

"Have fun," he said. "I'll be down in the rec room. Braves are in Chicago today."

I settled in with the documents, went through them one at a time. The financials all worked. None of the correspondence showed anything out of the ordinary. After a while I got up and had a beer and a turkey sandwich. My stomach was feeling a little better.

I went back and looked through the two due diligence memos. If anything was screwy about the deal, it should have showed up there. Nothing. Clean as a whistle. The amazing thing about it, knowing what I know about Roger, was that it was so well put together. This guy Harvey Zell that was helping Roger with the limited partnerships at Excor, he must have had his shit together. It was a pretty deal.

When I was done, I put the papers back in the banker's box and sat back, the funky periscope chair digging into my spine. I finished my beer, trying to figure what I was missing. Whatever it was, it wasn't in that box.

Ray came up the stairs from his subterranean rec room, making a slapping noise with his K-Mart slippers. "How's it coming?" he said.

I just shook my head. He went into the kitchen, came out with two beers. He popped one, set it in front of me, popped the other one and took a pull on it.

"Bobby," he said. "Time to get you a good lawyer."

"I was starting to come to that conclusion myself," I said.

"Problem is," he said. "Good criminal lawyer, you gonna have to put up a retainer. Ten, fifteen grand, just to get in the game."

I took the check out of my wallet that I had gotten from Jordan Foote's office manager, the ten thousand dollars that Jeannie had promised me, and set it down on the black marble next to Ray's beer.

He picked it up, squinted at it, then looked at me for a minute. He had a funny look on his face. I think he was wondering why I was worth so much money to Jeannie Richardson. That thought had crossed my mind, too. Ray folded the check in half.

He said: "Let me go make a phone call."

CHAPTER 2

Next morning I got a call from Sarah. How about meeting her for dinner at a restaurant called Faux Pas—did I know where it was? Over on Piedmont Road? Her friend from Tate Keenan's office had something interesting to tell me.

After that I went to visit my new lawyer, a guy named Dick Bloom, the one Ray had set up for me. He was your typical trial lawyer—extremely full of himself. He had a look on his face all the time like there was something he knew that you didn't. A hard guy to put up with. On the other hand, he had kept a long list of guilty sleazeballs out of jail.

First we talked fees. He said he liked to get that straight so there wouldn't be any problems later on. It was usually fifteen grand up front, but he and Ray had talked and ten would be okay for now. Fees were a hundred and a half an hour for himself, ninety-five for his associate, forty-five for his paralegal, to be applied toward the ten. If and when the ten gets eaten up, we would talk again. Ten, he said, wouldn't get me through a trial. Not even close.

I asked him how he felt about representing a disbarred lawyer, whether that might bother him in some way. He peered at my bank draft for ten thousand dollars and said, "What, is there a problem with the check?"

After that he told me that Jackie Shane, the public defender, was an idiot; that the arraignment was screwed up; that I never should have made a statement to the cops, and for God's sake not on videotape; that under no circumstances was I to leave the state; that under no circumstances was I to talk to the police again; that under no circumstances was I to talk to members of the press; that under no circumstances was I to talk to representatives of the district attorney's office; that under no circumstances was I to talk to anyone connected with the case, in particular friends and associates of the deceased. And furthermore, having been a lawyer, I should have known all of this already and not fucked everything up so badly.

I said, "I didn't practice this kind of law. Criminal law's kind of outside my range of expertise."

Bloom gave me a tell-that-to-the-jury look.

"Also," I said, "I have a problem with that last one—not talking to friends and associates of the deceased." Bloom said that was too bad. If I wanted the benefit of his representation, I played by his rules. Period.

I thought about it for a minute, about whether I should tell him about my arrangement with Jeannie. If I told him that my freedom was conditional on my rooting around for information for Jeannie, then he was going to say: Fine, then go back to jail so I can defend you properly.

I decided to be a typical client and lie to my lawyer. "Okay, I guess I can live with that," I said. It didn't feel very good.

I talked for a while, giving Bloom the lay of the land. I told him about getting hit over the head behind Ray's Rent-2-Own. Bloom thought that it was a weak story, and that it was very very unfortunate I had told it to the police. Conspiracy theories, he said, frame-ups, these are very very difficult concepts to convey to a jury. It was very very unfortunate, also, that I had talked to the police; that was going to be very damaging, very damaging indeed. *Indeed*—his very word. I told him about the fact that Roger was embezzling huge amounts of money from the limited partnership.

Bloom wanted to know how I knew all of this about Roger. Hadn't I said that I hadn't seen him since the trial? True, I said, but I had asked around, you know, old friends, that kind of thing. Bloom said don't do it again. No more old friends, no more asking around. You talk to people, they end up on the D.A.'s witness list. Talking to people is what investigators are for. Bloom had one of them on retainer, a very very competent guy who wouldn't fuck things up like I was liable to.

I told Bloom about Ed Mance's Scenario Two theory, the one about how there was a second man in the car (leaving out the fact that it was Ed, a cop, who came up with the idea). The motive, I said, was that somebody knew Hawley was stealing all this money from Health Systems, and they wanted it for themselves. They figured they could frame me, take off with the money. Kill two birds with one stone, that kind of thing.

Bloom thought it was a very weak theory. Very very weak. In the absence of a great deal of very admissible and very unimpeachable evidence, he said, it was going to be very very difficult to convey that to a jury. Very difficult indeed. No doubt, he was right. But still, I believe he would have thought any theory I presented was weak: Like everybody else, he was sure I was guilty—and a liar. As a good member of the defense bar, he naturally didn't give a shit. He just wanted to find some way of getting me off the hook. He didn't need inconvenient theories. They would just get in the way.

The thing is, it was the only theory I had.

Bloom asked about evidence. I told him I was weak on evidence. There was an anonymous phone call, sixteen hours after the murder—a voice on the 911 tape. Why would somebody wait that long to call unless they had been involved? Some neighbor peeping through the window? Not likely. I told Bloom that the 911 tape was my only piece of evidence to show some kind of frame-up conspiracy.

Bloom tapped on his desk with a pencil, said he was going to do what he could. First he'd get the case record from the public defender, review the documents, the autopsy, lab reports, fingerprints, all that, then he'd file some motions, see if he could slow this thing down. It would be a couple of days, he said, before anything developed. "Just go home," he said. "Relax."

"Sure," I said.

I noticed a photo in a gold frame on his credenza. It was a picture of him hugging a young woman in a black robe. The young woman looked familiar.

"Who's that in the picture?" I said.

"That's my daughter, Leslie," Bloom said. "She was graduating from law school, University of Texas."

Then I made the connection. She had been the U.S. attorney who had prosecuted me three years ago. "She sent me to jail," I said.

Dick Bloom said: "Sure. That's her job."

* * *

I left Dick Bloom's office, ate lunch, and went straight to Excor—doing exactly what he had instructed me not to do.

I told the receptionist who I was. She talked into the phone and a pudgy guy who looked like he was made out of pressed-together potato peelings came out to meet me. He put a miserable smile on his face, said that he was Truman Shore and that he wondered how could he help me.

I came back at him with my biggest, dumbest grin. "Well," I said, "Ms. Richardson sent me over to kind of take a little peep at the Health Systems books."

"Ah," he said. "I see. Maybe we should go sit down, work out just *exactly* what it is you're looking for."

We walked back to Truman Shore's office through a hallway of paintings of machinery, gears, smokestacks, that kind of thing. I wondered who had the sense of humor around there. It obviously wasn't this guy.

Truman Shore's office was the perfect showplace for a guy with no personality, no balls. Rosewood desk (clean) with a calendar/blotter thing square in the middle, one matching credenza, one reproduction auditor's lamp with a green glass shade, one pastel abstract that might have been ripped off from a Mariott Hotel hung dead center on the wall behind the desk. The only things that would distinguish this office were three pictures, gold framed, sitting next to the phone: two ugly kids, one frightened wife. This guy was no deal maker.

Truman Shore offered me a seat. I kept grinning, trying to look like a harmless idiot.

Shore gently adjusted his desk blotter from the near corners, just to make sure it hadn't gone out of true while he'd been gone from the room. "Jeannie phoned me, if you will, contacted me briefly this morning. We, I believe you understand, this is kind of a delicate, what you might call a delicate situation. In terms of some type of intensive scrutiny prior to your trial? The evidence, potential evidence in there, I'm not sure this is prudent, this type, intensive scrutiny type of thing." He was one of those guys who can't spit out a full sentence at one throw. What he was trying to say was that he wasn't too happy being leaned on by Jeannie. I didn't blame him.

"Intensive!" I said. "Oh, by all means, no. Good gosh! No,

sir. We just wanted a little independent confirmation, won't take any time at all. I'll maybe make a photocopy or two and be out of your hair in a flash."

"I suppose under the circumstances we can allow it. Our concern, I understand Ms. Richardson's desire in terms of confidentiality. . . ." He petered out. "Our concern, naturally, is that your interests are restricted to the Health Systems investment and we do, of course, have many other, well, projects in one stage or another, one phase or another if you will. Naturally we've got various confidential situations, confidential information here to contend with. . . ."

"By all means!"

"I'd hate to just open our kimono here without, I believe, without . . . adequate assurance. Adequate assurance, if you will, nondisclosure type thing. Plus your criminal situation, excuse me your *alleged* criminal charges, it puts us, if you see what I'm saying, it puts us between a rock and a hard place."

"Yeah!" I was enthusing. I was full of beans. "Confidentiality! That's an issue, all right. That's sure enough an issue. Hey, I been there before. You can bet on it! Let me just give you my personal assurance that you have nothing to worry about. Absolutely none! You need to get me to sign some kind of waiver or nondisclosure agreement, whatever—hey, by all means. Sit a girl in the room with me, fine. We're flexible." I paused, let my goony smile go away. "As long as Ms. Richardson's happy, I'm happy." Give this guy a little dig, just so he didn't forget who he was dealing with.

Shore winced. "Where did you anticipate, that is, where do you intend to start?"

"Oh!" I said, bringing back the smile. "Well. Gosh, might be good to start with Mr. Hawley's office! His files! Wouldn't it?"

Truman Shore said that, yes, perhaps it might be just as well. We walked to Roger's office.

I sat my old briefcase next to the window and looked around. "Hoo, boy," I said. "Where to start!"

Truman Shore stood in the door for a moment, watching, like he was worried I might start pocketing the knickknacks. "I must say," he said, "when Ms. Richardson contacted me, I was a little, well. . . . Let me ask you this, sir, just what is it Ms. Richardson is looking for?"

I turned off the smile again, looked him dead in the eye. "I guess you better ask *her* that."

Truman Shore didn't say anything. He watched me a minute, picking nervously at the nonexistent lint on his jacket, then went away. I heard him talking to Roger's secretary outside. The secretary came in with some files, set them on Roger's desk. She went away, too.

I looked around. Roger's office reminded me of pictures of a famous takeover guy that you might have seen in business magazines. I've seen the guy in a bunch of photographs, a bunch of magazines, but he always looks the same: He's always sitting in an antique chair, sipping pensively out of an antique teacup, holding the saucer in his left hand, his teeth clenched in a kind of bogus patrician grimace. Like he grew up floating around on the Mediterranean in a 114-foot boat instead of playing stoopball in Brooklyn. That's what Roger's office put me in mind of, that guy getting his picture taken, always the same pretentious pose. Roger always had that same look—like he was checking himself in a mirror the whole time he talked to you.

Take Roger's desk. It wasn't a desk in the normal sense. It was what I believe is called a secretaire. Or maybe an escritoire—I'm not sure. In any case it's the most nonfunctional flavor of desk you'd be likely to run into. It was an antique, the real McCoy here folks, about half the size of your standard Power Desk, with rickety little legs, carved and fluted, and one dinky drawer. No room for files in this one, babe, just enough space for paper clips and a couple pens. Of course, Roger didn't even bother with that. The drawer was empty. Did he do work here, or did he just sit behind the desk and pose?

The escritoire, whatever you call it, was mostly made of some kind of dark wood, but the top, the writing surface, was inlaid with a close-grained blond veneer, leaves, and jungly-looking vines. It's the kind of desk you imagine the fabulously beautiful contessa sitting at, writing a note to her doomed lover, Fabio, you know, before she plunges the poisoned blade into her heaving and ample bosom. No desk calendar on this sumbitch. No favorite coffee mug, no pictures of the kiddies—just an inkwell, hewn from living Eye-talian marble.

Next to the escritoire was a round table, same height, same mode, with a delicate wooden box sitting on it. The box had pictures inlaid on it (mother-of-pearl)—guys with powdered wigs and spears, stabbing wild pigs from the comfort and safety of horseback. Inside the box, Roger had artfully hidden a telephone with lots of buttons on it.

And on the walls? None of that English hunting print shit for Roger. No, ma'am. Roger got himself some paintings! *Oil* paintings: more French nobility attacking pigs. The paintings were dark and murky looking, rough and cracked on the surface, the Frenchmen's wigs and stockings floating like bits of sunlight in a thunderhead. They were the Real Thing, by God. No fooling here. No repros from the Smithsonian book shop for Roger.

And so on: draperies, rugs, gewgaws, cabineted china—all of it old, rare, coy. Thankfully, the hog-killing motif had not been extended to these other furnishings.

I sat down in the Louis the Umpteenth chair at the escritoire, with my stack of files in front of me, and for a minute I felt kind of sad. Sad for Roger because it was all so patent, so obvious, so contrived, so—what?—silly, I guess, is the only way to describe it. Did poor old Roger—B.S. in Accounting Sciences from Clemson University—think the world was so dumb and easily bamboozled that it would mistake him for some stranded Count de Rothschild, thrown up by a freak tide on the Chattahoochee River and dumped off in Atlanta, Georgia? What in hell was going through that guy's mind?

And maybe I felt sad for myself, too. Sad and ashamed. Because somehow back there he had taken me in. That silly, obvious guy had—in fact—bamboozled *me*. Right out in the open. I don't mean the illegal things he had gotten me to do, and I don't mean throwing me to the Feds. It was deeper than that. Somewhere along the line, he had convinced me that I should want things, need things, pursue things that I didn't really much give a damn about. During those years that I was around him, I guess I started to imagine myself just as he imagined himself: perched behind my escritoire, nosing into a snifter of thirty-year-old brandy while someone from a business magazine took my picture. The Deal maker. The Hotshot. He saw that I had lost some essential inner resource of courage or belief, that I had started operating according to rules and precepts that didn't make sense—and so he had sold me on a whole way of life . . . without my even knowing it!

And I had to go to jail, lose my wife, my Williamsburg house with the eagle over the door, my chicken smoker, my job, my vocation, my own sweet children before I realized that it was all a sham.

How can you explain something like that? How can you get over it?

There was only one modern touch in the room: a batch of Lucite-encased tombstones—little announcements of done deals that get printed in the *Wall Street Journal*—sitting on a table near the escritoire. Most securities people cut them out and display them like trophies, kills they've made in the great blood sport of deal making.

There were about twenty of them on the table. All of them looked about the same, most of them three or four inches square. I picked one up, looked at it. At the top in tiny print it said: *All of these securities have been sold. This announcement appears as a matter of public record only.* Underneath it said:

500,000 Shares
Class A Convertible Preferred Stock
Hi-Top Security, Inc.
Price $6.25 per Share

The undersigned advised the issuer and arranged for the private placement of these securities.

Excor, Inc.

The tombstones were the only sign that someone had actually worked here, that a human heart had beat within these walls.

I set the tombstone gently back on the table, then started

going through the files, tracing everything back, looking at who Roger had talked to and what he'd done in the course of putting together the Health Systems deal. A lot of the material I found there duplicated the documents that Sarah had given me at Foote's office. Most of the correspondence was Roger's although there were also a couple of letters from his partner Harvey Zell. There was some correspondence with the hospital company; a couple of exchanges with the equipment manufacturers; some letters to Tate Keenan, Roger's lawyer; an exchange between Roger and Jordan Foote; letters to and from some of the other limited partners; letters to and from the bank.

By the middle of the afternoon, I had about exhausted the possibilities in the stack of files. There was nothing really interesting there. It was time to look at the financial material. I had Roger's secretary dig out the pro formas as well as the information on the bank accounts used by the partnership.

Pro formas are basically just projections of what a company's financial condition is likely to be. You do your balance sheet, cash flow statement, income statement, and so forth, based on certain assumptions about your market, your product, interest rates, whatever, and then you just shoot them out as far into the future as you like. They were pretty easy to do for a setup like Health Systems.

It was a nice profitable deal. Excor got about half a million in fees, plus a unit in the partnership, which would pay out in quarterly distributions. The partners, including tax deductions and distributions, were going to return between thirteen and fourteen percent per annum on their money. Which is a damn good return, in case you don't follow this kind of thing.

Again, unfortunately, everything looked squeaky clean. No surprises.

I looked at the bank accounts. There were three of them, each one at a different bank. The first one had been opened about a year ago with a deposit of a thousand dollars. Presumably that was when Roger had gotten the idea for the partnership. They had probably incorporated a shell at that point just to have something to play with if the deal started to come together. For the first few months, the thousand dollars just sat there. The other two accounts opened in Septem-

ber of last year, again with a thousand dollars each. Two
months later, the first account got a deposit for eight million
dollars. Jeannie's money. During the next several months,
more deposits were made at a hundred thousand apiece: the
other limited partners.

Occasionally small accounts, generally less than ten thousand each, were moved to the other two accounts. From there
small checks were written against the two accounts. Presumably these were for partnership expenses—stationery, legal
fees, whatever. After the deal closed in December, two large
checks were written to the manufacturer of the CT scanners,
along with a half-million check to Excor for the general partnership fees. The total balance of the three accounts at that
time was a little under eight million. Then about April, something strange started happening. Checks were being written
from one account to the other. Large amounts. Each account
was periodically being drawn down all the way, and all the
money moved to one of the other accounts. The account record doesn't show who was doing it, but it must have been
Roger.

As the money started going round and round, occasional
checks were written to an account with no name attached to
it, just a number, an account other than the three Health Systems accounts. Classic check kiting: money chasing money.
The way check kiting works is that anytime someone—an auditor, for instance—notices that some money is missing, it's
immediately covered by another check. Which is covered by
another check. Which is covered by another, *ad infinitum.* As
long as the money keeps moving, it's damn hard to figure out
what's going on.

By July 11, the day Truman Shore called Jeannie, over half
a million dollars had disappeared into the numbered account.

On July 12, three final transfers were made, this time by
wire rather than by check, direct to the same numbered account. That was when Roger cleared out the accounts. Presumably, the numbered account Roger sent them was to his
personal account.

So there it was: Apparently Roger had been embezzling
money in dribs and drabs, moving things around to distract
anybody who might be checking up on him. It wasn't a very

sophisticated maneuver, but I suppose it gave him the one-day lead time he needed.

Then Shore had caught onto what he was doing. Roger had probably figured out that Shore knew—maybe he overheard the phone call with Jeannie or Jordan Foote. So he made the wire transfers rather than writing a check: The exchange was instantaneous. No wait for the check to clear.

It all made perfect sense. Except. . . .

Except who killed him?

Suddenly we're back to Ed Mance's Scenario Two: The other man in the car. There was somebody else working with Roger, someone completely ruthless, willing to kill. Whether this mysterious somebody had been in the car with Mr. Crowbar or not didn't matter. What mattered was that somebody was working with Roger, somebody who knew that Roger had just taken eight million dollars out of the Health Systems account.

So what else is new? Same theory, no more evidence, one day closer to trial.

I opened the box with the pictures of French pig hunters on it, took out the phone, punched 0, and asked to speak to Harvey Zell. The receptionist was sorry, but Mr. Zell was out of the office for the day. Would I like to leave a message?

I wouldn't, thanks. I put the phone back in the box, looked at the stack of files heaped up on the escritoire. What else was missing here?

I stuck my head out the door. Roger's secretary was sitting at her desk outside looking bored. Her name was Lisa.

"Not much to do now, huh?" I said.

Lisa jumped. "Oh! Mr. Vine. You scared me. Was there something you needed?" She had that look in her eyes—not sure how to respond to the guy who was supposed to have killed her boss.

"Actually, yes," I said. "Did you keep Roger's calendar?"

Lisa frowned. "Yes and no," she said. "I kept some of his appointments, but not all of them. He had a little book. Like a Day-Timer? He had one of those. I kept as much as I could, but sometimes. . . ." she shrugged ". . . he'd forget or something. Plus his personal life. He never made me set up dates with his girlfriends or that kind of thing."

"You mind if I see it?" I said.

She took out a desk calendar and showed it to me.

"Could I get a xerox of that?" I said. "Going back to, like, last August?"

"Sure. Would you like it now?" She seemed glad to have something to do that would get her out of close proximity to me.

I told her now would be great, then I went back into the office and called Dick Bloom. I asked him to check with Handlin over at the Sheriff's Department to see if Roger had his pocket calendar with him when he died.

"You think there's something there?" Bloom said.

"Could be," I said.

"You're at home?" he said. He sounded suspicious, like he knew what I was up to.

"Just going out," I said. "I'll be back in a few minutes."

Lisa came in with the copies of her desk calendar. "Would you happen to know where he might have left his personal calendar?" I said. "I mean, if he left it here?"

"Gosh," she said. "I just don't know." She poked around for a while and gave up. "Sorry." She shrugged.

"No problem," I said.

"He always carried it with him," she said. "He never went anywhere without it. It had phone numbers in it, everything."

I thought about that for a moment. "Good," I said. "Then I'm sure it'll turn up."

I drove back to Ray's house. The light was blinking on the answering machine.

"Bobby, it's Dick Bloom. The time is, let's see, three forty-five P.M. I just got off the phone with Handlin down at the Sheriff's Department. When he was found, Hawley didn't have a calendar on his person. No dice."

CHAPTER 3

If you follow Peachtree Road north out of downtown Atlanta, you get to Buckhead—this being the yuppie part of town, where all the German cars live. Lots of people in their thirties and forties who look like they were born in flannel suits. *Pretentious* is maybe the word that gets closest to what Buckhead is all about. Not pretentious in some kind of sneering, Frenchified way, but pretentious in a kind of naive, corn-fed, rah-rah American way.

Faux Pas, the restaurant where I was meeting Sarah and her friend, was a pure, full-bore expression of what Buckhead was all about. It was a little funky—stark black and white decor, shiny checkerboard tiles on the floor, lacquered bar, extravagant orchid arrangements—but not so outrageous that a guy in a Hickey Freeman suit would feel nervous there. All the waiters looked gay; all the patrons looked straight; everyone's hair was neat, well-crafted.

I got there early, had a scotch at the bar, watched the bartender flirt with a guy who looked like Ernest Hemingway. You know—red-faced, Hermes tie pulled down, sleeves rolled up. A money artist.

As the scotch settled into my belly I started thinking about Sarah, feeling excited and apprehensive like I used to before a date in junior high. I hadn't expected that. Man, how long had it been since I'd felt that sensation? Years and years and years. Half a lifetime almost. Jesus, how could that be? How could those years have gotten away from me?

I had never cheated on my wife, never even let myself get infatuated or feel that dumb head rush that comes when you make the first tentative moves with a woman. Strange, given all the other things I had done back then. That says something about me—I don't know what, exactly—because looking back on it, Carla and I hadn't done a lot for each other. Fifteen years we had spent together, fifteen years of empty pleasantries and dull routines and dry desires, fifteen years of living for the images we had of each other—until by the end you couldn't have squeezed a half-pint of blood out of our relationship. When it had all fallen apart, it had seemed . . . well, I don't know how it had seemed; I didn't let myself consider it too much.

I had thought about Sarah a couple of times since we met at her office—not really concentrating on her but just letting her float through my mind. There was something about her that had stuck with me; maybe it was the way she got right there in your face at the first sign of bullshit, not letting you get away with lying and fraud. Then again, maybe I just wanted to go to bed with her. I'd gone so long without feeling much besides fear that it was hard to sort these things out real clearly.

Sarah and her friend came through the door eventually, running a little late. She looked as good as I remembered, her hair pulled up, so you could see her long neck. She wore a simple sleeveless black dress that showed off her lean frame. It surprised me how glad I was to see her.

"How are you, Bobby?" she said. Her friend was a nervous woman, chubby, with a dark Latin look.

"Full of bad thoughts," I said. "Full of meanness."

Sarah laughed, and her friend looked like, *oh, God, here we go again.*

Sarah said, "Bobby Vine, Rosie Saiz." I nodded at Sarah's friend. "Rosie is a paralegal at Tate Keenan's office." Rosie shook my hand, tried to smile, but couldn't pull it off. She seemed kind of jumpy and told us she wanted a table in the back of the restaurant, where she wasn't likely to be seen. I said that was fine with me.

We went back, sat down. Sarah drank bourbon on the rocks and Rosie wanted a Sprite. She said, "Thank you, sir," to the waiter. I tried to make a little conversation, loosen things up. I did the Attorneys Anonymous joke, along with a few other semifunny quips I use when the unpleasant subject of my disbarment and attendant legal troubles comes up. I even made up a couple of new, fairly ornate lines—none of them funny

enough to become a permanent part of my defensive reper-
toire. Rosie didn't crack a smile. She was too distracted to
even talk, her eyes going around the room like she expected
someone to be following her, snooping on our conversation.

"Okay, Rosie," I said. "I guess you came here to share
some things with me. Do you mind if I go ahead and ask you
a few questions?"

Rosie's gaze flicked here, flicked there—everyplace but
my face. "I'm sorry," she said. "Okay, I guess." She spoke
with a soft, nasal accent. Mexican, maybe.

"I know you're nervous," I said. "If you aren't comfortable
telling me anything, I understand. Just tell me if I cross that
line. But let me just add this for the record: I'm not going to
trot out in court with anything you say to me . . . or even to
my friends or my lawyer. What I'm looking for is some background on people involved in this case. That's it."

"Okay," said Rosie. She was studying her Sprite.

"I'll put this bluntly," I said. "I have been charged with
murder. Right now I am the only person in the world, besides
the guy who did it, who knows that I didn't commit the
crime. I can't prove jackshit. I don't have even a *shred* of evidence that would implicate anybody else. Nothing. I have to
turn over every stone, find out about everyone connected to
Roger Hawley so I can figure out who had the motive and
who had the means to take a piece of steel and hit him in the
head until he died. Okay?"

"Okay." Rosie was still working on the Sprite, rotating it,
looking at the different angles.

"So what I'm saying is, I understand your concerns about
your job and I understand there are plenty of sound ethical
reasons for you not to talk to me. But if you can help me—"
I stopped. It made me feel worn out, making this tired appeal
again. "If you know anything that can help. . . ."

Rosie was still looking at the Sprite. "I'll do my best, if I
know anything," she said. "But you know, Mr. Vine, I got a
little baby son. I got a baby son I got to take care of."

I nodded. "Thank you," I said. "I appreciate everything
you're doing. And there's no need to call me mister. I gave
up mister a couple years back. I like to think of myself more

as plain old Bobby now." Trying to use kind of a light touch. She still didn't seem to think I was especially amusing.

"Okay," she said. She glanced up. "I'll try to help."

Sarah put her hand gently on Rosie's arm. "Maybe you should start by telling Bobby about what you do, who you work for, that sort of thing, and then he can ask you some questions."

Rosie started rotating the Sprite again. "I'm a paralegal. I work direct for Mr. Keenan. Day-to-day, I don't know, I do different things. Organizing clients' documents. LEXIS searches on the computer. Lots of times working with printers. Like with a prospectus. Sometimes I have to be at the printer all night, leave my little boy with my sister or something. It's a lot of hours."

"Sure," I said. "I know what paralegals do."

"It's like being a junior attorney, sort of. Only I get paid about half what they do." Rosie showed her teeth, smiling at something unsaid. She had big dimples in each cheek.

"Then you've worked with Excor?" I said. "And with Roger?"

"Oh, yeah. All the time."

I thought about it, trying to think how to ask the next question. "Rosie, how would you characterize their relationship, Roger and Tate's?"

"They get along okay. You know, Roger comes over: talk, talk, talk. That's how he is. Then Mr. Keenan tells him what to do. Then Roger shuts up and goes away."

"Tate tells Roger what to do? Isn't Roger the client?"

"Sure, but there's more to it than that."

"More to it? How do you mean?"

The nervous look came back. She hesitated, communing for a few seconds with her Sprite. Then she looked up, right at me. "Mr. Keenan owns Excor."

"What!"

"Yeah, sure," she said. "Maybe not a hundred percent, but he was the main investor. Like sixty, seventy percent. The rest comes from the other three—Mr. Hawley, Mr. Zell, and the other man, the accountant guy."

"Truman Shore?"

"Right. Mr. Shore. He looks like he never goes outside, never had a good time in his life. Anyways, they put up some money, but most of it comes from a dummy corporation controlled by Mr. Keenan."

"Right out in the open?" I said. "The bar would have a fit if they found out about it. That he owns one of his own clients? There's so much room for conflict of interest there it's not funny."

"Of course not out in the open. Anyway, who's going to find out?" Rosie said. She shrugged. "Very difficult to uncover. Excor is a corporation, sure, but nonregistered stock. Only four shareholders. They don't have to do any public filings, far as I know. No paperwork with the SEC, the NASD. Plus, the stock Mr. Keenan owns? It's not in his name. Like I say, it's a dummy corporation, limited partnership. Without subpoenas, some type of lawsuit or something, nobody's ever going to find out that Mr. Keenan controls it. Maybe not even then."

She was right. It wasn't hard to do. A partnership can own stock—or any other asset for that matter—but it's pretty difficult under Georgia law to figure out who controls a partnership. Without inside information or some kind of legal action, then no one would—or *could*—ever know that Keenan controlled Excor.

Unless the Securities and Exchange Commission came in and started tearing Excor apart. They'd find out pretty quickly in that case.

I explained what I was thinking to Sarah.

"But with Roger dead and a few million dollars missing, that just might happen," Sarah said. "The SEC probably will show up."

"In which case Tate could end up getting some shit on his boots."

This didn't make Rosie happy. She couldn't stop messing with the Sprite. "You promise you're not going to tell anybody what I said to you?" she said. Her voice was low, quiet.

"Scout's honor."

"I got my little boy. If I lose this job, I'm not going to find one that pays this good again. My little boy's got day care, insurance, everything. I need this job."

"I promise," I said.

"Okay," she said. "Okay." She seemed unconvinced.

Our *salades* came. Faux Pas is the kind of place where

they don't have salad, they have *salade*—radicchio and bitter lettuces, small portions scattered across a big plate.

"By the way," I said. "You remember the name of this dummy corporation?"

Rosie snapped her finger, trying to think of the name. "Like a tree," she said.

"A tree?"

"You know, like Pine Tree Associates or something. Bush-wood, I don't know." She looked away for a minute. "Wait. Evergreen! That's the name of it. Evergreen Partners."

We didn't talk for a while. Suddenly Rosie stood up, a terrible look on her face, like she was in pain. She jammed a napkin over her eye and ran down the stairs to the bathroom.

"Some dirt in her contact?" Sarah said. The main course came. I tasted Sarah's trout, but she wouldn't taste my veal.

"I'm on a veal embargo," she said. "Those poor little cows, they won't let them out of the stalls."

"Yeah, I heard that. But I keep forgetting. You know I haven't had veal in three years. I keep finding things like that, things I haven't done in three or four years."

"I guess so." Sarah looked around the restaurant.

"It's good veal. Undercooked potatoes, but otherwise it's alright. You don't want to try the sauce?"

Sarah shook her head, distracted. "I wonder what happened to Rosie."

"Maybe her contact fell down the drain or something. Here." I was spooning up the sauce for her to try.

Sarah stood up, dropped her napkin on the table. "Hold on. I'm going to check in the bathroom and see if she's okay."

I watched her walk to the stairwell. She was a graceful thing, not showing off, swiveling her hips, any of that—just walking to get there. A little tendril of hair had escaped from the comb on the back of her head. It was hanging down her neck, floating as she walked.

I worked on the veal, stole another piece of Sarah's trout. Sarah came back up from the bathroom, a funny look on her face, and walked out the front door into the parking lot. After a while I could see her through the window, looking around. One of the parking lot valets came up to her, said something. Sarah shook her head and said something back to him. The valet shook his head. The glass in the window was beveled, so that little slices of their bodies floated around in the air.

Sarah came back in. "She's gone," Sarah said.

"What happened?"

"I don't know, but her car's gone." Sarah stood next to me for a minute, looking down. "I'm going to make a phone call." She walked away again, back down the stairs, the little tendril of hair still floating down her long neck.

I looked around the restaurant. Women with straight teeth and good complexions, men with good complexions and expensive suits. Something about the whole thing bugged me. It all added up to money, being able to pay for the braces, the dermatologists, the trips to Cozumel. I couldn't stand being around people like that anymore. Maybe I'm bitter, resentful, pissed off because I can't be like them anymore, because I can't take Hickey Freeman suits and orthodontically correct teeth for granted anymore. But I don't think that's all there is to it. It's not the outward form, really: the perfect smiles, the Caribbean suntans, the imported flannels—all that doesn't bother me, finally. It's the look on these people's faces, that insufferable, pious, self-satisfied look. Like they couldn't imagine anything outside their own skulls: *Here I am; don't you wish you were me?*

There were a couple of men at a table near us, though, that were somehow different. They had the seventy-five-dollar cravats, sure, but not that oppressive air of correctness. They didn't look like nice people, I'll admit—but at least they seemed to have been squeezed out of a different mold. The younger of the two was about my age. He was a short guy with a wide mouth and big lips, and he never stopped talking. His suit was linen, double-breasted, a little too Italian looking, and he wore a diamond pinky ring. His black hair was starched up and swept back like a televangelist or maybe a car dealer. He put me in mind of a shark.

Across the table from him, his back to me, was the other guy, a little older. Maybe forty-five, fifty. It was hard to tell, since I could only see part of his face. He was stone bald and had one of those thin, taut faces—a guy with the lid on too tight, burning himself up all the time. He wore charcoal and pinstripes. He reminded me of somebody, but I wasn't quite sure who.

The young guy, the shark, kept talking, always in motion, waving his hands around, poking at his food, straightening his tie, never stopping. The bald man just watched him, only looking down to impale something on his plate. He was a mechanical eater, working his way in sectors across his plate. He turned once to look for the waiter, and I saw his eyes: hot, intense, hard.

"I'm worried," Sarah said. I hadn't noticed her come back. "She's not here, she's not at home. Her car's gone from the parking lot. I don't know what to do."

"Here's my thinking," I said. "Sit down. Finish your trout before it completely congeals. Then when you're all done, call her house again. It's only been ten minutes. She probably hasn't had time to get home yet."

Sarah looked at her watch. "Yeah," she said. "Still. . . ."

"Still, your trout's getting cold."

Sarah sat down and started eating. I kept watching the two men at the other table. I couldn't make out what they were saying, but the shark was trying to convince the bald guy of something. You could tell from the body language. The shark was leaning in, prodding at the air with his fingers, pushing and pushing. The bald guy wasn't having it though. He didn't say a word, just made war on his food, trenching across the plate like some grim World War I general. He hardly moved, everything in control.

Finally, the shark put the question to him, trying to close the sale. The bald guy finished off the last sector of his food and set his knife and fork down softly on the plate. They were lined up perfectly. He put his hands together, fingers intertwined, set one knuckle softly on the very edge of the table and leaned forward, maybe an inch. Then he said something. One word.

I couldn't hear him say it, but I could tell that was what he said. No. There was no mistaking it. No ambiguity in his posture, no appealing the decision.

The shark slumped back in his chair, defeated. One hand made a little spasm, flopped on the tablecloth like a grounded fish, still trying to make the sale. He started to say something but it was no good. The bald man said it again. No.

The short guy might as well have argued with a rock. There wouldn't be any appeal. It just flat wasn't on the menu with this guy. The shark shut up and started sawing on his fillet.

"You're staring."

"Sorry, what?" I said.

"You're staring," Sarah said.

"I was eavesdropping," I said.

"I know," she said. "But there's an art to it, Bobby. You're supposed to pretend like you aren't doing it."

"Maybe you're right. I never thought about it before."

"Sure I'm right." The smile appeared, the startling smile. Her face changed, became beautiful, then settled back into its normal angles. She had freckles across the bridge of her nose. I hadn't noticed that before.

"You look around this room," I said. "What do you think, Sarah? About all the people in here? What do you think?"

She looked around a little, fiddled with her hair. "Boring," she said finally.

"Okay," I said.

"Pompous?"

"Okay."

I waited, but she didn't say anything else.

"You know what I notice?" I said.

"What?"

"Teeth. Everybody here's got good teeth. The waiters, the busboys, all these assholes." I fanned the air around us.

I went on like that for a while, tearing everybody down. You would have thought I was Karl Marx, all the shit I was giving these people. I went on and on, talking about corner offices and Mercedes Benzes and MBAs and houses with rec rooms and eagles over the door. I was heaping it on, getting worked up. Finally I decided to shut up; I could see I wasn't getting anywhere.

Sarah looked at my face for a minute, her eyes narrowing, like she was trying to figure something out. "What is your problem? You're so pissed off . . . but why? It's not these people's fault you went to jail."

"Pissed off? Who's pissed off?"

"Look at you," she said. She reached across the table, put one hand on my face, and pushed back the corner of my lip. "Your teeth, Bobby, they're perfect. Straight. White. There's not a goddamn thing wrong with your teeth. Why are you ragging on all these people? There's nothing wrong with having good teeth. There's nothing wrong with clean children. There's nothing wrong with cars that don't blow a gasket halfway down to Florida. There's nothing wrong with a house where the roof doesn't leak. There's nothing wrong here! Damn it, this is real life, Bobby."

"You know what I'm saying," I said, feeling peevish.

She watched me for a while. "Yeah," she said. "I do know what you're saying. But I don't make a big deal about it. I don't have some chip on my shoulder all the time. What's wrong with being a happy white guy? What's wrong with being some yuppie jerk driving around in a BMW? Is that really so bad?"

"See? You said it yourself. You don't like these people any more than I do."

Her cheeks went red. "I don't know these people. I don't know anything about them. And if I were you, I wouldn't sit around all the time trying to fob off all your troubles on them. If you've got problems, Bobby, blame them on yourself. You caused them. You can fix them. Screw these people. They don't matter."

I felt a hot, raw shame. "Okay. Forget about it. I was just making conversation." The waiter came by, bused my plate.

"Is the other party going to be returning?" the waiter said, nodding his head at Rosie's plate.

I looked at Sarah. "Why don't you leave it a minute?" she said.

"Let me illustrate my point, okay?" I said. "There's a guy sitting behind us, he's got funny-looking teeth. Now to me, it makes the guy more interesting. Just turn around, look at this guy over there, the one with the televangelist hair. Look at his teeth. There, that's the one."

Sarah looked. "Oh, shit," she said. She had a funny look on her face, like she had just caught on to something.

"What?"

"When Rosie left? She was holding the napkin up to her face, like maybe she had something in her eye, right?"

"Right."

"But she didn't. It wasn't her contact. It wasn't her eye."

"How do you know?"

"She was covering her face so he wouldn't see her."

"What do you mean?"

"The bald guy," Sarah said. "That's Tate Keenan."

Freeze frame.

We sat there for a minute. So I was wrong. The bald guy wasn't fifty after all. He was about my age—not quite forty. I happened to remember his age, God knows why, out of some Bar Association newsletter I guess. It was amazing that you could do that to yourself, eat yourself up with ambition, work, fear, whatever it was that was going on inside him.

"Must have been a long time since I saw him last," I said. "He used to have hair."

"You've been out of circulation a while."

"He's a scary guy."

"Yeah," said Sarah. "He is."

Everything was awkward. I didn't know what to say. The waiter came, asked if we wanted desert. Sarah didn't, thanks.

"Can you give us a minute?" I said.

"May I tell you your choices for the evening so you can think it over?" He had his head cocked to the side, trying to act helpful. He had a perky look that reminded me of the receptionist at Sarah's office.

"In a minute," I said. "Two minutes." I held up a couple fingers, shook them around about eight inches from the waiter's perky face. Then I felt bad for being rude. The waiter went away.

I put my hand over my mouth, rubbed my face, looked down at the floor.

"Here's the deal," I said finally. "I don't want to give you excuses for how I act sometimes."

Sarah interrupted. "No. It's my fault. I know you're under a lot of pressure."

"Hear me out. Hear me out," I said. "And don't apologize for something you shouldn't apologize for. Don't do it. I guess I *am* bitter about some things. And I'm worried. This is a lot worse, this thing with Roger, than anything I was accused of before. But I've been through all of this bullshit— jail, courts, lawyers, all that. And I know that it won't break me. I know that now, because I've done it all already."

I stopped and drank some wine. I was trying to get a handle on some things I hadn't ever put into words before. "But that's not the point. The point is that when I was in jail, I thought—I don't know how to put this—I thought that I would get out and everything would be okay. That's the light at the end of the tunnel. Just getting out. I thought somehow that even with the divorce, and losing the kids, and my profession taken away—I thought that still I was going to come back, I was going to return to some kind of normalcy. You understand what I mean?"

Sarah nodded. I don't guess she did, really—but that was okay.

"But it's *not* normal anymore. You're right, see, you're right. I *am* like these people in a lot of ways. I'm bright, I still have some good suits, a couple sharp neckties. My teeth are straight." Sarah's face lit for a moment, went dim again. It was as though that startling smile took so much effort that she couldn't sustain it for more than a second or two.

"But things have all been busted up. All that stuff I used to believe in has gone away. I used to be *just* like these people. I mean, identical! All I wanted, I just wanted a nice place, a big yard for the kids, good school district, sit out on the back porch on the weekend and cook chicken. I used to have one of those chicken smokers. You know the kind I mean?"

"Like a black, barrel-shaped thing?" she said. "You put the charcoal in the bottom, then a bowl with beer and onions, then the chicken?"

"Beer? I never thought of that." I sat there a minute, imagining the smell of burning chicken, of beer, of cut grass. It made me feel weary as hell. "Yeah, I bought one of those things, those big chicken smokers, and in the summer, weekends, I'd set it up out back. Have a couple drinks. I don't know how to describe it. It was maybe the happiest I've ever been. The most complete?" I shrugged. "Just sitting out there with the bugs flying around, the kids yelling, running all over the place. Drinking Miller long necks. Remember? The champagne of beers?"

I didn't say anything for a while.

"You sound so sad, Bobby. Like everything is past tense."

I sat there feeling like everything that happened to me back there was obscured and distorted, like I couldn't see the whole field. But the worst part was that I couldn't *feel* it either, that I couldn't seem to mash it all together into one organic, undifferentiated whole and *feel* something coherent about all those things that had happened before. Everything was all splintered apart and painful.

I wanted, suddenly, to say all of this to Sarah. But all I could say was: "Yeah." And then: "I don't know what went wrong. I just want to get it all back. I just want the kids, the chicken smoker, the backyard, I want it all back."

"And the bank, the job, the law degree?"

"That never meant shit to me. Not really. At the time it seemed like it meant something, but looking back—" I laughed a little. "The nobility of The Law? Please! The adventure of high finance? That was all just a big specious put-on, a trophy to stand up on a shelf and point at so people could see what a grand guy I was." I smiled sadly, thinking back on it.

Sarah looked at me, pitying me, I think. It made me feel sick and weak and dirty, the expression on her face.

"What about your wife?" she said.

"Carla?" I said.

My wife, Carla. Jesus, I couldn't seem to get her in my head all at once. Just bits and pieces. I could see the bare, mysterious line of her hips at night; I could see the way she used to stare and stare into the mirror sometimes when she was making up her face, the eyeliner just sitting there in her unmoving hand; I could see this goofy old fly-fishing hat of her dad's that she used to wear when it rained; I could see that look of bewilderment and the dawning of understanding and fear in her eyes when I sat up there on the witness stand and lied my ass off. And then when these bits and pieces got there in my head, I started trying to add and subtract and weigh, tried to perform some kind of moral calculation: What was she worth to me? What did our life together *mean?* What rules described it?

Oh, Christ.

I shook my head, no. But I couldn't say the words. It was a terrifying thing to realize that, sure, I'd probably take my wife back, too, if she gave me half a chance. I had never realized that before.

I shrugged. "It doesn't matter. It's all gone, Sarah. I can't be like that anymore, can't have any of that anymore."

"Bobby. . . ." she said. She leaned forward, touched my hand, lightly, with the tips of her fingers. I couldn't stand the intimacy of it, the rush of pleasure it gave me, and I had to jerk my hand away.

"And even if I could," I said, "I'd grab it, and I'd hold onto it, and it would be like death. It would be bitter and I'd hate it and still I wouldn't be able to let it go."

"Bobby. . . ."

"Better not to be tempted."

"Bobby. . . ."

I looked into her black eyes, saw the same pain I was feeling—or at least some kind of recognition of it—after a minute I reached back across the table, put my hand on hers.

She smiled. Oh, man, that smile!

And for the first time in a long, bleak stretch of long, bleak days, I felt the terrible watch spring of fear and defeat and anger inside me start to unwind.

We got two huge pieces of cheesecake and we got some brandy in outrageously large snifters. We talked about divorces. Sarah'd had one of those, too.

"One week to the day after my devoted husband passed the bar," she said. "I was at the office, working at McCormick, Van Thuyl and Curtiss. That was where I met Rosie. Anyway I was in a deposition and I got this call from the front desk. I go up, and there's this nice-looking old guy in a windbreaker. He says, 'Are you Sarah Bryce?' I say, 'Yes.' He hands me an envelope and starts to walk out. I say, 'Thank you!' Being nice and polite. He turns around and looks back at me, you know, with this look on his face like *don't thank me yet,* and then he goes hustling out the door, I mean really moving. You'd have thought he was one of these Domino's delivery guys. Well, these giant smoked-glass doors close behind him, and this guy's gone. I open up the envelope and look inside. He's just served me the papers. Petition for Divorce. I go running through these giant glass doors. I'm yelling *'Wait! Wait!'* "

"Yeah," I said.

"Like if I could just give the papers back to the guy in the windbreaker, the whole thing would never have happened. *Wait! Wait! Wait!*"

We laughed a little.

"I supported him all the way through law school. Clipped coupons, paid the bills, fixed his dinner. All that Suzy Homemaker shit. The only thing I didn't do was his shirts."

"In gratitude for which. . . ."

". . . he screwed me. Royally. He had passed the bar, but he didn't have a job yet. See what he was doing? So he could go to the court, plead hardship and not have to pay any alimony. I found out later he'd had a girlfriend already for close to a year. And a job offer. He made a special deal, took a deferred salary the first year, just long enough to get the alimony issue settled while he was still broke and making practically no money. An extremely effective negotiation strategy. Gee whiz, Your Honor, nothing in these pockets but lint!"

"This," I said, "being the reason you think lawyers are scumbags?"

"One of but a long, long list."

I laughed and she favored me with the amazing smile.

I offered to drive Sarah home. She gave me directions, sort of, and I headed off down Piedmont. We were a little drunk.

Some asshole behind me had his bright lights on. I moved my head over so the light wouldn't reflect out of the mirror.

"You're kind of far away," I said.

Sarah looked at me for a minute. "Yeah?" she said.

"That's just my reading of the situation."

Sarah slipped out of her seat belt, slid across the vinyl bench seat, right next to me. I drove, concentrating on keeping it between the lines. After a while I put my arm around Sarah's shoulder. She hoisted my arm back onto the wheel. "Eyes on the road," she said.

But after a minute she started doing things to my neck, little things with her fingers, little things with her lips. I felt something wet and delicate crawling up the side of my neck. I was having a hard time, all those lines, lights moving around, blinking. This thing that was happening to my neck.

I took my hand off the wheel again, trying to find her leg. Sarah hoisted it back onto the wheel. She said, "Concentrate."

"I am reckless," I said. "I am more reckless than hell."

"Left at the light," she said. I turned, too fast, off Piedmont onto Monroe. We made a screeching noise. There were lights all over the place, lights moving around, confusing me. Sarah slid her hand down the front of my shirt, feeling around.

"Man," I said. "Oh, man." I couldn't come up with anything else to say. I took my hand off the wheel again. This time she didn't do anything when I found her leg. She didn't have stockings on. It was nice. I moved my hand up past her knee, up the inside of her thigh. She had goose bumps. Lights going by, houses in a blur.

"Right at the sign. It's a yield. It's a yield, you don't have to stop."

"This guy behind me," I said. "He's had his damn high beams on the whole way. I can't see the things, the signs."

"Well move the mirror, butthead." She did it for me, twisted the rearview off-kilter so the light wasn't shining in my face. I couldn't see anything behind me anymore. Then she slid her tongue up the side of my neck, into my ear. "Is that better?" she whispered.

"Yeah," I said. "No more high beams."

I slid my hand up her thigh, as far as it would go.

"You want to rut?" I said.

"What?" She still had her lips up there, wet against my ear, breathing into it.

"You heard me," I said.

"Maybe," she said. "Left at the light. See? You're on North Highland now." I was conscious of pink lights off to my right. They were fuzzy-looking. Cars were going by. A big red light swam up in front of me.

I stopped for the light, started kissing her.

"Green light," Sarah said. "Green light! Go go go!" She whapped on my bare chest with her palm.

I went. She took a handful of shirt, pulled it out of my belt.

"I hope we're close," I said. She put her hand into my shirt, down into my pants. My concentration weakened.

"We are," she said. "We're very close. We're very, very, very close." We drove down North Highland, past all the fuzzy houses, through some fuzzy lights.

"Where?"

"Right. At the light." I drove under a fuzzy orange light, turned left, dipped past a synagogue with a blurry and inexplicably Greek facade and down a long hill.

"It's amazing," I said. "This guy behind me is going the exact same place we are. It's really, I mean, it's amazing how sometimes two people are going to the exact same place."

"Who?"

"The guy with his brights on. He's been right there behind us the whole time."

"Cosmic," Sarah breathed it into my ear. I was having a darn good time, let me say. We drove down a long dip, snaked upward toward a tight turn. Sarah was inside my pants again.

As the road bottomed out, headed upward toward the turn, I heard something behind me, a roaring noise. The car behind us had downshifted, swung out to the right like it was going to pass. There was a big V-8 engine back there, you could tell by the sound of it. The high beams flashed out beside us. It was big as hell, maybe a truck.

"What's this jerk doing?" I said. It was a tiny residential street, no room to pass. I was mad. I was mad drunk. I was going to demonstrate! I was going to *show* this truck, no sir, by God, he wasn't going to pass me on the inside going up some blind curve on a hill. No way, my friend. There was principle involved!

I stomped on the gas. If I'd had any sense; if I had drunk any less; if it had been any other day—I never would have done it that way. I probably would have slowed down, honked, lifted the finger, let the guy pass. But there was too much alcohol, too much sex in my blood. I was a testosterone fool. I was reckless. The headlights were swimming up in my right side view, high up, like a good-sized truck.

I stomped, stomped on the gas. The Aries downshifted to second, hesitated, bucked, downshifted into first, bucked again. I was pushing the gas pedal, and yelling, *"Aaaaaaaaahhh! Fuck yooooouuuu!"* That Dodge four-cylinder was yowling right along with me, *Aaaaaahhh!* and the headlights were coming, swimming up, making tracks on the right. The Aries finally gave some power, the sad little engine screaming up the hill, the car bucking, trying to throw us up the hill and the headlights were coming up, the head-lights were making tracks on the right.

And there it was, a big van beside us, a black shape against the blue-black blur of trees, and that big V-8 was screaming, beating the Dodge into the turn. There was no room.

I yelled: "Aaaaaaaaaahhhhh!"

The big shape, the van, the big black shape was looming over us. The van was swerving into us, the black shape, crashing into us, driving us sideways. Metal crunched on metal—the van hit us!—the Aries slammed to the left, into the oncoming lane, blind curve, four cones of light sailing out in front of us over the guardrail, the metal grunting and scrap-ing, the wheel gone dead in my hand, the turn gone tighter and tighter, and the guardrail swimming up, tighter and tighter, swimming up on the outside, tighter and tighter, guardrail steel blur and—shit!—we were into it, metal on metal, pinned by the black shape, scraping, scraping. And. . . .

We stopped.

Two taillights swung out in front of us.

The van was driving away.

We were stopped.

We were jammed up against the guardrail in the oncoming lane, blind curve. It was a bad situation. The engine of the Aries made a clunking noise. I turned it off. Our headlights ran up along the guardrail, as it bent around the curve. The trees on the other side of the guardrail looked flat, white-green, in our headlights, like the leaves had been daubed on canvas with a pallet knife.

The taillights of the van moved away from us, stopped.

The white van was right in our headlights. I could see the blue oval on the back door: a Ford.

We sat there breathing. We were surprised. We breathed in and out. Sarah made a funny noise, a kind of puffy sound, letting out her breath.

The van's reverse lights winked on, lighting up the dirt bank on the inside of the turn. He was coming back. What for? The reverse lights went off again. He had changed his mind.

The big V-8 spooled up, blowing leaves out from under the front of the white van. The taillights got smaller, disappeared around the bend. The van was gone.

I said: "Shit."

Sarah said: "Vee-Jay-Vee-Seven-Four-Nine."

"What?"

"Vee-Jay-Vee-Seven-Four-Nine," Sarah said. "The license plate number. Vee-Jay-Vee-Seven-Four-Nine."

I started the engine again. It was still clunking, but it worked. Maybe a twisted fan blade. We drove a couple more blocks and reached Sarah's place. She lived in an attic apartment in the eaves of a big yellow stucco place owned, she said, by a maxillofacial surgeon.

We parked the Aries at the curb and sat there on the empty street of that rich old neighborhood, the dark oaks and maples towering over us. Sarah was still making the funny little puffing noises, like she was doing Lamaze exercises.

"Are you okay?" I said.

She nodded a little. Her eyes were open wide, the pupils huge.

"They were trying to kill us," she said finally. "God*damn* those people. God*damn* them." Her shoulders quivered, rocked for a second, collapsed. I held her while she cried. She didn't make any sound at all now. There were just the spasms in her shoulders, her wet face pushing into my neck. After a while, she stopped.

"We would have gone down into the ravine," I said. "We would have gone down if I hadn't acted like such a jerk. I should have braked, you know. I should have braked when that guy started to pass." I thought back: The lights swimming up next to us just before we got to the guardrail.

"What do you mean?" Sarah said.

"If I had braked, if I'd had any sense, even kept going the same speed—they would have hit us about thirty, forty feet earlier. We wouldn't have hit the guardrail. We'd have gone down into the ravine. If I'd had any sense, we'd probably be dead now."

We got out of the car. It seemed as though nothing bad could ever happen in this rich, silent neighborhood with its big houses and ancient trees and neat yards full of crocuses and trimmed azaleas. The dull slam of my car door seemed uncouth there, like coughing during a quiet part of the symphony.

I put my arm around her and we walked awkwardly across the big lawn in front of the cheese-colored house, then climbed an iron staircase behind the garage, up to her small, spare apartment. I held her again in the darkness, smelling the cigarette smoke from the restaurant on her skin. It kept surprising me, the feel and smell and solidness of her.

"What's going on here?" she said.

I knew what she meant, but all I could bring myself to say was, "I guess we better call the police."

A couple of late-shift Decatur cops showed up after a while, carrying clublike flashlights and small, worn notebooks in their hands. They talked to us, wrote things down, went away. From the reverent way they held them, those big flashlights seemed to mean a lot more to the cops than anything that got written down in their notebooks. I don't think they believed me when I told them how the wreck happened.

I stood in the doorway, watching the police car drive off. My blood was still going; I couldn't calm down. Nothing added up: It was all just a big nonsensical swirl. I was afraid, but it wasn't the Big Fear just then; it was a smaller, quieter fear, like maybe I had found something in this place, something that I needed. And I was tired of getting things and then losing them, sick to death of that. I turned from the open doorway and looked at Sarah, looked into her soft black eyes. There was only one thing I was sure of at that moment, but I was afraid to say it, afraid even to make a move toward her.

I think Sarah understood, though.

"Stay?" she said.

I still couldn't say the words. I just nodded.

Sarah closed the front door, took my hand, led me into the dark bedroom with its inward-sloping walls. We took off our clothes in silence, lay on the bed in front of her black and white TV, and watched some old, foolish movie starring Victor Mature.

CHAPTER 4

"Vine, son, how you doing?" It was Ed Mance on the phone. I was back at Ray's, where I'd gone after Sarah left for work.

"Okay, Ed. What you come up with?"

"Hate to say it."

"Nothing?"

"Zero. M.O.'s no good. Blunt instruments are all over the place. It's not enough to go on." Ed paused. "You sure this boy wasn't a Latin? Potto Rican, something like that?"

"I'm telling you. . . ."

"All-American nigger."

"Black," I said. "Could we go with black?"

"Okay. *N* for *Nee-gro*. I got it right here on the computer request form. Your last lead, Nee-gro hit man, known to of been in the employ of *C* for *Caucasian* in the past. We got about five in the whole U.S. All five is currently serving life sentences in one state prison or another."

"Anything else?"

"I hope you got a smart lawyer."

"Dick Bloom," I said.

"He's pretty good," he said. "Good Jew lawyer."

"Whatever," I said. "Look, I got another one for you."

Silence.

"Ed?"

"Okay."

"Easy one. I got a Ford van, big V-8 engine, tag number Vee-Jay-Vee-Seven-Four-Nine."

"New development?"

"You could say that. Guy tried to kill me last night. Ran me off the road."

"On purpose."

"Hell yes, on purpose!"

"You tell Deputy Handlin?"

"For what it's worth, sure."

"All right. I'll pull it off the computer," Ed said.

"Ed?"

"Yeah?"

"Soon?"

Silence.

"This afternoon," Ed said. *"Maybe* this afternoon."

"I appreciate it, Ed. You know I do."

The line went dead.

I called Jeannie, reporting in. I told her I couldn't find Hawley's desk calendar. She asked, did I check his house? I said, what did she mean by that? I couldn't get into his house. She didn't say anything, just let me listen to the phone hiss. Meaning, why don't you break in, Bobby? Only she didn't say it. I told her I'd keep working on that angle. "Good," she said. "You do that."

I called Ray. Ray asked, where in hell was I? I told him, explained what had happened last night. He told me some story I couldn't follow about an ad he was doing for TV. Something about the guy who was doing postproduction on the ad. I didn't understand the story.

"I got to go," I said.

"Oh, yeah?" he said. "What do you got to do, you in such a big hurry about?"

"I'm going to break into Roger Hawley's house."

"Hey, good idea!" Ray said. "I'm not bailing you out when you get put in jail for that, either."

I drove to Roger Hawley's house. It was out in Gwinnett

County, looking the same as it had the last time I saw it: a big, white clapboard thing—you'd call it pseudoplantation, maybe. White columns, big, useless front porch, big, useless brick gateway out by the drive. A lot of square footage—and him the only person living in it. It was in a development called Tara, a bunch of huge houses crammed together on quarter-acre lots.

I parked across the street, walked down to Roger's house, looking to see if anybody was around. Everything seemed okay. He had planted a little cast-iron pickaninny out front, a new addition. The pickaninny's face was painted green. It was adorable. There were a bunch of pickaninnies in the neighborhood, all painted green, so you wouldn't mistake these high-tone suburban crackers for racists.

I knocked on the front door for the benefit of any neighbors who might be watching, looked around, slipped on a pair of gardening gloves and gave the knob a good heave. No luck. I walked around back. Back door, locked. Patio door, locked. No key under the doormat. No key under the loose brick. No key in the gas grill. I wandered around the patio. There was a conch shell in the corner next to a dead potted plant. I lifted the shell: bingo, a rusty key.

As far as I could remember Roger didn't have an alarm. But he might have gotten paranoid since then. I looked through the sliding glass door, trying to see if there was an alarm contact along the inside of the door frame. It looked clean. I went to the other door, turned the key, walked in. No alarm.

It was the same inside as it had been three years before. Nothing, I mean not one iota of difference. The living room was carpeted in a cream color. There was cold Danish furniture scattered around the room, a couple of vacant, modern canvases clinging to the walls.

I wandered around, looking at everything. There was nothing out of place, nothing dirty. *Architectural Digest* and *Southern Living* on the coffee table. It was so labored, so fake—as though Roger had slipped through life without leaving any traces of himself behind; like one of those perfect Olympic dives: You see the guy spinning and twisting, then he's in the water, and he's gone. No splash, not even a ripple on the surface.

Then, there it was in my head again, that same question that I'd had in his office: Who was this guy? I had once thought he was my friend. But looking around the house, looking at the things that were left, it seemed like I had never known him. Surely there had been more to him than just some ambling lust, some machine whose task was to fill empty rooms with expensive things. Surely, surely. . . .

But we can never know, maybe not just about Roger, but about anyone. I felt a heavy, creeping sadness again, thinking about Roger, thinking about things I had said to Sarah the night before. Admitting I wanted it all back, not just the kids, but the Williamsburg house, the new Oldsmobile. Wanting even my wife, who had been shabby and mean to me. Or maybe she'd done what any self-respecting human being would do when the person they loved had turned out to be foolish and weak and dishonest.

I thought about shame, my shame every day in prison, my shame at selling trashy furniture to people who couldn't afford it, shame at having to make Attorneys Anonymous jokes every time I met somebody new. Shame, every day; shame, shame, shame. Would a house full of smoked-glass tables, wide-screen TVs, microwave ovens, smart-looking toilets—would that make me feel more like a whole man again? I wasn't sure. It might.

Then I thought about Sarah, about lying in bed, naked, holding her hand last night. Maybe that was a start.

After I had been through the room with the English billiard table and the fine stereo that no one ever listened to, the cold bedrooms, the bright bathrooms with their impressive plumbing—after all that, I came finally to his office. I pulled on my gardening gloves again, pushed open the door and went in.

Inside there was a bookshelf, a beautiful rolltop desk, a computer, a picture of Roger's bewildered-looking folks, a phone, a fax, a little Xerox copier, a typewriter on an old metal typing stand. I looked at the books on the shelves: securities industry manuals, reference books, a thesaurus, a whole shelf of self-improvement guides. Yes, by God, self-improvement! Roger *had* lived here.

Down to business. I opened the big rolltop. Roger had it custom built, a beautiful piece of furniture, solid oak, with all kinds of pigeonholes and odd-shaped drawers.

I went through all the drawers looking for the calendar, looking for anything that had anything to do with Health Systems. There was a lot of stuff in the desk, mostly tax papers, receipts, bills, warranties, that kind of thing. Plus a few bits of string, orphan thumbtacks, rubber bands, a couple of pictures of Roger (skiing, sailing, standing in front of the Washington Monument with a woman I'd never seen, washing his BMW). He seemed a lot less dashing than I remembered him: just a sort of ordinary guy, brown hair, blue eyes, not especially square-jawed or memorable-looking. If anything, he looked kind of scared of the camera, like it was going to see through him somehow. It reminded me of the Wizard of Oz going, "Pay no attention to that man behind the curtain!"

His business records seemed to have been left at Excor, which is pretty much the way you'd expect it. I spent about an hour on all the pigeonholes, another hour on the drawers, looking at every scrap of paper. Anything that seemed even vaguely interesting, I xeroxed on Roger's home copier.

When I was finished, I hadn't made many copies at all. An ad for a discount broker with some notes scribbled in the margin, a couple of pamphlets about time-share condos in Florida, an airplane ticket stub—round-trip, O'Hare to Singapore—dated about four months back, a few pieces of paper with dates or phone numbers scribbled on them. Nothing I could make sense out of.

I turned on the computer, looked at his word processing files. Not much there. Roger was never the kind to spend a lot of time writing letters.

I turned off the computer, looked around the room. What hadn't I checked? The trash. There might be something there.

I rifled around the wastebasket. Some bills, a couple of things like that. And a fax.

The fax had been sent by someone named Ram Battachargee with a firm called Lee Hong Investments, Ltd.

Suite 4300, 13 Raffles Road, Singapore. There was a short list typed in the middle of the page.

> Singapore Harbor Zeros
> 9 ⅝ yield
> Due June 2000
> Noncallable
> U.S. $100 K face
> Bid U.S. $47.375 K
> 192 units
> Physical delivery upon your instruction.

Now we are getting somewhere. I dicked around with the fax machine, trying to see if it would print out a transmission report. It took a while, but I finally figured out how to make it work: The fax machine hooted and chirped, spit out three inches of paper. It was a report of all transmissions and receipts from the machine since the last time the power went out. There were about ten entries. The second to the last entry was dated July 12, 11:17 p.m.—a receipt from an international number. I checked the fax from Singapore. Same number as the one listed on the Lee Hong letterhead.

The last entry was an outgoing fax. Time 1:22 in the morning, July 13, the day Roger had been killed. One page. It was the reply to Ram Battachargee, whoever he was, in Singapore. Middle of the night, Roger knew the shit was coming down. It had to be the instructions for physical delivery. But where was the original? Where was the reply Roger had sent to Singapore telling this guy, Ram Battachargee, what to do?

I dumped the wastebasket out onto the floor, spread the paper across the carpet. A couple of bills, a travel brochure. No reply to Singapore. I started pulling everything out of the pigeonholes, throwing it in a heap. It was so goddamn close, I could feel it. Pretty soon all the pigeonholes were empty, paper piled up all over the floor. Nothing. No cover sheet, no letter addressed to Ram Battachargee, no scribbled time or date or place.

But it had to be there. It had to. I pulled everything out of the drawers, one by one, chucking the empties across the room. It had to be here, it *had* to. I pulled out the last drawer, turned it over. One piece of paper drifted out, fell toward the floor. I caught it in midair. This was going to be it. I could feel it: This was the one.

I turned the paper over. It was a letter, handwritten. *Dear Roger, I miss your cute buns so much I can't stand it.* I skipped to the bottom. *Please, please come and see me now!!!!! Love ya, Tori.* Signed with a little circle over the *i*. Old Rog, always a weakness for those brain surgeons.

"Shit," I said. My voice had a dull, flat sound in the little room. I picked up the drawer to put it back in the desk. Something made a clunking noise, and the drawer moved in my hand like it was alive. I turned it over again. Another clunk. Something moved inside. What the hell was going on?

Then it hit me: The drawer had a false bottom.

I set the drawer down on the floor, stomped on it twice. Nothing happened. It was a nice piece of joinery, solid as a rock. I came down on it again with my heel, this time dead center. The false bottom of the drawer shattered. I picked it up, ripped away fragments of wood and looked inside the hidden compartment. There were a couple things inside, neither of which was a fax to Singapore.

I put my glove inside the smashed compartment, pulled out one of the drawer's hidden contents. It was a little automatic pistol, a Colt .380. I set it down on the desk, put my hand in the hole, pulled out one more thing. It was Roger's calendar, leather bound, with his initials on the front. Even if I couldn't find the fax maybe I'd find what I needed in his calendar. I slipped it into my coat pocket. For no particular reason, I picked up the little Colt, checked the safety, stuck it in my pocket.

Alright. Time to get the hell out. I looked around the room, trying to think whether there was anything else here I should look at. The phone. I hadn't thought of that. It was one of these jobs that had lot of buttons—the kind with memory, speed dialing, all that stuff. I picked up the receiver, punched * 0: auto redial. Just out of curiosity, maybe I'd find out who Roger had made his last phone call to.

The line clicked, clicked, connected.

"Hi-Top Security," said the voice on the other end of the line, "could you hold for a moment please?"

"Thanks, no," I said. "I'll try again later."

CHAPTER 5

I went back to Ray's, made some phone calls. Jeannie wasn't reachable; Dick Bloom was out of town for the weekend. I put on a pair of shorts, picked up Roger's pocket calendar and a legal pad, and went out to the pool.

The pool was the only architecturally normal thing about Ray's house. It was rectangular, blue and white concrete, about fifty feet long, with a diving board at the deep end. Just a basic pool, nothing to it.

I sat on a canvas chair in the sun and looked at my belly. Prison pale.

I opened up Roger's calendar, looked through the last couple of weeks. He was a busy guy. Meetings with Tate Keenan, a lunch with Zell, a board meeting for Excor, lots of phone calls to people I'd never heard of. A couple of notes to call Ram Battachargee, the guy in Singapore. During the last week of his life, he had three lunches with a guy named Clement. Was that a first name or a last name?

I went back inside, came out with a beer. There were no clouds in the sky, not even a hint of haze. Time to cook myself a nice case of skin cancer.

Delivery date—that's what I needed. I flipped through the calendar. Monday the 13th, the entry: *Tell Clement—dummy bonds, Monday 20.* Underneath it said, *DeK/P'tree Aport, 3:30 p.m.* Who was Clement? Were these the right bonds?

I flipped through to the twentieth to see if there was anything there, anything that might explain the note. A tickler: *Call somebody name Winger about Braves tickets.* Winger was going to have to do without free tickets this year. There was nothing that seemed related, nothing about bonds, Singapore, Clement, Health Systems, anything like that.

Back to the thirteenth. *Tell Clement—dummy bonds, Monday 20.* Was Clement bringing the bonds on the twentieth? Picking them up? *DeK/P'tree Aport.* That had to be DeKalb-Peachtree Airport, a little general aviation airport northeast of the city. It was right off Buford Highway, near where Ray's main store was.

Monday, the twentieth. Day after tomorrow.

So who was this guy Clement? I looked in the back for an address. *C* for *Clement?* I got lucky: Clement Crews, two *C*'s, home and office.

I put the book down, lay back in the chair, felt the sun come down. Monday at three-thirty I was going to drive up to the DeKalb-Peachtree Airport and get back Roger Hawley's money. Hell, yes, nothing to it.

I drank the rest of the beer. After a while I fell asleep.

When I woke up, the sun had sunk in the sky. My chest felt tender and doughy. My brain was a little stupid at first, and I couldn't remember what I'd been doing. I looked down. My skin had turned a shrimplike shade of pink. Damn. Time to seek shelter.

I went inside, had another beer for the pain, checked the answering machine. There was one message: "Bobby. Ed Mance here. Got some good news and some bad news. Call me."

I called, but he was out of the office. Then I picked up Roger's desk calendar, looked up Clement Crews's phone number, tried the home number first.

"Hello, you have reached Clement Crews. Obviously I'm not here. Leave your message after the noise."

I hung up and tried Crews's work number. I got the same voice I'd heard this morning: "Thank you for calling Hi-Top Security. How may I—"

"Sorry," I said. "Wrong number."

Hi-Top, Hi-Top. Where had I seen that name before?

I tried Ed on the phone again. The cop who answered said

that he was sorry but Detective Mance was out. He was apprehending a reluctant witness. I asked when Ed would be back. The cop on the phone said: "Detective Mance—sometimes he's out a long time. Sometimes not." The cop had this tone of voice that grates on you, the kind of guy who thinks everything he says ought to make you laugh.

"Who is this, anyway?" the cop said.

"Never mind," I said.

"Never mind," the cop said. "I never heard of that name before." He was a funny cop. I hung up on him.

I went down to the rec room, turned on Ray's stereo and put on a George Jones disk. George Jones is the greatest, saddest country and western singer who ever lived. I fell asleep about halfway through a song called "She Thinks I Still Care."

When I woke up it was dark outside. I called Ed Mance, but the funny cop answered the phone instead. I didn't want to talk to the funny cop.

My chest was smoldering and itchy now. I felt like there were heat waves rising from it, so I went upstairs to get another beer. As I was opening the refrigerator, I heard Ray come in the door.

"Working late on a Saturday, Boss Man?" I said. "You want a beer?" I got two Michelobs out of the door.

"Come here, Counselor," Ray said. "In the living room."

"What?" I said. I went into the living room.

Ray was standing in the middle of the living room in his polyester suit with his arms raised, like Charlton Heston—or whoever it was—parting the Red Sea.

"Be totally honest," he said. "I want you to be a hunnert percent honest. A hunnert and ten percent honest, okay?"

"What?"

Ray turned around slowly, doing little ballet shuffles. His arms were still spread, and a thin sliver of white belly showed through a gap in his shirt.

"Be totally honest," he said. "Tell me what you see."

"You're acting a little weird. That's the main thing I'm seeing here."

"Come on Counselor, seriously now." He waggled his stumpy hands. "I'm talking appearance. I'm talking, clothes make the man." He took his arms down, hitched up his Sans-a-belt pants for emphasis.

"How do you mean?" I said. I had a hunch what was coming.

"What I'm saying, I see you come to work every day looking sharp as hell," Ray said. "Real professional. Nice-looking shirt, tie, good suit—the whole nine yards. Now I personally never paid a lot of mind to my clothes, you get what I'm saying?"

"Sure."

"I mean I wear a suit, try to make an appearance. But then I look at you and I say, being totally frank here, totally honest? I look at you and I say to myself, here's a fellow looks better than me. But I'm damned if I can figure out why."

"Well," I said. "I'm glad you think my appearance is more or less reasonable." Choosing the words, being careful.

"Point is," Ray said. "I'm looking for your opinion. I'm a pretty rich guy, Counselor, not ashamed to admit it. But I look at you, and I start thinking, hey, I could do better."

"Well. . . ." I said.

"Bottom line here," Ray said. He parted the Red Sea again. "Tell me how I look."

"Ray. . . ."

"I look like shit, don't I?"

"Ray. . . ."

"Don't jerk me around. What am I doing wrong here?"

"I don't know that *wrong* is necessarily the word I'd choose Ray." I was being feeble as hell.

"Bobby! Goddamn it! Tell me what to do here!"

"Okay," I said. "Okay, Ray. You want me to be brutally honest?"

"Be brutal."

"Okay, Ray. First, lose the two-tone loafers with the little gold thing on the top. And lose the shirt. That white-on-white thing is strictly bush league. No, Ray, lose the shirt. Lose the brown tie. Lose the green socks. Lose the suit. It's green, it's polyester, it's got elastic in the pants. The left shoulder's too high, it sags in the back, the sleeves hang down to your fingers. It's bright *green,* Ray. Bright green! You look like the seven fucking dwarfs."

Ray was starting to get a look in his eyes, kind of defensive. "You don't like the suit."

"Lose the suit, Ray. You really want to look like some hotshot asshole, you got to lose that suit."

"Green? You don't even like the green?"

"Lose the suit, Ray."

Ray put his hands down. The wretched, bright green suit hung off him like a sack. He looked pitiful and sad, like some strange little fuzzy-headed kid in his dad's leprechaun costume. I felt terrible.

"Give me that beer," he said. I gave him the beer. "Michelob? Did you buy these?"

"Ray. . . ."

Ray held up his hand, cut me off. "I ast you for a honest opinion. Honest, okay. You give it to me. I appreciate that."

"Ray. . . ."

"I'm serious," he said. "I ast any those fools out the store, you think I'd of got an honest opinion? Shit no. 'Oh, yessir, Ray, you looking good as hell! Looking expecially good today!' See, you I trust. I trust a guy that's willing to give me some bad news."

We took our beers downstairs. Ray turned on the TV. We watched a movie about a woman who was trying to kill a man who had raped her at Girl Scout camp when she was thirteen. The guy had just escaped from prison and was going to hunt her down and rape her again.

"I guess we got our work cut out for us," Ray said, about half an hour into the show.

"How's that?"

"You and me, we got to upgrade my wardrobe."

"What?" I said. I tried to figure out what he meant. "You want me to go clothes shopping with you?"

"Absolutely. Abso-damn-lutely."

I watched the program for a few minutes. The rapist was in the woman's house, but she didn't know it. She had turned all her lights off, wandering around in the dark. For some reason—despite the various spooky noises she kept hearing—she wouldn't turn on the lights.

When the commercial came on, I said: "You want me to go

out with you, pick out your socks, tell you this tie is good, this one isn't? You really want me to do that?"

"Hey, if you got a problem with that—"

"No," I said. "It's just. . . ." It's just—what? I wasn't sure. It just felt funny, like something women would do.

"How much is it gonna set me back?" Ray said.

"Depends on what you want."

Ray thought about it. "Assuming I start from scratch. Top to bottom. New suit for every day of the week. New shirts, ties, socks, shoes—hell, cuff links? Whatever it takes."

"Lot of money," I said.

"I *got* a lot of money," Ray said. "I got a whole shitload of money. I'm fifty-six years old, got no kids, no wife. You know, thing is, Counselor, I got nothing in my life *but* money." He had a distant, regretful look on his face.

"You sure you want to do this?" I said.

"Top drawer. Nothing but the best."

"You're talking custom made, Ray. Hand, by God, made. Tailored to your unique form. Minimize your flaws, maximize your strengths, fit you like a glove—all that shit. You choose the style, the cut, the finish, the cloth."

"Custom made," Ray said softly. There was a kind of girlish quality to his voice. "Damnation, I never thought of that."

Now the girl was in the rapist's house, a big turnaround. He didn't know she was there, but he had this big butcher knife under his pillow—you know, just in case. The girl didn't know that the gun she was carting around had a history of jamming when the clip was full. A police sergeant had conveniently explained this to another character earlier in the show. She had a full clip in there, too; she wasn't taking any chances.

"Can we turn this off?" I said.

"You know what?" Ray said. "I just ordered me a new TV, one of them projection jobs, got a six-foot screen." He punched the remote control, and the screen went dead.

I played the George Jones CD again.

"Kind of takes you back, don't it?" Ray said.

"I don't know," I said. We listened to a couple songs.

"So," Ray said. "You falling for this girl, the lawyer?"

"Paralegal," I said. "She's a paralegal. There's a difference."

"Oh, yeah, what's that?"

"About fifty grand a year." I sat there for a while, working on my beer.

"You didn't answer my question," Ray said. "About the girl."

"True," I said.

Ray looked at me out of the corner of his eye, then fooled around with the remote control, made it play "White Lightning" again. "White Lightning" is a stupid song, the kind of song that gave country music a bad rap.

"Me and some old buddies of mine," Ray said. "We used to get drunker than hell, listening to this song." He was going to tell me a story. He had that look in his eye. Then, all of a sudden, he changed his mind. "Wait a goddamn minute," he said. "You told me you was busting into Hawley's house today, gonna get this money or something."

I told him about breaking into Roger's house, told him about the fax and the calendar I found. I went upstairs, got the fax, and brought it down.

Ray looked at the fax, squinting. "Singapore Harbor Zeros?" he said. "This don't mean shit to me."

"Here's the deal," I said. "If I'm right, Roger had ordered some kind of bonds, Singapore bearer bonds. Government backed, nice safe investment. All this money that he stole, that he transferred to these Panamanian banks . . . it's all gone by now. The money went straight to Singapore to get these bonds, so the FBI isn't going to find squat in Panama. You know what a bond is, right?"

"I may look like a old coonass redneck," Ray said. "But I ain't a idiot. I know what a goddamn bond is. It's a IOU with interest. Like a pawn ticket for rich people."

"Well, that's the general idea. Here, where it says this stuff about nine and seven-eights yield, noncallable, so forth, it just means it's paying about ten percent interest. This is what you'd call a dollar-denominated zero coupon bond."

"Damn!" Ray said. "Where they come up with this shit?"

"A zero coupon bond is kind of like a savings bond. If it has a face value of a hundred thousand U.S. dollars per unit—that's what we've got here—then it's going to sell initially for a lot less than that. It only pays interest at maturity. Let's say Roger buys them for forty, fifty grand. In July 2000, they pay him back a hundred grand. You with me?"

"Sure."

"They would be selling at a big discount to face value, so, here, where it says 192 units, that would probably be about right to cover eight million. Actually it's a little more."

"Okay."

"Now these are also bearer bonds, unregistered. Meaning, if you have the bond in your hand, the actual piece of paper, you can sell it. Now, like I said, it's also a zero coupon, meaning there's no direct payment of dividends. Unregistered zero coupons, there's nothing they can trace, nothing the FBI can get its hooks into. You see the advantage for a guy like Roger?"

Ray said: "So if he got to take a quick trip, no forwarding address, go someplace that don't have no extradition treaty with Uncle Sam, then he's safe. Throw them bonds in the old suitcase, he's ready to rock and roll."

"Exactly. But to do that, obviously he needs to have the actual physical bonds, the pieces of paper, in the suitcase."

"Okay."

"So he needed physical delivery. See where it says here, *Physical delivery at your instruction?* Okay, now I checked the fax machine, found out that Roger sent a reply to Singapore a couple hours later, telling this guy in Singapore where to deliver the bonds. Now if he sent a fax, he had to write the instructions down on a piece of paper, run it through the fax."

"And that would tell you where the bonds were being sent."

"Right. Only I couldn't find it." I told him about finding the calendar in the secret drawer, then I told him about the note concerning Clement Crews. "So it turns out I didn't need the original that he faxed to Singapore, anyway. Monday at three-thirty, eight or nine million bucks worth of bonds are coming in on some private plane up at the DeKalb-Peachtree Airport. I guarantee it."

"What you gonna do?" Ray said. "Call the cops?"

"I'm going to go down there myself, see who picks them up."

"Then what?"

"Don't know." I hesitated. "I guess I'll think of something."

After the George Jones disk was over, Ray went upstairs. I went to the bathroom. Looking in the mirror, I could see I was going to hurt like hell tomorrow.

When I came out of the bathroom, Ray was standing in the middle of the room, holding the phone book out to me, draped over his hand like an evangelist would hold his bible on TV.

"Lookit here," Ray said. "Alfred G. Detwiler, custom tailoring. Biggest ad in the yellow pages. Suits, sport jackets, shirts. Wide range of fabrics."

CHAPTER 6

I didn't do much on Sunday, just sat around worrying and wishing to hell my sunburn would go away. Monday morning I got hold of Ed.

"Well, Bobby, we got some good news and some bad news."

"You said that on the message, Ed."

"Did I?"

"Those exact words."

"I be damn," Ed said. "Good news is we found out who owns the van tried to run you off the road the other day."

"Okay. Who was it?"

"Hold on. Hold on. Bad news, it was reported stolen, eight o'clock P.M. Friday."

"Two and a half hours before it hit us."

"Yeah," Ed said. "Tough break. It might of just been some crackhead out taking a joyride."

"I don't think so," I said. "It was too intentional."

"Whatever," Ed said. "Anyway, I got to go."

"They followed us all the way from the restaurant."

"Well, look," Ed said. "I got to go."

"Hey, Ed. Hold up a second. Just out of curiosity, who *did* own the van?"

"Let's see, it's on the report here." I could hear paper crackling. "Okay. Here it is. Commercial vehicle, owner's a outfit called Hi-Top Security. Never heard of it."

I didn't say anything.

"Bobby?" Ed said. "Bobby, you still there?"

A few minutes later the phone rang.

"Bobby, I'm sorry I didn't get back to you. I was tied up all weekend." It was Jeannie Richardson.

I told her about the bonds that were coming in by air at three-thirty. "Interesting," Jeannie said. I waited for her to tell me we had to notify the FBI or the police. But she didn't. "What do you plan to do?" she said.

"What I'd like to do is follow whoever picks up the bonds, find out who they are and what they're doing. And then get the bonds back."

"How?"

"I'll figure that out when I get there."

She thought about it for a minute. "You're sure this is where the bonds are?"

"Not absolutely," I said. "But it's a pretty good bet."

"Go ahead," she said finally. "Just make damn sure you find out who picks them up."

"Fine," I said.

Jeannie said good-bye.

"Hold on," I said. "I forgot. Have you ever heard of an outfit called Hi-Top Security?"

"High Top?"

"Right."

Silence. Then: "No, darling, I can't say it rings a bell."

I met Sarah for lunch at a sandwich place near her office.

I had turkey and Swiss, mayonnaise and mustard only. Sarah got roast beef all the way, the soggy kind that leaks oil and vinegar the whole time you're eating.

"You look awful," Sarah said.

"You should have seen me yesterday," I said.

"You're lucky you didn't get sun poisoning." She touched my face softly. It felt like she had light bulbs in her fingertips.

I told her about the bonds, about what I found at Roger's house, asked her if she'd ever heard of Hi-Top or Clement Crews.

"Hi-Top," she said. "I can't place it."

"Careful," I said. A trail of oil was running down her arm. "You're about to soil yourself."

"Never," she said. She licked the oil off her forearm.

"Neat trick," I said. "I never saw anybody lick their elbow before."

She gave me a sly smile. "What was the guy's name again?"

"Clement. Clement Crews."

Sarah shook her head. "Never heard of him."

I finished my sandwich, folded up the wrapping paper, and stuffed it into my empty cup. "Let me ask you this: Why does Jeannie use Jordan as an attorney? She doesn't seem to have much respect for him. I know it's in the terms of her father's trust that he acts as trust administrator. But why let him act as counsel to RichCo? Why have him represent her in her personal business?"

Sarah cocked her head to the side. "That's an interesting question. I don't know the answer. The only thing I can think of is that he's well connected to all the people on the RichCo board. She and the RichCo board don't always see eye to eye."

"How do you mean?"

"She tried to throw them out a couple years ago."

"Are you serious?"

"Oh, yeah. She was going to do an LBO, a recap, take the company private again."

"But she didn't. Why not?"

"Problems with the financing, for one thing. The board

pushed her into a corner mostly, though, I think. They were going to fire her if she tried to do it. I guess she just decided to scrap the whole deal. She's the kind of person who bides her time, waits until the right moment. She can be very patient when she has to." Sarah finished her sandwich, picked a few stray pieces of lettuce off the empty wrapper, and ate them.

"So who is this guy you asked me about?" she said.

"Clement Crews," I said. "Apparently he works at a company called Hi-Top Security. Roger had his work number written down in his calendar. I called the number and Hi-Top answered. He's supposed to pick up the bonds today. I just have this funny feeling that I've seen the name of this company before. Hi-Top Security. I can't remember where, though."

Sarah looked at her watch. "Oh, damn it. I'm late." She got up, threw her trash away, started hustling toward the door.

Suddenly it popped into my head. I slammed my fist down on the table.

Sarah stopped at the door and looked back at me. "What?" she said.

"It just came to me," I said. "Where I saw Hi-Top before."

I drove over to Excor. Truman Shore wasn't in. I said to the receptionist, how about Harvey Zell? Mr. Zell was in, but he was not to be disturbed. It would only take a second I told her. No problem, I'd find his office. There wasn't much she could do to stop me.

I walked back to Roger's office, went in, and picked up one of the Lucite tombstones, then I walked out. In the next office a squat, swarthy, black-haired guy was sitting behind a big desk heaped with paper. He had a filterless cigarette growing out of his hand.

I knocked on the door. Zell looked up at me, took a drag on the cigarette, and then stubbed it out in the ashtray. He had an annoyed look on his face, like I was smelling up his office. He stared at me suspiciously, not saying anything.

"Can I talk to you a minute?" I said.

"I recognize you from your picture, Vine," he said, finally.

"Why the fuck should I be talking to you?" He had a Brooklyn street-fighter accent.

I sat down in a green leather chair. "Nice to met you, too," I said. "I guess it's been a rough month."

Harvey Zell watched me. He had a broad face, heavy lips. His cuff links were bright red—a little too big, a little too loud. It was two o'clock, and he already needed a shave. Harvey Zell stuck out his tongue about a quarter inch, picked a piece of tobacco off of it with his thick fingers, flicked it into the air. "You still haven't answered my question," he said finally.

"Here's the deal," I said. "I don't know where the missing eight million is right now. But I think I know where it's going to be in about an hour and a half. You need the eight million; I need information. You help me; I help you. It's that simple. And don't give me any crap because you don't have any room to bargain. If that money floats away, Excor goes belly-up, and you know it."

Zell lit another Camel. It made a crackling noise when he sucked on it. "Let's pretend," he said, "that you're not totally full of shit." Smoke rolled out of his nostrils in two slow streams. "What kind of information would you want from me?"

"For now," I said, "only one thing. Tell me about Hi-Top Security."

A wary look crept into his eyes. "How do you know about Hi-Top?"

"I know a lot of things."

"Were you in with Roger on that one, too?"

I didn't know what he meant. "*In* with Roger? In what?"

"Yeah," he says. "We found out about Hi-Top. Roger was ripping that one off, too."

"Wait a minute," I said. "I don't know anything about that."

Zell looked at me, pulled on his cigarette, decided I was lying. "You got a bad sunburn," he said. "You sure you're feeling okay?"

"I'm serious. I came here to find out a little about Hi-Top. For purely personal reasons."

"In that case, I don't know shit about Hi-Top. In fact I never heard of it." Zell crossed his arms and leaned back in his chair. He had a mean smile on his face. His big enamel cuff links sparkled red at me.

I took the Lucite tombstone out of my pocket. I read: *"Five hundred thousand shares, Class A convertible preferred stock, Hi-Top Security, Inc. We the undersigned advised the issuer and arranged for the private placement of these securities.* Then down at the bottom it says *Excor, Inc."* I threw the tombstone onto the desk. It bounced off some papers and fell into Zell's lap. Zell turned the tombstone over in his hands—not looking at it, just thinking. He threw it back to me.

"Not my department," he said. "Ask Roger about it." He smiled.

"At three-thirty today," I said. "Eight million dollars worth of Singaporean bonds—Roger's money—are coming into town on an airplane. I don't know why or how. All I know is where. When I get my hands on those bonds, I have a bunch of choices. I can give them to the cops, start telling all kinds of stories, people embezzling money, poor financial controls down here—all kinds of wild shit. Or I could hide them, bring them out when I feel like it. Or I could trot on down here and hand them over to you. Which would you prefer?"

Zell looked away for a minute, shrugged. "What do you want to know?"

"Tell me about this company, Hi-Top."

Zell took another drag, stubbed out his Camel, lit another one. "It's a rent-a-cop company. They hire high school dropouts, retired cops—give these bozos a gun, a flashlight, a cute little blue polyester uniform, sit them at the front gate of some factory checking IDs. That kind of thing. They claim they do investigations, too. I wouldn't hire them to investigate my dog, personally." He pointed his cigarette at the tombstone. "It was Roger's deal." The way he said it, he didn't think much of the deal. Or Roger for that matter.

"Profitable for Excor?" I said.

Zell said, "Sure." He blew smoke up in the air so it drifted down around my head.

"Who owns the company?"

"The president is a guy named Crews. He owns maybe eighty-five, ninety percent."

"Clement Crews?"

"The very same. Roger owned the rest of it."

"Roger personally?"

"Sure. Part of the deal, he got equity."

"That's a little on the ethical borderline, wouldn't you say? Getting paid in stock?" I said.

"Ah," Zell said. "An ethics dissertation from a guy who's been tarred and feathered by the American Bar Association. How fucking ironic."

"But still. . . ."

"The stock, that was really just a minor side issue, something Roger set up. Excor got paid cash—a decent amount, too. I frankly couldn't figure out why Roger wanted the stock. The company's a bowwow."

"But now you know, right? He needed the equity to run some kind of scam with their stock. Am I right?" I said. Zell didn't say anything. "How? What was he doing?"

Zell said, "I don't think we got anything else to talk about."

"One last question. Who bought the preferred stock? It's a private placement, right. Who was the investor?"

Zell shrugged. "French vulture capital group. These fucking guys, let me tell you, they had top talent involved. I never did get why they put money into some scam like Hi-Top."

"Scam?"

Zell just looked at me.

"What was this group called, this French venture capital group?"

"The vehicle they were using, it's just some bullshit limited partnership."

"Called what?"

"Called Evergreen Partners," Zell said.

"Evergreen? Are you sure?" I said. That was the name of the company Rosie had talked about, the one that owned Excor. "Who's the general partner?"

"A lawyer," Zell said. "Guy by the name of Keenan. Tate Keenan." Zell drummed his fingers on the table, then clapped his hands together. He seemed sorry he'd talked to me. "Okay, Vine, time to say bye-bye."

I got up to leave. "Oh," I said. "I forgot. One last quick question. You have a personal stake in this business don't you?"

"Personal stake? I invested some money in Excor, sure."

"If Excor went belly-up, what would happen to you? Would you go bankrupt, lose your house, that kind of thing?"

Zell looked at me for a minute, pulled on his cigarette. "You want to make your point, Vine?"

"Let me put it another way. If you found out your partner was ripping you off, doing something that might cause you to lose your house, that kind of thing—how pissed off would you be?"

Zell had a flat, irritated look in his little black eyes. He stubbed out his cigarette, didn't say a word.

"Pissed off enough to kill someone?"

"You know what I think, Vine?" Zell said. "I think you been out of the deal-making game too long. One whiff, it smells so good you can't think straight."

CHAPTER 7

I drove out Buford Highway, past the discount carpet outlets and Burger Kings, the transmission shops and Vietnamese restaurants, the pawn shops and strip malls, thinking that in a funny way Zell was right. I missed the action, the game, the smell of the deal. Something else to add to my list of regrets. All that drama, that pressure, that feeling of making things happen—it was hard to put that behind you.

When you were in the thick of it, with the adrenaline pumping and the crazy late-night phone calls and the number games, you felt important and vital and charged up. You felt like you were tapped into the energy at the core of the universe. It sounds dumb—but, man, until you've been there, you can't know. It's an indescribable high. The only problem with deal making is it sucks you along so fast you don't have time for questions, for making sense out of what you're doing.

Anyway, first things first: Get the bonds back, see where that leads.

The one face that kept popping up, the one constant in this whole business, was Tate Keenan. He not only represented Excor, he somehow owned or controlled them through this Evergreen partnership. He also owned or at least had a major interest in Hi-Top.

And Keenan had talked to Hawley several times in the week before Roger was killed. It was right there in Roger's calendar. But I couldn't see any reason yet why he'd want to kill Roger. And from everything I knew about him, embezzlement was not his style. He was a smarter, subtler guy than that. There was still something missing.

I drove into the DeKalb-Peachtree Airport through a high chain-link fence. Maybe I'd find the answer here. Out across a big field, an orange wind sock hung limp in the hot, dull air. Not real auspicious.

There were a bunch of different buildings that said Hangar One on them. I wondered how there could be more than one hangar called Hangar One. It was hard to figure. There was a lounge where you could wait for people, another building that said Executives. The control tower was a tall, square, brick turret with tinted windows around the top.

I parked by one of the buildings that said Hangar One and got out. Where was this guy Clement going to show up? And how would I know him when he did? I didn't want him to see me, but I didn't want to miss him, either. I walked through the gate in a chain-link fence near one of the hangars, out to where I could see the whole airfield. It was a big place, acres and acres of concrete and grass.

There were a couple of guys standing about fifty feet away, in between two parked propeller airplanes. They had a good view of the entrance to the airport, so I walked over.

"Hi, guys," I said. I put on my happy goof smile. "Y'all fly these things?"

They were both dressed in chinos and golf shirts with blue

baseball caps and aviator sunglasses. One guy's hat said *Gulfstream.* The other guy's said *Astra* then, underneath that, *Leadership . . . by design.* Very gung-ho-looking guys.

Gulfstream told me they were both pilots for BellSouth. They told me that they flew the chairman, various other people, around the country. I was smiling, keeping my eyes on the parking lot.

Astra told me that they had gone in together, bought their own bird, which they flew for pleasure. "We were both off duty, so we drew straws today," he said.

Gulfstream pointed at Astra. "He got the big straw, goddarn it," Gulfstream said. He punched Astra in the arm.

I told them how I had always wanted to fly, but never got around to it. I had the day off today so I figured, what the hay, I'll go watch some birds up at Dekalb-Peachtree. I was grinning, yucking it up.

We shot the shit a little bit, and they told me all the places they had been. Gulfstream had been to Madison, Wisconsin, last week, a sleep-over, his first time there. He said I'd be amazed at all the weirdos they had in that town. Astra had been to New Jersey five times in the past two weeks. He had been forced to land ILS all five times, the weather was so bad. Wow! I said. I wasn't sure what ILS was. They told me about other places they had gone to. It was a long list. They toted it up, decided that between them, the only state they hadn't been to was New Mexico. They had flown *over* it, of course, many times—going out to San Diego, LAX, John Wayne.

I saw a car coming around from behind the control tower. It was going slow, like the driver hadn't figured out where he was supposed to park. A big car.

A champagne-colored Lincoln Town Car—tinted windows, curb feelers, opera windows.

It circled the control tower, drove into a lot about two hundred feet away, parked close by the fence next to a hangar, under a sign that said Executives, with an arrow pointed at the ground. Just seeing it made me feel all tensed up, like I was about to get in a fist fight.

Astra said that, hey, he'd love to take me up in the bird if I was interested. He showed me some maneuvers with his hands, told me he could run me through them, let me hold the stick, kind of get the feel of it.

"Gentlemen, if you'd excuse me for *just* one second," I said. "I believe I left something in my car."

I had a pair of binoculars in the glove compartment. After a few minutes, I pulled them out, kept them trained on the Lincoln. Inside, no one moved. All you could see was a vague outline through the tinted windshields.

Planes took off, planes landed.

It was five past three. Then it was three-fifteen. Then three-thirty-five. Inside the Town Car, nothing. The air shimmered over the hood. Two planes landed.

Three-forty. Three-forty-seven. Two birds up, two birds down. I was beginning to wonder if I had missed something, like maybe they had gotten out of the Town Car, gone inside a hangar.

Three-fifty-one, I heard jet engines, saw a little two-engine plane coming down, landing gear out, wings waggling. It hit the ground, engines singing, taxied around for a while.

Down by one of the signs that said Hangar One, it pulled in and stopped, maybe fifty yards from the Town Car. The cabin door popped open, stairs built into it, and a kid in a suit jumped out and secured the door. After that he climbed back up the stairs, went inside. A little breath of wind came up out of nowhere, tricked the wind socks all across the field for a few seconds. A minute later the socks all went limp again.

The kid in the suit came back out the door of the plane, trotted down the stairs. He had a shiny metal briefcase in his hand, the kind that looks like one of those Airstream campers.

The doors to the Town Car opened. Two men got out.

The driver was Mr. Crowbar.

Same little guru hat, same mustache, same sunglasses. It gave me a bad feeling looking at him again. A weird sensation, kind of like vertigo, washed over me—as though something bad were about to happen. Mr. Crowbar got out and stood next to the door, doing his hard guy pose—hunching up his neck muscles a little, hands over the genitals. The universal dipshit bodyguard pose.

The guy who got out of the passenger side I didn't recognize right away. He was a short guy with black hair and a baggy double-breasted suit. His mouth was too big for his face. Then as he walked out toward the jet, through the fence, I remembered: the pop eyes, the zoot suit, the Elvis hairdo. It was the shark man, the guy Keenan was eating with at Faux Pas the other day.

Out on the strip, the guy from the plane was walking out to meet the Shark. They shook hands. The Shark talked, moving his hands, twitching around. He had too damn much energy. The guy from the plane opened the briefcase, showed the Shark what was inside, then closed it and set it down. The Shark was looking around, scratching himself, straightening his tie. The guy from the plane handed the Shark a clipboard. The Shark signed, handed it back. The guy from the plane pulled a pink piece of paper off the clipboard, handed it to the Shark, headed back to the plane.

The briefcase sat there for a minute in the middle of the wide stretch of concrete. Eight million dollars worth of bonds would fit in a briefcase easily. It had to be the bonds.

The Shark picked up the briefcase and walked briskly back to the Town Car, his big Italian pants flopping around in another short-lived breeze. He got in, Mr. Crowbar got in, the doors closed, they drove away. I put the car in drive.

On the strip, the jet engines spooled up, and the plane moved off down the concrete. By the time the Town Car had reached the gate to the airport, the jet was airborne.

I popped the emergency brake and followed.

The Town Car drove out of the gate, left on Clairmont, down past I-85 into Decatur. I kept as far back as I could, trying to keep a couple of cars between me and the Lincoln. We drove through the outskirts of Decatur, past lots of brick ranch houses with American flags flapping next to the front door.

The Lincoln turned right on Scott, left on Ponce de Leon. We drove past all the beautiful old houses and on into the city. Ponce de Leon, after you pass Moreland, is wall-to-wall winos. They were sitting in the bus stops, sitting on the curb. It seemed like they were all eating oranges out of paper bags. The Town Car kept going, past all the wino hotels, the yuppie apartments with bars on the windows, the Majestic Diner, all that stuff.

We were in the far right lane. Just past Big Star, out of the blue, the Town Car turned left, laying over across all six lanes, pulling into a restaurant parking lot.

I kept going down the block, turned left into another parking lot. By the time I had turned around, the Town Car had shot back across the street again, into a big shopping center filled with Chinese stores. The Town Car drove across the parking lot and slid to a stop at the far end.

I jumped out of my car, ran across Ponce and stood at the edge of the parking lot. Mr. Crowbar and the Shark got out of the Lincoln. I ran across the lot, zigzagging from car to car, trying to hide. When I got close enough to see better, I stuck my head around the back of a delivery truck and watched.

Mr. Crowbar and the Shark were talking. The Shark had the metal briefcase in his hand. The Shark held the briefcase up to Mr. Crowbar, pushed it at his chest. Mr. Crowbar put his arms around the briefcase. Now it looked like a toy, tiny in comparison to this huge guy. Mr. Crowbar opened the driver's door of the Town Car, threw the briefcase in, sat down, and closed the door. The reverse lights came on.

I had to think. Should I follow the Shark or Mr. Crowbar?

Follow the money, wasn't that what they always said? Mr. Crowbar had the bonds, so I'd better follow him. As I threaded my way back to the car, I looked over my shoulder and saw the Shark taking his keys out of his pocket as he climbed up a flight of stairs along the outside of the building. At the top of the stairs was a big sign: HI-TOP SECURITY, INC.

I managed to get to my car in time to keep up with Mr. Crowbar. The Town Car turned back up Ponce. At the corner of Moreland, the winos had disappeared. Nothing left but orange peels scattered across the buckled tarmac.

The Town Car turned right. We drove through Little Five Points, past lots of white kids with silly haircuts and motorcycle boots. I saw one boy, smoking, with his head cocked back. He wore a T-shirt—black with white letters—that said

Eat My Shit. He was maybe fourteen years old. What's gotten into these kids?

We kept going down Moreland, turned left onto a road I'd never been on before. We cut through a black neighborhood, little four-room houses with tar-paper walls, falling-down porches, trees and vines overgrowing everything. There were no white people around, not even in the cars. After a couple minutes, going deeper and deeper into this place, I started getting nervous, fear welling up me—this clutching feeling that my safety was now in the hands of some tribe other than my own. I had never felt that way before.

We turned onto another street, past Little Lucy's Cut & Curl. Little Lucy had a sign outside, hand painted on plywood, that said she did Bo cuts and fades. I didn't know what those were.

We were on a big street now, a center of black commerce. Nancy's Soul Food and Jamaican Restaurant, Furniture Liquidators (Flea Market!), lots of gun-and-pawns. "We give cash for car titles." "Don't rent when you can buy!" Little A.M.E. churches, red brick, off to the side, here and there. Strip malls. All the buildings had iron bars on every window. There were lots of people with bags, satchels, parcels—no white people at all.

I was lost, no idea where I was.

After a few minutes the strip malls disappeared, the buildings got smaller, dingier, more of the businesses failed and boarded up. We were going deeper into the southeast side of town.

We made a couple of turns, and the Town Car pulled up at the curb, parked in front of a fire hydrant. There was a liquor store on one side of the street. On the other side there was a cinder-block building that had once been white, surrounded by a chain-link fence, rusty coils of razor wire draped across the top. A sign on the fence said *$$We Buy Auto Parts, Junk Cars$$*.

I parked about a block down the street, got out of the car, and locked the door. Behind me a bunch of kids were listening to rap music, shouting at each other, pitching pennies. I could hear their voices above the music, but I couldn't make out what they were saying, just one word: *Whiteman, whiteman, whiteman.*

I put the key back in the door of the Aries, opened the glove compartment. Roger's little Colt automatic sat there, gleaming, on top of a pile of maps. I took it out, put it in the pocket of my blazer. I was sweating hard, soaking my shirt.

Down the street, Mr. Crowbar came out of the liquor store carrying two paper sacks. He opened the Lincoln, took out the metal briefcase, crossed the street, walked through the open gate in the fence and in the front door of the auto parts store. I waited a couple minutes, crossed the street, went down the block.

There was a gate in the fence. I stood there for a second, feeling scared and isolated and maybe a little dumb, thinking I should get the hell out of there and forget about the whole thing. But when I thought about cutting and running, a cold feeling of dread came through me—the Big Fear starting to clench around my heart—and I knew I had to go on, had to fight with everything that was in me.

I walked through the gate. The front of the building had only one window—so choked with dirt and spiderwebs you could hardly see through it. There was a little office inside, boxes heaped up all over the place. A guy with his feet up on a desk sat near the window, his face turned away from me, watching TV.

I walked in the door, my heart beating hard. As soon as I was inside another wave of fear hit me, and I had a sudden, powerful need to take a piss.

The man with his feet on the desk looked up at me. He was maybe the scariest guy I've ever seen—a big black guy, bigger even than Mr. Crowbar. *Black* is not the right word, though. He was yellow. An albino. Maybe six-five, strong, but running to fat. It was a spooky combination: the heavy-featured face, the messy Afro, the yellow skin. He looked at me with mean pink eyes, not sure what to make of me.

I realized I had no idea what to say to him: I didn't even know Mr. Crowbar's name.

"Where's my main man at?" I said desperately, doing the jive white man thing. It felt completely ridiculous as soon as it was out of my mouth.

"Something you need?" he said.

"Where's my main man?" I snapped my fingers, trying to act impatient. The albino's little pink eyes flicked over my shoulder, trying to see if there were any more like me outside. I guess he figured I had a badge under my coat.

"Who?" the albino said. "Andre?" I noticed there was a shotgun, a twelve-gauge pump, propped up against the wall about three feet from his shoulder. I got the feeling they probably didn't sell a lot of auto parts here.

"Who you think?" I said. "Michael Jackson?" The albino didn't think I was especially funny. Understandably. I didn't think it was funny, either.

His lips flicked open for a second, a pink gash against his yellow skin. He looked back at the TV. He was watching one of these Japanese cartoons, the kind with jerky robots and kids with big heads.

"Andre in the back," the albino said.

There was a door in the back of the office with a Rigid Tool calendar pinned on it, November 1982, featuring a girl with Farrah Fawcett hair and a tiny red swimsuit. The Rigid Tool girl was holding a pipe wrench up to her cleavage, the humongous forty-dollar oil rig model. I pointed at her chest. "I'll just go on back there," I said. "See if I can find him."

"Man, you messing up my motherfucking reception," the albino said. His cartoon had gone all wavy.

"Let me get out of your way," I said. I started walking back toward the door.

"Hey!" he said, about the time I got to the door. I turned around. The albino was pointing his finger at me. His fist was more or less the size of my head. "If you fixing to do something you ain't spose to," he said, "I come back, break your motherfucking neck."

"No problem," I said. "Me and Andre got a little business to take care of. I'll be out in a jiffy."

"Jiffy? *Jiffy?*" The albino shook his head, disgusted. "Shee-it."

I stuck my head through the door, looked around. It was a dark storeroom full of shelves. There were a few boxes on the shelves—fuel pumps, alternators, stuff like that—but nobody had made a real strong effort to keep up the inventory. A hallway led off to the left. There was nobody in the storeroom. I walked through the door, closed it quietly behind me, one sweaty hand in my pocket, fingers around the butt of Roger's gun.

Dance music was coming from the hallway, muffled. I stood behind the doorjamb, looked down the hall. There were a couple of doors on the left, one door on the right. I had a sick, paralyzed feeling in my chest that oozed out into my arms. I went to the first door, stood there a minute, trying to make myself do something. I turned the knob, peeped in.

It was a bathroom, awful smelling, nothing inside but a toilet with no seat and a sink with a bar of oily soap in the drain. The walls were spray painted light blue.

I closed the door, walked down the hall. The other two doors were across from each other. The music came from the door on the right, strong bass, lots of synthesizers.

As I stood there, an ugly thought started worming its way into my brain: Something was way far out of whack here. Eight million in bearer bonds sitting in a briefcase in a southeast Atlanta slum? No way. I felt a terrible-tasting dryness in my mouth, like I had eaten a bag of lint. Why would the Shark have given eight million dollars to some thug like Mr. Crowbar? The answer was he wouldn't.

So now what?

I stood there frozen for a long time, trying to figure out what to do. I wanted to bail. Say good-bye to the albino, hope I had enough gas to find my way home. But then I thought, okay, forget the bonds. The guy who probably killed Roger Hawley was behind that door. I might as well go in and find out why he'd done it. I took a couple of ragged breaths and opened the door—just a crack—and looked in.

Across the room Mr. Crowbar was sitting on a couch watching a music video on a big color TV. A pregnant girl— she couldn't have been more than sixteen years old—was sitting on the couch next to him. On the TV a guy with a big necklace and no shirt was dancing around, making humping motions with his hips. I just stood there watching, afraid to move. Mr. Crowbar reached over and put his hand gently on the girl's belly.

"How you feeling, babe?" he said. His voice had that same

buzzing, beelike quality that I remembered, but now there was no edge to it. He sounded like a nice guy, a sweet guy hanging out, doing the nice domestic scene. His guard was down.

"Feel like my booty fixing to rip out," the girl said. She laughed, a nice strong laugh. She had square teeth and an amazing hairdo that looked like it had come out of a soft-serve ice cream machine.

I pushed the door open. The girl looked up. She looked up and she was afraid. Mr. Crowbar kept watching the TV. He said: "Yo, Whitey, man, I'm trying to have some family situation here. Get your big yellow butt the fuck outta my room."

The girl prodded his arm with her fingertips. "It ain't Whitey," she said.

Mr. Crowbar turned around and looked at me. His expression didn't change. "Ah, shit," he said. He was wearing a pink suit, no shirt, no shoes, no socks.

For a second I just stood there, no idea what to do next. Then I took Roger's gun out of my pocket and pointed it at his head. Fifteen feet away, I'd probably hit him if he didn't move too quick.

"You crazy as hell," Mr. Crowbar said. He wasn't letting any expression onto his face.

"Keep your goddamn voice down," I said, trying to sound tougher than I felt. I closed the door, locked it behind me. "Now. Tell me who hired you to kill Roger Hawley."

He showed a little expression, big eyes, trying to look like he didn't know what I was talking about. "Who?"

"Now," I said.

And as I stood there looking at him giving me that bogus innocent face, I felt a sudden wave of anger welling up inside me, stronger than I'd ever felt before, crowding out all the fear and the uncertainty. My vision kind of closed in, like I was at one end of a tunnel and Mr. Crowbar was at the other. It was as though all the anger I'd felt—at Roger, at my wife, at everybody else including myself who'd let me down—all that bitterness was boiling up inside me and had to get out.

And while I was feeling that rage coming on, Mr. Crowbar's hand was snaking down toward the floor. He came up with the Airstream briefcase, fast, threw it at me. It was too heavy, though, even for a guy as big as him: It missed me, banked off the wall, split open, fell to the floor. I looked down at the metal case, lying like an open clam at my feet. There was nothing inside it at all. Stone empty. No bonds. For a second I felt stupid and lost, the anger replaced by a feeling of impotence and futility.

Mr. Crowbar stared at me for a minute and then he laughed, laughed like I was one dumbass chump for thinking he had anything in that case that might have done me the least bit of good.

And then the rage came back. Maybe I *was* a chump and a dumbass and a fool. A fool for being there, a fool for a lot of things. But it didn't matter, because at that moment I realized why I'd come. Yes, maybe I wanted the bonds. Yes, maybe I wanted to make Jeannie Richardson happy. Yes, maybe I was trying to clear my name. But that wasn't why I was there. The reason I was there was a lot simpler: I wanted payback. For sneaking up on me and hitting me in the head, for framing me, for making me feel like people could push me around and make me eat shit and there was nothing I could do to stop them—for all this, I wanted payback.

I glanced down at the empty case, kicked it across the room.

When I looked up, Mr. Crowbar was coming at me—crouched over with about eighteen inches of timing chain hanging out of his hand. It was a big chain, maybe from a truck engine, and he was planning to put some serious hurt on me with it.

I felt no fear at that moment, no calculation, no sense of future or past, none of those clean, deliberate habits of consideration and logic that keep civilization knotted together; nothing but rage, a rage that was all the more crazy and uncontrollable for being clamped down and shut in and papered over for so long. It was nothing but me and him and that whirlwind of bone-breaking, thumb-in-the-eye, atavistic, biblical rage.

He was coming at me with that big timing chain, and I wanted payback. I wanted mayhem. I wanted death.

So I pulled the trigger.

I shot him in the chest, catching the pink peak of his left lapel. He sat back down on the couch, and squinted at me like a guy who'd been asked a trick question on "Jeopardy." He tried to clear his throat. It made a bubbling noise. He tried again, but the bubbling wouldn't go away. He put his fingers against his chest, tenderly, the way he'd felt the pregnant girl's belly.

"Who killed Roger Hawley?" I said.

The girl started to make a high, whimpery noise. She had a couple flecks of red on her shirt. The bullet had sprayed some blood across the couch when it came out Mr. Crowbar's back.

"Shut up," I told the girl. She made the whimpery noise again. I pointed the gun at her. She shut up. Her eyes were big around as shot glasses.

"Who killed him?" I said again. I had to hear it from his lips, had to get the answer.

"Man," said Mr. Crowbar. "Man, I'ma kill you." He stood up again, hefted the length of chain, started to come at me again. There was a sober, concentrated look on his face. Why didn't he just sit down? I shot him again in the chest.

"Who killed him, goddamn you?"

He came at me with the timing chain, raised his arm, but it was all slow motion, tired, no fury in it. I shot him again. He stopped, stood there for a minute. There was no blood on his chest, just three neat holes in the lapel of his pink jacket.

"Man," he said, "I'ma fuck you up." He cleared his throat, trying to get rid of the bubbling down there. Then his knees went, and he fell on his face.

"Mmmmmmmmm," he said to the floor, and his voice was like the whine of bees.

Then there was blood—blood on the linoleum, blood on his back, blood coming out of his mouth. Two of the bullets had gone all the way through him, making a red design on his jacket.

"Mmmmmmmmm," he said, talking to the floor again. And again there was the sound of bees—but this time warbly, like you were hearing them from inside a waterfall.

"Who are you?" I said. "Who the hell do you work for?" I kicked him. "Who killed Roger, goddamn you?" Then I was kicking and yelling, blind with all the anger. I was out of control. "Who are you working for, you son of a bitch?" I kept saying things like that, kicking him for a while. I couldn't help it.

Then it was all over. I stopped, wiped my face. There was water running out of my eyes. I crouched over the dead man, water leaking out of my face, dripping off my nose onto his pink suit. "Oh, Christ," I said, clutching him, trying to undo the terrible thing I had just done.

It was no use.

I wiped my face again, then pulled out his wallet, looked at his employee ID. I had just killed a twenty-nine-year-old male, Negro, black eyes, black hair, Terrance Andre Dupree. The card said he was an employee of Hi-Top Security, Inc., Atlanta, Georgia.

I looked at the girl. She was leaning back on the couch, frozen, holding onto her belly with both hands.

"I'm sorry," I said to her. "I'm sorry. He was going to kill me. You know he was." Her lips parted a little, teeth still clenched, and a sound came out of her mouth, a sound I'd never heard before. It was kind of a grinding hoot, like disk brakes make when the pads need to be changed. It went on for a while.

Then, abruptly, she stopped. "I know," she said. "I knew it was gonna happen sometime. I just didn't expect it so gotdamn soon." She was quiet for a minute, and then the grinding sound started coming out of her mouth again.

I stood there, paralyzed.

Behind me there was an explosive crunching noise. I turned around and saw the albino plunging into the room, smashing the door off its hinges, splinters of the ruined door frame sticking to his shirt. He had the twelve gauge in his hands, pointed at the middle of my chest.

The albino looked at Andre Dupree lying dead on the floor, then he looked at me. He shook his head like he couldn't believe some sunburned white guy could do this. There was a terrible, spent look in his eye. "That's my brother," he said. "Now you gone be dead, too."

"Hold up, Whitey. Not yet." There was a man standing in the doorway. Short guy, double-breasted suit. It was the

Shark, the guy from Hi-Top. "Give me the gun, Bobby," he said.

He stretched his hand out to me. He had a big ring on his little finger, the same one I'd noticed when he was having lunch with Tate Keenan. I put the gun in his hand. He pulled the slide, checked to make sure he had a round in the chamber.

"What to do? What to do?" he said to me. "Boy, but it's sure a mess, isn't it?" He spread his hands, a big theatrical gesture, grinning like a dancer in Las Vegas.

The albino looked at the Shark for a minute. "I tell you what I'm gone do," he said. He put the shotgun in my face.

"Hey, Pardner," the Shark said. "I got a better idea." He pointed Roger's gun at the albino's temple and shot him, point blank, through the head.

The big albino's body jerked, the gun slipped out of his hands, and he fell on top of his brother. Red stuff poured out into his orange hair.

I was in a state of shock already and couldn't seem to make sense of what was going on. I just stood there. The girl started screaming like hell now, no fooling around.

"Honey," the Shark said. "Do me a favor and shut up for a sec, would you?" Offhand, like he was telling the waitress, oh yeah, make it extra cheese on that burger. The girl wouldn't stop. She was in her own world now. The Shark hefted the gun, looked at the base of the clip.

"I used to know this," he said. "Colt three-eighty auto. That's probably, what, a seven-shot clip? Let's see, so that's three for Andre, one for Whitey—"

He pointed the gun at the screaming girl, shot her in the face. The bullet pushed her nose over to the side, gave her a third nostril and made a mess coming out the back of her head. I couldn't even look at it. And then the shock started fading, and I felt the Big Fear rising in me; my breath started coming in little jerks, too quick and shallow.

"One for her," said the Shark. "So that leaves, okay, two? Right, two for you, Vine." He was smiling at me. He could hardly contain himself, all the good fortune that was going around. He took the clip out, put it in his pocket, took out a handkerchief and wiped his prints off the gun. Then he threw it to me. I caught the empty Colt, looked at it. The Shark took another gun out of his jacket, a big revolver, pointed it at me.

"Have some fun!" he said. He waved his finger around the room. "Blam, blam, blam! Dawg, this is fun! Go ahead, dry fire it a couple times. Got to make sure we get your prints nice and clear on the trigger, huh?"

I wasn't scared anymore. It had gone beyond that now. My blood was roaring, a noise like a train, filling up my head. I started to see little spots, and then the blackness settled a notch or two deeper around the corners of my eyes.

"Hey, guy," said the Shark, his voice a long way away. "Steady there. Now give me the gun." He took a Ziploc bag out of his coat pocket. "Good thing I got my private investigator's equipment on me, huh?" I gave him the gun and sagged down on the arm of the couch next to the dead girl's feet. The Shark took the gun, dropped it in the plastic bag, stuck the bag in the pocket of his Italian suit. He had me. Roger's gun in his pocket, my prints on the gun, the bullets inside the dead people.

He looked around the room. "Look at this carnage. Man, you are armed and *dangerous!* I'm serious. If I didn't know what a sweet fucking individual you were, Bobby, I'd think you were a menace to society. What is this now, four counts, Murder One?" He was having a good old time, waving his revolver around.

I concentrated on breathing. After a minute my head started to clear.

"You know my problem, Bobby?" he said. "Sometimes, heat of the moment and shit, I forget my manners." He stuck out his hand. "My name's Clement Crews."

CHAPTER 8

We went outside and got into Clement Crews's car, a brand new Seville STS, flame red. He had the gun inside his coat, pointing it at my back.

"You like the Caddy?" Clement said when we got in the car. "Just bought it a couple weeks ago."

My mouth was dry, and I couldn't think about anything but that revolver in his pocket. "What are you going to do with me?" I said.

Clement shifted into drive.

"I used to have a 'Beemer'," Clement said. "Beautiful car, a 525? But it's getting old, you know, two years. Friend of mine, guy that sells cars up in Buckhead, says to me, 'You ought to take a peek at the new Caddies.' I said, 'You got to be shitting me.' Cadillac's an old man's car, right? Me in a Caddy, give me a fucking break. He says, 'Look, you pay thirty-something grand, you get a V-8, great low-end torque, rides smooth as hell, world-class air-conditioning, leather—shit, everything. Versus BMW, you get a nice ride, a decent little straight five, good handling—but, hey, where's the curb appeal?'"

We were driving through an awful neighborhood, wrecked businesses, worn-out buildings, beat-down people. Clement fiddled with the air-conditioning. "Seventy-three degrees okay with you?" he said, not listening for an answer. The digital thing he was poking on said 73. "Me, I like it a little chilly, makes me know I'm getting what I paid for. See the Krauts, they don't got to live in this type climate, so they haven't quite got this air-conditioning thing down yet. You put a Beemer at seventy-three, the goddamn engine explodes."

We stopped at a light. When it changed, Clement peeled

out, laid us back in the leather seats for a second or two. "Feel that, huh? No arguing with a V-8, pardner. I got a hell of deal on it, too." He turned left at the next street, past a weedy lot full of junked school buses.

"Take a guess," he said. "How much did I pay for it? Take a stab. Alloy wheels, leather, driver's side airbag, antilock brakes, the whole fucking deal? How much?" He was smiling.

My arms and legs were weak and tingling with fear. I didn't feel like playing guessing games. "I don't know," I said.

"C'mon. Don't be an asshole."

"Are you going to kill me?"

He gave me an innocent face. "Okay, okay, okay," he said. "We got a situation here, okay. We definitely got a situation. But that doesn't mean we can't be friendly. Am I right?"

We drove for a while, past a lot of pawn shops and discount furniture stores, little dingy businesses with bars on the windows.

"You're going to kill me." I felt tired, like I'd just run a marathon. It was an effort to talk or even think. I wanted to just melt and drain out of the car like water.

"Come on. Guess."

"Thirty-nine five," I said.

"Thirty-nine five!" Clement said. "What kind of dipshit I look like?"

I shrugged. Better not to get into that one.

"Thirty-nine five, that's full MSRP. Maybe more. Here's a hint, okay? I'll give you a hint."

"How did you know I was following you?" I said. "After you got the briefcase at the airport."

"Shit, Vine, I saw you back on Clairmont, two miles from the airport."

"I didn't think you'd notice."

"Sure," he said. "At the shopping center, I just put the bonds under my coat, gave Andre that metal briefcase. I figured you'd come after him. Who wouldn't, all that money?" He patted a leather briefcase that was sitting on the seat between us. "It's all right there," he said. "I had it all the time."

"Great," I said.

"What you need is a hint," he said.

"What?" I wasn't paying attention to where the conversation was going. My mind was too consumed with the thought that this guy was going to kill me.

"A hint. You need a hint so you can guess how much I paid for this luxurious American-crafted automobile."

"What about Friday night? Was that you in the van?" I said.

"That was Andre. He didn't do a real good job, did he?"

"Why?"

Clement looked at me, like he was trying to figure out what I was so worked up about. "Why what?"

"Why'd you want to kill me?"

"I saw you there Friday night, hanging around with that babe from Jordan Foote's office, that other chick, the Mexican, from Tate's office, I figured you were nosing around, trying to find out what was going on with Roger. I called Andre up, told him to call in the robbery, and then run your ass off the road."

Clement poked the dash, turned the air down to seventy-two.

"What I'll do," Clement said. "What I'll do, I'll tell you my philosophy of life, how about that? Then you can guess again, what I paid, having a more-informed type understanding of my personality, how it operates. Okay?"

"Fine," I said. "And then maybe you can pull over, no hard feelings, and let me walk away."

Clement stopped at a red light, gave me a vaudeville surprise face: jaw hanging down, eyes bugging out. "Let you off here? Southeast Atlanta? Pardner, you're safer in here with me than out with them Jamoakes on the street. I bet you couldn't find a white man in two, three miles of here." He pointed to some black guys in colored sweat suits standing on a corner in front of a place that said MO'S LOUNGE over the door. "These boys, they'd fuck you up in a New York minute."

"I'll take my chances," I said.

"Are you ready?" Clement said. "My philosophy of life. By Clement Crews." He said it like he was up in front of the class, doing show-and-tell. The light changed, and Clement stomped on the gas, throwing us back against the seat.

"Okay," Clement said. "My philosophy. You listening? Here it is: *Don't get fucked.*" He looked over at me, making sure it had registered. *"Don't get fucked.* Simple. Elegant. Is that a great philosophy or what?"

"That's it?" I said. "Don't get fucked?"

"Don't get fucked. Don't never never never ever get fucked. What I mean: Don't stand in line, don't take shit off people, don't follow the rules, don't pay list price, don't get involved in things that's none of your business. You do any of that, you're asking—hey, you might as well bend over and lubricate because, brother, you're just asking for it."

I nodded, pretending to listen. But all I could think about was that gun in his pocket.

"See, Bobby, this has been a real complicated deal. High stakes. Started out simple, ended up complex. But I've got rules that are like part of my philosophy. Rule one: no loose ends. That's why I had to take care of Andre. Like I'm saying, you keep your eye on the ball, you sweat the details, you keep your ass covered, every crisis has an opportunity built into it."

"Would I be right," I said, "if I guessed that Roger Hawley tried to screw you?" I was thinking back to what Glickman had said, that Roger was ripping off Hi-Top somehow.

Clement turned onto the 75/85 corridor. I didn't know quite how he had gotten there. We had come out somewhere south of Atlanta, heading north toward the skyscrapers. Clement took us over into the left lane, set the cruise on eighty. "You want to know the problem with Roger? His basic problem? He was a dishonest hosebag, which personally I can appreciate, okay, but he didn't understand that you can't fuck everybody in the world without it catching up to you."

"So you two were working together?" I said.

Clement looked over at me, studied my face. Then he shrugged, like he didn't care if he told me or not. "Sure. See initially what we did was cook the books a little at Hi-Top to get some seed money. He helped me out, showed me some creative-accounting type things."

"The seed money you're talking about—that was the preferred stock offering you did? To Tate's company, Evergreen?"

Clement was surprised. "You been doing your homework, man," he said. "Yeah, I was signing up some major accounts, and basically we'd book the deals before we got paid. It's kind of bending the rules, nothing serious, but you end up a little cash poor after a while."

"Which is why you sold the preferred stock?"

"Sure. It's kind of like a bank loan really. You just pay off the interest over time, retire the debt on some kind of schedule, nothing to it."

"Only Roger started stealing the money from the offering."

"It was me and Roger both. Only, I like to look at it as being that the cash demands of the management of my company turned out to be more extensive than anticipated."

"And then what? Take Hi-Top into bankruptcy?"

"Kind of like that. But there was one more step. We were going to do an initial public offering, raise maybe six, eight million and retire Tate's preferred stock. That would leave us about five mill to play with. So we'd expand a little, do some smoke and mirrors—whoops!—all the money's gone. Then *that's* when we go Chapter Seven and find us another sandbox to play in."

"Nice," I said. "Only you didn't know that Roger was doing the same thing over at Excor, right? You didn't know about Health Systems. So when the shit hit the fan there, he knew they would find out about Hi-Top, too."

"Yeah, he neglected to let me in on that little detail. See what he really had in mind was ripping us *all* off. Go to Costa Rica or something with ten million cash."

"How do you know that's what he wanted to do?"

Clement laughed, showing his pointy teeth. "The stupid fuck told me."

"He *told* you?"

"Yeah. See once Shore figured out that there was a problem with Health Systems, it was just a matter of time till they figured out what we were doing with Hi-Top, too. So what happens, me and Roger caucus on Sunday, I tell him, hey, you screwed this up, you got to make me whole at Hi-Top. Well, I don't have to tell you, he says forget it. You know, gives me some shit about how if I won't play by his rules, he's going to fold up his tent, ride off on his camel. See he's administrator of the Hi-Top investments. We had about a million two left in liquid assets from the Evergreen money. So

Roger goes: 'I'm going to clear out of here, take off with the million two.' That's when he tells me how much Health Systems cash there is, too. So I go: 'What about me?' He says, tough shit, he's history. And if I try fucking with him, he's going to go to the FBI and turn state's evidence. He told me how he'd done it before, got away with it." Clement laughed, making a kind of yip-yip-yip sound. "That's when he told me about you."

"And that gave you an idea, huh?"

"I don't got to tell you, that was a bad move, making threats to a guy like me. Anyways Roger goes: 'Okay, I tell you what, Clement, I'll cut you in on the deal if you do me a favor.' "

"Let me guess," I said. "He wanted you to pick up eight million dollars' worth of bearer bonds."

"You're a smart guy, Bobby. More like nine-two, though. You got the Health Systems money—that's eight—plus the million two from Hi-Top. He'd already cleaned that out, too."

"You kind of saw an opportunity here," I said.

Clement was feeling good, smiling to beat the band.

"So you and this guy Andre killed Roger, framed me. And you figured all you had to do was wait for the bonds to show up."

"That's about the shape of it," he said.

"There's something I'm curious about," I said. "You mind if I look at the bonds for a minute?"

"No harm in it, I guess," Clement said. "Just don't be a funny guy, try hitting me with the briefcase or some kind of shit like that." He put his pistol in his lap, finger on the trigger.

I reached over, clicked the latches, opened the case. There was a manila envelope inside. I took the envelope out, opened it, pulled out a stack of bonds a little under an inch high. The first bond said Singapore Harbor Authority at the top, lots of complicated engraving. Nine and seven-eighths yield, a hundred thousand U.S. par, callable July 2000, serial number 1017.

I flipped through the stack of bonds. There was something funny about them. I ripped off the red tape, pulled one of the bonds out of the middle of the stack, looked at the serial number.

"One-oh-one-seven," I said.

"What?"

I pulled out another bond. Number 1017. Another. 1017.

"Look," I said. I held the paper in front of Clement Crews's face.

"Yeah," he said. "So?"

I flipped the paper over. The back was blank. The bond on the top was real, but this one was a fake, a good old color xerox. All the rest: fakes. That was what Roger had meant when he said Clement was supposed to pick up the *dummy* bonds.

"Fakes," I said. "He had the real bonds salted away someplace else. He was just trying to buy time so he could get away from you."

"Fuck!" Clement slammed his fist into the dashboard.

We were heading through a tunnel downtown. Clement slalomed roughly around the bend, his face twisted with anger. As we left the tunnel, the late afternoon sun was flat and white, silhouetting the black skyscrapers. "So this whole thing was just a ploy? I guess I misjudged old Roger." Clement laughed nastily. "Not that it did him a whole lot of good."

We drove for a while, and Clement seemed to calm down.

"Tell you what," I said. "Why don't you just hang a right up here onto North Druid Hills and then drop me off at my place?"

"Yeah, right!" said Clement. "I made a couple mistakes here, but letting you go, man, that would be some insane shit, wouldn't it? I kind of like you Bobby, but I'm afraid you and me still got a date out at the Gwinnett County Landfill."

"Look," I said. "I've got a proposition for you."

"Forget it. Nice try, but forget it."

"Just listen," I said.

"Forget about it."

"Okay," I said. "Piss away your nine million dollars. Fine with me. But Roger's going to be up there smiling every time you drop the soap."

The Monroe and Buford loop was coming up on the right. Clement was five lanes over, doing eighty.

"One more exit," I said. "North Druid Hills."

We passed Monroe, went around a couple of big sweeping curves, under a bridge. We were heading up a long grade toward the North Druid Hills turnoff. Still in the far left lane, still doing eighty. Just as we were about to pass the exit, Clement turned the wheel, and the Cadillac cut across six lanes of traffic, slid onto the exit ramp.

"Talk to me," Clement said.

A wave of cooling relief ran through me.

"Finance," I said. "Finance is not your normal line of work, am I right Clement? And neither is securities law."

"Make your point," he said. "If you haven't convinced me of something by the time we hit Clairmont, I'm getting back on the highway, take you out to the Gwinnett County Landfill."

"I'm a lawyer, a finance guy," I said. "You're not."

"Last I heard, you were a furniture salesman."

"Okay . . . *ex*-lawyer. What I'm saying is, I can figure out what Roger did with these bonds, where he hid them, where he transferred his money, whatever. It's a paper chase. I can do it. You can't. You don't have a prayer in hell."

"Keep talking."

"Right on La Vista," I said. "Next to Dunkin' Donuts." Clement turned right on La Vista.

"I'll get the bonds for you," I said. "There's nothing I can do to you. You've got the gun that shot Andre and the albino and the girl—with my prints on it. I can plead the thing with Roger down to manslaughter. But four people? If you hand that gun in to the police, I'm history. You've got all the cards."

"Maybe."

"You give me time, I *will* find the bonds. But if I end up facedown in a garbage dump with a bullet in the back of my head, the GBI's going to be all over this thing. Worst case, they might even figure out you did it. And even best case, you'll never get the bonds back." I pointed to the next road. "Left up here."

Clement didn't say anything until we got to Ray's house. He pulled up and stopped. "Basically, Vine, I think you're full of shit," he said. He put the car in park. "But I kind of like you. So what I'm going to do, I'm going to let you off the hook. For now. But when you find those bonds, brother, you come straight to me. Do not pass go; do not collect two hundred dollars. Straight to me."

"So we've got a deal?" I said.

"You give me the bonds and keep your mouth shut, you get the opportunity to stay alive. And I might even be generous and hold off on showing the gun to the cops."

"It's a deal?"

"Deal," he said. He gave me his big shark smile. I felt suddenly as though there was oxygen in the air again.

I got out of the car, started to close the door. Once I was safely out of his reach I said, "You know, you never told me what you paid for the car."

Clement kept smiling. "Thirty-four nine ninety-two. Dealer invoice," he said. "Beginning of the model year, loaded factory options, hot new model, I got it at dealer fucking invoice. They didn't make a dime. The perfect deal. You know how I got the perfect deal?"

I sighed.

"Superior attitude," Clement said.

"Smile on your face, lots of positive thoughts, I suppose?"

"Not exactly. See, I drug out this big old army combat knife, sat there cutting my fingernails. After I'd thrown a pile of them on the sales manager's desk, I suggested real politely to the guy that if he didn't give me the car for dealer invoice, well, him or a treasured member of his family might just run into an accident in a dark alley that night." Clement waved his finger at me. "Superior attitude. That's the key to the perfect deal."

I looked at him for a few seconds. "You ever heard of holdback?"

"What?"

"Holdback."

"What's that?"

"The domestics," I said. "Ford, GM—they have this system called holdback. What they do, they invoice the dealer when the car hits the lot. The dealer pays the invoice. Then at the end of the quarter, the factory cuts the dealer a check, somewhere between three and five percent of invoice."

"Wait a minute—"

"That's right, Clement. They still made about a thousand bucks off you."

Clement looked at me for minute, smiling. "Damnation!" he said. "Holdback! I never heard of that."

"Superior knowledge." I gave the monster a nice big smile. "Key to the perfect deal."

5

Wendell's Deal

CHAPTER 1

"What you think?" Ray said.

He was punching buttons on the remote control, trying to make his brand-new, wide-screen, stereo-projection TV come on.

"It's big," I said.

"Shit, I can't get this thing to cut on. I got this integrated dingus, this remote control, I can't tell which is the stereo, which is the damn TV." Ray kept trying different buttons.

"Definitely big," I said.

"You damn right it's big." Still punching on the remote control. The stereo came on full blast, Hank Jr. doing another racist drinking song. It was loud.

"THE GREEN ONE!" I said.

"WHAT!"

"THE GREEN BUTTON! PRESS THE GREEN ONE!"

Ray kept punching, and Hank Jr. shut up.

"The green one," I said. Ray punched the green button and his Japanese monster TV came on. It was a terrible picture for something that cost five thousand dollars, grainy, with little points of light swimming around across the picture. The tiny lights gave you a feeling like you'd been hit in the head. A huge face dominated the screen; his lips were moving, no audio.

"You got the mute on, Ray."

Ray said, "Oh." He hit the button that said MUTE.

The face on the screen said: ". . . urther gang-related killings in southeast Atlanta. Three persons, two males and a female minor, were gunned down in the place of business of Rashad Dupree, thirty-three. Both Rashad and his brother, Terrance Andre Dupree, twenty-nine, were on parole for narcotics violations. Police have not released the name of the third victim, a seventeen-year-old girl, believed to have been. . . ."

"You want to change that?" I said. "It's making me nervous."

Ray changed the channel. Another talking head appeared on the screen—the host of one of these investment programs—a guy who, incidentally, has the worst haircut on TV. Worse even than Ted Koppel.

". . . with a bang or a whimper?" the host with the bad haircut asked. His head was five feet tall. The pits and creases in his face swam around in big grainy schools across the screen. "Here to answer that noisome question are our distinguished panelists. Today our guests. . . ."

"You want a beer?" Ray said.

"I need one," I said. I was thinking about Mr. Crowbar—Andre—lying on the floor with his life flowing out onto the linoleum. I couldn't get that sound out of my mind, the gurgling that his lungs had made.

"Molson? Michelob? We got Black Label, too, if you feeling adventurous."

"Whatever. Michelob's fine."

"You sure? Just cause you bought 'em, don't mean you got to drink 'em."

"Michelob is fine."

"You don't want no Molson? You sure now?"

"What the hell? You want me to drink Molson, give me a damn Molson."

Ray looked at me like he was going to ask what my problem was, but he didn't. He went up the stairs to get the beer, his slippers going slap slap slap on the stairs.

The Distinguished Panelists were addressing the question *Was the great leverage binge really dead?* Ray came back down and sat the bottle in front of me. Michelob.

"Sorry," I said. "I had a shitty day."

"What is this?" he said. He picked up the remote. "I can't feature this asshole."

". . . and I'll tell you why," said the second Distinguished Panelist. "Here's a scoop for you. Late this afternoon, RichCo, which as you know is a specialty chemical company based in Atlanta, was put into play by a bid from an international investor group. RichCo could be bought out tomorrow. That's what I'm talking about. Welcome to the nineties, folks. It's just. . . ."

Ray changed the channel, jabbing the remote at the screen. A new channel came on, with the toll-free prayer line in four-inch-high numbers at the bottom of the screen.

"Wait!" I said. "Go back!"

It took about five calls, but I got through to Jeannie. She was at Jordan Foote's offices. "Darling!" she said. "Do you have my eight million dollars?"

I gave her a cleaned-up version of what happened. I didn't see any point in bringing up anything about Andre and his albino brother, or anything about killing pregnant fourteen-year-old girls. I didn't bring up Clement either. It ended up being a fairly short story.

"The bonds were fake?" she said.

"Right. I still think I can find them." I *hoped* I could find them.

"Good."

"I just saw on the television," I said. "Somebody is trying to buy RichCo?"

"Hostile tender offer," she said. "We're going to kick their asses."

"When did this happen?"

"This morning, registered mail, I got a letter asking if we were interested in a friendly takeover. I called them to make sure they were serious. Then we called an emergency board meeting this afternoon. After the meeting we sent a fax back, saying *thanks but no thanks*. They announced the hostile tender offer at four-forty-five this afternoon. We have a team of bankers coming in from New York tonight. We may have to do a recap."

"A recap?"

"Recapitalize. Buy back stock, issue new debt. It'll make us a lot less attractive to an acquirer."

"No, I didn't mean that. I know what a recap is. I heard you had tried one a couple of years ago. A management buy out."

Silence.

"Jeannie?"

"Where did you hear that?"

"Let's just say I keep my ear to the ground."

"Mm," she said.

"Anyway," I said, "here's why I called. I just wanted to make sure that this doesn't affect our arrangement."

"No. Just find the money, Bobby."

"What about your other investment?"

"My what?"

"Your other investment. When you got me out of the lockup, you told me that you were heavily invested in some kind of deal. That you couldn't get out of it."

"Right," she said.

"So what's happening there? Are you going to be okay, now that RichCo is in play?"

"Knock wood," she said. There was something funny about her voice. She sounded a little too lighthearted. "Keep plugging, Bobby. I know you're going to find the money. I trust you." A phone range on Jeannie's end of the line. "Look, I think that's the bankers calling. Bye, Bobby."

"Oh," I said. "I almost forgot. Who's the other company?"

"Who?"

"The other company. Who's the company that's trying to buy RichCo."

"A French investment group," she said. "You've probably never heard of them. They're called Evergreen.

CHAPTER 2

I told Ray that I might be back that night, I might not, then I drove over to see Sarah. I couldn't seem to concentrate on the road.

"You don't look so good," she said.

"It's all just heaping up now," I said. "I don't know what to do. I keep thinking I'm almost out of the woods, and then things just get worse."

"No," she said. "I was talking about your sunburn."

She touched my forehead. It still hurt.

"Yeah. I still have sunburn." We stood there for a minute on the little landing outside the house. I said: "I know it's late. I had to see you."

"That's okay," she said, and we went inside.

She had a nice apartment, lots of funky-looking art on the walls—things made out of string, painted masks, neon-colored pictures that looked like cartoons. I wasn't sure if I understood the point of most of her stuff, what it was supposed to mean.

"I didn't find the bonds," I said. "Everything got screwed up."

Sarah put her arms around me. I held her for a while, held her a little too tight. I didn't know quite what I was doing there, what it was I wanted out of her. It was like I was on the edge of something, ready to plunge, and I needed her to help me. But I wasn't sure what it was I was on the edge of, or what she could do to help. Sarah stepped back, looked at me, trying to figure what was going on.

"You want something to drink?" she said.

"Decaf," I said. "If you've got it."

"Instant okay?"

"That's fine."

Sarah went in the kitchen. I sat down on the couch and watched her through the door. She had on a white T-shirt, blue running shorts, no bra, no makeup. Her hair was loose, hanging in a mess around her shoulders. At that moment, she was too beautiful to describe.

There was music playing, somebody I didn't recognize: a woman playing guitar.

Sarah came in with a mug of coffee, set it on top of a *Time* magazine. The coffee spilled all over Boris Yeltsin. Sarah sat down across from me in a canvas chair. She blew on her coffee, took a sip, burned herself.

"What's going on here?" she said.

I looked around the room at all the weird art, the stuff I couldn't identify, realized that she was a lot younger than me.

I shrugged. "Ray thinks we're falling for each other."

Sarah looked at me for a minute. "What do you think?" she said.

"It's a reasonable hypothesis," I said after a minute. What a stupid thing to say.

We sat there for a while. I wasn't sure if we had made any progress or not. Sarah just kept looking at me, waiting for me to say something. I tried the gray-colored, gray-tasting coffee. She had put skim milk in it.

"Good coffee," I lied.

"I don't know anything about you," Sarah said. "I don't know where you grew up, where you went to college, what you like to eat. You've got no history."

I took another sip of coffee, set it back down on top of Boris Yeltsin's pompadour. "It's funny you mention that," I said. "Because I'm not sure you'd learn much if I told you all that stuff. I mean, I don't feel real connected with any of that anymore."

"Parents?"

"Cancer." I shrugged. "Heart attack."

"College?"

"Clemson. I was in accounting. Sigma Nu. ROTC."

"I guess you went to law school."

"Vanderbilt. Middle third of the class."

"Where'd you grow up?"

"Six Mile, South Carolina. About a thousand people. Everybody lived in one-story brick houses. Except the rednecks—theirs were white, made of wood." I smiled thinking about it. "Actually we were all kind of rednecks, you get right down to it."

"See," Sarah said. "Now we're getting somewhere."

"I don't know," I said. "I'm not sure. I just feel so cut off from everything. I feel like half of me is dead."

"I felt that way once," she said. "I took some pills." She was being serious.

It took me a minute, trying to figure out what she meant. "You mean like suicide? Or like you got Valium," I said, "from a doctor?"

"Both. First as prescribed." She shrugged. "Then too much of it. I had my stomach pumped. I was okay."

"Jesus," I said.

"Yeah, well. I feel great now. It was right after my divorce."

I drank some more coffee.

"You remember at lunch," I said. "I asked you about this guy Clement Crews? And this company, Hi-Top?"

Sarah looked annoyed. "You keep avoiding something, Bobby. It's like there's all this stuff you won't talk about. *Cancer? Heart attack?* That's all you've got to say about your mother and father? Goddamnit, Bobby, you've got to make some effort here, too!" There was a terrible, hurt urgency in her voice, but I was paralyzed. I couldn't think about love or recollection or changing my life. Not right then.

I said: "I followed this guy, Clement Crews. He went to pick up the bonds, the money that Roger stole. I found out that Tate Keenan owns part of Hi-Top. This guy Clement killed Roger. Sarah, this guy killed a lot of people." Sarah sat balled up in her canvas chair, watching me with her chin propped up on her knees.

I kept talking, the words coming out of my mouth in no particular order until I couldn't talk anymore. The part about Andre and his brother and the girl, that part just stuck in my head and wouldn't come out of my mouth. I felt the tears running hot down my sunburned face. I was falling apart, popping at the seams.

Sarah took me in her arms again and I collapsed against her.

"We're okay, Bobby," she said. "We're alright." The woman on the stereo was singing this sweet, grim song about a waitress named Sylvia. I'd heard the song on a country station once of twice; but this was somebody different singing it.

I sat up and looked into Sarah's eyes.

"No," I said. "It's not alright. Today everything changed."

"How do you mean?"

I tried to breathe, the air coming hard into my lungs in little shuddering jerks, my face snotty and wet with tears. I wiped my nose.

"Today I killed a man. I shot a man to death."

Sarah closed her eyes, dropped her head back against the chair. "Oh, Jesus, Bobby. Why didn't you tell me?"

"I did," I said. "I just did."

CHAPTER 3

Early the next morning, Ray dropped me off to pick up my car, and then I drove to the RichCo building downtown, got there before seven o'clock. There was a man standing around in the lobby at RichCo, looking like he was waiting for an elevator—a middle-aged guy with an exotically large nose and lumpy hair. He wore a baggy gray suit, black wing tips.

"How you doing?" he said in a nasal, know-it-all voice.

"Going up?" I said.

"Oh," he said. "No, I'm just waiting. You need to press the button."

I pressed the up button.

"Heading up for the big Evergreen powwow?" he said. His face was excessively open and obliging-looking—like there was something he wanted out of me.

"Why?" I said.

"Jon Scheib," he said, and he put out his hand. "I'm with the *Journal.*"

"No comment," I said.

Scheib squinted at me. "Don't I know you from somewhere?" The elevator bonged and the door opened. Scheib poked his finger at me. "Wait!" he said. "Bobby Vine? Am I right?"

"It's possible."

"Don't tell me you're back in the game?" He was holding onto the door, not letting it close. I punched the button for the top floor. Back in the game. *Was* I back in the game? "How about answering a couple questions before you go?"

I shook my head.

"That's too bad," he said. "Because this is getting very interesting."

Scheib kept holding the door. I thought of something. "Tell you what," I said. "There's something I'd like to know. What is Tate Keenan's role with this Evergreen group? Is he an investor, deal maker, faithful counselor, what?"

Scheib smiled at me, got in the elevator pressed the close-door button, and flipped the little red stop lever. The overhead light blinked. "Why?" he said.

"There's no why," I said. "If you want to talk to me, you start by telling me what you know about Tate Keenan."

"Hard to say," he said. "We'd never heard of Evergreen before this thing with RichCo. I understand their money comes from one of the French bottled water families. They haven't done any deals in the U.S. before."

"Wrong," I said. "They haven't done any *big* deals before."

Scheib raised his eyebrows. He had a sly, ferrety look on his face. "Is that right?"

"Keep talking, maybe I'll share something with you."

"Fair enough. Keenan seems to be their advisor—legal and otherwise. It seems like it's more otherwise than legal, though. They've hired a big Wall Street firm to do the spade work. I think he's actually the one putting the deal together."

"That's what I thought," I said. We stood there a minute.

"Well?" Scheib said.

"Well, what?"

Scheib scratched his magnificent nose. "You implied that Evergreen has done some smaller deals over here."

"You'd never guess in a million years."

"Who?"

"They own a majority stake in Excor. Roger Hawley's firm."

For the first time Scheib lost his know-it-all look. "Holy shit," he said.

"You got that right," I said. I flipped the little red lever back to start, pushed the open-door button.

"You want to have some fun," I said, "go to Tate Keenan and ask him what happened to Roger's bonds? Okay?"

"What happened to Roger's bonds?"

"What happened to Roger's bonds."

The elevator door opened. Scheib held the door, took out a pocket recorder, put it up to his face, punched RECORD. "Question. Keenan. What happened to Roger's bonds? Question. What in hell is Bobby Vine doing at RichCo?" He turned the machine off and got out of the elevator.

"Have a good day, Mr. Vine."

They had set up a war room in the RichCo directors' suite. Jeannie was there. Jordan Foote was there. Everybody was there: investment bankers, lawyers, accountants crawling all over the place. One of the bankers had set up a laptop computer and a little printer and was tapping away on the keys down at the end of the thirty-foot conference table. There was paper all over—spreadsheets, forecasts, the usual accountants' lies.

At the far end of the table, sitting around the banker with the computer were the junior analysts, the staff accountants, the kids who did the actual work. They all wore dark suits, all seemed to have been pressed from more or less the same mold. They were scrutinizing various pieces of paper, making sure the lies in one part of the prospectus agreed with the lies in the other parts.

At the other end of the table were the big boys, disagreeing about something. There were four of them: Jordan, Jeannie, a guy with Coke-bottle glasses who I didn't recognize, and a guy with a beard. They all wore indistinguishable gray suits except Jeannie, who had on a red outfit with a black velvet collar.

The fourth man looked familiar. After a minute I placed him: He was the guy I had seen at Jordan Foote's office, the guy with the beard who had been pounding on the conference table. Now that I had a better look at him, I knew who he was. He was a hotshot New York investment banker, famous for throwing phones when he got pissed off. Bruce Something-or-other.

"I'll be with you in a moment," Jeannie said. Meaning, wait outside.

"Oh, great," I said. I gave everybody my dumbass smile and sat down next to Bruce, the phone thrower. Jeannie gave me a nasty look, but I didn't move.

Bruce was talking: "I frankly don't see that you have any alternative, Jeannie. If the board's going to be intransigent about this thing, then you're just pissing your capital out the window. You already did that once before."

The guy with the Coke-bottle glasses held up his hands. He wore a two-tone shirt, blue with white French cuffs. "Bruce, please," he said. "Let's explore the options here. Poison pill is a possible—a long shot, maybe, but still a possible. Let's not rule anything out based on previous representations of the board. We all know Jeannie's history there. But manifestly, she has convinced them to see things from her perspective before."

"The shit has hit the fan this time, Marty," Bruce said. "Definitively, Marty. I mean definitively."

Marty was the guy with the Coke-bottle glasses. "All I'm saying, Bruce, let's explore the options. The board hasn't given a final word on any of our proposals."

"That's bogus, Marty, and you know it. The shareholders know it, the board knows it, I know it, you know it. Christ!" Bruce looked around, maybe hunting around for a phone to throw.

Jeannie looked at Bruce. "Bruce. Shut up." She gave Marty the Sweet Briar smile. "Marty?"

They went on for a long time, talking about different strategies they could use, bitching at each other, talking about white squires and ESOPs and poison pills. Jeannie wanted, in effect, to buy her own company, but they couldn't agree on how they would raise the money. As best I could tell, they were also having trouble getting the board of directors of RichCo to approve whatever it was that Jeannie wanted to do.

After a while Jeannie stood, held up her hands. "Gentlemen let's take a step back here. In the past I have attempted to take this company private. I was thwarted by the board, who determined that my offer to the shareholders was insufficiently generous. Fine. That's history now. I believe the time has come to force the board to face that alternative again. Bruce, you say the board is intransigent. Well, we have not put them to the test. Last time I made a bid for RichCo, there was no competing offer. Now there is. We have spent too much time fucking around. Bruce? No more fucking around. Understood?"

Jeannie walked slowly around the table. Her high cheekbones were hot. The streak of white in her hair seemed to pulse like an old fluorescent bulb. "Bruce, I understand that you have been retained by the board of directors of RichCo and not by me personally. And I understand further that there is not unanimity among members of the board about what your charter is to be. Nonetheless, I am instructing you—*instructing you,* do you understand me?—I am *instructing* you to determine how we can maintain the independence of the company. I'm the chairman of this goddamn board and that's what I'm telling you to do. If you have a problem with that, if you need the board to vote every time you take a crap, every time you wipe, then feel free to get back on the goddamn plane and go home." She gave him the Sweet Briar smile, batted her eyelashes a little.

The kids down at the other end of the table were peeping at her over their printouts, loving it. "Do you think you can manage that, Bruce?" More smiling, more eyelashes.

Bruce glared at the kids at the other end of the table. "I don't frankly appreciate being put in this position," he said.

Jeannie touched a languid finger to her lip, looked down at him. She didn't say anything because she knew what he would say.

"Okay," Bruce said. "Here's what we can do. I can get things lined up, Marty and I can work out which kind of vehicle—ESOP, recap, buy out, whatever it is—give you some recommendations, maybe even set up a couple dog-and-pony shows for the lenders. But we can't go forward without a vote by the board. You know that, and I know that."

"And we also know that the reason I am paying your absurd fees," Jeannie said, "is that if I want, for instance, to present the board with a fait accompli, then you will do what it takes to make that come to pass."

Bruce drummed his fingers on the table for a minute. "I need to talk to my people," he said.

Jeannie waved her hand at the room. "It's all yours. I'll be outside." She gestured to the door with her head. "Bobby. Outside."

We went through the big oak doors. Jeannie stood in the corridor with her arms crossed. "What in the hell are you trying to pull?" she said.

"What?" I said. Giving her the dumb look.

"You know damn good and well that I don't want my association with you made public. Now what in God's name do you want?"

I kept smiling. "Having a little trouble with the board of directors? Not as pliant as we'd like them to be?"

Jeannie crossed her arms, scowled, looked at me for a long time. "I did not bring you out of the jail to get mixed up in my affairs. I brought you out to find my money. That's your job. I don't have to tell you that that eight million can make or break my ability to fund the recapitalization of RichCo. If you think your job is to come into these very delicate negotiations and ruin my reputation as a respectable member of the business community, then you have made a tragic mistake. Because my reputation is more important even than this company. If you play one more little trick like that, then it's bye-bye Bobby. Back to jail. And the hell with the bonds, the hell with the eight million." Her voice went down to a hiss. "Because I will *not* be dragged through the mud by someone like you."

Someone like you. Maybe it was just bluster . . . but, man, you have to actually hear it, actually have somebody say it to your face, to know what that feels like. *Someone like you.* It was so vague, so all-encompassing, a complete dismissal of everything I was. It's the closest I've ever come, as an adult, to hauling off and busting someone in the face.

I just stood there, hoping that I'd think of something smart to say.

"Fuck you," I said. It was weak, it was juvenile, but it was all I could think to say. "Fuck you, Jeannie. I hope Tate Keenan throws you to the wolves."

I turned around and walked down the hall, past the gloomy

oil paintings of Jeannie's father, her grandfather, some old guys in celluloid collars. I had gotten almost to the elevator when Jeannie called out.

"Wait!"

I looked at the elevator door. I wanted to push the button, but I didn't have the courage.

"Wait! Bobby! I didn't mean it that way."

I kept staring at the elevator button. It was made of mahogany, to match the boardroom doors, with a little plastic arrow glued to it, pointing at the floor. Beat down, once again. I had no choice. Comply, comply, comply. I shrugged, looked up at her. Jeannie was standing under a bright well of light, the streak in her hair lit up, her face cut up into planes of white and black. It wasn't a good light for her. She looked old—old and calculating.

"What?" I said. "What's the point? I'm never going to find that money."

Jeannie looked at me, a fragmented person, black here, white there. "I got a phone call last night," she said. "A call on my private line."

"And . . . ?"

"They said they knew where the bonds were."

"Who was this?"

"They wouldn't say."

"But they said *bonds?* They said the word *bonds?*"

Jeannie nodded, the shadows slicing down through her face. "Bonds. They said they knew where the bonds were."

"Well? Where?"

"They didn't say. They said that the bonds were being transported to a new location. That's why they couldn't tell me exactly where they were. They said as soon as they found out where they were, they'd call again."

"Anonymous caller?"

Jeannie shrugged. "A woman. Kind of a foreign accent."

I poked the button and the door opened. "Call me," I said.

When I got back to Ray's house there were two messages on the machine. I pushed PLAY. "Vine, this is Harv Zell, it's about ten-thirty, Tuesday morning. Aren't you supposed to have something for me?" The machine beeped.

Second message: "Hello, Mr. Vine, this is Rita Flynn at the law firm of Faulkner Keenan & Williams. Mr. Keenan would like to meet with you at your earliest convenience. Please call."

Scheib must have moved pretty fast. I wasn't sure what to do, what I should say to Keenan at this point. I decided to not to return his call.

I put on some number fifteen sun block and went out to the pool. Back in the game, I kept thinking. Back in the damn game! Only I wasn't quite sure whether this was a good thing or not.

Ray was sitting under an umbrella talking on the phone. When he saw me he put his hand over the mouthpiece. "Ay, guess what, Counselor!"

"What?"

"Ten o'clock Thursday morning I got us a appointment at the tailor," he said. "We gonna get me a wardrobe!"

CHAPTER 4

That night Sarah and I went out to Marietta to a country and western dance bar. It was a big place, two stories, built to look like something out of a cowboy movie. Boardwalk, hitching post, bat-wing doors, all that hokey shit.

We went in, walked up to the balcony level, and looked down at the dance floor. They were playing black music, rap, with lots of bass. A phalanx of these chrome-plated rednecks were down on the dance floor, all facing in one direction, dancing the same steps. About every eight or ten bars, they'd stomp their right foot, do some kind of little move, pivot ninety degrees. It didn't make any sense. It looked like a cross between disco, buck dancing, and a Hitler Youth physical fitness routine.

"What's going on?" I said. "I thought this was a country bar."

"You never heard of line dancing?" she said, laughing.

I didn't get it. After a while the rap music went away, and they put on some country, a song by Randy Travis. That was better. Sarah and I drank scotch, tried to talk for a while. It was too loud. Everything seemed awkward, dislocated.

We danced a little, then drank some more. I was sucking down doubles and after a while I got pretty drunk.

We got up and went down to the dance floor again, holding hands. I stumbled on the stairs, banged into a guy on the way down. A curtain of gloom was coming down on me.

We got on the dance floor. They were playing a Clint Black song, the song about how the lights were on but nobody was home. I was slopping around, banging into people. Sarah had this look on her face, wincing, like she was sorry we were out there.

After we'd danced a while, this old John Conlee tune came on, "Back Side of Thirty." It was about a guy whose life is wrecked and who doesn't feel like it's going to get any better. I clutched onto Sarah, pulled her to me. We were getting in people's way. The floor was wobbly and kept shifting under me, making me lose my balance. Too many doubles.

And then I was lying on the floor, looking up at the black ducts and braces on the ceiling, the wagon-wheel light fixtures. Without any intervening space of time, no slip, no fall, no impact, I had gone from upright to flat on my ass. Sarah was bending over me, saying things, hauling me up by my arm.

"Hell," I said. "Somebody must have spilled their drink, some beer or something."

"Come on," she said. "Up and at 'em." People were looking at us, but I couldn't see their faces. Everybody was underwater, blurred. They were accusing me of something, accusing me without putting it into words. Sarah was closer, not as deep in the water.

"I think I better go outside," I said. I had a pain in the back of my head. Sarah took my arm, and we walked outside. There were a lot of people in my way, people bumping me with their shoulders, their elbows. Accusing me.

We got outside, into the warm, wet air, and I sat down on the curb, propped my head on my hands. I wasn't sure whether I was going to throw up or not. I could still hear John Conlee through the door. The song was about a guy getting old, about watching everything he believed in fall apart.

"Sarah," I said. "I keep screwing up. What's happening, what's going on with me?"

"I don't know," she said. "I wish I knew what to say."

We sat on the curb, listened to the muffled music coming out of the building. We were on the edge of a parking lot filled with pickup trucks—full-size, American-made pickups. Jacked-up, chrome-plated, fog lights, step bumpers, roll bars, big tires with raised white letters. Trucks for men who didn't really need trucks. The whole world was underwater.

"You know what I like about this place?" I said.

"What?"

"Teeth," I said. "All those people in there, a bunch of snaggly toothed sons of bitches."

Sarah sighed, the kind of sigh a woman makes when she thinks, Why is it I keep getting stuck with losers? She put her head on her knees, stared down at the ground.

"Forget I said that," I said. "I'll start all over."

"Don't bother," Sarah said. "I wouldn't want you to strain yourself."

A car pulled out of the parking lot, V-8 engine, throwing up some gravel and then screeching when it hit the pavement. You could hear it shifting, shifting, shifting up into the distance, the big engine farting each time it popped out of gear.

"Let me ask you," I said. "Let me ask you something." I had to talk slowly to get the words out. My head was throbbing, mixing up the sounds as they came out of my throat.

Sarah's shoulders moved up and down once. She kept looking through her knees at the ground.

"You ever—do you have, I don't know, some kind of approach, some kind of theory? To how you live your life?" I was back to my survey again, seeing if I could have somebody explain it to me, a valid set of principles for how to live your life and so on.

"Bobby, what difference does it make?" she said after a little bit.

"I'm just curious." I started talking about legal ethics and stuff, about how my life had gone all haywire because I had gotten carried away with this legal mind-set, with all these fine distinctions about what was okay to do and what wasn't, blah blah blah, going on with all that self-pitying slop about why I'd screwed up my life. She looked away from me and then started shaking her head, shaking it so slowly that you almost couldn't see she was doing it. I shut up for a minute and then said, "Look I'm just *curious* is all, trying to find some answers."

"Well the answer is there's no answer," she said. "I don't have some kind of rule book. Life is not like law. You can't just flip to page 712 and look up the answers. That's bullshit, Bobby, looking up the answers."

I stared around the parking lot at the blurry shapes of the dude pickup trucks. Sarah sat up, tossed a pebble over a green Camaro.

"Bobby, if there's anything I've learned in my life—and believe me it took some real pain and some real effort and some hard times to figure this out—it's that there's no rule book. No precedents. No laws. No simple answers. Each day you have to get out of bed and just go to it."

"Okay," I said.

"You have to look at everything for what it is, and then you have to look in your own heart. If you look hard, I mean if you look unwaveringly at your own heart, you'll see what you're supposed to do. But it's no good to just find some kind of answer and let it sit there. Then it's just more bullshit. It's like some kind of moral exercise, like lifting weights but never using your muscles to actually do anything. You see?"

"I'm not sure."

"Bobby, you have to take control. That's all I'm saying. Looking for some neat, shiny, legalistic, philosophically defensible answer—that's just evading responsibility. 'Cause the world, finally, doesn't yield to that shit."

So maybe she was right. Maybe I was being a fool to think that what happened to me before—jail and all—had happened just because I didn't hew religiously enough to the right set of rules. Maybe I'd just lost hold of myself. Maybe everything was a lot simpler than I was making it out to be. Or, hell, maybe not. There was too much liquor in my head to take a clean swipe at the problem.

"Sure." I said it off-hand, like a joke.

"Oh, Bobby, spare me please from that patronizing crap."

I was feeling pissed off suddenly, the old rage boiling up again. "You think your divorce was hard?" I said. "Taking some pills? Well I've got news for you, I've been through all that, and it ain't the worst thing in the world. You couldn't begin to understand what it's like to think, hey, I might be on death row come Christmas. Death row! Merry Christmas, Mr. Vine. Merry fucking Christmas! Tell me how to take control of that."

Sarah looked at me, her face crumpling. But she didn't say anything. She just took my hand and held it between her knees for a while. More V-8 engines came and went. People swam by, looking down at us. Nobody was talking.

"You just keep missing the point," she said softly.

We just sat there a while, people clomping by us in their Dan Posts and their Tony Lamas. Eventually I calmed down some, and my mind started drifting, putting pieces together, seeing what fit and what didn't. Putting what she was saying together with everything else that was going on in my life. It started making some sense. "You know what I think?" I said.

"No," she said.

"I think it's time to change the playbook."

"You're not listening, damn it. It's not about playbooks. It's not about circles and arrows. It's not about rules of civil procedure."

"What I'm saying—"

She turned and grabbed my arm. "See? The thing you're looking for, it's just—" She shook my arm, digging her nails into it. "—this! This is all there is. It's right here." She held my hand up to her breasts, and her black eyes were dulled by a sad impatience. "I don't see what the goddamn mystery is, Bobby."

"I got to change the playbook," I said woodenly. "Got to go on the offensive."

Sarah stood up, took a deep breath, like she was tired of waiting for me to get the picture. "You want to go?" she said wearily.

I stood slowly, and we started walking across the parking lot. We were close together, but we weren't holding hands, weren't touching at all.

When we got to the car, I stopped and said to her, "I heard what you said. Don't give up on me, okay? Because I promise I was listening."

"Okay," she said, but she wouldn't meet my eye.

"Please," I said. "Don't give up yet."

Then I pulled out my wallet, fished around, found a business card that said Rosita D. Saiz, Legal Assistant. At the top of the card, big letters, it said FAULKNER KEENAN & WILLIAMS.

"I need to make a phone call," I said.

Sarah sighed, shrugged, leaned against the car.

I lurched back over to the club, over to this pay phone bolted to the wall up on the bogus Dodge City boardwalk. I could feel Sarah's eyes on my back. But I had to do this thing, had to do it right now, while I still had the high drunken urgency in my blood.

I dialed the number on the card. The computer told me that if I wanted to leave a message for a member of the firm, I should use the buttons on my touch tone phone to spell their last name. I punched in 5–3–3–6–2–6.

A man's recorded voice told me to talk after the tone.

When it beeped, I hesitated, almost chickened out. But I knew Sarah was right. It was time to start taking responsibility, time to stop letting myself get carried along by the current.

So I said: "Yeah, this is Bobby Vine. I just called to say, sure let's get together one of these days. Oh, and guess what, Tate. I'm taking you down."

When I got back in the car, I said, "Have I told you what a fine woman you are?"

"Actually, no." Her face tight, hands gripping the wheel: ten o'clock, two o'clock.

"Well," I said. "I'm telling you now."

She was still pissed off at me, but I could see a smile budding inside her lips.

CHAPTER 5

I spent the night at Sarah's, then drove back over to Ray's first thing in the morning. Ray was in the kitchen in a pair of shorts, no shirt, cooking breakfast.

"Want some cheese eggs?" he said.

"Thanks, no. My stomach's not up to that." I checked the phone—no messages—and walked back to the kitchen. "Ray," I said, "did anybody call me last night? Or this morning?"

"Nah," he said. "Hey, look. I got a question."

"Okay."

"This tailor thing?" Ray waved his spatula gently, dripped some cheesy goo on the floor. "What you supposed to wear to the fitting? I mean I don't want to look like I just fell off the cabbage truck. The suits I got—I don't know."

"Don't wear a suit then," I said. "Wear something else. Wear a pair of blue jeans."

"What about a golf type outfit? You know, pair of pants, shirt type of thing?"

"Careful. Your eggs are about to scorch."

Ray turned down the burner. "You see what I'm saying? A golf outfit, you know, is that too casual? Too, I don't know, a little too loud, something like that?"

"Ray," I said. "You pay a guy twelve hundred bucks to make you a suit, he doesn't care if you come wearing a sheet."

Ray stared at me, purple bags under his eyes. "Say what?"

"I said, you pay a guy twelve hundred bucks to make—"

"I heard you," Ray said. "You never told me it was gonna cost no twelve hundred dollars for one suit."

"You didn't ask. You said you wanted the best, I said go tailor-made."

"Five suits, man, that's six grand. Plus the shirts, the ties, socks, that's crazier'n hell."

"How much money you got in your checking account, Ray?"

"What's it to you?" His little eyes were pinned on me.

"I'm just asking a leading question," I said. "How much?"

Ray shrugged. "Sixty-five, seventy grand."

"Jesus, Ray, I never heard of anybody with that kind of cash lying around. You don't even have to *charge* it. You can go in, buy fifteen suits, write them a check. What's the big deal?"

Ray looked at me like he couldn't figure out where I was coming from. "What the big deal here is, is *principle*. It's a matter of principle, Bobby."

"So go back to J.C. Penney, get another sixty-nine-dollar suit," I said. "You sure those eggs aren't ready yet?"

Ray was scraping the pan with the spatula. "I like 'em dry, can't take them loose eggs—feel like I'm eatin' snot. Man, I hate that shit. I like 'em *real* dry." He took the eggs out with his spatula, heaped them on a plate. They were bone dry, little pellets of egg the size of kidney beans. "Ah, man, I forgot to make the God-durn toast," he said.

The phone rang.

"You mind getting that?" he said. "I got to get the toast done before the eggs get cold."

I answered the phone.

It was Tate Keenan. I had never talked to him, but I could tell it was him. It was a thin, quiet voice. Not harsh exactly, but completely controlled, squeezed down, no modulation, no particular tone. It was like ice on a pond, cold, smooth, brittle-sounding. Tate said he thought that the two of us ought to get together and talk. Now.

I told him, sure, I might as well. Nothing to do but watch a guy eat his cheese eggs. I hung up.

"Got to go, Ray," I said. Ray was sitting in one of his black Euro-chairs at the far end of his twenty-four-person dinner table eating his cheese eggs. The little stalk of chair back peeped over his head at me.

"I'm going to this guy Tate Keenan's office," I said. "If I'm not back in a couple hours, send the cops."

Ray looked up from his cheese eggs. "You being serious?"

"I don't know," I said. "I think he's the one. I think Clement is working for him."

"Can you prove it?"

"Nope." I stood there for a minute.

Ray lifted his fork at me, showing off a little pile of egg pellets. "It'll really fit like a glove? Maximize your strengths, minimize your faults, all that shit?"

"That's what the twelve hundred bucks is for."

"I think I'll go with a golf type outfit," he said. "To the fitting, I mean. Man-of-leisure type of look."

Tate's secretary showed me into the room. It was a corner office, views of downtown and the 75/85 corridor—a nice view if concrete's one of your turn-ons. Tate was not in the room.

There were filing cabinets along one wall, nothing decorative about that, and law books on the other. He had a normal wooden desk, nothing special, with a computer on one side, phone on the other, some law bibles and correspondence stacked up in the middle. It was pure, boiled down, functional.

I stood at one window and looked down at the interstate, miles of it, twisting in and out—ten, twelve lanes across sometimes. Middle of rush hour, clogged with cars. We were way up, forty stories, the cars looking pretty small from here. I was nervous, wondering what Keenan was going to say. I had to try and push, get him pissed off so he'd say something he shouldn't. Maybe I could jar something out of him.

I heard a noise behind me, a toilet flushing. As I turned, Tate Keenan came out of a door on the other wall, next to all the filing cabinets. He was zipping his fly.

"That was quick," he said. But his face didn't show any particular surprise. He sat down in his chair in front of the computer. "May I offer you some coffee? Tea?" He had a strange way of speaking, maybe like a foreigner who had the accent down pat, but still hadn't quite figured out how to string the words together fluidly.

"I'm fine," I said.

"I spoke to Mr. Scheib," he said. No transitions, no small talk. Bang. Right to the point. "Of the *Journal*. He said that you gave him a tip, instructed him, so to speak, to ask me a question. That question was, *What happened to Roger's bonds?* I would like to know, sir, what you meant by that."

I studied his face, trying to see what he was up to. I might as well not have bothered; he wasn't giving anything up. He was just a thin bald guy, tight lips, intense eyes. But they had an even intensity, like a cutting torch flame—no flicker, no excitement, nothing you could latch onto.

"Seems like a clear enough question to me," I said. "No big words in it, nothing you'd have to look up in the dictionary."

He kept watching my face. He was trying to figure me out, too—like some Japanese engineer, taking me apart piece by piece, looking for the weak links.

He said, "You have a reputation as a bright man, a capable man. *Solid* is a word I've heard to describe you, your criminal record notwithstanding." We watched each other.

"And?"

"I must assume, therefore, that you had a clear purpose when you spoke to a representative of the *Journal.* Jon Scheib is in a very influential position. I believe that you, in a circuitous way, were implying to him that I am somehow involved in the unfortunate situation at Excor."

"You are," I said.

"Oh?"

"I know for a fact that Evergreen provided the seed money for Excor. You represent Evergreen and have done so since its inception."

Keenan raised his shoulders slightly, lowered them. "That is true. It is also true, however, that we are passive investors in the narrowest sense. Nevertheless, your implication, I believe, went far beyond that. You were attempting to taint me and my client Evergreen Partners with Roger's misprision. That would be incorrect, however, Mr. Vine. Also, rather unwise. In fact, as you are obviously aware, Evergreen has a great deal of potential exposure—in the event, for instance, that the stolen funds are not recovered."

I waited, seeing where he was going.

"What puzzles me about my supposition here, Mr. Vine, is why you would wish to undermine the attempt of my client to acquire control over RichCo. On the face of it, this seems inexplicable. Would you like to explain?"

"No."

That one didn't faze him at all. I assume he anticipated it, since it's the same response he probably would have given if he had been in my shoes. I looked down at the interstate again. It reminded me of a network of veins and arteries, splitting, spreading, channeling blood from here to there, there to here.

"Good. After considering those facts of which I am aware," Keenan said, "I conclude that you have no stake in RichCo's future. Further, I proceed from the premise that you have discovered certain information which, if incorrectly or incompletely analyzed, might falsely implicate me and/or my client Evergreen as having some role in Roger's misdeeds at Excor." He stopped, evaluated me for a moment, looking for a reaction. "Would you like to fill in the blank here?"

"Hm," I said. I had a hunch where he was going. "Interesting. But no, I'll let you finish."

"Let me paint a scenario. First you plant some obscure allusion to Excor with a highly motivated and resourceful member of the press. You do so in such a way as to raise his suspicions while giving him information which he cannot use directly in any way, other than to come to me and ask me the question you fed to him. I will understand more fully than he the potential results of the allusion, while also realizing that it is essentially meaningless—a kind of challenge, insupportable by Scheib should he attempt to dig up something with which he can go to press. Roger had nothing to do with bonds, a fact of which Mr. Scheib is unaware. I, however, will understand the nature of the challenge. I will read between the lines, recognizing how potentially damaging half-true revelations to the press about connections between myself and Evergreen, on one hand, and Excor, Roger, and Hi-Top, on the other, might be." He stopped, waited. I didn't say anything.

"Your intent in this scenario, then," Tate continued, "is to extort from me or my client certain advantages. If we refuse to grant you these advantages, you will continue to leak information—both true and untrue—to the press. If the press jumps to the wrong conclusions in the middle of a course of action as sensitive as that which Evergreen is pursuing, the results could naturally be devastating for my clients.

"I examined the scenario and asked myself what advantages you might obtain from Evergreen. Initially my hypothesis was that you needed legal resources to pursue your acquittal. Naturally I checked to find the status of your legal representation. When I found that you had retained Dick Bloom, with, I might add, a substantial retainer, I discarded that as a motive. My fallback hypothesis, then, is that you simply wish to accumulate a substantial amount of money. I conclude, therefore, that you wish to disappear. Honduras, Indonesia, Poland, God knows where."

Keenan stopped talking. I felt him looking at me, feeling for a reaction. I kept watching the cars circulating through the city. It was an interesting approach Keenan was taking, pretending to see all sorts of complicated motives behind my comment to Scheib. Was he trying to milk information out of me, provoke me into showing my hand? I turned around, sat down across the desk from Tate.

"Ingenious theory," I said. "You have a lot of imagination."

Keenan's face was as blank as ever. "Quite the contrary, Mr. Vine. I have very little imagination at all."

I had the feeling he was waiting for something. But I was damned if I could figure out what it was. I sat there, arms crossed, and waited.

Keenan looked at his watch. "I have things to do," he said. "No more discussion. Name your price."

"My price?"

"How much do you want from my client for your silence about our connection to Hi-Top, Excor, and Roger Hawley?"

"Jesus," I said. "Blackmail?" I hadn't expected this at all. I thought for a minute. How much was I worth to Tate? He must be pretty worried that I was close to finding something. "Let's just imagine, for the sake of argument," I said, "that you're right. Let's just imagine that I'm trying to blackmail you. How does a million and a quarter sound?"

Keenan didn't even blink. "Done."

I couldn't believe it. "You're prepared to cut me a check

for one million two hundred and fifty thousand dollars? Right this minute, just to get me out of your hair?"

"So to speak." Keenan's eyes were burning. The one thing I could read, the one thing I was sure of, he didn't like me at all.

"This is a weird one," I said. "All the things I expected, this was not it."

"What are you saying, Mr. Vine?"

"I'm saying: no way. I don't want your money."

"How much, Mr. Vine? If you play games with us, we will have to resort to other means to deal with you."

I shook my head. "No, no, no. You don't get it. There is no price. There's no magic number. I don't want your money."

It was the first time I had seen any emotion on Keenan's face. You could see it dawning on him that he had somehow guessed wrong about me entirely. Another look crossed his face, just for a second, something I couldn't read, and then his face went blank.

"What *do* you want?" he said.

"Did you listen to my message?" I said. "On your voice-mail system?"

"A threat. Part of your game."

"No, not a game. Just a threat."

Keenan was thinking. His eyes were looking dead ahead, nothing going on inside them. It was like a mask he pulled down to cover up what was going on in his head. After a minute he stood up, walked to the window where I'd been standing.

"I can see you think that you can play cat and mouse with us, that you can negotiate. I'm afraid, however, that it's not going to work that way." He stopped, kept looking out the window, down at the interstate. "I have a great deal of power, a great deal of influence. I can destroy you."

"Whatever you say."

"Let me share some thoughts with you, Mr. Vine, about how I believe the world works. Ordinarily I would not waste my time on this, but I think that you are receptive, that you are intelligent, that you may profit by listening." He paused, looking down at the great serpentine swathes of reinforced concrete below us. "Power. Power is what life is all about. Collection, accretion, distribution of power. Every man, every organization, every society, nation, company—every one of them has power, stores it, wields it, loses it. Some of us have very little, some a great deal. Society is a great mechanical construct, one yielding to laws analogous, say, to Newtonian mechanics. I exert influence on you; you exert influence on me. For each action there is an equal and opposite reaction. Simple physics. If you learn the rules, you can bend them to your will. If you don't, you'll simply be rolled around like a bowling ball—always an instrument in someone else's game."

"Yeah, yeah, I get the point," I said. "Now you're going to tell me that if you drop a bowling ball on an orange, it's going to turn into orange juice, something like that, right?"

Tate looked at me, not amused. "That's not my point at all. My point, Mr. Vine, is that you and I are not so different as you might think. Either one understands and uses the rules . . . or one is exploited by those who do."

"Meaning what? That if I don't take you up on one of your offers, you'll have Clement Crews come after me with a crowbar?" I got up and headed for the door.

"Mr. Vine!" Keenan called out to me as I reached the door. "I checked into something. While you were in prison, you filed an appeal to the American Bar Association. An attempt to reverse your disbarment. They tabled the appeal, I believe."

I didn't say anything.

He raised his eyebrows. "All that power I was just talking about," he said. "I could use it to your benefit."

I waited, let him keep talking.

"I could see to it that your appeal was taken off the table, that you were reinstalled to the bar. With conditions, of course. Perhaps some community service, some selfless *pro bono* work on behalf of the indigent and the downtrodden."

Blindsided, my eyes must have widened. I had pretty much given up hope about the appeal. The thought of it gave me a weird feeling: What if? Jesus, what if?

"That's all it would take," he said, "to put you back in the game. The revivification of Bobby Vine, deal maker."

"No that's not all it would take," I said finally. "You're missing the most important thing. Nothing, *nothing* matters until I find the person who killed Roger."

"Ah. And who do we suppose that might be?"

I smiled grimly. "You."

CHAPTER 6

I told Ray: "The son of a bitch wanted to bribe me. Said he could get me restored to the bar, put me back in the deal-making game."

Ray was doing some kind of paperwork, sitting it on his knees while he watched his gigantic TV. He was ticking things off on a computer printout, and then drawing lines through other things on a different printout, going back and forth between the two. "I thought you gave up on that," he said. "That whole way of life."

"I did ... I think." It was hard to be sure.

Ray went back to his paperwork.

"He kept going on about power," I said. "Saying power and influence were as predictable as physics. I mean, to some degree he's right: He's powerful and I'm lower than bug shit."

"You're saying you're S.O.L.?"

"I'm saying what I need is something I can move the guy with. Like in physics. I need a lever."

"You don't need no lever," he said, not looking up. The top of his head looked like a hairy sponge. "What you need is a goddamn miracle."

"Thanks for the encouragement," I said.

"Hey, no problem," Ray said.

The phone rang. It was Jeannie.

"Bobby, thank goodness," she said.

"Did our mystery guest call back?"

"Yes. She said the bonds came in today."

"Who has them?"

There was a pause. "This is a very great shock to me," she said. "I was physically ill, I mean I was literally physically ill when I found out who has the bonds."

"Who?"

"Tate Keenan."

So. There it was, finally. I felt like a big weight had been tipped off my shoulders. "Did they say where? I mean, physically what location?"

"Down to the last detail. She said they were in a filing cabinet in Tate's office, second filing cabinet from the left, bottom drawer, inside a gray lockbox."

"Did you record the voice?" I said.

"No, why?"

"You need to get the cops over there with a warrant. I don't think they'd do it with no evidence. You need something tangible they can issue a warrant on. You're going to need to get the SEC involved, the FBI, whatever."

There was silence on the line.

"I didn't think of that." More silence. "Bobby, we're so close." There was an edge in her voice.

"Well, what are we going to do? We need to smoke him out somehow. We need some time."

Silence again. I saw it coming again. "Bobby, we don't *have* time. The tender offer expires next Monday. You're just going to have to get them back somehow."

"No sir, nohow, no way. Not the break-in routine again. Not in a law firm with alarms, not with security guards and cameras in the lobby. Roger's house was bad enough."

Silence.

"Bobby. Be reasonable."

"Be reasonable, shit! I'm not going. Hire a P.I. Send Jordan over there. Pull some strings with the cops."

Silence.

"Bobby." She didn't say anything else. She didn't have to. It was simple: Do it or get sent back to the Fulton County Jail.

"Ten grand," I said. "It'll take another ten grand. Cash."

"Just do it," she said. "Jordan will handle the money."

"Fair enough," I said. "I think you just gave me a lever."

"A what?"

Ray was still working on his printouts, crossing things off. Top of the second, Otis Nixon on the TV, taking a practice swing. You could see him sweat, see every piece of lint on his uniform. The Braves were already down two-zip.

"Got a question, Ray," I said.

"Yeah?" Ticking and crossing, shuffling the papers.

"You know anybody that's good with alarm systems? Like, a burglar?"

Ray looked up at me, blinked as though I had just made some kind of moronic joke. Then he looked back at his computer printouts.

CHAPTER 7

The burglar's name was Wendell, and he was late.

Ray and I were sitting in a booth at the Kollege Klub down in College Park. All Girl Staff, the sign said. Ray was giving me an ugly look. He wasn't happy about this situation. Wendell was reformed. Wendell had been *mainstreamed*, turned into an honest merchant, doing a good job managing one of Ray's stores down in Newnan. The whole thing was against Ray's principles.

Our booth was semicircular, pea-green upholstery with geometrical patterns in black and silver printed onto the fabric. I didn't see the All Girl Staff. There was a bartender, a fat guy with a cigarette in his mouth, watching the Braves, who were now down five-zip. The All Girl Staff came out after a while. She was about forty, kind of drained out and saggy looking, wearing a high-cut red leotard, fringed at the crotch, with gold stockings, shiny gold pumps, about nineteen inches of heel. She was carrying a little round drink tray.

The All Girl Staff didn't say anything, just walked up and leaned one hip against the table. When I told her I'd have milk, she didn't even smile, just wrote MILK on her little pad. Ray didn't believe he wanted anything, thanks. She didn't say a word, just teetered off, showing us some varicose leg. After a while, she came back with the milk, a small glass, set it down on a little cocktail napkin.

"Two and half bills," she said.

I was tempted to laugh, but I wasn't sure if it was funny or not. I gave her three dollars and she teetered away, no change.

Wendell finally came in, sat down across from us, took off his mirrored sunglasses. He had blond hair, not cut recently, bad skin, pop eyes. He was too thin, the veins sticking up in his arms, and he wore a skinny, leather, pulled-down necktie and a cheap yellow shirt. A nervous-looking guy.

"Nice place," I said. "You been a member for a while?"

"Yeah," he said, straight-faced. "They serve on Sunday."

"Here's what's going on," Ray said. He pointed his fat little thumb at me, showing off the tattoo on the back of his hand. "We got a guy here, good friend of mine, got hisself in some trouble. He says to me, you know any B&E men? I say, yeah, I know a good one, but he don't break no more and he don't enter no more. I told Bobby that you was out of the bidness."

"Where's the girl at?" Wendell said. "I need me a beer or something." He hadn't said hello, hadn't shook my hand.

Ray said: "My point is, Bobby here, he told me to call up this B&E man cause he needs to break and he needs to enter. He says he needs to do this in a big way. I said, okay, I'll call Wendell, let Wendell make his own choice."

Wendell was looking around for the All Girl Staff. She was hiding. "Hold up a sec," he said. He went up to the bar, got three bottles of Bud, came back, and set them down. "Here," he said. "Y'all making me nervous, drinking milk."

"I don't want to encourage you to backslide, mess up your life, take up a life of crime again," I said. I heard the words come out, sounding like Kojak, some idiot on TV. "On the other hand, I could pay you a lot of money."

Wendell drank about half his beer in one swallow. "Man!" he said. "Don't that hit the spot!" He looked at me. His pop eyes were washed-out blue, moist-looking. "You don't look like the regular type guy wants to go bust into a jewelry store."

"I'm not," I said.

"Yeah, well. How much is a lot of money?" He winked at Ray, gave him this smarmy-looking smile. "Just while we're sitting around pretending I might do it."

"Three thousand dollars." I came up with the number on the spot. "Just get me in, shut down the alarm and go away."

"Three grand! Shit! You hitting a damn bank?"

"A law firm."

"Law firm? What in hell for?"

"To get some papers," I said.

"Get some papers." Wendell blinked at me. He finished his beer. "Three thousand dollars, must be some damn tasty papers."

"They are."

"You gonna drink that?" he said, flicking my beer with his middle finger.

"Help yourself," I said. "I kind of overdid it yesterday."

He took a long pull on my beer, leaning into it with his jaw. When he set it down, the beer foamed up all the way to the top of the bottleneck. Ray was watching, drumming his fingers.

"How 'bout I let you in on something?" Wendell said. "There's about fifty, sixty companies that make alarm systems. XTruder, ATC, U.S. Protective, whatever. They all work the same way, most of them. You got two contacts on a window, door, whatever. You pop it open, this little magnetic thingy drops in the contact. Any dipshit can get around that, long as he got the tools, knows where the contact's at. But once you get in a building, they could have foot treadles, ultrasonics, infrared beams, all kind of freaky shit."

"Sure," I said.

"There's all kind of variations. If it's some kind of standard brand, I can do it in my sleep. But if it's some high-end system got a fire alarm, phone in/phone out, tiered access, whatever, it gets real complicated. Nah, I take that back. It gets impossible."

I thought about it. "What you're saying, Wendell, hypothetically, is that you can get me inside anyplace—I mean *in the door.* But you can't guarantee the alarm won't go off if they have motion detectors inside. Is that it?"

" 'Bout the size of it."

"And if I trip the motion detector, how much delay before the alarm goes off?"

"No delay. The door, you got forty-five seconds, so the first person to enter in the morning can punch in the code. Some systems, a minute. Motion detector, bang, it goes off, no delay."

"How long would it take the police to get there if the alarm went off, forty stories up in a Midtown office building?"

"Cops, two minutes minimum. Maybe five. Maybe more than that. Then you got security in the building. That could be something or it could be nothing." Wendell finished my beer. "Man! Thirsty today!" He was looking happier now.

"Three grand," I said. "What do you think? We go up, you open the door. If it's an alarm you know how to defeat, you defeat it. If not, I give you five minutes to get out of the building, then I go in and take my chances."

"Three grand." Wendell made a snapping noise with his mouth. "You got a awful good haircut, you know that? Drinking milk? I don't know."

"So?" I said.

"Nothing personal, okay, but you remind me of my brother-in-law? Big milk drinker. He got a nice haircut, too."

"I'm sorry to hear that," I said.

"Neat, nice haircut, sharp as a tack, huh?" Wendell was grinning at Ray. "My brother-in-law, he's in the fucking FBI."

Ray jumped in: "Bobby ain't FBI, son. You can forget that. He did two terms, three to five concurrent, down at Maxwell."

"*Federal* pen? What you do, break into somebody's mailbox, steal their Sossal Security?"

"I violated Securities and Exchange Commission Rule

Number Ten, Section B, Subsection Five," I said. "Among other things."

"Rule what?" Wendell looked over at Ray, a blank look on his face. "Who the fuck is this guy?"

"Three grand," I said. "We go up, scope it out. If you don't like it, we don't do it." I took out two hundred cash, the one-day limit on my bank machine, and set it in front of Wendell. "Earnest money. Thirteen hundred more outside the building. Another fifteen hundred if you get me in the door."

Wendell looked at me. "What time?"

"How does midnight sound? The SouthBank Building on Peachtree."

"Meet me there, eleven-forty-five. Wear blue khaki pants, white T-shirt, work boots."

Ray was watching, an ugly look on his face, like somebody had done something cheap and mean to him.

Wendell looked over at him. "Ray. Three grand, cash, that's two months work. I'm sorry, man, but Rhonda done run up the Visa card, I'm starting to get phone calls." He got up, walked out of the Kollege Klub, drinking Ray's Budweiser.

We drove home in Ray's Mark VII. He wouldn't talk to me. "I'm sorry," I said. "I wish it didn't have to be this way."

Ray didn't say anything till we got back to the house. "It's the goddamn principle of the thing."

"You got any better suggestions, Ray? Do you?"

I called Jeannie. "Tonight," I said. "I'm going in tonight. I'll call when I get back with the bonds."

Jeannie Richardson said: "What time?"

"Midnight."

I was getting ready to go downstairs and catch the end of the Braves game when the phone rang.

"Bobby?" It was Ed Mance.

"What's going on?"

"I got a little problem, is what's going on."

"Yeah?" I had a nervous feeling, this nasty sound to Ed's voice.

"These three niggers they killed down near Carver Homes?

Two men, little pregnant girl? You maybe seen about it on the TV? More what they call drug-related violence." He waited for a second, seeing if I'd chime in. "The thing is, I was talking to this buddy of mine, Homicide Squad, he says one of these boys worked as a security guard. I say, 'Oh yeah?' He says, 'Yeah, place called Hi-Top.' He says, 'You ever hear of it?' You know what I said?"

"What?"

"I said, 'No, never heard of it.' "

I didn't say anything.

"But still I thought, out of curiosity, run the niggers through the DMV computer, what the hell. The younger boy, he's got a vehicle registered to him, you want to take a stab?"

"Tell me."

"I'm reading here: Make, Lincoln. Model, Town Car. Year, 1981. Let's see. We got number of doors, number of cylinders, odometer, VIN, what else you want to know?"

"Okay, okay," I said.

"Bobby, I been a cop long enough, I know this ain't a coincidence. Even so, I'm thinking, maybe so, maybe not. I just thought I'd call. But you remember what you said, how you promised you wouldn't lie to me?"

"I remember," I said. I sat there a minute, trying to think what to say. I told him about the kid I shot, about Clement Crews killing the other two, putting the gun right up to the albino's head. I laid it all out. I told him about the gun with my fingerprints on it, the gun in Clement's plastic bag. "I know I'm putting you in a bad position," I said.

Ed was breathing on the other end. It was maybe worse than he'd expected. Or maybe not.

Finally he said: "It ain't my case, so for now it's just between you and me. Since you kept your word, didn't lie to me."

"I appreciate that."

"And Bobby? We treading on some damn thin ice."

I said: "Ed, I'm walking so light these days—I mean, I can't remember how to leave a decent footprint anymore."

I drove over to Sarah's. She met me at the door, looking good. "I'm taking control," I said. "Taking responsibility."

"Come on in," she said.

I looked at the weird art hanging off the walls, told her what I was going to do tonight. Then we sat there a while.

"Are you sure this is the right thing to do?" Her voice listless because right or wrong didn't matter. She knew I was going.

I didn't answer.

After a minute she got down on her knees, unlaced my shoes, took off my socks. Then she led me into the bedroom.

CHAPTER 8

Eleven-forty, I parked my Aries on a little street near the Arts Center MARTA station and walked down two blocks to the SouthBank Building. There was nobody around, not even cars going by—like the whole city had been closed for repairs. The air was nice and cool for July, with a little breeze.

The SouthBank Building was maybe fifty stories high, glass and tan concrete, nothing special about it. The bottom floor was built over a bias with the cross streets slanting down from Peachtree on both sides. Walking in from Peachtree, you'd go into the lobby, a big glassed-in place with black marble floors. There was a lot of light in there and a security guard.

The parking garage was in the basement, with an access on each of the cross streets down at the bottom of the hill. Big steel gates, the kind that come down out of the ceiling, were pulled down over the entrance on the nearest hill. A security guard sat in a little Plexiglas booth just inside the door. I kept away from the light, wondering where Wendell was. Whether he was going to show.

"Hey! Vine!" It was a voice, whispering to me. I looked

around. There was a shadow, human-shaped, over by a big bush. Wendell. He was carrying a tool kit.

"So what's the plan?" I said. "I figure we can tell the guard upstairs that we're electricians or something."

"You crazy, man?" Wendell said. His face was dark, nothing showing but a little gleam off his pop eyes. "They got a list, approved contractors. They wouldn't even let you in the door."

"Oh," I said. I hadn't even thought of that. "Well, what are we going to do—cut through that thing with a torch?" I pointed at the steel gates.

"Shit no," Wendell said. We walked up the sidewalk about thirty feet. He stopped at the edge of a big metal grate in the sidewalk, set the tool kit down, took out a big pair of bolt cutters. "Where's the lock at?" he said.

We looked until we found a lock recessed into the face of the grate. Wendell looked around, pushed the bolt cutters down into the little lock well, heaved on the cutters a couple of times. Finally the hasp popped and a loud noise went clanging through the whole grate. Wendell took out a flashlight, shined it straight down. Underneath the grate, there was a concrete chute about thirty feet deep, a metal ladder running down the side. Water glistened up from the bottom.

"After you," Wendell said.

About fifteen minutes later, we were at the bottom of the parking garage, next to the elevator shaft.

"Okay," Wendell said. "So much for the easy part."

I walked to the elevator, punched the up button.

"Hey!" Wendell said. "Whoa. You outta your fucking mind?"

"I'm getting the elevator," I said.

"You crazy?" he said. "They probably got a camera in there. We go up in the elevator, we got our faces in the news tomorrow."

"Wendell," I said. "This place is on the fortieth floor."

Wendell showed his yellow teeth, held out his tool kit. "I don't mind," he said. "You the one gonna be carrying the iron."

"Great," I said.

"Oh, yeah," he said. "I forgot." He took a blue jacket out of the tool kit, handed it to me. It said U.S. PROTECTIVE on the back. I put it on.

"Who's this supposed to fool?" I said.

"From now on, you're Woody and I'm Blair," he pointed at a little white oval on the left breast of my jacket. It said WOODY, stitched in red letters. Wendell's said BLAIR. "Just in case. It's like when I was in the Corps, you got to put up a perimeter defense, interlocking fields of fire, so you got a little room to drop back, regroup, you know what I'm saying."

"Okay," I said.

We went up the stairs. Every two landings there was a red door, numbers stenciled on the back in black paint. Stair, landing, stair, landing, door. Stair, landing, stair, landing, door. It kept going and going.

"Hold up a second," I said. We were in front of a door that said 15. "My arm's about to fall off."

"I was hoping you'd say that," Wendell said. He had a sour nervous look and there was sweat pouring off his face. "I ain't young enough for this shit anymore."

I set the toolbox down. It made a loud clang that raced up the concrete stairwell and then cascaded back in a wave of echoes. Wendell took out a pack of Marlboros.

"Smoke?" he said.

"Gave it up," I said. "Long time ago."

Wendell thumped the pack with his finger, and a cigarette popped out. He lit up, took a long, ragged drag. Wendell carried a smell with him, like the inside of an old bar.

"You really went to Maxwell?" he said.

"Twenty months," I said.

"Hard time," he said.

"I guess," I said.

Wendell sucked on the cigarette, pulling it deep into his lungs. "Did you ever . . . ?" He was going to ask me something, but then he didn't.

"No," I said. "I was lucky."

"Nah," he said after a minute. "Me neither." He had a sad, dreamy look in his eyes, thinking back about it.

"You said something about thirteen hundred on the outside," Wendell said after a couple minutes.

I took out a stack of fifties I'd gotten from Jordan after dinner, counted out twenty-six of them into Wendell's hand.

"Thanks," he said. He folded the bills once, stuffed them in the front pocket of his pants.

"Wait," I said. "Here." I handed him the rest of the stack, the full three grand.

"We ain't finished yet," he said. "Hell, we ain't hardly even started."

"That's okay," I said. He folded the rest of the bills, put them in his pockets. I thought about Maxwell, about what it was like being there. I didn't want that again, never again. I didn't want anybody to go through that. "Can I give you some advice, Wendell?"

"Blair." Wendell pointed to the stitching, Blair, inside the white oval on his jacket.

"Can I give you some advice?"

Wendell shrugged, dropped his cigarette on the floor.

"My advice," I said, "don't ever do this again."

Wendell stepped on his cigarette, ground it into the metal plate at the lip of the stair. He looked at the name stitched on my jacket. "Sure, Woody," he said. "Whatever you say."

We stood on the landing in front of a metal door, the number 41 stenciled on it. After Wendell finished his third cigarette, ground it into the concrete, he said: "Here's how it works. If anybody comes up to us, asks us what we're doing, I do the talking. We're from U.S. Protective, twenty-four-hour response team, had a battery failure on the silent alarm circuit. Okay?"

"Okay."

"They ask you anything technical, just say something about how we got a defective microprocessor, whole mess of them from Hong Kong, keeps draining the battery on the silent alarm."

"Defective microprocessor draining the battery."

"That's good, Woody. Don't say another goddamn thing. Not another goddamn word. That clear? Just smile, act relaxed."

Wendell took a tool belt out of his kit, hung it around his waist, and peeked out the door.

"It's cool," he said, and we walked out into the hallway. The elevator bank was beside us, two elevators on each side of the hall, plush carpet on the floor, peach color. At one end of the hallway was an oak door. At the other was the standard wall of smoked glass, double doors in the middle of it. The name of Tate's firm was etched into the glass on the left side of the door with a little gold border running around it.

Behind the doors sat a small desk with carved legs, nothing sitting on it but a phone. There were two groups of furniture, chairs, some couches, two coffee tables—nice reproductions. They were shooting for the English gentlemen's club look. A couple hunting prints, heavy-shanked horses straining o'er hill and dale. Two hallways led back from the sides of the lobby.

Wendell set the tool box beside the door, rapped on the glass a couple of times, making a lot of noise.

"Hey," I said. "You trying to wake up the neighborhood?"

"You got to do that," he said, "just in case some dingbat's in there hanging around at midnight. I've even had people let me in once or twice." We waited. Nobody came.

"So what's the program?" I said.

Wendell ran his fingers along the bottom of the door. "Nice work. We got a contact embedded in the floor, that'll take a while. Then we go in, find the console. It'll be back in one of those hallways somewhere." Wendell pointed. "Then probably we got ultrasonics after that. If I can defeat the console, you'll be okay. First thing, though, I got to pick the lock." There was a brass lock on the door, belly height. Wendell bent down and looked at it. "Not too bad."

He took a flat leather case about the size of his hand out of the toolbox. Inside the leather case were some flat pieces of steel, two prongs bent ninety degrees at one end, along with a bunch of tiny steel wires that looked like miniature allen wrenches.

Wendell took out one of the flat pieces of steel, tried to slide the prongs into the keyhole. Too big. He tried another, and it slid in smoothly, leaving a space in the center of the keyhole. Then he took one of the little wires and slid that into the keyhole so that about three inches of it stuck out.

"Okay," Wendell said. "I'm a little out of practice, but I'll give you maybe ninety percent with this type of lock. If I can't get it in four, five minutes, you gonna have to go through with a sledgehammer."

He leaned over the lock, looking down at it, took the flat piece of steel in his left hand and applied a little pressure. Then he took the little bent wire in his right hand, the end of the wire cushioned in the palm of his hand, and started flicking it gently with his index finger, pulling it slowly in and out of the keyhole. I looked at my watch. Twenty-one past twelve.

Wendell kept flicking and flicking, scraping the little wire in and out. It seemed like it took forever, in and out, with this scraping noise. Wendell stopped, shook his head.

"Shit," he said. "I just realized I was turning it the wrong way." Twenty-six past twelve.

Wendell started again, this time pulling up gently on the piece of steel. In and out, in and out. Twelve-thirty-two.

"You weren't serious about the sledgehammer, were you?" I said. Wendell stopped, turned around, and gave me a pissed-off look. His eyes were wet and bloodshot, and I could smell beer on his breath.

Wendell said, "Man, Woody, I got to have me a cigarette before I die."

"Fine, take a break," I said. But he was already gone, back into the stairs. I picked up his tool kit, hustled back to join him. I didn't want to stand there any more than I had to.

Wendell didn't look too good. The veins were standing out on his arms. His face was blotchy, dripping sweat. He was scared.

"I thought you were supposed to be some king-hell B&E man," I said.

"I'd get about a A-minus on alarms," he said. "But locks, shoot, maybe a C-plus." He tried to smile but it didn't come off too well. He was dragging hard on the cigarette, then letting the smoke dribble out his nose.

"Come to think of it," he said. "I'd really hate like hell to go back to prison."

"Come on," I said. "I gave you the whole three grand already. At least get me through the damn door."

"No," he said. "It's not that. I'll do what I said. I ain't fucking with you." He shrugged—a kind of sad, worn-out gesture. "I was just thinking, that's all. Just thinking."

He finished the cigarette. I felt bad for bringing him here. Ray was right. He shouldn't have come.

"You ready?" I said.

"Yeah," Wendell said. "Let's do it, brother." He smiled, his face lit up like a flashbulb, then the smile was gone again.

He slouched back to the door, slid the tools into the lock, started flicking the wire, in and out, in and out. Twelve-forty. Twelve-forty-three. Twelve-forty-seven.

Wendell had dark blue circles under his arms, sweating all the way through his jacket. The wire scraped, scraped, scraped. It sounded like a dental instrument, made my teeth hurt.

Then there was a noise, BONG, the elevator doors opening.

I said, "Shit."

A loud click shimmered through the glass. It was the lock. Wendell had it open. Wendell looked at me for a second, panic on his face. It was the moment of truth. If we closed the door and stood there looking like fools, the worst that could happen to us would be some kind of bullshit charge, felony trespass, something like that.

On the other hand, if we opened the door, bluffed a little bit, maybe we could pull it off. But if our bluff didn't work, the charge would be breaking and entering, a big-time felony. Enough to put a loser like Wendell back in jail for a while.

Enough to put me back in jail for good.

Wendell was thinking the same thing, calculating, you could see it all running across his face.

"Fuck it," Wendell said. He pushed the door open.

Three men and a woman—all of them decked out in Brooks Brothers suits—walked out of the elevator. Midnight, they looked like they'd had a long, long day.

Wendell turned around, smiled. He looked, I don't know, relieved somehow.

He said: "Hey, great, fellows! Glad to see you!"

The four suits looked at us, the bag of funny tools, the wet boots. They didn't know what to think.

"Excuse me?" one of the suits said. He was about thirty, with horn-rimmed glasses, thinning hair.

"U.S. Protective! Twenty-four-hour response team," Wendell said, full of juice all of a sudden. "May I ask if you gentlemen—ma'am!—if you folks were here approximately twenty-seven minutes ago?" He looked at me. "Twenty-seven? That right, Woody?"

"Yeah," I said. I had no idea what he was talking about.

"Silent alarm went off here, our sensors back at the central office said twelve-twenty-two A.M. Were you folks here at that point in time? Notice any suspicious activity?"

The suits looked at each other. The woman said, "Oh. No, huh-uh. When did we leave? Eleven-thirty. Sorry."

"I tell you what," Wendell said. "I'm a little curious—"

"Look," the guy with thin hair said. "I'm sure you've got it under control. We've got an important conference call coming in about two minutes." He gave us a patronizing smile. "International."

"Okay," Wendell said. "Let me know, you see anything suspicious, anybody might of breached the perimeter."

"It's those microchips again," I said, "the ones from Hong Kong."

The suits hustled off down the hallway on the left. "Oh, wait!" Wendell called after them. "Punch in the code before the dang thing goes off again."

The guy with the thin hair looked back at us, a funny look on his face. "Peculiar that the alarm went off that way," he said. "We forgot to turn it on before we left."

After the suits went away, Wendell said. "Oh man oh man oh man." He had a used-up look on his face.

"You okay?" I said.

"I think I'm gonna lose it," he said. "My nerves are shot."

"Hit the road," I said. "Get while the getting's good."

Wendell looked at me for minute, shrugged. He looked like he'd aged ten years since this afternoon, tiny creases stacked up in the skin around his eyes. His hair was wet with sweat, and little red veins had started to light up at the end of his nose. "I can't do this again," he said. "I just can't do it, I can't."

"And thanks for the help," I said.

"I'll make a deal with you," he said. "When you see Ray, tell him I decided not to come. Tell him I never showed."

He took the roll of money out of his pocket—the twenty-eight hundred I'd given him on the stairs—and set it on the antique reproduction receptionist's desk.

Wendell walked out the door, down the hall, the tool kit banging against his leg. Then he was gone.

I picked up the two rolls of fifties, squeezed them together in my hand. The cash was warm, damp with sweat, and smelled like stale beer.

"It's a deal," I said.

I went back into the dark hallway. It turned right, down a long, straight hall. That was Keenan's office at the far end. I hedgehogged it from doorway to doorway, hearing the voices of the suits coming from somewhere. I couldn't see where they were. A streak of light shot down the hall. Someone opening a door. I jumped into a dark office. The door closed; the light went away.

I went down to the end of the hallway. Tate's door was open, but the office was dark. I went in, closed the door just enough that no one from the hallway could see me.

The moonlight was strong in the room. Strong enough I didn't need any lights on. I got my bearings, looked at the wall of filing cabinets. Second from the left, bottom drawer. This shouldn't be too hard. I had a little pry bar, eight inches long, in my back pocket. I bent over the cabinet, slid the pry bar into the lip of the drawer, right next to the lock.

I was about to give the bar a yank when I heard voices, voices coming down the hall, muffled footsteps. Was it just the suits? I couldn't take that chance. The voices were getting closer. There was no good place to hide. Under the desk? Behind the couch over by the window?

I noticed the door next to me, the door to Tate's private bathroom. The voices were getting louder and louder. I opened the door to the bathroom, jumped in, closed the door.

A ribbon of light appeared around the margin of the bathroom door. Voices in the room. I crouched behind the door in the half dark. There was a shower stall with a glass door next to me, a vanity, and toilet next to that.

The first voice was Keenan's. "I would appreciate your taking no action without my attorney present," Keenan was saying. "I am very disturbed about this."

"We got a warrant, feel free to take a look at it." It was a laconic, take-no-shit voice. A cop. "It's a good warrant. You can bring down your attorney or not, sir. That's not my concern. But we gonna make the search right now, sir."

"I think that would be unwise, Sergeant." Tate's voice.

"We got a warrant, we gonna make the search, get out of your hair. End of story."

I heard the squawk box come on, beeping as Keenan punched in a phone number. A sleepy voice answered, asked who the hell it was, twelve-thirty at night.

"This is Tate Keenan. I'm at my office. I would appreciate your coming down immediately."

The sleepy voice changed. "Ah! Tate! Absolutely. Any explanation as to what this is about?"

"Immediately," Tate said, and the dial tone came on.

"Excuse me, do you have keys to these filing cabinets, Mr. Keenan?" Another cop, this one a little more deferential.

"Those are sensitive files. Those files are protected by attorney-client privilege."

"Contraband," said the first cop. "Contraband, sir. That isn't covered by attorney-client privilege, you can look it up. Now we got a warrant here, been worked out real carefully. Judge wasn't happy about us coming, okay, so the warrant's detailed out real clear, what we *can* do, what we *can't*. We look one place, we look for one thing. If you got the thing we looking for, it goes out with us. If you don't, we close the drawer and get on out of here. Now, sir, you want to supply us with the key to this here file drawer or you want us to bust the lock?"

There was a pause. "One moment," Tate said. I heard a drawer opening, a jingle of keys.

This was too much. Unless I was way offtrack, somebody had been issued a warrant to find the bonds. The question was who? And how did they know the bonds were there?

"It's one of these three," said Keenan.

"You want to do the honors, Johnny?" said the first cop.

I heard the keys jingle, some grunting as the second cop tried them out, one after the other. Then I heard a click, metal scraping on metal, a drawer opening.

"Lookee here," the second cop said. "Just like that warrant says."

"Gray metal box," the sergeant said. "You want to take it out, Johnny, set it on the desk?" Something clunked, metal on wood. "Got anything you'd like to say about this box, Mr. Keenan?" the sergeant said.

"I think we'll wait on that until my attorney arrives."

"Johnny, you can close that drawer now, give the keys back to this gentleman," the sergeant said.

The file drawer made a scraping noise, closed with a thump. The keys jingled again.

"We got a couple brief questions we need to ask you, sir," the sergeant said. "We could take you down the station if you prefer, but since your lawyer gonna be coming anyway, we could do it here, save you the trouble."

We waited. In the other room, no one spoke. I was afraid to move, afraid they could hear me breathe, hear my knuckles crack, my bones squeak. My leg started to cramp. I rocked back against the shower door, slowly shifting my weight. Everything was absolutely quiet. I looked at my watch. One-twenty-five. One-thirty. No one was talking in the other room.

Twenty till two. Where the hell was Keenan's lawyer?

"Sergeant," Tate's voice. "If you have no objection, I'm going to use the rest room."

"Be my guest." The sergeant making a wise cop joke.

What now? I stood up, slid the frosted-glass shower door open. It sounded as loud as a gunshot to me. I got in the shower, closed the door, tried to mash myself into the corner.

The door opened, the light came on, a dark shape passed in front of the frosted glass, was gone. I heard Tate unzip, water flowing into water, another zip. The toilet flushed, the tap came on.

The dark shape appeared in front of the shower again. The blob where Tate's head was changed colors, from brown to pinkish, then brown again. My heart was going crazy. Tate stopped. His head went from brown to pinkish again. He was looking at the shower door. He just stood there a minute, looking. Another pinkish blob swam up, materialized into a hand. Tate was holding the shower door handle. He stood there a second, opened the shower door.

He wore a blank expression on his face, the closest he came to looking puzzled. Then he saw me. His face didn't change at all. He just looked at me, stared straight into my eyes.

"Sergeant?" Tate said in his monotone voice.

"Yes, *sir.*" The cop, with that ironic sound to his voice.

Tate stood there for another second, looking at me. I couldn't tell what was going through his mind. He just stood there watching, trying to figure things out.

Then he closed the shower door.

"Never mind," Tate said. "I just thought of something. But I believe it can wait until my attorney arrives." He turned off the light, walked out, closed the door.

I sank down in the corner and huddled into a ball.

The lawyer finally showed at about ten till two. He and Tate stepped outside to talk then came back into the office.

"Sergeant," said the attorney, "I'd like to know what you intend to do next."

"We got about five questions," the sergeant said, "that we'd like to ask your client here, and then we'll be on our way."

There was some whispering between Tate and his lawyer.

"I would request that I be able to record this conversation," the lawyer said.

"Fine," the sergeant said. "Johnny, you taking this down?"

"Yes, sir."

There was a click, the lawyer turning his dictaphone on.

"Okay. Mr. Keenan, do you reconnize this box? I'll identify it since we on tape here, gray metal cash box, what would you say? Fifteen by twelve inches?"

"No, Sergeant, I have never seen that box in my life."

"Mr. Keenan, do you own this box?"

"No, Sergeant, I have never seen that box in my life."

"Does it belong to anyone you know?"

"I have no knowledge of that one way or other. I have never before seen this box."

"Mr. Keenan, do you know what the contents of this box might happen to be?"

"No, sir, I do not."

"Now you did see us remove that box from this filing cabinet, correct?"

"Correct."

"And would it be accurate to say this is your personal filing cabinet?"

"It belongs to the firm. But, yes, it is for my exclusive use."

"And who might have access to this drawer besides yourself?"

"My secretary certainly. But anybody in the firm potentially could have access. If the door were unlocked. If no one were paying attention to who came and went." Pause. "Or if someone broke into my office. It could be anybody."

"Uh-huh," said the sergeant. "Thank you, sir, I believe that'll do it." The tape clicked off. "Johnny you want to give the gentleman a receipt for the box. Then bag it and tag it."

There was some scuffling around.

"Oh, yeah," the sergeant said. "Out of curiosity, you seen anybody tonight, anybody wandering around that's not supposed to be here. Alarm going off? Anything suspicious?"

There was no sound in the room. No sound but my heart hammering against my ribs. I felt the sweat on my chest, my forehead, my scalp.

"No," Tate said. "Nothing out of the ordinary."

"You always work this late?" the sergeant said.

"Not infrequently," Tate said.

"Gracious!" the sergeant said, still playing wiseass. "Y'all have a good evening." I heard the policemen's footsteps, moving down the hall.

Tate had a brief conversation with his lawyer, then the lawyer went away, too.

"You may feel free to come out, Mr. Vine," Tate said.

I came out. Tate was sitting in his chair, arms crossed, looking at me.

"Tell me about the box," he said.

"You're a funny guy," I said. Tate kept watching me, nothing showing. I said: "Why didn't you tell them where I was?"

"Instinct," he said.

"Instinct? You, instinct?"

"It is rather uncharacteristic, isn't it?" he said. He came close to smiling. But he didn't, not quite. "Seriously, Mr. Vine, what was in the box?"

"You know what was in the box," I said. "Nine point two million dollars worth of Singapore Harbor bonds. Roger's bonds."

"You just keep surprising me," he said. "I'm just not sure what you gained by planting them here."

"Planting them?"

"They didn't get there by magic."

"Tate," I said. "Tate, old buddy of mine, I didn't come here to plant them, I came here to *steal* the damn things."

Keenan put a hand to his chin. "Fascinating." His face as emotional as slate. Then, after a few seconds: "Bobby, I'm going to have to do something about you."

"Yeah," I said. "But not tonight."

And I got the hell out of there.

6

Tate's Deal

CHAPTER 1

"**L**et me ask you this, Ray," I said. "Let's say you've got something that's not yours, let's say a stolen TV, hidden in your office. The cops show up, they have a warrant to look for the TV. Now just as they're about to haul off and ask you some questions, you find some guy in your bathroom, somebody who's broken into your office. What do you do?"

"I don't know," Ray said. "I kind of like the dark one. With the big stripes." He was standing in front of a dressing mirror at Alfred G. Detwiler Custom Tailoring. He had his arms up in the air, frozen in this orator pose, a long swatch of cloth hanging off each shoulder—like Huey Long in a pinstriped Batman cape. The tailor, an Armenian guy with pins in his mouth, was smoothing down the fabric.

"I tell you this," the tailor said. "Very impressive fabric. Ninety-seven threads to the inch. Very continental, you think?"

"Chalk stripes," I said. "I don't know. That's pretty strong."

"Tell you the truth," Ray said, "I'm confused. I don't get the point of your story."

"Yeah," I said. "I guess not."

"Maybe something double-breasted, mmmm?" said the tailor, talking out of the side of his mouth. I wondered if he ever swallowed the pins. "What do you think, what do you think, mmmm?"

Ray looked over at me, trying to get some arbitration. The Armenian was upselling him, going for the two-hundred-buck-a-yard English flannel with the chalk stripes. That was going to cost him close to two grand if he went pleated, cuffed, double-breasted, all that stuff.

"It's not going to be cheap," I said. I was thinking about last night, about why Keenan didn't turn me in to the cops. I couldn't figure it out. The whole damn thing just didn't add up.

"Hey, Counselor, you only live once," Ray said. "Let's go with them big stripes, Mr. Zadigian. And, ah, tell me about this double-breasted thing."

"Like this," the tailor said, crossing his hands, flat, in front of his belly button. "Button here, button there, mmmm? Double-breasted? Very impressive."

"Let's do it," Ray said. He was still posing with the fabric, hands in the air. Zadigian, the tailor, took the samples off his shoulders, gave them a big showy snap, doing a little routine so we'd see how hard he was working for us. Ray put his arms down. "Where are we, Counselor?"

"Suit number four," I said. "Thursday, I guess."

"Perhaps a houndstooth check, mmmm? Glen plaid? Something like this?"

Ray looked at me. That was how it worked. The tailor talked to Ray; Ray looked at me; I told the tailor what to do. "Glen plaid, yeah," I said. "But, tell you the truth I don't know if Ray's ready for houndstooth yet."

"We got just the thing, mmmm? Several weights. Very impressive." Zadigian flipped the cloth under his arm, trotted through the canvas drape at the back of the fitting room.

"The cops are in the office?" Ray says. He's standing on the riser in front of the dressing mirror, looking like Jack Nicklaus on a frisky day: bright yellow pants, shiny white shoes with tassels, a shirt you'd put somewhere in the vicinity of cranberry. "You're in the office? This guy Keenan catches you while the cops are pulling this cash box with the bonds in it out his file drawer? Is that what I'm hearing here?"

"Right. I'm in the bathroom, Tate comes in to take a leak and finds me. Nowhere to go, right? Tate starts to call the cops in there, and then he changes his mind."

"Stolen shit in his files, you just broke into his office, cops in the room?"

"Right."

Ray thought about it. "He should of called the cops—'Officer, holy shit, there's a man in the crapper!' type thing—

told them you must of planted it. Been easy to blame the whole thing on you."

"That's what I was thinking."

Zadigian came back with four bolts of glen plaid. "Feel, mmmm?" he said. "Marvelous hand, drape like a sculpture."

Ray rubbed the cloth dubiously. "Sound to me," he said, "like old Tate didn't know what the hell was in that box."

When we got back from Alfred G. Detwiler Custom Tailoring, the message light on the answering machine was going crazy. I hit PLAY. Four messages from Jeannie, progressively more urgent. One from Ed, one from Sarah, one from Clement, one from Scheib, one from Zell. One from Dick Bloom, pissed off. Two from Jordan. He sounded scared about something.

The shit was starting to hit the fan.

I called Jeannie first. "What happened last night, Bobby? You never called." She was annoyed with me.

"Sorry, I tried this morning first thing. I must have missed you."

"What happened?"

I told her about Tate, about the police showing up before I could get to the bonds.

"The police!" she said. "What were the police doing there?"

"I am extremely, extremely curious to get the answer to that myself," I said.

"Did they arrest him?" she said.

"Nope. Just asked some questions."

"My God," she said. "What was going through their minds?"

"They didn't even open the box, I don't think. I'm not even sure the police knew exactly what was in it." There was a short silence. "How's the deal going?" I said. "Are you lining up the financing okay? It ought to help, having the bonds back."

"Well, they're not back yet," she said. "Not as far as the banks are concerned."

"I've got a message from Zell. Since Excor is general

partner of Health Systems, the police probably contacted him first," I said. "I'll let you know what I find out."

"We've got to get him, Bobby," Jeannie had a harsh rasp in her voice. "We've got to nail him to the wall."

"Who, Zell?"

"Who do you think? Tate Keenan. He's behind all of this. He's behind it all."

"I agree," I said. "But I'm not sure quite how to go about it."

"I'm going to wreck him," she said.

I called Jon Scheib.

"You read the article?" he said.

"Nope."

"First section, page two, column five. You're gonna love it. After you read it, maybe give me a call?"

I called Ed Mance.

"Ed."

"Bobby. I been keeping tabs on your case. Them bonds you told me about. They showed up last night."

"Oh." I wasn't sure what to say.

"Guy called in, said he had evidence that stolen property of his was in this lawyer's office. He said not only that, we had to move fast, they were about to move the bonds, hide them someplace. Said we needed to catch them right at midnight. We had some trouble getting the warrant, this lawyer's a real bigshot asshole, right, so they had to arm wrestle a little with the judge. Anyway they get there late, but they're still in time to find the bonds."

"Who called in this complaint?" I said.

"Guy that worked with Roger, I forget his name."

"Zell? Harvey Zell?"

"Sounds about right."

I thought about it. "Twelve o'clock? Zell said they should go in at twelve o'clock?"

"Yeah," Ed said. He waited a second. "You know anything about this?"

I called Sarah.

"Thank God," she said. "You're safe."

I told her what happened the night before.

"Tate *saw* you?"

"That's right."

"Oh, Bobby. Oh, Bobby. I don't know what to say. That's terrible."

"The good news is the bonds are back. The bad news is that I'm not any closer to putting Clement in prison for killing Roger. Or any closer to Keenan, either."

"Oh, Bobby."

"Yeah, I know. Look," I said. "I've got a question. What have you been working on lately?"

"The last few weeks?" she said. "Mostly the RichCo deal. Why?"

"Not the last few days," I said. "The last few weeks."

"I *have* been working on RichCo for—well, at least two weeks now."

I thought about it. "Do me a favor," I said. "I know you're busy, but if you have a spare minute could you write down kind of a chronology of the deal—what happened when."

"I guess," she said.

"Just fax it over to me," I said. I told her Ray's fax number. "Oh, and while you're at it, have you seen any of Jeannie's financial statements lately?"

"Sure. They're part of the recap circular we're putting together."

"Could you send them, too?"

"I don't know, Bobby. I mean strictly speaking that's kind of privileged stuff."

"It's okay," I said. "I've already been disbarred."

Sarah snorted. "Okay, Bobby. Okay. The financials, too."

"I owe you."

"And I will collect," Sarah said. "Maybe even tonight."

I had written down a list of the calls. Bloom, no, didn't feel like talking to him. Clement, maybe later. I was going to have to come up with a damn good story to keep him from going to the police with the pistol. Jordan Foote. He sounded pretty hot about something.

I dialed his office. "Bobby!" There was a shrill edge to his voice.

"What's going on Jordan?"

"I have uncovered something," he said. "Something unbelievable. I've miscalculated about you. Miscalculated drastically."

"What? Tell me."

"I can't talk here," he said. His voice was low, strained.

"Are you okay, Jordan? You sound a little shaken up about something."

"I'm afraid I'm in a terrible dilemma," he said. "An ethical dilemma. I need to speak to you. Alone."

"Fine," I said. "Where?"

"I don't want anyone to see us," he said. "Not together. It can't be my office."

"Whatever. Name the place."

"Piedmont Park," he said. "Do you know the bridge that comes in from Monroe?"

"The one that goes over that big drainage ditch?"

"Yes. Can you be there in ten minutes?"

"Make it twenty," I said.

"I'll be waiting."

As soon as I set the phone down, it rang again. It was Harv Zell.

"So you got the bonds back," I said.

"Yeah," he said. "I guess I owe you an apology. It's looking like something else was going on than I thought."

"I hear you were the one who called in the dogs."

"It's weird. I got a phone call last night, a lady who wouldn't give her name, said she knew where the Health Systems money was. She said Roger had converted it to bonds, passed it to Tate. Told me where it was, the whole schmear. I mean exactly where it was."

"This caller, she didn't say who she was?"

"Wouldn't say. She had a funny accent."

"Funny how?"

"You know, foreign."

"French, German, Chinese, what?"

"I'm from Brooklyn, what do you want. It was fucking foreign."

"Give it a wild guess."

"I don't know, maybe Spanish, Puerto Rican, something like that. Why?"

I drove down to Piedmont Park. The place Jordan was talking about was a little stone bridge that went into the parking lot next to the pond. I drove over the bridge, didn't see Jordan, parked in the lot. From where I was standing I could see the bridge, the algae pond, the paths radiating out across the park, the big trees, the back of the Piedmont Driving Club. No Jordan.

I looked at my watch. Twelve-thirty-five. I was late. Jordan was later.

I walked over to the bridge, sat down on the curb and waited. It was a nice little bridge, gray stone, arched over a concrete trough about fifty feet below the center of the bridge. A couple of guys, gay weight lifters with tank tops and crew cuts, walked over the bridge. A black kid, maybe seventeen, rode by on a bike. He wore an L.A. Raiders hat, backwards, and his bike was too small. He rode slowly around the parking lot, standing up on the pedals because the seat was too low.

Over by the little boathouse on the pond, a guy was dancing around on roller skates. He had a boom box on the ground, but I couldn't hear the music. He was pretty good, but he danced like a sissy, throwing his hips around. Sometimes he rolled his head back so his sunglasses reflected the blue-white sky.

I started getting hot, annoyed, wondering what was going on with Jordan. He said he would be there in ten minutes. It had taken me more than twenty minutes because of the call from Harv Zell, and Jordan still wasn't here. My shirt started to get sticky, and I could feel the sweat beading up in my eyebrows.

The kid with the Raiders cap rode back across the bridge on his little bike, humping up and down. He slowed when he got close to me. " 'Scuse me," he said. "Y'all know what time it is?"

I looked at my watch. "Twelve-forty," I said. "Twelve-forty-two." The black kid looked at me, appraising me. I don't know what for.

"Yo, thanks," the kid said. He humped up on the pedals again, getting ready to ride off.

"Got a question," I said.

"Yeah?" He looked at me, his eyelids hanging heavy over his eyes. He had that city look, taking no shit.

"You been around here for a while?"

He shrugged, looked off into the distance.

"Why I'm asking," I said. "I was supposed to meet a guy here a few minutes ago. White guy, good tan, probably wearing a nice suit. He looks kind of gay."

"Man, it's faggot city around here," he said. "Lot a faggots."

"In a suit? Standing on the bridge like he was waiting for somebody?"

He shrugged again. Not his problem. "Sorry, man," he said. "Maybe ax Honey Bear."

"Honey Bear?"

"Dude on the skates." He lifted his chin at the dancer over by the pond. "He watch everybeddy," the kid said. He humped off on his little bike.

I waited another five minutes, then walked over toward the dancer on skates. One hand was flat on his belly, the other floated in the air like he was cradling a brandy snifter. He was grinding his hips, sort of a solo lambada on wheels. There was Latin music on the boom box, loud, so the bass was distorted and crunchy-sounding. Honey Bear had a dancer's build, no fat on him, a tight red tank top, black and yellow biking pants. His skin was a shiny black. You couldn't tell if he was watching you or not, because of the mirrored sunglasses.

"You Honey Bear?" I said.

He stopped doing the lambada with himself, skated around in a couple of lazy, effortless circles. I could feel him looking at me behind the glasses. "Who told you that?" he said.

"Kid on the bike." I pointed over at the bridge, but the kid was gone.

"He making some shit up, girl." Honey Bear's shoulders

were still dancing, the muscles snaking around under the skin. He had a little pout to his lips.

"It doesn't matter," I said. "I just wanted to ask if you had seen a guy hanging around over there. White guy in a suit. Maybe fifteen, twenty minutes ago."

"I couldn't say," he said.

"Meaning what?"

Honey Bear pursed his lips. "Now don't get disappointed. I think he got a date already."

"A *date?*"

"Under the bridge, girl. Under the *bridge*. Him and his date went under the bridge."

"Are you saying he met somebody already?"

"Lot of boys go under the bridge. Ain't nothing wrong with that. It's a popular place. Him and a little dude with black hair went under the bridge. I didn't see either one of them come back up, but they bound to had they fun, be finished by now."

"Black hair?" I had a bad feeling all of a sudden. "A short guy, black hair?"

"Yes." He said it primly, like a girl in school. Another move, some more lambada. The dancer's hand was crawling across his belly toward his groin.

"Shit!" I said. I turned around and sprinted back toward the bridge.

"Girl, don't be so sensitive," the dancer called after me. "He just having some fun."

There was a little path down the side of the bridge, underneath some trees. I ran down it, stepping over a bunch of bottles—Thunderbird, MD 20/20, 190 grain. Wino country. A pair of men's underwear, ripped in half. An alternator, rusted.

A tree at the bottom of the path had funny-looking fruit hanging off it, long, wrinkly translucent things—like some kind of bean. Most of the fruit was a dull yellow color; some was green, some was red. When I got closer, I saw it wasn't fruit at all. The tree was a little dogwood, its branches hung with condoms.

I skirted by the rubber tree, down into the concrete drainage ditch. It was about forty feet wide, a V-shaped slot with a soft slope down to the center. A green, scummy path trailed down the middle, where the runoff built up. It was quiet down there, like the city had gone away.

I slid down into the center of the concrete ditch, walked toward the bridge, which was about fifty feet away. There was all kinds of junk heaped up under each end of the bridge. From where I was, I couldn't make out what the piles were. When I got closer, I saw an old bureau, half the drawers missing. A couple of chairs. Some rags, bottles, boxes. No Jordan Foote.

I got to the bridge, walked up to the left, the park side. At the top of the trough, there was a red dirt bank, eroded, rocky—no grass, just a little moss. Next to the chest of drawers sat a wooden chair, the rattan seat rotted out. Piles of crap, all over, like homeless people were living under here, accumulating bits of stuff no one else wanted. A shirt, cigarette butts, McDonald's bags. The remains of a couple fires.

Above me the bridge hung low and dark, birds' nests built into the iron superstructure. The ground was mottled green and red, striped here and there with blue-white bird droppings.

"Jordan?" I called. My voice made a clangy echo and then died away. "Jordan?" Nothing. Something didn't feel right.

I walked down the bank, across the concrete trough, over to the other side. More bottles of cheap drink. More McDonald's bags. Whoever lived here was probably filching them from the park, eating scraps out of the trash. There was an office chair, the foam back ripped off of it, sitting behind a card table with wooden legs, a cardboard top. Like an office, presiding over the end of the world. It was a sad place, a place you wouldn't want to end up.

A mattress lay next to the table, the stuffing ripped, the springs showing through. It had a big lump under it, like it was lying on top of a log. There was a lot more depressing junk, half rotted. I won't go into it. It didn't matter. I could see that Jordan wasn't there. A roach scuttled out from under the mattress. I had to get out of there.

I scrambled back down into the concrete sluice and started walking away from the park, thinking maybe Jordan had gone that way. Then I stopped, had a bad thought.

I ran back to the bridge, up the bank, my wingtips slipping on the red clay. The ruined mattress. I picked up a corner of the mattress, hauled on it. The stuffing gave like moist bread, ripping off in my hand. I got a grip on one of the springs, pulled the mattress a few feet, let it fall to the ground.

There was a brown rectangle on the clay where the mattress had lain. In the middle of the rectangle was a man, lying facedown, with his arms up beside his head, one leg canted off to the side at an odd angle. He wore a seersucker suit. You'd have thought he was sleeping, except that the side of his head was leaking red all over the ground. There was a stick next to him, four feet long, an inch or so thick, the end of it blackened and glistening.

"Christ, Jordan," I said. "What did you do?"

It just kept happening. It wouldn't stop. The Big Fear ran through me, coming up out of my belly, running around in my head. There was nothing but death, nothing going on but death.

I couldn't breathe. It was starting again, the fear, the panic. I was dying. I was next. This was all a preamble: Roger, Jordan, Andre, his albino brother, the girl. I felt death coming, running through my heart, my guts, my lungs.

I crouched on the ground—didn't even have the strength to move. I just dropped down on my heels, feeling all this death rolling around inside of me. My breath came too fast and shallow, my heart was kicking and squalling, the tumors were sprouting everywhere. It was all caving in.

I huddled there for a long time.

And then it was over. I got up and looked down at the body, and didn't feel anything, didn't feel anything at all. It was like my emotions had all been cleaned out, everything—good, bad, indifferent—had been purged, sluiced away.

I rolled Jordan's body over, faceup. His eyes were open, one pupil full of blood, the other clogged with dirt. I checked the pockets of his jacket to see if he had brought anything, anything that he had planned to show me. Two tickets to a string quartet at the Arts Center. I wondered vaguely who his disappointed date would be. Nothing else in the jacket. Nothing in the wallet, nothing in his pants. I rolled Jordan's limp body back over on its face. There was nothing else I could do here.

I was going to go back down the bank when I saw a piece of yellow paper sticking out of his fist. I pulled his fingers open, one by one. There was a scrap of yellow paper clenched in his hand. It was about three inches wide, six inches long, perforated along three edges. I put it in my pocket and stood up.

Behind me I heard a noise, a footfall. My heart jumped, and I whipped around. Silhouetted against the brightness outside was a man. He was standing about twenty feet away, looking at me. It was a crazy-looking wino with a red, torn-up face. His pants were held up with a piece of wire.

"Uh-oh," he said.

I looked at the crazy man and then down at the body. "I guess we better call the police," I said.

He looked at me for a minute, like I was nuts. "You may call the po-lice, my friend," he said. He had a soft, deliberate way of speaking, like a Baptist youth minister. "Me, I'm getting the fuck out of here."

CHAPTER 2

I drove over to the Hi-Top Security office on Ponce de Leon, got there about one-thirty, and asked the receptionist if Clement was in. She buzzed him, said he'd be out to see me in a few moments, he was on the phone with a client.

I sat down on a god-awful orange suede couch and picked up a copy of a magazine called *Secure!* from the coffee table. It was full of guys advertising guns and flashlights and kevlar vests, everybody looking serious as hell. I put it down after a minute or two. It was too much. I noticed there was also a copy of the *Journal* on the table. I opened it, looked for Jon Scheib's article. Page two, column five, just like he said.

Board Rift Weakens RichCo's Odds for Independence

ATLANTA—A divided **RichCo** Corp. board of directors failed to respond to the $22-per-share offer by **Evergreen Partners,** L.P., a French-backed investment group, increasing the likelihood of a successful takeover by the partnership.

Analysts had expected an announcement of a competing bid by a management-led group yesterday, but no such announcement has been made, nor has the RichCo board formally responded to Evergreen's offer.

According to a source within RichCo, the board of directors is deeply divided over the Evergreen bid. On one side are supporters of a management buy out led by Chairman Jeannette Richardson.

On the other side are several long-time directors originally appointed by Ms. Richardson's father, Charles G. Richardson, the deceased former chairman of the company. This "old guard" apparently favors accepting an offer from an outside bidder if the offer is deemed reasonable by their bankers. The board has not yet taken a formal vote on the issue.

According to attorney C. Tatum Keenan, an advisor to the French investor group, Evergreen is confident it will complete the deal in short order. "We believe the board will evaluate the offer and accept it. We approached them informally several weeks ago. The response to our initial offer was weak, so we sweetened the pot based on those discussions."

"Their chances for remaining independent are slim right now," says Tinsley Post, a chemical industry analyst with A. G. Edwards & Sons. "It's widely known Jeannie [Richardson] wanted to do an LBO several years ago and couldn't muscle it past the board. I think they've spent too much time bitching at each other and haven't kept their eyes on the ball."

There was some other stuff about bond ratings, stock price history, that kind of thing. Nothing else real important.

"Bobby, Bobby, Bobby!" It was Clement in his little hotshot Italian suit hustling out to see me. The baggy pants and the padded shoulders made him look even shorter than he was. He had his hand out, wanting to shake. I ignored it. "Come on back," Clement said, not bothering to take offense. "We got some shit to talk about."

We went back to his office. It was just an ordinary office, ordinary desk, ordinary LeRoy Neiman print on the wall—a guy hitting a tennis ball, flecks of yellow paint flying out of his head. I expected something flashier, something weirder out of Clement. The only funny thing, he had a picture of himself, framed, sitting on the edge of his own desk. It was a black and white three by five, inside a Lucite frame. He was smiling.

I sat down and looked at Clement's face. He didn't look nervous, angry, worried, juiced up—none of the emotions you'd expect out of a guy who had just killed someone. I picked up the Lucite frame, looked from the picture to the real guy and back.

"*Secure!* magazine," he said.

"What?"

"I was in *Secure!* last month, big feature they called 'Faces to Watch in the Nineties.' Up-and-comers, you know what I mean? They sent me a copy of the original so I figure, what the hell, put it on my desk. Good picture, huh?"

"Well," I said, "it looks like you anyway."

"Ha ha," Clement said. "You got a sense of humor. So what's going on?"

"You tell me," I said.

Clement looked at me like he was trying to figure out what I was talking about. He shrugged. "Let me guess, you made zero progress on getting Roger's bonds back."

"The cops found the bonds," I said. "They're giving them back to Zell over at Excor."

Clement's eyes widened, then he got a pissed-off look in his eyes. "Shit!" He smacked his palms down on the desk, his big lips screwed up and ugly. He stood up, cussed for a while, grabbed the edge of his desk with both hands like he was going to pick the whole thing up and throw it at me.

"You know who had them?" I said.

Clement didn't say anything.

"Tate Keenan," I said.

Clement stared at me for a minute, then sat back down. He had a distant look in his eyes, almost like he thought it was funny. "No kidding?" he said. "No damn kidding?"

I just sat there.

"Okay," Clement said. "Okay. We got some thinking to do, huh?"

"Is that right?" I said.

"Sure. I got to figure out what to do with you." He tried on his shark smile for size.

"Nothing. You've got the gun in the bag, my prints on it. You're still holding all the cards, Clement. There's nothing I can do to hurt you."

Clement thought about it, twitching around, drumming on his desk. "Man," he said finally. "Nine mill, out the window."

"Uh-huh."

He shrugged, spread his big lips. "Easy come, easy go, huh? What a bummer. You remember my philosophy? If you can't win, smile?"

"I thought your philosophy was—"

Clement waved his hand. "Yeah, well, I got a bunch of philosophies."

"Yeah," I said. "Easy come, easy go." I was thinking about Jordan Foote, his head beat in with a stick.

"So I guess it's sayonara for you and me," Clement said. "Back to business, huh?" He gave me the shark smile again. "This thing with Roger, what a tragedy. Maybe I'll mosey down there, see you on death row one of these days."

"That's sweet of you," I said. "But before I go ... what were you doing today? About, say, twelve-thirty?"

Clement narrowed his eyes. "Twelve-thirty. Why?"

"Curious," I said.

"I was down at the health club," he said. "What are you getting at?"

"Health club. Definitely at the health club?"

"Yeah. What are you getting at?"

"I just saw a guy in Piedmont Park about twelve-thirty. Reminded me a lot of you." I studied his face. He was wearing a kind of puzzled look.

"Not me. I left here about quarter till twelve, sometime around then. Went straight over, worked out till about one."

"You got a witness?"

Clement's eyes got thin. "Do I need one?"

"I don't know," I said. "You might."

"Then I got witnesses out the ying-yang." He held up three fingers next to his face. "Scout's honor, my son. You can call. Buckhead Health & Fitness, ask for Judy, the head trainer. We were working on my glutes together."

"Glutes?"

"Gluteus maximus. You know, the muscle in your ass." He winked, gave me a poon-hunter smile.

I reached into my pocket, pulled out a little piece of yellow paper. It was perforated on three sides, cut clean on the other: a check receipt, the carbon copy off a check register. A check for five grand. There was a line printed across the bottom, PAY TO THE ORDER OF written next to it. Handwritten above the line, carbon copy, it said HI-TOP SECURITY.

I read the name off the corner of the check receipt I'd taken from Jordan Foote's dead hand. "Turnkey Investment Corp. You ever heard of that, Clement?"

"Turnkey," he said. He looked up into the distance like he was thinking about it, twitched, buttoned his jacket, unbuttoned it again. He shook his head. "Turnkey, Turnkey. Rings a bell, man, but I just can't place it."

I looked at him, trying to see into his head. All I saw was a little short guy with an Elvis hairdo, a pinky ring. "That's just what I was thinking," I said. "It rings a bell, but I can't place it." I looked at Clement, looked at the picture on his desk, the one from the magazine. It was a good likeness.

Clement looked at his watch. "Bobby, I got to go. I got to call on a couple clients. You know, taking care of business." He stood up, started out the door.

I picked up his picture off the desk, looked at it for a second. Clement smiling, big grin. It was a spooky picture.

I slid the photo into my pocket.

Back at Ray's the fax had come through from Sarah. It was sitting in a little rolled-up pile in the rec room. Following

Sarah's cover sheet were a financial statement and a handwritten sheet that said RichCo Chronology at the top.

I looked at the financial first.

Unaudited Statement of Net Worth
Jeannette Richardson
Dated June 31, 1993

ASSETS

Cash and liquid securities.........	$12,345,777
Nonliquid securities (limited partnership).............................	8,000,000
Annual trust payment (estimated unpaid quarterly installment)	366,000
Home equity...............................	327,456
Other real estate........................	405,211
Tax loss carryforwards...............	26,373,877
Other assets	596,000
TOTAL	48,414,321

LIABILITIES

Home mortgage..........................	$ 46,312
Investment real estate mortgages..	275,488
Consumer installment credit......	12,467
TOTAL	334,267
NET WORTH	$48,080,054

It was a weird financial statement. Somewhere along the line, she had taken a bath, lost twenty-six million dollars. That was what the tax loss carryforwards were. She was allowed to write that amount off on her taxes in the future. It was, strictly speaking, an asset, but it wasn't much use in raising money to buy RichCo stock. I wondered where she had lost all that money.

The rest of it was pretty straightforward. The eight-million-dollar nonliquid securities item had to be her Health Systems investment. The rest was houses, cars, the usual stuff.

What it told me was that, even with a lot of leverage, a lot of borrowed money, Jeannie Richardson wasn't going to be able to pull off a buy out of RichCo by herself. Back in the mideighties it had been possible to turn ten or twenty million in hard assets into three or four hundred million (which was about how much it would cost to buy RichCo from its public shareholders). But these days lenders were not putting up money for deals with that kind of leverage. If she didn't come up with another hundred million or so, somehow, Evergreen was going to get RichCo and there would be nothing she could do about it.

No wonder there hadn't been an announcement about a management-led buy out yet. Jeannie didn't have the cash to do the deal by herself. She was stalling Tate Keenan. Or just plain old bluffing.

I read over the chronology of the deal that Sarah had put together for me, and then rewrote it on a legal pad, adding some dates of my own. This is what the final product looked like:

RichCo Chronology

Initial discussions between Evergreen and J. Richardson	July 7
Board retains investment bankers (Wexler Brothers) to advise and/or raise money	July 7
Evergreen offer made privately: $20/share	July 9
Roger's scam is discovered	July 11
J. Richardson proposes management buy out	July 12
Roger is killed	July 13
Board votes down Jeannie's LBO as proposed	July 13
I'm arrested	July 14
Jeannie bails me out	July 16
Evergreen announces tender offer $22/share	July 20

So Jeannie knew that Tate Keenan was coming after her company a full week before she bailed me out of jail and two weeks before the tender offer was officially announced. That was a lot of time, under the circumstances. I was a little confused about some things. When she sprang me, Jeannie said that she was in the middle of a deal, but she didn't say what the deal was, that it was RichCo itself she was trying to buy.

I drove over to Piedmont Park. There were cops swarming around the bridge, stringing up yellow plastic tape. I looked for Honey Bear, the roller-skate dancer, but he wasn't there—not next to the pond, anyway—so I walked around the pond, over toward the big stage where they have the weekend jazz shows, summer pops series, that kind of thing. When I got to the other side of the pond, there was Honey Bear, radio on the ground, dancing.

I called to him. "Honey Bear!"

He looked over at me. "Shit!" he said, and he started skating away from me, hauling ass.

"Wait!" I said. But he wasn't listening. He even left his radio. What was he afraid of? I ran after him, yelling his name. He started skating up the path toward the Driving Club, losing speed on the hill. I gained on him, my lungs straining. But even though I had closed the gap to maybe twenty feet of him by the time he hit the top of the hill, it wasn't close enough to catch him before the path leveled off and he was able to pick up some speed.

Then he was crouched down again, going flat out with his arms swinging up over his head. He worked up a nice speed-skater rhythm, covering a lot of ground. He had gone maybe a couple hundred feet, leaving me in the dust, when he made his mistake. He looked over his shoulder, just to make sure he was free.

I guess he was going a little too fast. Maybe when he looked back at me, he didn't notice something in front of him—a rock, a twig. Or maybe he just lost his balance. Whatever it was, he went flying—pitching over headfirst, flipping twice before he stopped.

He lifted his head once or twice, then laid back down. I ran up, leaned over him. "You okay?" I said.

He had ripped a nice burn down the side of his face, blood welling up on his cheek, and his sunglasses had popped off. He just lay there for a minute, breathing raggedly.

"Honey Bear," I said. "Honey Bear, are you okay?"

He sat up slowly. "Girl, I am so embarrassed," he said. "I have not fallen, I mean, in *years*." He felt the side of his face, softly, pressing on it with two fingers.

"Good thing you had the elbow pads on."

"You got that right." Honey Bear stared morosely at the ground.

"Look, I have to ask you a question," I said.

"Man, that dude you was axing me about, he got killed. Cops found him under the bridge."

"I know. I'm trying to find out who did it."

"You a cop. I knew you was a cop." Honey Bear took his fingers away from his face, looked at the slick red liquid on the pink tips of his fingers. "Ahhh, shit. This gone *ruin* my complexion. I worked so hard, get a even complexion."

I pulled the picture out of my pocket that I'd stolen off Clement Crews's desk, stuck it in Honey Bear's face. "The guy that went under the bridge, the short guy with black hair. Is this him?"

"I think I spraint my ankle or something." Honey Bear started taking off his roller skates, undoing the fluorescent yellow laces.

"Is this the guy?" I gave him my prison voice, torquing up the threat level a couple notches.

Honey Bear stopped unlacing, looked at the picture. "Nah, that ain't him."

"You sure? You're not fucking with me?"

"Yeah, man, yeah! Dude at the bridge was darker. Darker complexion. Might of been foreign."

"What kind of foreign?"

"I don't know. Mexican, maybe, I don't know. He was a long way off."

"Absolutely, totally sure?"

"Go on, girl! You think I'm blind? Little Mexican dude, that's what it was." He pulled off his skate, felt his ankle, winced.

"Thanks," I said.

Honey Bear looked up at me, giving me the pitiful face, big eyes. "Girl, can you be a sweetheart, go get my radio? Before somebody be perpetrating it?"

* * *

I drove to Buckhead, found the Buckhead Health & Fitness Center on Pharr Road. Inside it was all mirrors and chrome, guys with huge lumpy chests, like they'd stuffed potatoes under their skin. There was a smell in the air, a smell I can't quite identify except to say I associate it with sex and high school athletics. Body fluids and perfumes, I guess.

I walked up to a big desk at the front.

"Can I help you?" It was a smiling girl with a big chest, a tiny waist, arms like Bruce Lee.

"I'm looking for Judy," I said.

"I'm Judy." She kept smiling, blinking like she had grit in her contacts.

I took out my picture of Clement Crews. "I'm Sergeant Armbruster, Atlanta police. Can you identify this gentleman?"

"Who, Clement?" She pursed her lips, looking concerned. "Did something happen to Clement?"

"No, ma'am," I said. "Just a routine check. Did you happen to see Mr. Crews today?"

"Sure." She pulled a clipboard off the wall, ran her finger down the list. The muscles in her forearm were hard as bridge cables. "Twelve o'clock. He came in at twelve."

"That's what your clipboard says. Are you sure that's when it was?"

She put a look on her face—click, click, click, thinking!—the gears going round and round. She smiled: Bing!—the answer. "It was right before twelve. I remember because he was kidding around with Donnie, my partner. Donnie goes to lunch right at twelve. He's, you know. . . ." Her eyes widened, and she leaned forward so I could see down the front of her sweatshirt. "Punctual."

"And can you tell me when Mr. Crews left here?"

"He finished about twelve-forty-five, probably took a shower, then left right before one. He did supersets today."

"And you're sure he was here that whole time? From twelve to twelve-forty-five."

Judy blinked, smiled. "Sure. I was working on his glutes today."

"Yeah, so I heard."

* * *

I got back to Ray's, checked the machine. Three messages from Jon Scheib at the *Journal*. He had heard a rumor, wanted to confirm it with me. Fine. I'd wait on him. Another message from Dick Bloom.

I called Bloom's office.

"You're making me very, very annoyed, Vine," he said.

"What did I do?" I said.

"Give me one good reason why I shouldn't drop you on your ass right now."

"Your well-known charitable nature?" I said.

"I'm very very serious, Vine."

"I know you are," I said. "I know I lied to you, I'll admit it right now. But I'm onto something, okay?"

"Like dead people under bridges, for instance?"

"Nobody can connect me with that," I said. "Anyway, I think I know who did it." This was stretching the point. I had thought it was Clement, but now it didn't look like that at all.

"That doesn't matter right now," Bloom said. "Right now what you have to worry about is stuff like this bullshit at Tate Keenan's office."

"How did you find out about that?"

"Tate told me, what do you think?"

"Oh," I said.

"You might as well tie a rope around your neck and hike down to the state pen right now, the shit you're pulling. I'm dropping you, Vine. I'll even give my retainer back."

I thought about everything that had happened during the day. I just needed a little more time. "Don't do it yet," I said. "Give me one more day. Then I'll come down, explain everything."

"One more day for *what?* Explain *what?* I mean, what's the point here? Exactly what's the point?"

"The point here, Dick, is that I didn't do it. I didn't kill Roger Hawley! I'm out here, I'm bailing water, trying to get the charges dropped. I know who killed Roger, and I know why. I just can't prove it yet. Maybe I've only got one chance in ten of beating this thing, doing it my way. But if I do it your way, the best we're going to manage is getting me sent up on a manslaughter charge. Right?"

Bloom didn't say anything.

"Manslaughter, Dick. That's a lot of hard time for an innocent man."

"Everybody's innocent, Vine. Everybody I handle is innocent." Dick Bloom sounded worn out all of a sudden, like a guy who'd had a discouraging day.

"No. Wrong. Bullshit," I said. "And, Dick? You're still my lawyer. One more day and I'll explain what I'm doing."

"Forget it, Vine."

"One more day."

I hung up on him.

I called Excor, asked for Harvey Zell.

"Bobby. I'm kind of busy, here."

"Quick question," I said. "What happened to Tate after the bonds got picked up? Did he get charged with anything?"

"Funny you ask."

"Oh?"

"I find out the bonds are locked up in Tate's desk drawer or something, I think, great, now they're gonna arrest the son of a bitch for stealing them. Right?"

"Right."

"Wrong. I call the guy, the sergeant who went in with the warrant, he acts like I got a disease, he's busy, got a call on the other line, a bunch of shit like that. I say, 'Hey Sarge, you just found ten million bucks in a guy's desk drawer, you at least gonna play twenty questions with him, right?' He says, 'Mr. Zell, we already took care of that. Mr. Keenan indicated he had no knowledge of the contents of the box.' Just like that. I say, 'What?' He says, 'No, sir, we asked him all about it, he indicated he had no knowledge of the box or its contents.' "

"Jesus," I said.

"No shit. He indicated he had no knowledge of the box or its contents? Kind of shit is that? I hung up on the guy, started making some calls. You wouldn't believe it. It's like nothing ever happened. Tate who? *What* nine million worth of bonds? *What* little gray box? Nobody's heard of it, nobody wants to talk. I mean the D.A., you name it, right down the line. Vine, we got some weird fucking shit going on down there. Somebody's been pulling some strings at city hall. Big time."

"Tate?"

"Who the fuck else?"

"Jesus," I said.

"Believe it. Truth is stranger, you know what I'm saying?"

"Speaking of bad news," I said. "Jordan Foote got killed today. Got his head beat in under a bridge down at Piedmont Park."

The line was silent for a long time.

"You still there, Harv?"

"My advice, Vine? If I were you? Get in a fast car, drive straight to Honduras."

"You might be right," I said. "Are you guys going to survive this thing, now that the bonds are back? Excor, I mean?"

"I got a second mortgage, cleaned out the savings account, everything," Zell said. "I don't know, Bobby. There's so much shit coming down, I need a hat."

"One more question."

"Yeah?"

"How tall are you, Harv?"

There was silence on the line. "About five-six on a good day. Why?"

CHAPTER 3

There was a knock on Ray's front door. It was Jon Scheib, the reporter from the *Journal.*

"Got a couple minutes?" he said.

"Sure," I said. "Why not? I don't know that I've got anything to tell you, but you're welcome to come out and enjoy a little iced tea by the pool."

We went out back and sat on a couple of white plastic

chairs next to a table with a beach umbrella sticking out of it. It was a nice day, clear and a little cooler than it had been for the last few days. Cooler, meaning eighty-eight instead of ninety-five.

"Real unique place," Scheib said perfunctorily, looking around at Ray's weird house. He set his briefcase down on the table with the umbrella, pulled out a legal pad and a pocket tape recorder, and laid them down in front of him.

"It's not mine," I said.

"Probably just as well. I bet the roof leaks." He picked up the tape recorder, pulled out the cassette. "You mind if we get this on tape, Bobby?"

"Okay with me."

Scheib peeled the wrapping off a fresh cassette and slipped it into the machine. He clicked the buttons, set it on the table next to the briefcase. "July 31. Interview with Bobby Vine. For the record, you have no objection to my taping this conversation?"

"Correct."

Scheib leaned back in his chair, squinting against the afternoon sun. "Roger's bonds," he said. "You want to tell me what you meant by that?"

I thought about it. "Let me respond to that, Jon, by asking *you* a question. How did Tate answer you when you asked him about the bonds?"

"He didn't. He said, *Bonds?*—you know, like he'd never heard of bonds before. He said he didn't know what I was talking about. So I asked if he had some sort of business connection to Roger Hawley. That's what you were implying, wasn't it Bobby?" Scheib's eyebrows bounced, once, up toward his hairline. He was looking at me carefully.

"I wasn't implying anything," I said.

"Oh, I'm sure you weren't," Scheib said. He looked off at the sky. "Okay, let's take this from a different angle. Let's forget about RichCo and Evergreen for a minute, start from ground zero."

"Ground zero?"

"Right. Bobby, did you kill Roger Hawley?"

"No."

"Do you know who did?"

"Off the record, yes."

"Who?" Scheib was still looking off into the distance, a sort of nonsmile on his face, squinting, his lips pulled back.

"There's no point in my telling you that right now."

"Okay. Okay. Do you know why this person killed Roger Hawley?"

"Let's give that a rest," I said. "My attorney told me not to talk about that stuff about Roger. I've disregarded his advice about a lot of things, but I think he's right on this one. No comment. How's that sound?"

"Who's your attorney?"

"Dick Bloom."

Scheib picked up a pencil, wrote something on his legal pad. Then he leaned back in the chair again, started tapping the pencil against the palm of his hand. We didn't say anything for a while. Then Scheib looked up.

"Hi," he said. He was talking to someone behind me.

"Jon," I said. "Meet Ray. He owns the house."

I turned around. It wasn't Ray; it was Clement Crews.

"Vine," Clement said. "What the hell is going through your little pinhead mind?" His face was red, and his jaw was tense, mean-looking. This guy made me nervous. No, *nervous* isn't the right word. He scared the shit out of me.

"What are you talking about?"

"You didn't see me in Piedmont Park at lunchtime today, and you damn well know it."

"True," I said.

Clement looked up at Scheib like he'd just noticed him. "Give us a couple of minutes here, would you, buddy?"

"Sure," Scheib said. He picked up his things off the table, put them in the briefcase. "I'll take a little walk around the neighborhood." He left the briefcase and walked off. Clement watched him until he disappeared around the corner of the house.

"Who's that?" he said.

"Guy from the *Journal.*"

Clement sat down in the chair where Scheib had been, put his elbows on the table. "I ought to just wax you right here and now," he said.

"Good idea," I said. "That's probably your one shot at ever getting your face on the front page of the *Journal*. It'll be your Warholian moment, your magic fifteen minutes."

Clement stared at me. "Who you think you are? Trying to get me on the hook for wasting this lawyer. I just found out about that guy in Piedmont Park, put two and two together. You're trying to frame me for it. You must be out of your freaking mind."

I smiled, trying to look tougher than I felt. "It's an appealing idea. But that's not what I'm up to. You have to admit, all the bodies that have piled up so far seem to be connected to you."

"Not this one," he said.

"I know," I said. "I checked. It wasn't you."

Clement's eyes narrowed. He was the kind of guy that assumed, no matter what you said, that you were lying to him. He was lying most of the time, I guess he expected it out of everybody else, too.

"What's your game here, Vine?" he said.

"No games," I said. "I found an eyewitness, a guy that saw who went under the bridge with Jordan Foote. I showed him a picture of you; he said no, different guy. I checked with Judy, at your gym, she said you were working out the whole time. I was there about five minutes behind whoever killed Jordan, so I know the exact time of the murder. You couldn't have done it."

"Murder!" Clement said. "Man I hate that word." He twitched around in his chair, thinking.

"You got any thoughts?" I said. "Any thoughts, who might have done it?"

"Piedmont Park? He was a faggot. Probably went down there, got whacked by some butt-boy lunatic."

"No," I said. "That's bullshit. He was going to meet me there and tell me something. He's not an idiot. He didn't run off under the bridge to get a blow job from some crackhead hustler. That's not what he was there for."

"Yeah," Clement said. "You're probably right."

"So who do you think did it?"

Clement shook his head, didn't say anything for a minute.

"You said you got an eyewitness? What did the guy look like who offed him?"

"Short guy," I said. "Black hair. You see why I thought it was you?"

"Anything else?"

"Well, the guy said foreign-looking, Mexican, maybe. He said dark skin."

A funny look went across Clement's face.

"Who is it?" I said.

Clement shook his head.

"You know who it is don't you, Clement?"

Clement sat still for a while. I'd never seen him do that before: Usually he was moving all the time, twitching, tapping on things. But now he was still as a sculpture.

"You lied to me in the car, didn't you?" I said. "After you killed the albino guy and the girl. You were bullshitting me weren't you? Or at least not telling me the whole truth."

"I never said I killed Roger," he said.

"Sure you did."

"No. I inferred it, okay. But I never came right out and said it."

"So you're saying you didn't kill Roger?"

"Actually hit him over the head? Nah. I just set it up."

"You want to tell me what really happened?"

"Not especially."

"Maybe you need me on your side then," I said. It was feeble, but what the hell. "Who was it?"

"You're crazy. No way."

"We can help each other."

"Yeah, right!" Clement sneered. "The last thing I need is a loose cannon like you, Vine. Poking your nose into everything, talking to reporters, following people around, all that kind of shit. I need you like a fucking heart attack."

"You're not going to get out of this by yourself," I said. "If this guy—whoever killed Jordan—if he comes after you, it sounds to me like you're going to get screwed."

"No way, Jose."

"If we put our heads together," I said, "maybe we can come up with a plan, something that'll put us in the clear."

Clement was just sitting there, fiddling with his pinky ring, turning it round and round on his finger.

"Clement," I said. "Who killed Roger Hawley?"

Clement told me.

After Clement had explained everything, told me what had happened to Roger, we sat there for a while.

Then Clement got up, spit in the pool, looked at me. "Be careful, Vine," he said. "Next time it could be you or me under that bridge." He walked away, not saying good-bye.

I sat there a few more minutes, listening to the sound of the air conditioner, the birds, not thinking about much in particular—except, maybe, for a general sense of relief that Clement was gone. I heard something click in Scheib's briefcase.

The tape recorder. Scheib had left the tape recorder going. I pulled it out from under the legal pad. He had left the end peeping out, the end with the condenser mike on it. The click I heard was the sound it made when it ran out of tape, shut itself off automatically.

So now I had it all on tape, Clement's explanation of how Roger was killed.

Footsteps sounded behind me. I turned and saw Scheib ambling around the side of the house, hands in his pockets.

I held up the tape recorder. "You're a sneaky guy," I said.

Scheib smiled proudly. Maybe he saw that as a compliment. I popped the cassette out and stuck it in my pocket.

"Hey!" he said. "That's my tape!"

"Tape?" I smiled back at him. "What tape?"

After Jon Scheib finished the interview, I went inside and called Dick Bloom.

"Dick, you're never going to believe what happened," I said.

"Do I know you?"

"Cut the shit, Dick. Listen, I just found out exactly who killed Roger Hawley, how it happened. I even got it on tape."

"I don't think you're my client anymore."

"Just listen," I said. I told him everything that Clement had told me, told him how I'd gotten it all recorded on Scheib's tape.

"Why is it I don't believe you?"

"I swear. . . ."

"Nice try," he said. "But, look, even if you're being square with me, Bobby, there are all kinds of admissibility problems with secret tape recordings—especially when you stole the tape from somebody else in the first place. It's an evidentiary mine field. Eight to five it'd never make it into court. And even if it did, we've got big-time hearsay problems because Clement says he didn't actually witness the killing. See you around."

"Wait—" I said. But Bloom had already hung up on me.

CHAPTER 4

About six o'clock Ray came out the back door with a couple of beers, sat down at the other side of the table.

"Second fitting's on Monday," Ray said. "Did I tell you that already?"

"Yeah," I said. "You did."

"What do you think of double-breasted? Little too, I don't know, is it a little too . . . ?" Ray made a little circle with his hand, showing me his tattoo.

"A little too fruity?"

"Dressy. Little too dressy for a guy like me?"

"No, Ray. You're going to look great."

Ray drank some beer. "I appreciate you saying that," he said. He took another swig. "Nine grand, huh? Lot of money for clothes. Course, I got the shirts, too. It would of been less if I didn't get all them shirts."

"Let me ask you a question, Ray," I said. "Suppose you were me, okay? Suppose today you found out who killed Roger Hawley, why they did it. You got names, dates, faces, and you got it all on tape."

"I'd say you ought to be one happy sumbitch."

"Okay, but suppose the tape isn't admissible evidence. No use in getting me off the hook."

"Sound like you back to square one."

"Maybe."

We finished our beers. "What do you think of paisley?" Ray said.

"Paisley?"

"Sure. For a necktie. As opposed to maybe stripes? Or dots?"

"I've got to be able to do *something* here, Ray," I said. "I got the whole thing on tape. I know everything now. Or at least I know a lot of what happened. I just can't use it in court."

"Then don't use it in court."

"What good is it if it can't be used as evidence to get the case dismissed?"

Ray rubbed on the back of his hand for a minute, still working on the tattoo. "Paisley is kind of screwy-looking," he said, finally. "It's all jumbled up, you know what I'm saying."

"Yeah." I didn't want to talk about neckties.

"Explain to me how this thing works, Counselor."

"What thing?"

"RichCo. You say Tate wants to buy RichCo. Right? But so does Jeannie. Now how does all that fit together?"

"Okay," I said. "RichCo is a public company. Meaning that it's owned collectively by all the people who own its stock. Now the board of directors of RichCo is responsible directly to the shareholders. The job of the board is to make the most money for the people who own the company."

"Sure."

"But at the same time Jeannie wants to buy the company herself. As chairman of the board, she's supposed to represent the shareholders, get the most out of the company she can. As an independent investor, she wants to sell the company to herself as cheaply as she can. So she's got kind of a conflict.

"Now here's her problem. Some of the people on the board don't like the idea of her raping the shareholders by selling the company to herself on the cheap. So they're not giving her a lot of support. No, I take it back: That's her first problem. Her biggest problem is that she doesn't have enough money to buy the company all by herself. She'll have to borrow a shitload of money . . . and so far she hasn't been able to pull that off."

"Hell, I thought she was richer than God."

"She is and she isn't. Most of the money from her dad—the money he made selling the company to the public in the first place—is in a trust fund. Technically, it isn't even hers. She can't spend it, can't pledge it, can't borrow against it. All she can do is sit back and let the checks roll in. So she has to use her personal money. Now, even though she has several million dollars, it's not enough to buy RichCo. She could probably wrangle *something* if she had enough time. But the problem is she doesn't have much time. So she needs to be able to slow Evergreen down and raise enough money to do the deal herself. Or come up with some way to make Evergreen go away completely."

"How would she do that?"

"Simplest way, buy back the shares that Tate bought, throw in an extra twenty, thirty million."

"Two weeks' work, twenty million bucks?"

"Yeah."

"Inneresting," Ray said. He got up, went inside, came out with two more beers.

By the time we finished the second beer, the sun was going down. "You know," Ray said. "This tape. You never did tell me who it was that killed Roger."

I told him, explained why they did it.

Ray sat for a minute, thinking. "Damn," he said. "What a snake pit."

I looked out across the pool, the trees pushing up in a ragged black mass at the pale pink sky. "Yeah."

Ray went over and switched the pool lights on. The glow turned his face blue, made his eyes go black and impenetrable. We sat there for a long time.

"Here!" Ray said suddenly. He was getting ready to make some kind of point. He poked the air near my face with a fat blue finger. "Here! What do all these people got in common, Counselor?"

I shrugged. "Money."

"More than money, Counselor. I got money, but I ain't like them. When I didn't have money, I was like all these people you're talking about. Roger, Jeannie, Jordan, Tate, Clement, Zell, all these people. Now I *do* got money and, thank Christ, I ain't like them anymore." Ray stared at me with his little black eyes. "What's the answer, Counselor?"

"I don't know. You tell me."

Ray had his whole blue face concentrated on me. *"Greed!"* he said. "They all a bunch of greedy sumbitches."

"Greed, yeah. But what good does that do me?"

"You know what a greedy person's weak point is? Think about it. Think hard, because it's happened to you. It's happened to both of us."

"I don't know, Ray." I didn't like this kind of little guessing game. It made me nervous.

"Here's their weak point. You ready? The weak point of a greedy person is ... *greed!"* He leaned back in his chair, his smiling teeth lit up, blue, from the pool lights.

"Are you going somewhere with this, Ray?"

"Here's what I'm saying. The way to catch some greedy asshole off guard is to offer him more than he expects. More than he expects!" Ray spread his arms wide, then brought them together, fast, into a tight circle. "He'll dive for it! I mean put his butt in the air and dive!"

It was beginning to dawn on me, what I could do.

"By the time that sumbitch figures out he shouldn't of jumped, buddy, he's flying through the air with a string around his balls. And who's holding the end of that string? *You are!"* Ray was happy, showing me his little blue teeth.

I thought about what he was saying. Ray was a smart guy.

"Tape to tape," I said. "Can you record from one tape to another on your stereo?"

Ray looked at me, still smiling. He said: "Took you long enough, didn't it?"

CHAPTER 5

"**I** think I'll make a phone call, Ray," I said. I went inside and called the RichCo offices, got through to Jeannie.

"Bobby," she said. "My god, Bobby, Jordan's dead."

"I heard," I said. "I'm sorry to hear it."

"I know," Jeannie said. She sounded tired and old. There was a tremor in her voice. "I never really liked him. But this, my god. . . ."

"I understand," I said. There was silence on the line. "Jeannie, I found out who killed Roger."

She waited a second. "Oh?" She didn't sound interested.

"Yeah. I'd like to meet with you tomorrow morning. Briefly. Ten o'clock. There are some things we need to go over."

"Bobby, you know I'm very busy. Who killed Roger?"

"This is important. Have you got the financing put together yet?"

"No," she said. "We're still working on it. Jordan's death has set us back several days. Who killed Roger?"

"I think we can resolve this all tomorrow," I said. "The murder *and* the deal. It all fits together. We can save RichCo."

"Bobby. Answer me. Who killed Roger?"

"Ten o'clock," I said. "Your office."

Jeannie didn't say anything for a minute. "This meeting," she said finally. "I don't think it's such a good idea right now."

"Ten o'clock," I said.

"Damn it, who killed Roger?"

"It was Harvey Zell," I said.

I called Zell at home.

"Harv," I said. "Can you make it over to Jeannie Richardson's office tomorrow? One o'clock?"

"What for? I got a bankruptcy lawyer coming in tomorrow."

"It's come to that?"

"Exploring the options, as they say. What's this meeting?"

"Two things. First, Jeannie Richardson is going to make sure you don't go bankrupt."

"Hmm," Zell said, like he didn't believe it. "Second?"

"Second, I'm going to accuse you of murdering Roger Hawley."

"You're shitting me."

"I'm serious."

"You're a funny guy, Bobby," he said.

"You going to be there, Harv?"

"I wouldn't miss this for the world."

I went down to the rec room, made two copies of my conversation with Clement on Ray's tape-to-tape machine. Then I got two manila envelopes out of Ray's office, put one tape in each envelope. I wrote on them with a marker: DICK BLOOM on one envelope, JON SCHEIB on the other.

Then I called Sarah.

"Bobby," she said. "Did you hear what happened to Jordan?"

"I've heard a lot of things today," I said. I told her about Clement, about the tape, about who killed Roger.

"Jesus," she said.

"Yeah," I said. "Look, I've got a favor to ask."

"Ask away."

"Staying late tonight?"

"Probably. It could be eleven before we get finished."

"How'd you like to work all night, Sarah?"

"What do you mean?" she said.

"I have a plan," I said. I told her what Ray had said about greed, told her what I was going to do tomorrow.

"Isn't there an easier way to do this?"

Maybe there was. Or maybe there wasn't.

"Be careful, Bobby," she said. "You're the one who told me this wasn't a game. Now you're acting like some big player again, pulling the strings so you can make everyone dance."

Was that what I was doing? Letting myself be seduced by the game again, sucked back into it? Hell, maybe it was. But, man, it felt good! Making plans, making calls, studying the angles. Making something *happen* for God's sake. I was tired of letting things happen *to* me. Bobby Vine, deal maker— back from the dead. And why not? Stranger things have happened.

"I'll be over around ten or ten-thirty," I said. "Oh, and can you convince a lawyer to stay there? One of the associates? I've got something I need to have worked on."

I sat down with a legal pad, started drafting a letter of intent between RichCo and Evergreen Partners, stating the conditions under which Evergreen would buy RichCo. It covered the main points, described who was going to manage the company, capital structure, that kind of thing. The letter took about an hour to finish—all the angles squared away. The final product was five pages, handwritten. I tore the pages out of the legal pad, set them next to me on the couch.

Then I drafted another letter. This one only took about a minute. I set the stack of yellow paper on the table next to the phone and called Faulkner Keenan & Williams. Ten o'clock, Tate was still at the office.

"Tate," I said. "I'm afraid I was wrong about you. You didn't kill Roger after all."

"Of course not."

"Have you heard from the RichCo board?" I said.

"No. It appears they are giving Jeannie two days to set up a competing offer."

I heard Ray come in through the sliding glass door. He watched me, a little fragment of smile stuck to his face.

"Then I've got a proposition for you," I said.

"I'm not sure you have anything to offer me," he said. "At least not anything that I want."

"How about RichCo?" I said. "Half-price sale, today only."

"Be serious."

"I am."

"Yet again, you surprise me. Come on over."

"I'll fax over a draft of the plan," I said.

I hung up. While I was faxing the first letter over to Tate, I explained to Ray what I was doing.

Ray had his hyena smile going full strength. "More than they expected," Ray said. "More than they *ever* expected!"

Keenan didn't look up when I came into his office. He was wearing little half-glasses, reading the fax I had sent over. There was another guy sitting across the desk from him, a rumpled-looking guy in a handmade suit. He was a famous investment banker, a guy you might have seen on TV. There was a rumor a few years back that he was going to be indicted—but it turned out not to be true. His eyes were dark green, flecked with gray.

I introduced myself. The Famous Investment Banker shook my hand gingerly, like I had just wiped my ass with it. I guess he knew who I was, that I was supposed to have killed a guy. Or maybe it was my disbarment that scared him. Investment bankers, they're almost as bad as lawyers that way. We sat down and waited for Tate to finish reading. After a while he took off his glasses, set them on the table, handed the fax over to the Famous Investment Banker, who let it unroll down to his trouser cuffs.

When he was finished, he shrugged dismissively.

Tate looked at me. "This is a waste of time," he said.

"Point by point," I said. "You tell me why it's a waste of time, and I'll tell you why you're wrong."

"First," he said. "Jeannie won't agree to let us buy RichCo. The reason being that she will not retain total control of the company."

"She doesn't have much choice," I said. "She can't raise enough money by herself to beat your bid. The only way she can beat you is by getting an equity partner. She's looking for one right now—but as far as I know, she's been unsuccessful. This may be her last hope."

"If you're right," said Tate. "If she can't find a partner, than we've already won. Why should we accept a compromise when we can have it all?"

"Certainty," I said. "Certainty. She'll sign this tomorrow.

But if you give her two more days, you never know, she may find a white knight who'll bail her out. It's a quick kill."

Tate looked up at the ceiling for a moment, then looked back at me. "Second," he said. "Your plan does not give Evergreen total control over RichCo. While we get one hundred percent of the initial equity, the Class B convertible shares that Jeannie receives potentially gives her forty-nine percent and two members on the board."

I said: "Which, in and of itself, is absolutely useless. It's only a concession to her. You have to give her something. It costs you nothing and only acquires value in the event that the company is sold off or that you sell a portion of your interest to an outside buyer."

Tate put on his half-glasses, wrote something on a legal pad, took off the glasses, looked up at me. "Third. Your plan requires Evergreen to give Jeannie Richardson an ironclad contract as chief executive and chairman of the board. This is ridiculous. We can't commit ourselves to such a thing. The whole point of this exercise is for us to gain absolute control of the company."

I opened my briefcase, took out my second letter—the one that was only a couple of lines long. I put it on Tate's desk. Tate put on his glasses, read the letter, looked back at me over the top of the glasses. "What makes you think she'll sign this?"

I gave him a reason.

"Holy shit," said the Famous Investment Banker.

Tate took off his glasses, set them on the desk again. "You can't be serious."

"Dead serious."

"Hm," he said. He didn't say a word for at least five minutes. Then, all of a sudden: "Fourth, regarding the convertibility of the Class B preferred shares, it seems to me that the date for initial conversion should be—"

"Let's forget about the details," I said. "Assuming we can work out the details to your satisfaction, what do you think?"

"Nice quick kill," the Famous Investment Banker said.

Tate looked at him, no expression. Then he looked at me. "Feasible," he said to me.

I said: "Will you do it?"

"Yes," Tate said.

"I'm going to have a guy over at Foote's office working on cleaning up the details," I said. "What I gave you is just my first stab at it. Caucus with your people, call France, whatever you need to do, put together your own version and fax it over to Sarah Bryce at Foote's office. We'll get the details worked out tonight. We'll need an acceptable version, ready to sign, by ten o'clock tomorrow morning. Have we got a deal?"

Tate only had to think for a moment. "Done," he said.

Sarah was waiting for me in the lobby of the law firm. She had a young guy with her, a tired-looking blond kid in shirtsleeves and a bow tie. Everybody was tired these days. No wonder, it was almost eleven o'clock.

Sarah introduced me to the kid in the bow tie. His name was Brad.

"Okay, Brad," I said. "Here's what I'm doing. I've worked out a proposal from Tate Keenan to Jeannie. What I want you to do is work with Tate to hammer out the final document."

Brad was confused. "Wait a minute. Jeannie didn't say anything about this. Nobody told me to work on this. I mean with Jordan dead. . . ." He ran out of mental fuel.

"That's because Jeannie doesn't know about it."

Brad was confused. "Then I really can't."

"You're my client," I said. "I'm paying you to represent Jeannie's interests. Hypothetically."

The kid spluttered some more. Sarah took his hand, looked into his eyes. She said: "If you can't handle it. . . ."

Brad flushed. The way he looked at her, I could tell he couldn't have resisted her if he'd tried. And he didn't even try. "I can handle it," he said. "I can *handle* it!"

I handed him the draft of the first letter, the long one. "Here's my draft. I've shown it to Tate, and he agrees with the concept, but obviously he has some comments, some changes he'd like to make. I'm going to have Tate work directly with you. If he tries to jerk you around, call me. I'll be with Sarah."

"Tate? Me? I'm supposed to work *directly* with *Tate?*"

I smiled. "Welcome to the big leagues, son."

* * *

We went back to Sarah's office. She had a bewildered look on her face as she picked up a pile of stationery that was sitting on the chair next to her desk and threw it on the floor. It was RichCo stationery, something for the deal, I guess. I didn't sit down.

"God, I'm tired," she said. Her face was pale, with blue bruises showing under her eyes. She leaned her sharp elbows on the desk, put her head in her hands. A few wisps of hair hung down over her fingers.

I put my hands on her shoulders, kneaded them, trying to put some life into her. There were a lot of bones under the skin.

"I can't believe they killed Jordan," she said.

"Don't think about it."

She sat up. "I can't not think about it! Don't tell me not to think about it. My god, Bobby, he was murdered! They beat him to death. He was, today, I saw him, he was here, and then, I . . ." She stopped. I put my hands on her face, felt the tears run down through my fingers. I stood that way for a while, holding her head and feeling her body quake against me. It had been a sad, tedious, nasty couple of weeks.

Eventually Sarah's body stopped moving. She reached up, held my hand against her face for a moment, then wiped the water from her eyes. "I just want it all to go away," she said. Her voice was soft but clear.

I walked over to the window, looked out. Outside the world was dark and empty. "I know," I said. "One more day. Just one more day."

Sarah stood, put her arms around me, kissed me on the back of the neck. "Where do we start?"

"First thing, does someone in the office keep a log or a bible with all your Federal Express invoices in it?" I said.

"I suppose. Maybe the mail room, or the office manager."

"Good. I need you to go through all your incoming FedEx invoices—FedEx, UPS, Express Mail, registered mail, anything like that. July ten through July twenty. If you find anything with any of these names on it, pull it and make eight copies." I wrote down a list of names on a piece of paper.

Sarah looked at the names. "Okay, what else?"

"Outgoing courier invoices. Not Fed Ex. Local courier.

Same dates. Look for these names." I wrote more names on the paper.

"Eight copies also?"

"Right. Let's see, I also need to look at Jordan's correspondence, his chron file, everything coming in and going out."

"I don't really like doing this, Bobby."

"Neither do I," I said. "But it's better than the alternatives. What about check registers for trust accounts?"

"I don't know."

"If you could help me locate those two things, I'll go through them while you're pulling the invoices."

"Anything else?"

"Just one thing," I said. "I think you're the most beautiful woman in the world."

She looked at me, blinked as though I'd said something shocking. And then she smiled. The fear, the fatigue, the tension—it was gone. Her high cheeks lit up with a pale red fog, and her eyes were bright. She kissed me hard on the lips. I took her in my arms, felt the bones in her back with my hands, felt the hard thrust of her against me.

"Oh my god," she said.

"Later, Sarah. Later."

She was still smiling when she found the first invoice.

By midnight I had dredged up all the correspondence I needed, made eight copies of each letter, put them in a pile.

I went out and checked on Brad, the kid with the bow tie. He was on the phone, looking nervous. When I came in he smiled, gave me a thumbs-up. The troops were rallying.

I waited till he finished.

Brad started talking: "You should have heard me, Mr. Vine. I was great! I stopped him cold. Instead of convertibility on the Class B? He wants to issue warrants, you know, bundled but detachable from the Class B shares so that—"

I waved my hand. "It's okay. I believe you. I'm not trying to steal your thunder, but I'm too tired to concentrate on that kind of thing."

"You should have heard me," Brad said. "I was awesome."

"Keep it up," I said.

I went back to Sarah's office, took a piece of paper out of my briefcase. It was the original order for the bonds that I had taken from Roger's office. I dialed the number listed at the top of the page.

A voice at the end of a long, distant tunnel answered. "Lee Hong Investments." It was a woman with a vaguely English accent. Vaguely English, vaguely Chinese. She connected me.

"Hello, sir. This is Ram Battachargee speaking." Vaguely English, vaguely Indian this time.

"My name is Robert Vine," I said. I used my Texas lawyer accent on him. "I'm Roger Hawley's attorney."

"Yes?" Vaguely Indian, vaguely suspicious. "We had expected to hear from Roger earlier."

"Sure," I said. "In reference to that, old Roger's run into a little health trouble."

"Nothing serious, I trust?"

"Head injury," I said. "Boy's been flat on his back."

"Gracious! How distressing."

"The doctor says the worst is over," I said.

"Oh, super! Marvelous! Well! What may I do for you, sir?"

"Glad you asked. See, what happened here, Mr. Hawley got the bonds you sent, of course, but we needed some kind of record of the order. Tax purposes, you know."

"Sir? He should have received that with the shipment."

"Oh, sure, he did, he did. But, you know old Roger. He threw the goddamn thing away. Details, they never been his strong suit."

"Mm," said Ram Battachargee. "I'm afraid I shall have to check round the office. I'm not certain I can post it to you immediately."

"I hate to push you, son, but we got the auditors, goddamn IRS in here, Roger's flat on his back. The tax people gonna attach his checking account, I mean crush his *cojones,* if he doesn't come up with some type of documentation on the bonds."

"Perhaps . . . if it's strictly necessary."

"Strictly, hell, you better put a top priority on this one, my friend. Fax it to me here at the firm." I gave him the fax number at Foote Shelby & Foote.

"Very well."

"Oh, yeah. How about an invoice, too. Shipping record."

"Shipping record? I fail to see—What time *is* it over there, sir? You are suggesting that you have government employees performing an audit . . . at midnight?"

"That's what I'm telling you, amigo. *Top priority.*" I hung up on the poor guy, hoped for the best.

About two-thirty, the fax from Ram Battachargee arrived. Confirmation slip, record of payment, FedEx invoice. I made eight copies of each page.

About the time I finished, Brad came into Sarah's office, sat down in the spare chair.

"How's it going?" I asked him.

"We're getting close. I penciled up the draft they sent over, faxed it back. Now I'm waiting to see what they say. Hopefully we'll be able to kind of flyspeck it, get the language tuned a little bit, and we'll be in business."

"You're a good man," I said. "The only improvement I can suggest, get rid of that damn bow tie."

"Go to hell," he said, very polite about it.

I took all the copies Sarah and I had made, distributed them into eight piles. I put the first six piles into manila file folders. Then I put the folders into my briefcase and took out the two envelopes: JON SCHEIB and DICK BLOOM. I put one pile in each envelope, then I sat down and wrote a note to each of the two men whose names were on the envelopes. They were pretty long notes, explaining a lot of different things. I put the notes in the envelopes, licked the flaps, and sealed them.

"Done!"

I looked up. It was Brad, smiling. His tie had wilted, and his shirt was wrinkled all to hell, but he looked like he was having the time of his life.

"Give me two originals and go home," I said.

He handed me the copies, stapled, fresh out of the printer. "Already got them."

"Thanks," I said. "Thanks for everything. Now go home."

He was leaning against the door frame. The energy had

started oozing out of him. "How am I supposed to bill this?" he said. "I put in five point three hours."

"Go home, get some sleep."

He looked at me and then looked down at the floor. Sarah was lying on the carpet, her head under the desk. She was beautifully, peacefully, dead asleep. Brad sighed. "You're a lucky bastard, Vine," he said. "I'll see you later."

He was pulling off his bow tie as walked down the hall.

There was only one more thing to do. I took out the second letter I had written, the short one, picked up a few pieces of RichCo stationery from the stack on the floor next to Sarah's desk, and went out to find a typewriter.

I was bone tired. It was a short letter, only one sentence, but it still took me five attempts and half an hour of two-finger typing to get the letter done with no mistakes. I took the finished letter back to Sarah's office, put it in my brief-case, and closed the door. My watch said it was 4:22 in the morning.

I lay down on the carpet next to Sarah and thought vaguely about what she had said that afternoon. Was I just going through this production because I was addicted to the drama? Or because I wanted to prove that I could still trade licks with the big boys? It reminded me of something I'd forgotten—that as soon as the deal-making action cooled, the whole thing had always seemed hollow, a depressingly empty exercise.

And then . . . the emptiness of sleep.

CHAPTER 6

At six-thirty I woke up, sun pouring in the window. Sarah was still sleeping on the floor next to me. I nudged her, and she woke up suddenly, wide-eyed, like she didn't know where she was.

"Show time," I said.

At eight I drove over to Dick Bloom's office, found him behind his desk reading the *Journal.* He looked up at me for a second, then looked back at the paper. He was reading the third section, probably figuring out how to invest the ten grand I'd given him.

"Good morning," I said.

He said: "Who are you?" Not looking up.

I put my briefcase on the desk, opened it, took out the two manila envelopes. "Here," I said. I dropped the envelopes on the desk.

Bloom was playing it up. He let the paper droop a little, so he could see what was on the desk, then he lifted the paper up again, hid behind it. I wasn't in my usual playful mood. I took his third section by the corners, yanked it out of his hands. Bloom was looking up at me, trying to be cool.

"On your desk, Counselor," I said, "you will see two envelopes. On one envelope I have printed your name. That means that you may open that envelope and read its contents." I folded the third section of the *Journal*—doing a neat, slow job of it—set the thing down on the desk. "On the other envelope I have printed the name Jon Scheib. Mister Scheib is a reporter with the very newspaper that you were recently enjoying." I sat on the edge of his desk, showed him a lot of happy teeth.

Bloom held up his hands, surrendering. "Okay, okay, okay. What's in the envelope?"

"The tape I told you about, along with some documentation regarding stolen bonds, certain payments, shipping, invoices, etc.—all of which demonstrate the motive, opportunity, and method behind the murder of one Roger Hawley." I made a fanning motion with both hands. "Be my guest. Read."

Bloom tore open the envelope, read the letter on the top, looked through the stack of photocopies underneath. When he was done, Bloom looked up at me. "Okay, what of it?"

"Is that going to get the charges against me dismissed?"

Bloom sighed. "It's not a sure bet, but, yeah, I suppose so." He picked up the other envelope. "What do you want me to do with this?"

"In the next twenty-four hours, if I should end up dead under a bridge, get hit by a runaway automobile, something like that, I want you to give it to this guy Scheib."

Bloom got up, opened a cabinet behind him. There was a safe inside. He opened the safe, put the envelopes inside, closed it, spun the knob. The lock whirred chastely.

Bloom sat back down, picked up his paper.

"Oh, yeah," I said. "One more thing. Can you get a private investigator to take some pictures for me?"

Bloom sighed, shook his head. "I give up," he said.

I scribbled a list of people on a scratch pad sitting on his desk. "Here's a list of names, where they work, that kind of thing. Just send the guy around, walk up, take a snapshot."

"What kind of prints you want? Twelve by fifteen color glossies? Poster size? Maybe some retouching, some airbrush?"

"Polaroids. I need them by noon."

"Oh, sure. Noon. Right."

"Noon. Delivered to Sarah Bryce at Foote Shelby & Foote."

CHAPTER 7

Nine-fifty-five, RichCo, the boardroom. Jeannie said: "Would you do me the favor of explaining what the hell this is all about?"

What she meant was, Why was Tate Keenan at her office, sitting across the table from her? Tate was there with one of his partners, the Famous Investment Banker, along with a couple guys in spiffy European suits who didn't say a word the whole time they were there. Jeannie had Marty the lawyer with Coke-bottle glasses, and Bruce the phone thrower with her.

By way of an answer, I stood up, got myself some coffee, started my boardroom speech: "I appreciate your agreeing to meet with me here today. As you may or may not know, I have been tangentially involved in this deal as a result of certain unfortunate events in my personal life. For reasons which, in the fullness of time you will understand, I have taken an interest in RichCo's predicament—and, for that matter, in Evergreen's predicament as well."

Everybody was looking at me like I was the transmitter of some unspeakable disease. I blew on my coffee, smacked my lips. Fuck 'em. This was my show. Maybe the last chance I'd ever get to do this sort of thing—so by God I was going to enjoy it.

I continued: "It seemed to me that surely there was a solution to the problem which would not involve burdensome debt for RichCo, nor the gutting of the RichCo enterprise, nor layoffs, proxy fights, spin-offs, trim-downs, asset dispositions, and. . . ." I took a moment to smile at all the suits. ". . . exorbitant legal and bankers' fees." The suits didn't take this to be a joke.

"To that end, I spoke briefly with Mr. Keenan—with whom I had already had reason to be in contact regarding my personal situation, I might add. I suggested, in broad outline, a possible solution. Mr. Keenan refined that proposal, and is now here to discuss it with you." I took another sip of my coffee and sat down. "Mr. Keenan?"

Tate stood. "I have a few remarks to make regarding our motives for being here today, after which time I would like to outline our proposal, Jeannie. I realize that this proposal has arrived in a rather unorthodox fashion. But there is nothing I can do about that." His voice was soft, calm, no dynamics or color to it.

"Jeannie, as you know, I represent Evergreen Partners, an equity fund raised by European investors. As you also are aware, I'm sure, the climate and mores of business in Europe are generally somewhat less antagonistic than in this country. Hostile takeovers, if I may use that phraseology, are less common, less well-thought-of there. It was my client's intention from the first to consummate this acquisition in a noncombative manner."

Tate looked from face to face, going on in the same monotone, sounding like he was reading off a script, his fingertips resting softly on the tabletop in front of his pants pockets. Lulling them to sleep while he moved in for the kill.

"Therefore, my clients have requested that we make every effort to amicably consummate this acquisition." Tate paused, looking around the room. Jeannie stared at him, hate sparkling like tears in her eyes. "I have to thank Mr. Vine, who has brought us together, and who, as he just intimated, furnished the germ of the proposal that we will now present."

He nodded at his partner, a young guy with hard eyes and garish embroidered suspenders. The partner opened a manila folder, took out several copies of the letter of intent that Brad had finished earlier in the morning, and passed them across the table, one for each member of Jeannie's entourage.

"In summary, the proposal is as follows. Evergreen will acquire all of RichCo's common stock for twenty-five and one-half dollars per common share, transferring RichCo's assets into a holding company that will be wholly owned by the Evergreen partnership. This holding company will issue a five-year noncallable preference stock with a bundled warrant. This entire issue, which we will call Class B common, will be subscribed to by the RichCo management group. Exercise of the warrants would allow the RichCo management group to acquire up to forty-nine percent of common stock in the new holding company at a price of forty dollars per share. In return for providing the capital to fund this preference stock, current management will be awarded an ironclad, five-year contract to manage the company."

He went on for fifteen minutes, going through the letter of intent point by point. "We have furnished you, Jeannie, with an original version of a letter of intent describing the manner in which we anticipate consummating the acquisition, signed by myself. I think you will find this to be a fair proposal, one that leaves you adequately protected and free to manage the company, while giving our investors the opportunity of a fair return. And, Jeannie, I might add that it is our intention that you remain at the helm of the RichCo organization."

"If you are prepared to present this to your board of directors for an immediate vote, we will accept your signature at any time prior to seven o'clock today." Tate sat down.

His voice, which had gotten softer and softer as he spoke, was now a whisper. He put his elbows on the table and leaned toward Jeannie. "If your board approves it, then we will have the deal done by the end of the day, and your ongoing presence at this company will be assured. But if your board feels the necessity to change one provision, one word, one comma of that letter, then the deal is off."

His black eyes stared straight into Jeannie's. "Make no mistake, Jeannie, this is a final offer. If you attempt to stall, renegotiate, or otherwise undercut this proposal, I will come back, and, so help me God, I will take your company away."

Jeannie was holding the letter in her hands. It danced and wobbled in her grip. The white streak in her hair played like lightening above her face. "Damn you," she said.

"I expect you'll need this room to meet with your board of directors," Tate said. He looked at his watch. "If you are agreeable, we will return at one o'clock." Tate nodded at his clan. They stood, filed out the door.

"Damn you," Jeannie said again. This time she was talking to me.

"Things aren't always the way they seem," I said, after Tate left.

Jeannie stared at me, her face white and taut, like a dummy in a store window. The only things about her that seemed alive were her trembling hands, her hate-filled eyes.

"Let's start with this fact," I said. "There's no way in hell you can keep this company. Not *status quo ante bellum*. If you haven't found an equity partner yet, you're not going to. Tate had you. And if not him, then somebody else."

Jeannie didn't say anything. She knew I was right.

"Let me explain something to you," I said. "Tate was able to suppress the thing about the bonds in his office. It took a lot of clout to do it, and he probably had to call in some chips. He should have been charged with something—we both know that. But he got away with it. Fine. That's past tense. But there was more to those bonds than just a stack of paper in a metal box. There's a paper trail behind those bonds. It stretches from Roger to Zell to Jordan Foote."

"Jordan?" Jeannie's eyes narrowed. "What are you talking about?"

"If you trace the paper trail—invoices, confirmation slips, whatever—you can find out exactly what happened to the bonds. Now I haven't found everything, but I've pieced together most of the trail. It included Jordan Foote. He was working with Tate. He was working with Roger. He was working with Zell. I haven't got it all put together, but I will. Zell killed Roger because Roger was stealing money from their company. Roger was going to destroy Excor, and Zell had to stop him. He didn't realize that Roger was working with Tate."

Jeannie had a funny look on her face, trying to figure out where I was going.

"Now here's why I hooked you up with Tate. If you get this five-year management contract, then he can't push you out of RichCo, right? Now just imagine what would happen if Tate were suddenly implicated in a murder, in the stealing of nine million dollars worth of bonds, in securities manipulation. What would happen then?"

Jeannie smiled. It was a thin, cold smile, like a crack in an ice floe. "Then I would have gained absolute control over RichCo, without having put up but a fraction of the money."

"Exactly." I said. "And Evergreen, which is owned by a couple of French guys who don't know shit about your company, becomes a passive investor that you can manipulate at your pleasure."

Jeannie thought about it, then finally she shook her head. "It won't work. Bobby, you've already said that Tate has the clout to stop that sort of thing from happening."

"Uh-uh. Not this time. You get enough evidence, some of it's going to get out. In fact, I've already got a packet of very damaging stuff ready to hand off to Jon Scheib, the guy from the *Journal*. It's not quite a direct link, but it's close enough to get him in hot water."

"And Jordan? He was working with Tate?"

"Indirectly, yes."

"How did you find this . . . this paper trail?"

"There's a lot of paper out there. You just keep digging, it's amazing what you can find. Now there's only one thing left."

"What's that?"

"I've figured out—I won't bore you with the details—but I've figured out that the real smoking gun is at Excor. Jordan collected several invoices showing where the bonds were shipped and gave them to Tate, who gave them to Zell. Now the final recipient of the bonds is also responsible for Roger's death. They have to be. If I get those last invoices, I'll have a clear record of who stole the bonds. Therefore, I've got Zell. And if Zell falls, he's going to reach up and pull Tate down with him."

Jeannie watched my face. "What are you going to do?"

"Zell is going to be out of the office during our meeting with you at one o'clock. In fact I called him to come to the meeting. As you might expect, he's in some deep financial trouble right now. I've promised him that in the course of this deal, you're going to take care of him, make him whole. He'll be out of the office between one and three or so. So I'm going to give him a few minutes, get somebody I know to go in and steal the invoices around one-thirty or two. Excor is about to go bankrupt, and right now they only have a skeleton crew at their office. With Zell gone, there'll be nobody there to stop us from stealing the invoices."

"What kind of invoices are you talking about?"

"Federal Express," I said. "They'll be easy to find. Description of contents, gray box containing valuable securities. Nothing to it. One-thirty, we'll have everything we need."

Jeannie shook her head. "Bobby, I just keep underestimating you and underestimating you." She laughed, making that high electric organ sound. After a while it started to get a wild screechy warble in it. She laughed and laughed until the tears came out of her eyes.

"Yes," I said. "You're right about that."

I went back to Ray's, tried to eat lunch, but couldn't even

make it all the way through a ham sandwich. I was too strung out, my stomach too sour to hold anything down.

I called Deputy Handlin down at the DeKalb County Sheriff's Department.

"What do you want?" he said.

"I solved the murder," I said.

"Good for you," he said. "We solved it a week and a half ago."

I explained to him all the evidence I'd gathered, where it all was leading. It took a while to explain everything. When I finished Handlin didn't say anything.

"Well?" I said.

"I'm thinking," he said.

"While you're thinking, I need you to do me a favor, okay?"

"What's that?"

I told him.

"You out of your mind?" he said.

"Just do it."

I called Sarah at the office. "Sarah, how are you feeling this morning?"

"Like somebody dropped a piano on my spine. How about you?"

"About the same. Did you get the pictures delivered to you? The Polaroids?"

"Oh, that was you? I was wondering who sent them."

"Yeah, it was me. Listen, I've got one last thing I need you to do. . . ."

CHAPTER 8

At one o'clock the RichCo boardroom was cool, dim, full of investment bankers and lawyers, along with a couple of the RichCo directors. The suits milled around, heads close together, speaking softly and looking around with cardshark eyes. The paneled walls, the deep dark carpeting, the high ceiling ate up their words, so that the room seemed to be making a sound of its own, a sound like a waterfall inside a cave.

At five after one, Jeannie Richardson came in—Marty and Bruce, the New York hotshots, riding shotgun. The suits stopped talking, holstered themselves in their green leather chairs. Jeannie sat directly across the table from Tate Keenan.

The air was heavy with the pure, hallucinogenic smell of the deal. It was intoxicating.

Marty, the lawyer, sat his big black document bag on the table. There was no noise, just the rush of the air-conditioning, the slap of the leather flaps on the bag. Marty took out a folder and a pen, set them in front of Jeannie Richardson, took the bag off the table, sat down.

Jeannie picked up the pen, hesitated, looked up at Tate and smiled. It was a grim, hateful smile. Tate looked back, nothing readable in his eyes.

Jeannie signed, the pen scratching on the page.

She looked at the page for a moment, then pushed it slowly away from her, just far enough that Tate had to stand to pick up his copy. Jeannie signed the second letter of intent, her copy, handed it to Mary. Marty put the letter in the folder, put the folder back in the black bag.

Jeannie stood. "On behalf of the board of directors of RichCo Incorporated, I have just signed a letter," she said, "expressing the intention of this company to recommend that our shareholders tender all outstanding shares of RichCo Incorporated to Evergreen Ventures, Incorporated, a subsidiary of Evergreen Partners, Limited, at a price of twenty-five and a half dollars per share.

"The current management of RichCo will remain intact, and current operations will continue uninterrupted. Top management of RichCo will be offered a binding contractual relationship to the company for five years. RichCo is still in business, and. . . ." She looked around the room, lifted one hand to her bosom, smiled her best Sweet Briar smile. ". . . and I am here to stay."

She looked at Keenan. "Is there anything you would like to add, Tate?"

Tate looked over at me.

"Jeannie," I said. "I have one minor item here. I'd like to step outside and bring in Harvey Zell."

Jeannie thought about it, looked down at Tate, sitting across the table from her and smiled, sweet as rose-hip syrup. "Why not?" she said.

A secretary was waiting for me in the hall, standing next to Zell. "Are you Mr. Vine?" she said.

"Yes."

"Two messages. They both said they were urgent." The secretary handed me two slips of pink paper. One had Sarah's name and number on it. The other said Detective Edmund Mance. Funny, I never knew his real name was Edmund.

I thanked the secretary and then looked at Zell. "Go on in," I said. "I'll be back in a second."

I called Sarah. "So did you find Honey Bear?"

"Bobby, can you please tell me what we're doing?"

"There's no time. Who was it that went under the bridge with Jordan?"

There was an annoyed silence. Then she told me.

"I thought so," I said. "But I just had to make sure. Come on over to RichCo, okay. With the pictures."

"Bobby," she said. Pause. "Maybe now's not the time to say this. . . ."

"Look—what?—I need to get back to the meeting."

"What I'm saying, Bobby . . . I'm not sure I like the guy you turn into when you're playing this Master-of-the-Deal thing."

I looked up and down the mahogany-paneled hall, this cold corridor of power, and then said, "I'm not sure I like him either. But he's about to save my ass."

I called Ed.

"Bobby. Handlin get there yet?"

"Not yet."

"Well, anyway, you were right. We found the guy trying to bust into Excor, just like you said."

"What are you going to charge him with?"

"Nothing."

"Nothing!"

"Bobby," Ed said. "He just walked in the front door—just like you told Handlin he would. You can't put people in jail for walking into a legitimate place of business."

"That's okay," I said. "It doesn't matter. I just had to know that he'd be there."

"Okey-doke," Ed said.

"Thanks a million," I said. "Here comes Deputy Handlin. When are you going to make it out here?"

"Give us about ten minutes."

I went back into the boardroom, walked up to the head of the table. "Ladies and gentlemen," I said. "I just have one more minor item of business." I took the one-page letter out of my briefcase—the one I'd typed at four o'clock that morning. I walked down to Jeannie and set it down in front of her.

Jeannie read the letter, looked up at me. There were white spots at her cheekbones, and her eyes were wild, furious. She lifted the letter by the corner, like it was burning her fingers, threw it into the middle of the table.

She spit out the words: *"What . . . is this?"*

"It's a letter," I said, "RichCo stationery, dated September first. It says, as I recall, 'Effective immediately, I am resigning from RichCo Incorporated.' It has your name at the bottom." I smiled. "All it needs is your signature."

The suits were all looking around at each other, nervous lines cutting into the skin around their eyes.

"This is preposterous," Jeannie said.

"Actually not," I said. I took out the six folders I had put together in the middle of the night. I put one at my place; then gave one to Jeannie; one to Bruce, the phone thrower; one to Marty, the lawyer; one to Tate. Then I opened the door of the room, a big mahogany thing, and let Deputy Sheriff Handlin into the room. I gave him the last folder. He sat down at the far end of the table, away from the suits.

"I have a story to tell you," I said. "A story that will explain precisely why Jeannie Richardson is no longer fit to run this company." I strolled around a little bit, my hands behind my back, taking it slow. It felt good.

"About two weeks ago," I said, "Roger Hawley was found dead, his head beat in, in my house. He'd been dead for fifteen, sixteen hours. When the cops got there, I was watching a soap opera. It was an open-and-shut case." I walked down, put my hands on Deputy Handlin's shoulder, grinned at everybody, smiling like a fool.

"This fine representative of the law enforcement community, having received an anonymous tip about this murder, rushed over and solved the case." I snapped my fingers. "Man, I mean, solved it like that. And why not? Like I say—open-and-shut case." I whopped Handlin on the shoulder one more time, walked down the row of suits. They wouldn't look me in the eye.

Jeannie Richardson was watching me, nothing moving but her eyes and her trembling hands. It was like I had run a stick through her, pinned her to the chair.

"Now, no sooner had I been put in jail for this murder, then I was bailed out by Jeannie Richardson. It seems that the guy I'd allegedly killed, Roger Hawley, had taken off with eight or so million dollars of Jeannie's money." I put my hand on her shoulder, felt the bones moving under the slack skin. She twisted out of my hand like a snake.

"Bobby," she said softly. "Get your fucking hands off me."

I smiled again, giving everybody the dumbass grin, spreading it around. "Now, Jeannie bailed me out, she said, because she thought I could locate the bonds. Well! I tried to find those bonds, you wouldn't believe what I went through. I broke into houses, offices, got guns pointed at me, you name it. But I never found those bonds."

I walked down to my end of the table, opened up the folder. "If you'll bear with me, I'd like those of you with folders to turn to the first page. It's a copy of a faxed letter from a Mr. Ram Battachargee, a broker in Singapore—of all places. He is confirming that he was purchasing bonds, worth somewhere in the neighborhood of ten million dollars, on behalf of Roger Hawley. Bonds primarily purchased, of course, with Miss Richardson's money. Now, where would I get such a letter? Out of Roger Hawley's trash, of course.

"But here's a funny thing. I couldn't find a copy of the letter that Roger faxed back. See, here it says that Mr. Battachargee needs to know details of the 'physical delivery.' What he's saying is: 'Where do you want me to send these things?' Now, when you turn to the next page, I want you to think about the fact that I couldn't find the letter Roger sent back.

"Okay. Next page. It's a little report that I printed out on Roger's fax machine. Look at the last two entries. Next to the last entry, incoming fax, dated July twelve, late at night, from an international number. You'll find it matches the one on the stationery of the previous page. Last fax. Outgoing. Destination, Singapore. Early, early the next morning. *That was the order.* Are you with me? That was the letter in which Roger instructed Battachargee where to send the bonds. But let me reiterate: The original letter, the reply Roger faxed to Singapore, was not in his office. I know because I looked."

Tate sat still as a board. He didn't look happy, sad, nothing. He was just watching Jeannie, seeing what she would do.

"Next page. Fax of Roger's account record from Ram Battachargee's firm in Singapore. It records, definitively, the sale of these bonds to Roger Hawley. Just for reference, you'll note that this is one day before Roger was killed.

"Next page. Fax copy of an international Federal Express invoice, air bill number 5277743717, Singapore to Atlanta, sent to Foote Shelby & Foote. Care of Jordan Foote. Sender copy. Next page, same thing, but it's an original taken from a file at Foote's office. Mr. Foote, as you know, was Jeannie's attorney."

Jeannie wasn't looking in her folder.

"Next page. Cover letter. Also taken from a file at Foote's office. It says re: Richardson Trust Account at the top. From Ram Battachargee to Jordan Foote. Quote: *'Dear Mr. Foote: Enclosed is a gray metal box. Please send this box, unopened, to Mr. Roger Hawley.'* You see what Roger did? Those of us here who know anything about this case know this gray metal box had the bonds in it. Roger had the bonds forwarded through somebody else—somebody who would never in a million years be suspected of helping him embezzle this money—so they couldn't be traced to him. Ingenious!"

One of the suits nodded. I was starting to pull them over to my side now.

"However, note the date stamped on the letter by Jordan Foote's secretary. July sixteen. By that time, Roger was two days' dead. Next page. This is a courier slip from Jordan's office. Contents of package, I'm quoting here: 'gray metal box from R. Battachargee, Singapore.' Flash Courier Service, sent from Jordan Foote to. . . ."

I stopped, smiled at Jeannie. She met my gaze, silently hating me.

"Sent from Jordan Foote to . . . *Jeannie Richardson.*"

There was a murmur from the suits.

"July sixteenth," I said. "Remember that date. It's the same day that she bailed me out of jail. Ostensibly to look for the very money that she had just recovered. This is inexplicable! Am I right?"

I walked around the room. These goons couldn't get enough of it. Marty had started taking notes. Some of them were stretching their necks a little, trying to see what was in the folders.

"Inexplicable. . . ." I said. "Unless! Unless . . . Jeannie Richardson didn't want to have the bonds recovered just yet, thanks. She wanted to have them, of course. She just didn't want anybody to *know* she had them.

"Now let me back up a minute. You remember I said that I couldn't find the original letter that Roger had faxed to Singapore, the one instructing them where the bonds should be sent? Okay, and a second item. Why didn't Jordan send the bonds over to Roger's offices at Excor? He didn't know what they were. The letter said to send them to Excor. But he didn't do it.

"These two items only make sense in one scenario: I'm going to take a stab here and say that somebody broke into Roger's house before I did, found the original letter, and knew the bonds were coming to Jordan. So what did they do? They instructed Jordan—or maybe even just his secretary—to send the little gray box over to Jeannie's house.

"And who was it that did all this breaking in and so forth? Jeannie? Don't be ridiculous. It was a little guy named Akio Sugiyama, Jeannie's bodyguard and driver." I walked around to Jeannie. "This guy Sugiyama is also a martial arts expert. He trains Jeannie in kendo which, for those of you who don't know, is the subtle Japanese art of hitting people with sticks."

"This has gone far enough," Jeannie said. Her voice was tight but hard, just barely under control. She stood up and faced me. "I'm having you sent back to jail. You're a murderer. This is absurd speculation. You can't prove any of this nonsense. Call security and have him thrown out of here."

Marty reached up to her, put two soft fingers on her arm. "Not just yet, Jeannie," he said.

Jeannie looked around the room. All the hard-eyed suits looked away, afraid to face her. Only Tate met her gaze.

Then, strangely, he smiled. Only for a second, but it was enough. A smile from the man who never smiles—it means everything.

A thin, high sound slipped from Jeannie's lips and she slumped back her chair.

"Motive," I said. "Motive. What's going on here? Why would Jeannie hide the bonds—bonds she needed, indirectly, to finance her own attempt to buy RichCo?

"The answer is that sometime on or about July fifteenth, Jeannie Richardson realized that she would never raise enough money to save this company." I looked around the room. "You guys were here. You saw how little leadership she gave. You all know what a wild-goose chase this was. She was just going through the motions."

I saw Bruce nod a little. He was with me now. Marty had filled four or five pages of legal pad with notes. He was thinking shareholder class actions. Creditor suits. Bad press. He was a worried little guy.

"Jeannie Richardson has just been hanging on for the last few weeks, waiting for the other shoe to drop. But *what* other shoe? Once she realized that she couldn't buy the company, she figured—and I have to give her credit, this was smart— that the best thing to do was drive off the buyer. Not with money. No sir, Jeannie's playing for keeps. She was going to frame Tate Keenan, make it look like he and Roger and I were conspiring, that we were divvying up all that stolen money among ourselves. And killing each other off to boot."

A wave of muttering swept through the suits.

"She didn't have to *prove* it. Not in a court of law. All she had to do was scare off the banks, scare off the French guys behind Evergreen, get the SEC and the FBI running around throwing up mud. It wouldn't take much to make the whole deal fall apart. But how? How would she do that?" I looked around.

Tate said: "By getting you arrested in my office with the bonds." Tate's eyes were boring into Jeannie's head. But she wasn't looking at anybody now. She was slumped over, staring down at the table.

"Another story," I said. "On July twenty-first, Jeannie Richardson told me that she had received an anonymous phone call—anonymous phone calls, they're all over the place lately—she had received an anonymous phone call, saying that Tate had the bonds. So I told Jeannie that I was going to break in and get the bonds. She wanted to know exactly what time I was going in. And I told her. Only I ended up running a little late.

"By a strange coincidence, the cops charge in while I'm sitting in the bathroom next to Tate's office, and they've got a warrant to search the one place where the bonds happen to be. This warrant arrived thanks to another anonymous phone call—this one to Roger's partner, Harvey Zell.

"Now at the time, I didn't think too much of it. But looking back, it's perfectly clear. *Jeannie* was the anonymous caller. *She* called Harvey. *She* had Sugiyama or somebody plant the bonds, *she* had it all set up. Only, I was late, and instead of the cops finding *me*, they found Atlanta's tireless King of Spin, Tate Keenan. Still at his desk at midnight. They wanted to charge him with something, but Tate squashed the whole thing. If they had caught me there, a convicted stock fraud and alleged murderer, Tate could never have hushed it up. Only it didn't work out that way. Strike one for Jeannie.

"Next page. This is taken from Jeannie Richardson's personal financial statements, list of investments and liquid securities. You'll note there, oh, ten or twelve lines down, Turnkey Investments, Ltd. One hundred percent owned by Jeannie Richardson.

"Let's go to the next page. What you see is a check receipt. This piece of paper was found in Jordan Foote's dead hand. Check for five grand paid to a company called Hi-Top Security. Dated July twenty-first, one week after Roger's murder. Issuer of the check, Turnkey Investments, Ltd."

I took a portable tape player out of my bag, slipped a tape into the machine. "A little background on the tape I'm about to play. I'm speaking here with a guy named Clement Crews, the president of Hi-Top Security. Clement was also involved in a scam with Roger. They were using Clement's company, Hi-Top Security, to skim money off an investor. Remember the name on the check receipt? Hi-Top. Anyway, the investor, interestingly enough, being ripped off by Clement and Roger was Tate Keenan.

"The fact is, I was convinced originally that Tate killed Roger, one way or another. And that Tate was the guy who had the bonds. I was wrong.

"But let's forget about the bonds. I think I've demonstrated fairly persuasively that Jeannie had the bonds. But maybe a more important question hasn't been answered yet."

Tate filled in the blank: "Who killed Roger Hawley?"

I nodded, then punched the play button. My voice came out of the speaker a little tinny-sounding.

VINE: Clement. Who killed Roger Hawley?

CREWS: You're never gonna believe this.

VINE: Who was it?

CREWS: It was Jeannie Richardson.

Jeannie's head flew up. "You just wait a goddamn minute!" she hissed.

I hit the pause button. "Jeeee-sus Christ!" one of the suits said. Marty stopped taking notes, a kind of washed-out look on his face, and threw his pencil helplessly into the air.

Everybody started talking at once. Jeannie was screaming and yelling, not making any sense. It was like a roadhouse, Saturday night. Marty took Jeannie by the shoulders, forced her down into the seat. The mayhem went on for a couple of minutes.

Finally Zell stood up, yelled. "HEY! SHUT THE FUCK UP!"

And they did, everybody staring at him.

"Thanks," I said.

Zell shrugged. "I just want to hear what's on the damn tape."

I hit the pause button.

VINE: You're saying Jeannie personally killed him.

CREWS: On a stack of Bibles, I swear. Not on purpose. It was an accident.

VINE: Come on, I don't believe that for a second.

CREWS: Here's how it was. I get a call at the office from Jeannie. She says come over, she has an emergency. I'd done some work for her before, I guess she knew I was willing to take on, you know, more challenging type work than most people.

I drive over, that little Jap guy Sugiyama meets me out front. He's wearing this weird black outfit, you know, with, like, a skirt on it. We get out back, there's Jeannie wearing the same weird ninja shit. Black outfit with shoulder pads, arm guards. It's some kind of martial arts gig, right? Kembo, kenpo, kampo, something like that, hitting each other with sticks.

VINE: Kendo.

CREWS: Anyway Jeannie's out there behind her house, she's freaking out. Sugiyama, he takes me over to the pool, there's Roger lying on the ground, bleeding all over the place.

VINE: Jesus.

CREWS: I'm telling you. I say, "Whoa, guys, what's going on here?" Jeannie finally calms down, explains everything. What happened is this: Roger came over—I guess he was trying to figure out some way of scamming Jeannie—anyway he gets there while Jeannie and Sugiyama are doing this kembo shit.

VINE: Kendo.

CREWS: Whatever, yeah. So Roger starts telling Jeannie that unless she fixes his problems over at Excor, I don't know, gives him some money or something, he's gonna take off with all that cash from Health Systems. Needless to say, she's getting pretty cheesed off. Well she's standing there with this stick in her hand. You seen that kendo stick? It's like a bunch of bamboo strips kind of tied together?

VINE: Right.

CREWS: Well, she's getting more and more pissed off. I don't know exactly what finally does it, but all of a sudden she just hauls off, pops him a couple times with this stick. So Roger's just laughing at her, holding his arms in front of his face. She keeps swatting him, he backs up, trying to get away, he loses his balance, gives her an opening—she's trained, right?—she gets her opening, *whammo,* catches him a good one upside the head. Right in the temple. Roger goes down like a fucking tree.

VINE: You're telling me she killed him with a bamboo stick?

CREWS: I'm getting there, Vine. Hold your little horsies, man. *Bam,* right in the temple, Rog goes down like a tree. When he hits, I mean he bounces! Out cold. What happened, his head hits one of these things, like you put a rubber tree or a shrub in?

VINE: A planter, something like that.

CREWS: A planter, sure. Sharp corner on the planter. Pop. Busts a hole in his head, he's dead in about five minutes.

VINE: So they don't call an ambulance, they don't call the cops, they call Clement Crews. Because he likes a little challenge.

CREWS: Strange but true.

VINE: I'm skeptical.

CREWS: The point is, Jeannie wants me to get rid of the body. I say, "Come on, Jeannie, what if there's a witness, somebody saw him come here, whatever? We can't just toss him in the trash." Jeannie thinks about it, says, "Well let's dump him downtown, make it look like a mugging." I say, "Come on, we got to do better than that." Reason I say this, just between you and me, Bobby, is that if and when the cops figure out what me and Roger been doing together at Hi-Top, I'm gonna be suspect number one, right?

So I say, "Hey, Jeannie, has he got any enemies you can think of? Like somebody we could frame?" First name out her mouth, Bobby Vine. I kid you not. She says, yeah, she read all about this guy Vine in the paper, man, he'd be perfect. Been in jail once already. Way she heard it Roger testified against him, something like that. It's a natural. She makes some phone calls, I make some phone calls, we do it.

VINE: You do what? Explain it to me.

CREWS: First we take the body back to your place, stick old Roger in your kitchen. That's when Sugiyama beats his head in with the crowbar. We had to leave some evidence there, some kind of weapon, okay? Meantime, me and Andre Dupree go out, snag you from that shitty little furniture place, bust you on the head, put some Pentothal in you, take you home. We get your prints on the crowbar, get the hell out.

VINE: Coroner's report going to bear you out on this?

CREWS: What, that Roger got hit in the head after he was dead? I guess so. He hadn't been dead too long, though.

VINE: What about Jordan Foote? You know who killed him?

CREWS: I was wondering about that myself.

I turned off the tape recorder. There was no sound in the room. Jeannie looked up, finally. "This is insanity," she said. The resignation letter sat in the middle of the table. Everybody was watching the letter, waiting.

"One more thing," I said. I walked over, opened the big mahogany door, let Ed Mance and Sarah into the room. Ed went to the end of the table, sat down between Glickman and Handlin. Sarah was carrying an envelope in her hand. "You want to introduce yourself?" I said.

"Sarah Bryce," she said. "I'm a paralegal at Foote Shelby & Foote."

"Tell us what you just did."

"I went down to Piedmont Park," she said. "I interviewed an eyewitness, a man named Clydell North—nicknamed Honey Bear—who saw Jordan Foote go under the bridge where he was killed. This eyewitness saw Jordan go under the bridge with another man immediately before the murder." She turned the envelope upside down, spilling four Polaroid pictures onto the table. "I showed the eyewitness pictures of four people. He identified one of those people as the man who had gone under the bridge with Jordan."

I picked up the first picture, waved it around the room. It was a picture of Clement Crews. "Was this the gentleman the witness identified, the man who went under the bridge with Jordan at the approximate time of Jordan's murder?"

"No," Sarah said.

I picked up another picture. It was Tate Keenan. "How about this one?"

"No."

I picked up the third picture, Harvey Zell, showed it to the people at the table. "This one?"

"No."

I picked up the last picture. "Was this the one?"

"Yes. That was the one."

I walked down, showed it to Ed Mance. "Is this the same gentleman that you just apprehended breaking into Harvey Zell's office?"

Ed Mance squinted at the picture. "Yup. That's him."

I walked back to the middle of the room, tossed the last picture onto the table in front of Jeannie Richardson. She looked at the picture, then at her resignation letter, then at the picture again.

"Now you understand why I brought Zell here?" I said to her. "Now you understand why I told you it was him? I just had to make sure I was right. See, Jeannie, you were the only person who I told about the evidence at Excor, the missing link that would establish definitively who had the bonds. You were the only person who would want to make sure I didn't get my hands on it." I smiled at her.

"The thing is, Jeannie, there *wasn't* any evidence at Excor. There was no missing link. I made that all up. The real evidence was right here." I tapped my finger on her unopened folder.

Jeannie said nothing, but when she looked up at me, it was like there was no one left behind her eyes. She was a used-up shell, nothing left inside there but blind hate, hopeless rage.

"You want to identify this man, Jeannie?" I said. But it was all over. She had nothing left to say. "Okay, help me out, Marty. Turn the picture over, read us the name on the back."

Marty's small blue eyes blinked from deep inside his glasses. He picked up the fourth Polaroid, looked at the man in the picture. It was an Asian-guy—a calm, content look on his face. The only thing that would put you off, his eyes were little pink dots, reflecting the flashbulb. Marty turned the Polaroid over.

His voice was slow and careful as he read the name.

"Akio Sugiyama."

After that the only sound in the room was the scratch of pen on paper.

7

A Done Deal

CHAPTER 1

This story was on page one, column six, of the *Journal* August twenty-third of this year. There were cute drawings of Jeannie and Tate set into the text with their names printed in italics underneath the pictures.

RichCo's Richardson Maintains Control of Family Firm

ATLANTA—In a surprise move today, Jeannette Richardson announced her purchase of **RichCo,** Inc. from the French-controlled partnership **Evergreen,** L.P., which had taken it private just last month.

Scant weeks ago this story had appeared to be a closed book. Richardson's attempts to raise money for a management buy out had failed; her attorney and close advisor, Jordan Foote, had been murdered; and Evergreen had forced her to sign a letter of intent allowing Evergreen to buy RichCo at what many analysts thought was a bargain price.

According to some sources, Ms. Richardson had even been pressured into signing a postdated letter of resignation.

The death of Mr. Foote, however, turned out to be a blessing in disguise. His death invoked an obscure clause in a trust document, releasing the assets of a huge family trust for use at Ms. Richardson's discretion. In effect, she became almost half a billion dollars richer overnight.

Ms. Richardson quickly came to an understanding with Evergreen, buying out its interest in RichCo.

For Evergreen, it meant an instant profit, estimated by most analysts to be approximately $50 million. For

Ms. Richardson, it was the realization of what apparently was a lifelong dream: ownership of RichCo.

It was a pretty long article, heavy on innuendo and light on substance. The story implied—ever so gingerly—that Jeannie was linked to the killings, that her reputation would never be the same, that she'd be isolated and discredited, blah blah blah. I guess Scheib took it as far as the legal department would allow.

And maybe she would be isolated. Maybe she would be discredited. But I doubt it. Time and money seem to have unusual curative powers—even on the worst reputations.

CHAPTER 2

"Tell you what I hate."

A grating voice on the phone, a couple weeks after the story in the *Journal*.

"What's that, Clement?" I said. Just the sound of his voice made my lunch start roiling around in my stomach.

"Loose ends. Hate the shit out of loose ends."

"What do you want, Clement?"

"Got a proposition for you. How about swinging by my office this afternoon?"

"Proposition? Like what?"

He told me.

I said, okay I'd come. It didn't like it, but I'd come.

I walked in the door of the Hi-Top office in that Chinese shopping center off Ponce de Leon. It was hot inside, like the air-conditioning was broken. A funny smell hung in the air, hard to explain—like there was too much dust collecting, not enough activity. Like something dead but not yet rotting.

There was nobody at the receptionist's desk. I stuck my head into the hallway behind the desk.

"Hello? Anybody home?" My voice had a flat, compressed sound in there, like it had been shrunk somehow. I waited a minute. The whole thing made me nervous, like maybe it was some kind of setup. "Anybody here?"

Still no answer. I sat down, my heart beating hard, picked up a copy of *Secure!* Something kept telling me I shouldn't be here, that this was a bad idea. But I had to get this whole thing resolved; I didn't like loose ends any more than Clement did.

I was about halfway through this article, tips on buying a bulletproof vest, when I heard footsteps coming down the hall. It was Clement Crews. He was wearing cowboy boots, blue jeans, a Phillips head screwdriver sticking out of the front pocket. You would have figured him for a truck driver or supervisor of a plumbing crew.

"Vine," he said. "My favorite ex-lawyer." He looked tired.

"What's going on?" I said. "Where is everybody?"

"You didn't hear? We went Chapter Seven, liquidating the company."

"Gee, what a dirty rotten shame," I said.

Clement watched me, no expression on his face. He was leaning on the receptionist's desk like he was too worn out to stand up. "You about got my ass sent to jail, the shit you pulled with that tape," he said.

I shrugged. "I had to bring it out to get myself off the hook. Anyway, with all those heavyweights involved, I knew there wasn't a chance you'd get nailed. You walked. Sugiyama walked. Jeannie walked. I knew nothing would stick to anybody. Why do you think I went to all that trouble trying to ruin Jeannie? Hell, even that didn't work."

Clement didn't care why I'd tried to ruin Jeannie Richardson, didn't care that it hadn't worked. "I got to get all this furniture broke down so I can ship it off to the liquidator," he said. "So let's get this over with."

I took a manila envelope out of my jacket pocket, held it close to my chest. Clement watched the envelope.

"What good does this tape do you?" I said.

"I have no interest in getting stuck with an aiding and abetting charge. No interest in that at all."

"Yeah, but Jeannie's already. . . ."

"That's Jeannie. This is me. Like I said on the phone, I don't like loose ends. It's your only copy?" he said. "You swear to God."

"Yeah, but I still don't see what good it'll do you," I said. "The cops have another copy."

"Not anymore." He smiled his shark smile. "Little fire in the evidence room type of thing. Very mysterious."

"And your tape just happened to be there?"

"Along with a bunch of other stuff that might seem to incriminate Jeannie and Sugiyama. Fibers, sticks, pieces of paper, all kinds of goodies. Might interest you to know your lawyer, Bloom, and that guy Scheib, that reporter, they recently suffered break-ins, many valuable documents and records turned up missing. Funny coincidence, huh?"

"Who was responsible?"

"Sure as shit wasn't me," he said, reaching for the envelope. "I don't have that kind of juice." I slid the envelope back into my jacket before he could get his hands on it.

"What?" he said.

"You know why I came," I said. "Go get it."

Clement looked at me a minute, ran his tongue across his upper lip, laughed dryly. Then he disappeared down the hallway, his footsteps trailing off in the distance. After a while he came back, a Ziploc bag dangling out of his hand. He held it out to me. The gun gleamed, blue-black, inside its plastic womb.

See, the one thing that had been bothering me was that I figured Clement would eventually get busted for something. And when he did, he'd look for a way of copping a plea or trading information or whatever . . . and guess what happens then? Out comes the little plastic bag with the gun that killed Andre Dupree and his girlfriend and his albino brother. And *my* fingerprints are all over it.

I stared at the bag for a long time, then finally grabbed it—it was heavier than I remembered, maybe weighed down with the three lives it took—and shoved it in my pocket.

"The envelope," Crews said.

I handed it to him.

Clement tore through the paper, stuck the cassette into a pocket tape recorder, played it for a few seconds—the part where he was describing how Jeannie killed Roger—then turned it off. He popped the cassette back out, pulled eight or ten yards of tape out the cassette. When he had a big wad of the silvery ribbon in his hands, he tossed the whole thing into a pail that sat next to the desk.

"So much for aiding and abetting," he said.

"What's in the pail?" I said.

"Toilet bowl cleaner, got hydrochloric acid in it. Eats the metal right off the tape." Clement flashed me his carnivorous smile, then stared down into the pail for a minute, watching the acid do its work.

"See you around," I said.

"I hope not," he said.

I turned to go, stopped, my hand on the door. "Just one more question."

Clement looked up at me—not with much interest—and then stared back into the bucket of toilet bowl cleaner.

"After I went to the cops," I said. "How come you didn't give them the gun like you said, throw some blame on me?"

Clement shrugged, blew some air out through his lips. "Too much hassle," he said.

"I don't think that was it."

"Oh? Well, what *do* you think?" He wasn't smiling, wasn't looking at me with any particular expression on his face.

"It wasn't Jeannie, was it?" I said. "It was you."

Clement didn't say anything for a while. "You wearing a wire, Vine?" he said, finally.

I shook my head.

Clement kept looking at me. Finally, he said, "No, I guess you wouldn't be."

"You killed Roger, didn't you?"

Clement, peering into the bucket again: "Sure. It was pretty much like I told you the first time. He was gonna take off with the money, so things got out of hand a little, ended up I hit him in the head."

"What threw me off was that check receipt," I said, "the

one I found in Jordan Foote's hand. I figured that was payment for framing me. But it wasn't, was it?"

"It was for putting this little gray box in a filing cabinet at Tate's office. Jeannie hired me to plant the bonds."

"You didn't know what was in the box?"

"You shitting me?" He laughed again. "Would I be here today if I had known what was in that box?"

"So how come you lied the second time?" I said. "How come you made up the stuff about Jeannie killing Roger?"

"She killed Jordan. I figured, why not Roger, too?"

I thought about it. "No." I said. "That's not it. You didn't know that she had killed Jordan at that point. You didn't have any idea about that. Even I didn't know. At the time I thought it was because he knew she'd killed Roger. But actually it was a coincidence. Jordan had found out that you planted the bonds. But that's not why she killed him. She killed him to dissolve the trust with all her father's money in it."

Looking sheepishly down at the pail: "Nobody likes killing people, man. You think I'm some kind of monster, well maybe I'm not a nice guy, but I'm not a damn killer."

"What do mean? You killed him didn't you?"

He shrugged halfheartedly. "Well, I mean . . . it's not like I *enjoyed* it. You see what I'm saying? It's not a turn-on."

"And that albino guy, Andre's brother? And the girl?"

"It was just something I had to do. It was like self-defense, you know what I mean?" Another shrug. "After I let you off the hook, remember? In the Cadillac, when I dropped you off? After that I had to pull over and hurl, man."

"You didn't look too worked up about it while I was in the car."

"Looks can be deceiving. I mean, I didn't kill *you* did I? I could've. Probably should've. But I didn't."

"You're telling me you made up this whole thing about Jeannie just so I'd think you were a nice guy? Is that what you're telling me?"

He took the Phillips head screwdriver out of his pocket, listlessly stirred the handle around in the bucket of toilet bowl cleaner.

Next thing you know, his hand disappeared behind his back, came out with a snub-nosed revolver. Clement closed one eye, sighted along the barrel at my left temple, pulled back the hammer with his thumb. For a long, terrifying moment I had a feeling that this had been a mistake after all. My legs got rubbery. Christ, I should have known better.

But then Clement Crews just winked at me, smiled and shoved the gun back into the waistband of his pants. "What," he said, "you think I don't have feelings, too?"

The only satisfaction I had as I walked across the parking lot to my car was knowing with dead certainty that Clement Crews was closing in on his own personal endgame. No question about it. Looking into those empty shark eyes, I could see a man breaking down, the centrifugal forces of his character slowly ripping him apart. The last awful move— whatever it turned out to be—was damn sure not far away.

I was just glad I wouldn't be around when it happened.

CHAPTER 3

Sarah and I decided to shack up for a while. We got a little house together in Virginia Highlands, a six-month lease, fig- ured we'd see how it went. If it worked out, it worked out.

It was a little quick, I guess, but these were strange times for us both. It was good being with another human being again. I'd been cut off from humanity for a long time, cut off even from myself. I felt like I was recovering from some kind of blind sickness, just starting to get out of the woods.

We talked a lot, kissed, made love in the kitchen, listened to Sarah's records—all these bands, singers I'd never heard of. When the Big Fear hit me, I'd go stand out on the back porch, sometimes walk around in the woods at the edge of the yard. Then it would be over, and we could be together again.

As far as being a player goes, being a deal maker, I figured to hell with that. Tate offered to try and get me readmitted to the bar, see if he could con the NASD into letting me back into the securities business. But the thing was Sarah was right: I didn't like the guy I became when I was caught up in that stuff. He sucked you dry. That guy, whoever he was, wasn't the man I was trying to be. Best to let go of Bobby the Deal Maker, Bobby the Lawyer, Bobby the Hotshot, let that guy wither and rot with the dead.

We were sitting out back in the yard, nighttime, two folding chairs next to each other, holding hands, an Indian summer night. Sarah had the Indigo Girls on the stereo, coming out the window. They were an Atlanta band, two girls with big acoustic guitars.

Ray came out of the house, one of my Michelobs in his hand. We hadn't invited him over; he just showed up. He turned on the porch light—one of those yellow bulbs that fail miserably to fool the bugs—and held out his arms, doing his Red Sea thing.

"Where'd you come from?" I said.

"How you like it, Counselor?" He had one of his new suits on, charcoal gray with pinstripes, paisley tie, spread-collar shirt, contrasting cuffs. He still looked like Ray, though, a fat little white guy with an Afro. Which was good, I guess. His tatoo had turned black under the bug light. "Nice, huh?"

"Looks sharp," I said.

Ray screwed the top off his Michelob, threw it behind a bush. "I got an announcement," he said. Ray was grinning, smiling like a stone fool.

"I think you're in love," Sarah said. She had a soft, spooky thing going on in her eyes.

"No," he said. "I'm retiring."

"Oh, Ray," Sarah said.

"Now all I got to do is find somebody crazy enough to take over the business. Somebody got Real World Skills? A take-charge type guy—you know, understands Negotiation, Selling Skills, that type of thing."

"Ray," I said.

"Somebody I can trust, Bobby." He had that *look* in his little eyes.

"Ray, I'll talk to you in a minute," I said. I was starting to have that bad feeling again, like I couldn't breathe. I went inside, got Roger's gun out of the box full of old pictures and mementos where I'd been keeping it, put it in my pocket, walked back out in the yard.

"Bobby? Bobby?" Sarah had a worried look on her face.

"It's okay," I said. "I'm just going down to the woods for a minute."

I walked to the end of the lawn, into the dark stand of trees that butted onto the back of the yard. The world faded into various shades of black, all crowded together so I couldn't separate one thing from another. I felt brambles cutting at my legs, little tree limbs smacking into my face. The only sound was my feet, dry leaves shattering as I went down the hill.

Then at the bottom of the hill I heard water underfoot, felt it leaking into my shoes. When I was a kid, I used to build dams in a creek just like this one, wading around and ruining my sneakers. It was good to be there, the water soaking my feet. Threads of silver, barely visible, wound around underneath me, snaked slowly between my legs.

I took Roger's Colt .380 out of the Ziploc bag, ejected the clip, thumbed the bullets one by one into the water. They made hollow splashes, like a trout hitting a fly. I wiped my prints off the clip with my shirttail, dropped it in the water. The creek was nice, a good place to end this thing.

I sloshed down the middle of the creek, fieldstripping the little gun, wiping the prints off each piece as I went, dropping each of them into the water. When I was done, I reached down, scooped up some water, poured it on my forehead, felt the coolness on my nose, my lips, my chin, running down my chest. There were no words and no rules and no fine distinctions—only water. Only water and nothing else.

Back at the house, Sarah and Ray were talking in soft voices. They looked up at me as I trudged back across the yard—my muddy shoes, the water running down the front of my shirt—and they didn't know what to say. I stood there like a fool for a minute, grinning and dripping on the concrete patio, full of something that I didn't yet understand or know how to describe.

I wanted to sum everything up, to tell them how if they hadn't been there, I don't know how I would have made it, stuff like that. But it all got raw and lame and embarrassing-sounding when I tried stringing the words together in my head.

They kept looking at me, serious, wondering what was going on. Then Ray smiled.

"Smells good as hell out here," he said. "What's for supper?"

And Sarah, standing there next to our new chicken smoker—she was smiling, too. Her face, lit up with that yellow bug light—man, it was as fine and exquisite a thing as I'd ever seen.

"We're smoking us a couple hens," I said. "Sit down, there's plenty."